CRY FOR JERUSALEM

BOOK THREE: 67-69 CE

GROWING ANARCHY

WARD SANFORD

PUBLISHED BY STADIA BOOKS LLC

WWW.CRYFORJERUSALEM.COM

Cry For Jerusalem

Book Three: 67-69 CE

Growing Anarchy

Ward Sanford

CRY FOR JERUSALEM
BOOK THREE: 67–69 CE
GROWING ANARCHY
WARD SANFORD

PAPERBACK ISBN: 978-1-950645-04-6

PUBLISHED BY STADIA BOOKS LLC
WWW.CRYFORJERUSALEM.COM

CRY FOR JERUSALEM is a work of fiction that has been inspired by eyewitness records of historical events. Some characters, many scenes, and most of the dialog have been fictionalized for dramatic purposes.

WHAT PROFESSIONAL REVIEWERS ARE SAYING ABOUT CRY FOR JERUSALEM BOOK ONE AND TWO

"The story sweeps across a first-century world that's diverse, gritty, and laced with tension. Majestic and colorful landscapes such as Jerusalem, Rome, and the many places in between, both on land and sea, are richly detailed. I loved the maps that are included at the beginning. Sanford uses his characters well. Men and women have strong influence on the plot, including women who interacted with and changed their circumstances despite social constraints. Everything is supported by an incredibly well-researched foundation. The time period and social customs are delightfully developed... there is political and religious strife, moments of ancient beauty, and well-developed characters to carry the plot forward. Sanford is a talented author with an exciting new series to get lost in."

--Historical Novels Review Issue 91 February 2020

"In this first installment of a series, Yosef comes to realize what a tinderbox the political situation has become. As Roman leaders become increasingly authoritarian and hungry for tax proceeds, Jewish militancy increases, setting the stage for a brutal confrontation, a historical predicament vividly and intelligently depicted by Sanford. And Nero, looking for an excuse to rebuild Rome, raise taxes, and consolidate his power, takes Florus' advice to burn the city to the ground, starting the "most extensive and destructive fire that Rome had ever experienced." The plot is as gripping as it is historically edifying, remarkably authentic, and rigorously researched. At its conclusion, readers will be left impatient for the book's sequel. An impressive blend of historical portrayal and dramatic fiction."

--Kirkus Reviews June 2020

In this historical novel set in the first century, the lives of four unlikely friends are threatened by the gathering war between Emperor Nero's Roman Empire and the Jewish population in Jerusalem. Nero has nearly bankrupted Rome as a consequence of relentless prodigality, diminishing the empire's power and sending many of its provinces into mutinous discontent. His devious plan is

to manufacture a war with the restive Jewish population—
especially in Jerusalem—in order to plunder its treasury, and he's
prepared to deceive his own generals in order to accomplish this.

In this second installment of a four-volume series, Sanford deftly
depicts the historical conflict by chronicling four intersecting lives.
All of these characters meet by sheer happenstance but form a
potent bond: Cleopatra; Nicanor, a Roman centurion; Sayid, a
Roman solider in Nicanor's legion; and Yosef, the military
commander in charge of Galilee. Nicanor participates in a major
loss against the rebels at Beth Horon under the leadership of Cestius
Gallus, who entrusts the centurion with a packet of documents
substantiating his suspicions that his campaign was purposely
sabotaged by his own advisers. Meanwhile, Yosef tries to unite
Galilee to oppose the inevitable Roman invasion but is despondent
that his own people visit so much violence upon themselves, an inner
conflict subtly portrayed by the author: "Yosef did not know who he
hated more for what had happened—the Romans that had pushed
the situation in Judea to this point or his own people who, for selfish
reasons, had killed the innocent or let them be killed. They were
driving them all toward inevitable death and destruction."

Sanford's historical rigor is impressive and his account of the age's
troubles, nimbly nuanced, unburdened by any calcified moral
strictures. One caveat: For readers unfamiliar with the series
opener, this will be a difficult (though not impossible) novel to
follow. But the sequel is a captivating treat for those who enjoyed
the book's predecessor.

A thrilling blend of powerful emotional drama and meticulous
historical scholarship.

--Kirkus Reviews August 2021

About Cry For Jerusalem

A four novel—historical fiction—series based on the writings of Yosef ben Matityahu (Titus Flavius Josephus). Yosef's (Josephus's) work as a historian provides valuable insight into first-century Judaism and the background of early Christianity. He has specific details on the First Jewish—Roman War, which he not only witnessed but took part in at a high level. The story takes place from late 63 to 70 CE, a little over one-third of the way into 200 years of increased and sustained internal peace and stability for Rome, though not without lesser wars, conflicts of expansion, and revolts. This *Pax Romana* was first broken by the Jewish (Judean) first war of rebellion. First-century Judea was a time of new belief systems, persecution, and economic upheaval. Ruled by Rome's puppet-King Agrippa, the Judeans had fragmented into three factions under the Romans: the status-quo pro-Roman Moderates; the nationalists, Zealots who wanted Judean and Jewish independence; and the Sicarii, a violent splinter group who not only wanted freedom from Rome but also had a goal to kill all pro-Roman collaborators.

Two thousand years ago, men and women were driven to act—as they are today—by the same emotions, needs, and wants. In Cry For Jerusalem, we experience how such actions forever changed the world for Jews and Christians through our main cast of characters: In Book One, we meet Yosef, a Jewish scholar, sent from Jerusalem to free priests imprisoned in Rome; Nicanor, a Roman centurion; Lady Cleo, a Roman noblewoman whose marriage is arranged to Gessius Florus, a man who becomes the new Judean Procurator; and Sayid, a legion auxiliary serving in the lady's escort. A shipwreck—fate, it seems—brought them together to become unlikely friends and, upon their rescue, to experience the great fire that destroyed much of Rome. Afterward—having gone their separate ways back to the Roman Judea and Syria—they find themselves reconnected by fate that is not yet finished with them.

Synopsis of Book One: Resisting Tyranny

Yosef, Nicanor, Sayid, and Lady Cleopatra's (Cleo's) shared experience forms an unlikely bond of friendship tested throughout the four novels in the series. Was it fate, destiny, or some divine plan that brought these four very different travelers together to survive a shipwreck while traveling to Rome?

In Rome, the reader meets Emperor Nero and is introduced to the intrigue that permeates the empire. At the suggestion of Gessius Florus and to serve his own purpose, Nero sets Rome afire while shifting the blame onto the Christians. This sets events in motion to replenish Rome's depleted treasury by igniting a war in Judea to steal the vast treasure believed held in the Jewish Temple in Jerusalem.

Yosef, Nicanor, Cleo, and Sayid experience the Great Fire of Rome and its aftermath. Then each separately returns to Judea, where their fates further converge: Yosef to report the release of the Jewish prisoners and to attempt to stave off the increasing militancy of the anti-Roman factions, hoping to find a peaceful resolution with Rome; Nicanor—having avoided the Praetorian Guard duty he did not want—to return to his beloved legion duties in Antioch; Cleo, now married and accompanied by her husband; Gessius Florus, who is to become the new Procurator of Judea; and Sayid, glad to return to auxiliary duty in a land where he feels at home, is assigned to Lady Cleo and often thinks of Yosef and Nicanor.

In Jerusalem, the reader meets Miriam, Yosef's sister, who survives a tragic attack by Roman soldiers that changes her forever, turning her into something and someone she could never have imagined, which becomes a dark secret she must hide from her family.

In Judea, Gessius Florus shows his true colors. His oppressive actions were designed solely to squeeze more tax revenue and heighten tensions between Jerusalem's factions and Rome. He creates situations and events—including a massacre in Jerusalem shortly after Passover—that lead to chaos and the birthing of a full-blown war. All were intended as justification to steal the Jewish Temple treasure and to further his plan to keep a large part of it for himself and send the rest to Nero.

In Antioch, the reader meets Cestius Gallus, governor and commander of the 12th Legion. Circumstances and the rebels' actions forced him to lead his legion and allied forces into Judea for an ill-fated—ultimately aborted—attack on Jerusalem and one of the worst defeats of any Roman legion during their retreat through the pass at Beth Horon.

Yosef, Nicanor, Cleo, Sayid, and their family and friends, play critical roles at a focal point in the history of Western civilization. As the winds helped to spread the great fire in Rome, they also carried embers to Judea, where they threatened to ignite a conflict that would forever change the world for Jews and Christians.

SYNOPSIS OF BOOK TWO: AGAINST ALL ODDS
The epic saga continues its sweeping arc from Rome to Jerusalem, Antioch to Galilee. Ancient history comes to life—and events become plausibly explained that history has left unanswered—through the

actions of historical figures in the aftermath of the 12th Legion's retreat from Jerusalem and defeat at Beth Horon. The Romans: Nero, Gessius Florus, and Tigellinus, each has agendas. Cestius Gallus, former commander of the 12th Legion, bears the ultimate burden... and the fate of his actions. And we meet Vespasian, who has taken over the campaign against the Judean rebels at Nero's order.

Cleo suffers at the hands of Gessius Florus while continuing her secret attempts to let other Romans know her husband's role in inciting a war that could have been prevented. Nicanor and Sayid, meanwhile, find themselves reluctant messengers drawn into the intrigues of powerful Romans whose sole purpose is the self-enrichment only found in the chaos of war. The Jews: Yosef ben Mathias (Josephus), who becomes the military commander in Galilee, commits to lead and fight in a war he knows his country can never win. A rebel leader, Yohanan ben Levi (John of Gischala)—seeking power among the Jews—confronts and obstructs Yosef in Galilee. While in Jerusalem, Yosef's sister Miriam descends deeper on her dark path of revenge and retribution.

The reader witnesses the Siege of Yotapta (Jotapata), where thousands of Jews died fighting Roman legions—against all odds—in one of the bloodiest battles in Jewish history. All of which was experienced and chronicled by the famous Jewish historian Josephus.

The story behind the legendary (but real) Copper Scroll further develops. Considered "the most unique, the most important, and the least understood" of the Dead Sea Scrolls, it describes the locations of the Temple treasure moved from Jerusalem to be hidden—assumingly—from the Romans. But the treasure has never been found).

The factions and dissension grow and weaken Jerusalem, while the intrigues within the Roman Empire lead up to the Year of Four Emperors and the civil war that shaped the empire for decades.

CONTENTS

DRAMATIS PERSONAE

YOSEF BEN MATHIAS
A young, upper-class, educated Jew sent—in Book One—to Rome as an envoy to free imprisoned priests. Returns to Judea, and when the war begins, in Book Two, he is assigned to become military commander of Galilee. Captured by the Romans, he is now a prisoner.

REBECCA
Yosef's mother who has a lineage of Jewish royalty from the Hasmonean dynasty.

MATHIAS
Yosef's father and a leader in the Sanhedrin, the governing body of the Jews in Judea.

MATTHEW BEN MATHIAS
Yosef's older brother, an officer in the Jewish Temple Guard, plays a vital role in the plan to save the Temple treasure from the Romans by hiding much of it.

MIRIAM
Yosef's younger sister, her betrothal broken off due to tragic events in Book One. Her personal transformation continues in Book Two as she embraces becoming a Sicarii assassin known as The Hand. Her secrets lead to a deadly outcome.

EHUD
An old friend of Matthew and Yosef's who is also Miriam's former crush. His family had left Jerusalem years before and has business connections with the Romans in Alexandria. Gessius Florus forces him to become another spy, or his family will be killed.

LEAH
Yosef's cousin, mutually attracted to Yosef at age sixteen and afterward... but married to an abusive man.

RACHEL
Leah's younger sister, who develops feelings for Yosef.

YOHANAN BEN ZACCAI

Member of the Sanhedrin, respected by both Moderates and rebels, who had become Yosef's chief advisor in Galilee. He continues to help in the effort to hide the Temple treasure from the Romans.

ZECHARIAH

A virtually blind craftsman and skilled warrior who once lived in the Lower City and befriended Miriam. He was killed saving her a second time. Yet still looms large in Miriam's heart and mind. She uses his shop, where she feels safe, to practice the martial skills he taught her.

HANANIAH

A master bladesmith and killer-for-hire who hates Jerusalem. Gessius Florus has brought him from Alexandria to serve as his spy master and to hunt down and kill the Sicarii assassin, The Hand.

ARIELLA

A Galilean woman, daughter of a veteran Jewish soldier, who came to Yotapta to help fight the Romans and marries Levi ben Altheus, Yosef's chief lieutenant. Captured in the final battle of the siege, she holds Yosef responsible for Lev's death and swears she'll get revenge.

ELAZAR BEN YAIR

Leader of the Sicarii, who begins to focus on Masada as the Sicarii's final redoubt. He wants Miriam to continue to find and kill Roman collaborators within Jerusalem.

YOHANAN BEN LEVI (OF GISCHALA)

A rebel leader from Galilee, often at odds with leadership in Jerusalem. His refusal to accept Yosef's appointment as commander in Galilee resulted in death and disruption in the region. He abandons his city to the Romans and flees to Jerusalem, where he incites more dissension and tries to gain control of the city.

ELEASAR BEN ANANIAS

Captain of Jewish Temple Guard, a rebel leader, though not an extremist. He is assigned responsibility for Jerusalem and southern Judea's defense against the Romans. He is also Matthew's key partner in hiding the Temple treasure.

SIMON BAR GIORA

Top rebel leader from Judea and a competent field commander. He led the rebel force that—in Book One—defeated the 12th Legion and took their *aquila*, battle standard, at Beth Horon. He becomes increasingly involved with trying to gain control over Jerusalem and at odds—ultimately in conflict—with Yohanan ben Levi of Gischala.

YONATAN

Leah's husband, a rebel with a dislike of Roman collaborators and who holds a grudge against Yosef and his family.

ESAU BEN BEOR

A leader of the Judean province of Idumea whose secret hatred of Jerusalem enabled Florus to leverage him to become his spy within the Sanhedrin. As The Hand, Miriam killed him in Solomon's Quarry, which led to her first encounter with Hananiah, Gessius Florus's embedded killer in Jerusalem.

NICANOR

A Roman centurion who befriends Yosef. His father was also a Roman legionary, and his mother was Greek. Beginning in Book One and continuing in Book Two, he becomes entangled in the intrigues of Rome and the agendas of powerful men in the empire. He returns to Judea on Vespasian's staff, but after the fall of Yotapta, he returns again to Rome on a mission from Vespasian and to enlist the help of Lord Marcus Otho to help save Cleo from Gessius Florus.

GRAIUS

Lady Cleo's retired former major domus, who Nicanor discovers has a surprising background as he joins Nicanor on his journey to meet with Marcus Otho, governor of Hispania Lusitania, to seek his help in protecting Lady Cleo from Gessius Florus.

CLEOPATRA (CLEO/YA'EL)

A young Roman noblewoman and an admirer of Jewish culture. She had toured the eastern Roman provinces before wedding Gessius Florus, who would become newly appointed Judean Procurator. In Judea, married to a man she fears and hates, things grow worse. With Sayid's help, Cleo escapes from Gessius Florus but misses her opportunity to flee her husband and return to safety in Rome with Nicanor. Now she's stranded in a country at war with Rome, hiding among its enemies where she goes by the Jewish name Ya'el.

SAYID

A young volunteer Roman army auxiliary whose father was a Roman soldier of African descent who fell in love with his mother, a Syrian. Once assigned to Lady Cleo's retinue in her travels, after Cleo's marriage, he is soon attached to the 12th Legion. And—like Nicanor—finds himself drawn into helping the legion commander, Cestius Gallus, and then his friend, Lady Cleo. After saving her from Gessius Florus, he returns to the army, hoping to continue the search for his father.

ELIAN

A young slave boy who had been a servant in Lady Cleo's new household in Ptolemais. When she flees Gessius Florus, Cleo can't leave him behind.

ANTONIA CAENIS

Joined with General Vespasian in a *conturbernium*, a civil union and not a marriage, Antonia Caenis is a politically savvy advisor. She has connections throughout the empire and helps Nicanor in Rome.

GNAEUS BATIATUS

Owner of a gladiator training school, and a friend to Antonia Caenis, he provides a safe place for Nicanor in Rome.

MARCUS ATTILIUS

A freed man, a Christian who is also a skilled fighter, in debt to Gnaeus Batiatus, who wishes to turn him into a gladiator. He becomes a close friend to Nicanor in Rome.

FLORIN

A legion auxiliary was Nicanor's clerk and messenger when Nicanor was previously assigned as a watch captain at a prison in Rome. He now serves as Nicanor's personal aide.

CESTIUS GALLUS

Once the Roman legate (governor) of the eastern Roman provinces, including Syria and Judea, and commander of the 12th Legion. His attempts to alert the emperor to his concerns about how the war was provoked and his suspicions of Gessius Florus led to his death.

OCTAVIA

Widow of Cestius Gallus, a friend of Cleo, who sympathized with provincials over which Rome rules. She has returned to Rome—a villa far outside of the city—where Nicanor finds her to discuss Lady Cleo's predicament in Judea.

VESPASIAN

A formerly victorious but out-of-favor and retired Roman general recommended to Nero by the Praetorian Prefect Tigellinus to take over the Judean campaign to crush the rebels.

TITUS

Vespasian's son and field commander of three legions in his father's campaign against the Judean rebels. Ultimately, he leads the final assault that leads to Jerusalem's destruction.

GESSIUS FLORUS

A Roman tax collector who married Cleo to become the Judean Procurator, then Nero's Imperial Tax Collector in the region, who also plans to steal much of the Jewish Temple treasure. Empowered by that assignment, he abuses Cleo and is a deadly enemy to anyone in his way.

QUINTUS

A mercenary sea captain and another henchman/killer for Gessius Florus. He is sent on a mission to find Cleo and track Nicanor in Rome and kill him.

DRUSUS

Hired by Gessius Florus as a courier of messages to and from his spies in Jerusalem, he is also an abnormally strong and cruel man. Gessius Florus finds more uses for him better suited to his brutality.

KRATEROS

A merciless killer and leader of the Thracian mercenaries hired by Gessius Florus to watch for Judean rebels hiding shipments of the Jewish Temple treasure. He later focuses on assassinating targets given him by Florus.

NERO

Despotic Roman emperor who brought the empire to the verge of bankruptcy. Under his reign, Rome was nearly destroyed by a great fire. He pursues Gessius Florus's plan to replenish the Roman treasury by stealing from Judea under the guise of war.

OPHONIUS TIGELLINUS

The more publicly prominent co-Prefect of the Praetorian Guard, who is closely aligned with Nero and equally intent on self-enrichment, also has a vested interest in the success of Gessius Florus in Judea. He, too, will be enriched by the theft of the Jewish Temple treasure.

SERVIUS GALBA

The governor of Hispania Tarraconensis when Nero is finally held accountable for his misrule of the empire and forced to commit suicide. With support from northern province legions, Galba becomes the new emperor. Only to anger those who once supported him. He becomes the 1st new ruler in the Year of Four Emperors.

MARCUS OTHO

The brother of Lady Cleo, governor of Hispania Lusitania, and an early supporter of Galba. As the outcry against Galba grows and the new emperor—an old man—chooses another as his successor, Marcus Otho recruits enough support from within the empire to instigate Galba's assassination. He then becomes the 2nd new emperor in the Year of Four Emperors.

GALERIUS SENNA

Senior Military Tribune of the 12th Legion. Becomes its commander when Cestius Gallus is relieved of his duties by Nero. Gessius Florus controls him.

TYRANNIUS PRISEUS

Former camp-prefect and now First Centurion of the 12th Legion. He is also controlled by Gessius Florus.

HISTORICAL BACKGROUND

By the fall of Jerusalem in 70 CE, the culmination of ***Cry For Jerusalem***, Rome had much of the known world under its control. The empire reached its largest expanse in 117 CE under Emperor Trajan.

THE ROMAN EMPIRE CIRCA 117 CE

The empire encompassed an area of three million square miles. It stretched from the British Isles across western, central, and southern Europe, northern Africa, and western Asia. Its estimated 60 million inhabitants would have accounted for between one-sixth and one-fourth of the world's total population. It was the largest unified political entity in the West until the mid-19th century. More recent demographic studies suggest the population could have risen to 100 million at its peak. Each of the three largest cities in the empire—Rome, Alexandria, and Antioch—was almost twice the size of any European city before the 17th century.

The Romans had occupied greater Judea since the invasion of General Pompey in 63 BCE. Many large buildings and a grand Temple complex in Jerusalem were constructed by King Herod the Great from circa 20 BCE until well after he died in 4 BCE. After

Herod's death, the greater province was divided into four tetrarchs ruled by Herod's descendants, who functioned as Roman-controlled governors.

VIII

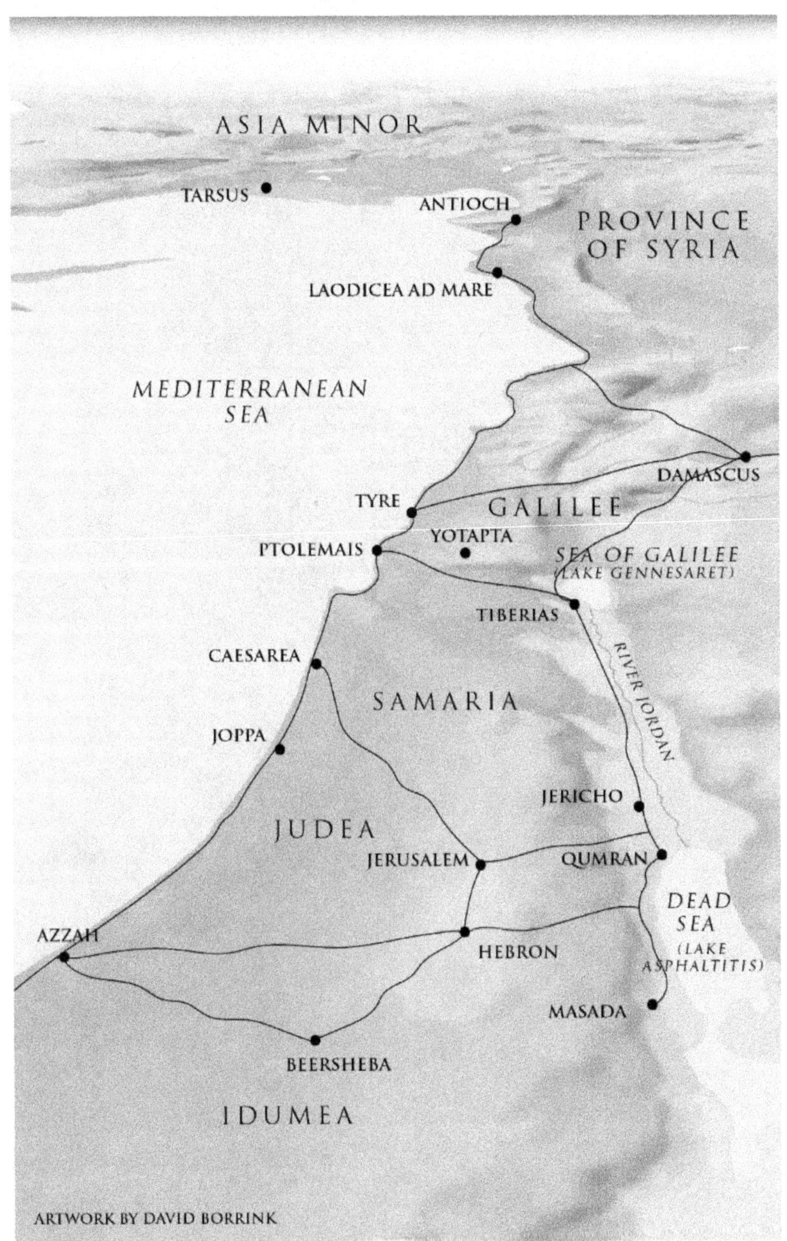# MAP 1 – EASTERN MEDITERRANEAN COASTLINE

MAJOR CITIES, TOWNS AND ROADS IN THE FIRST CENTURY CE

MAP 2 – JUDEAN PROVINCES

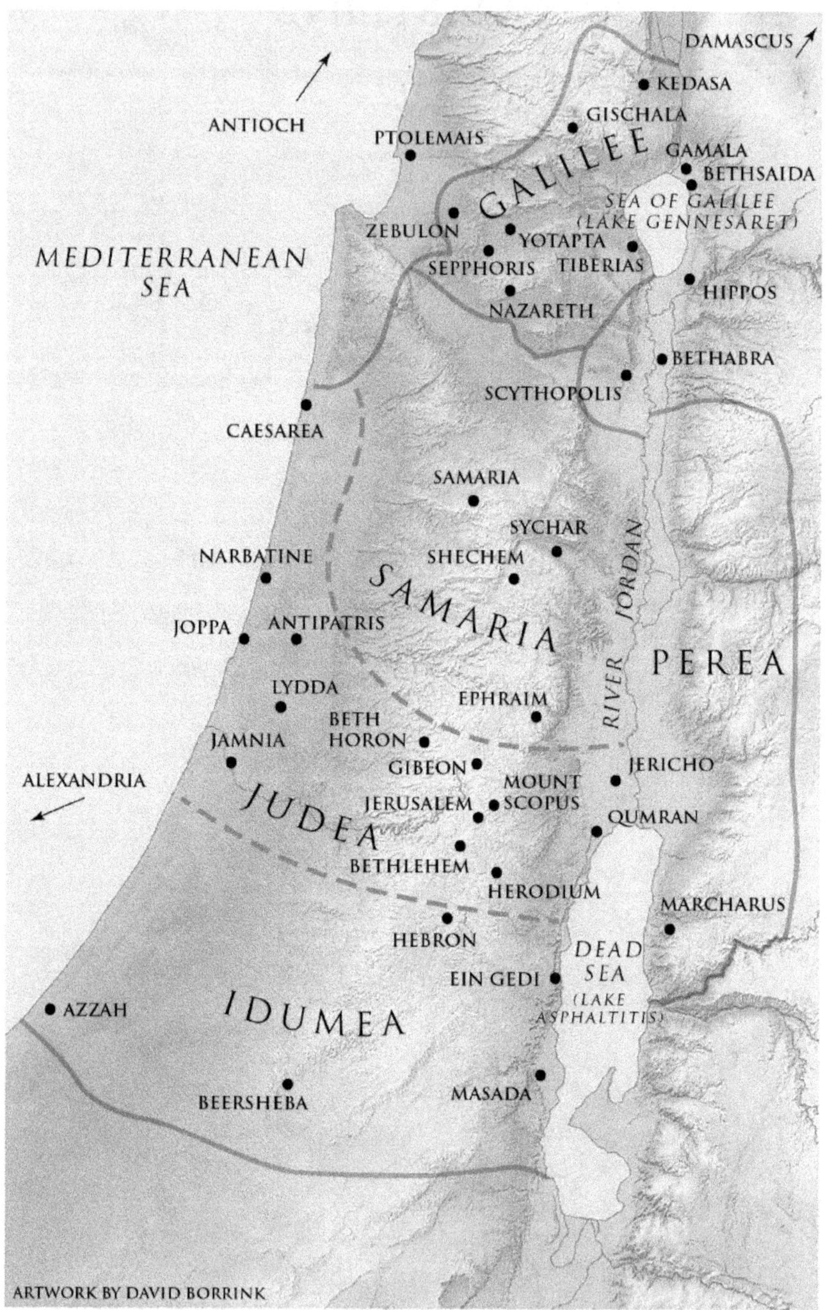

THE JUDEAN PROVINCES IN THE FIRST CENTURY CE

MAP 3 – GALILEE

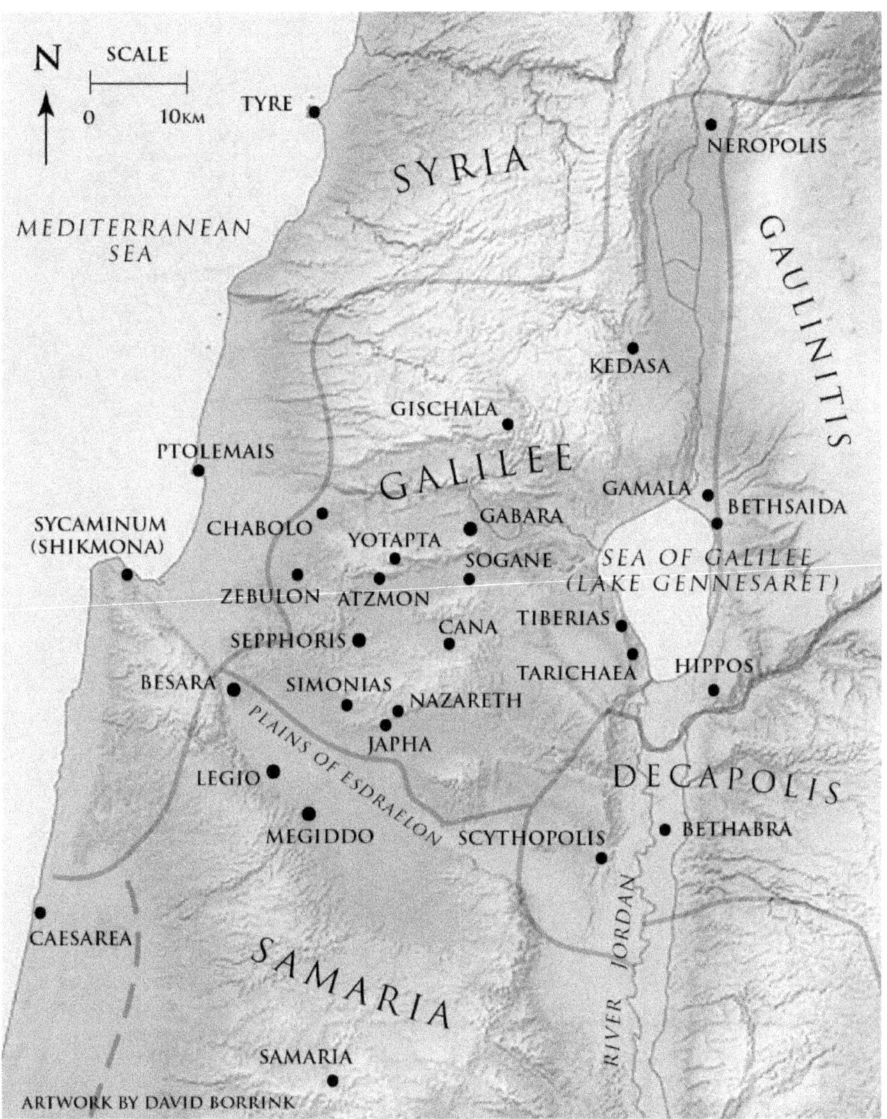

CITIES AND TOWNS AND THE SURROUNDING REGIONS IN THE FIRST CENTURY CE

MAP 4 – JERUSALEM

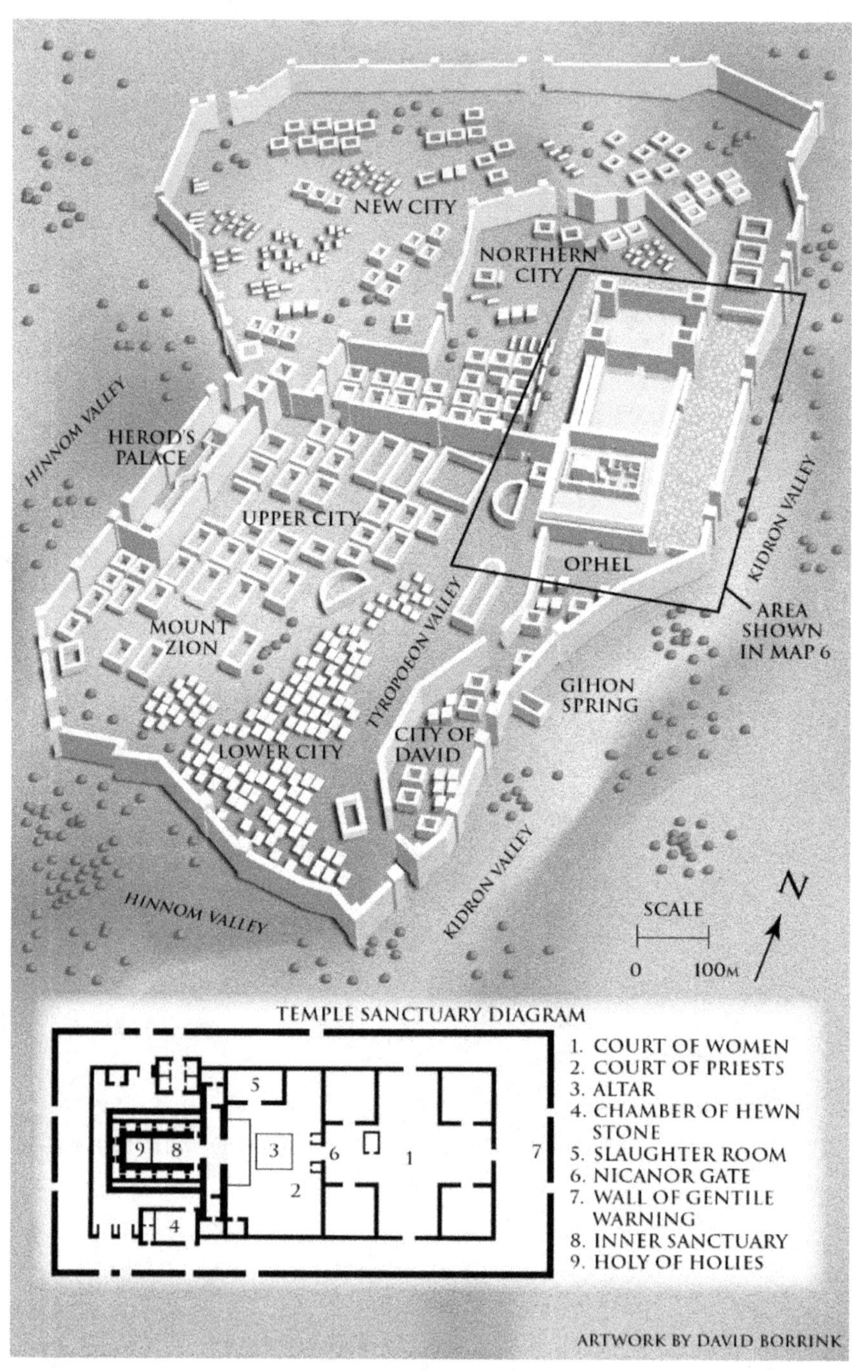

MAP 5 – THE TEMPLE COMPLEX

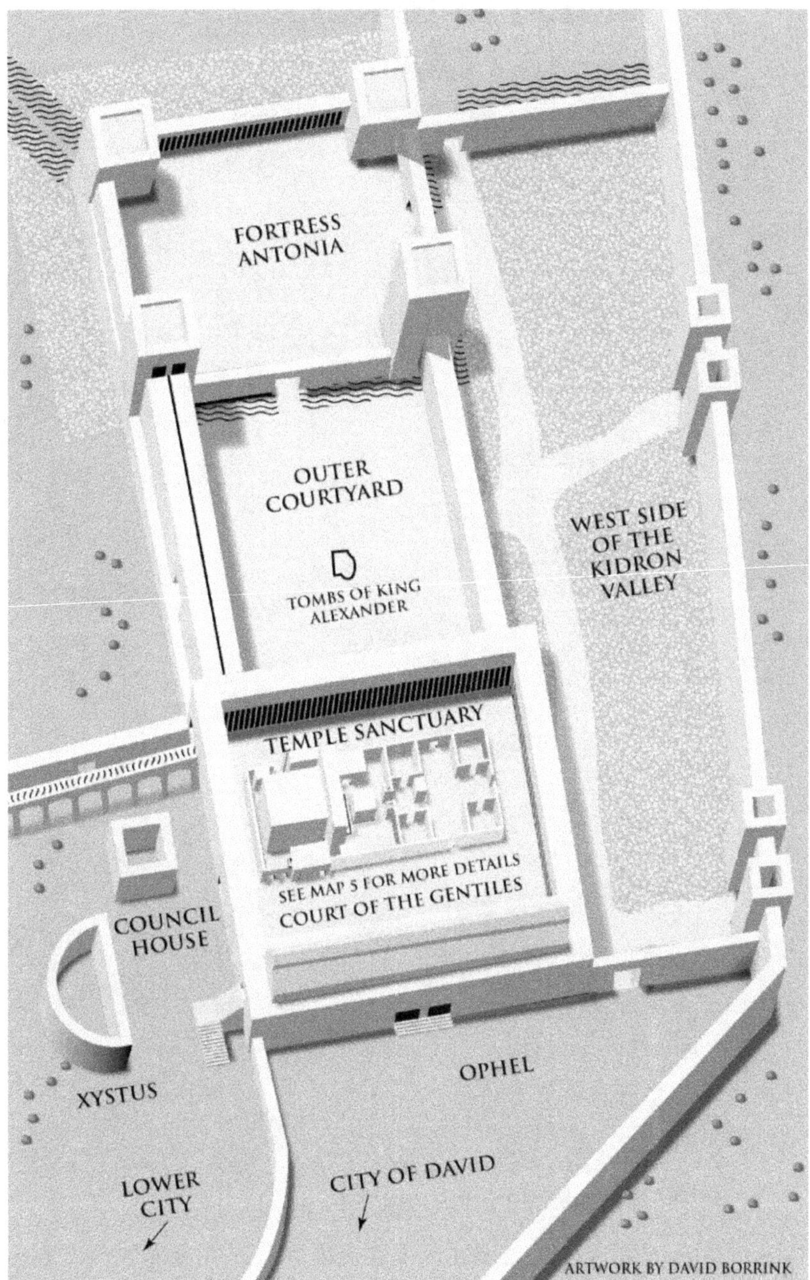

HEROD'S TEMPLE COMPLEX AS ENVISIONED BY JOSEPHUS SCHOLAR THOMAS LEWIN

MAP 6 – THE SEVEN HILLS OF ROME AND ITS 14 REGIONS

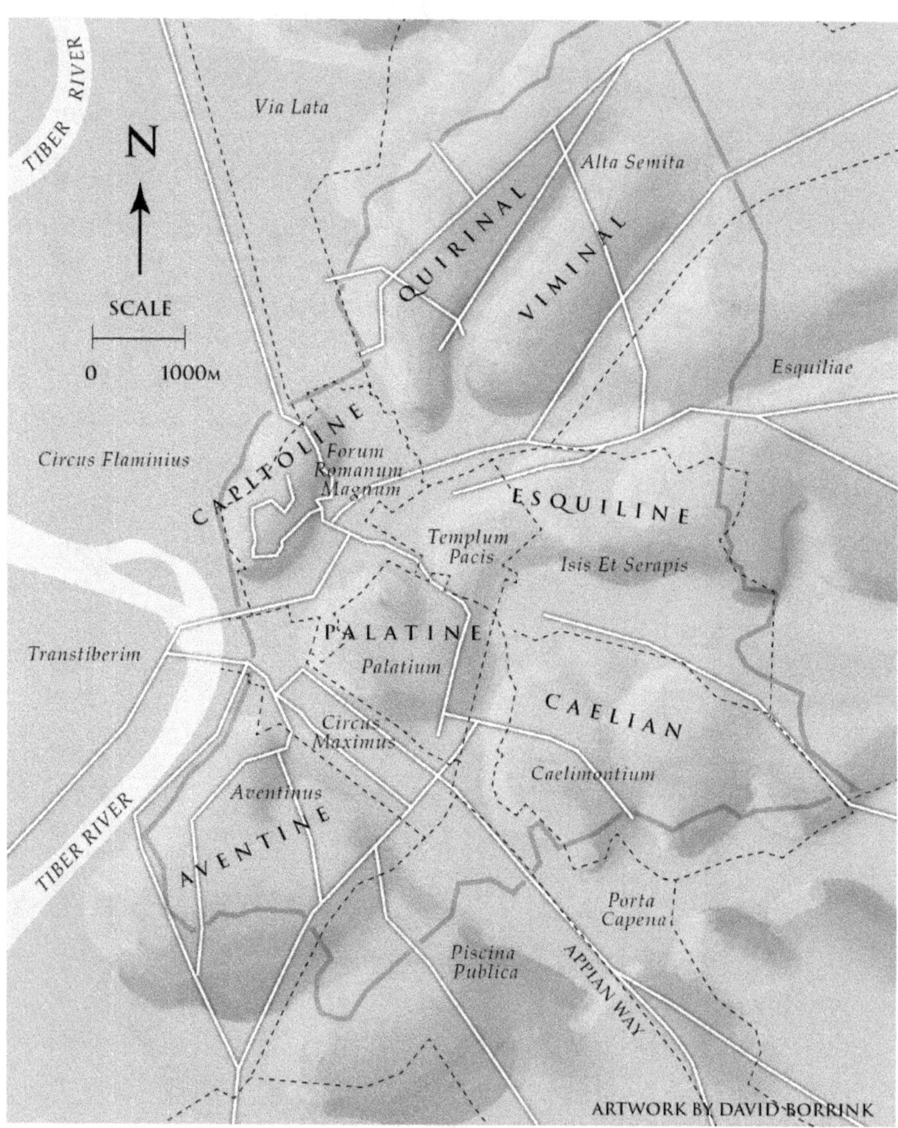

THE WALLS (SOLID LINE) AND ROADS (OPEN LINES)
OF FIRST CENTURY ROME

MAP 7 – THE CENTER OF ROME

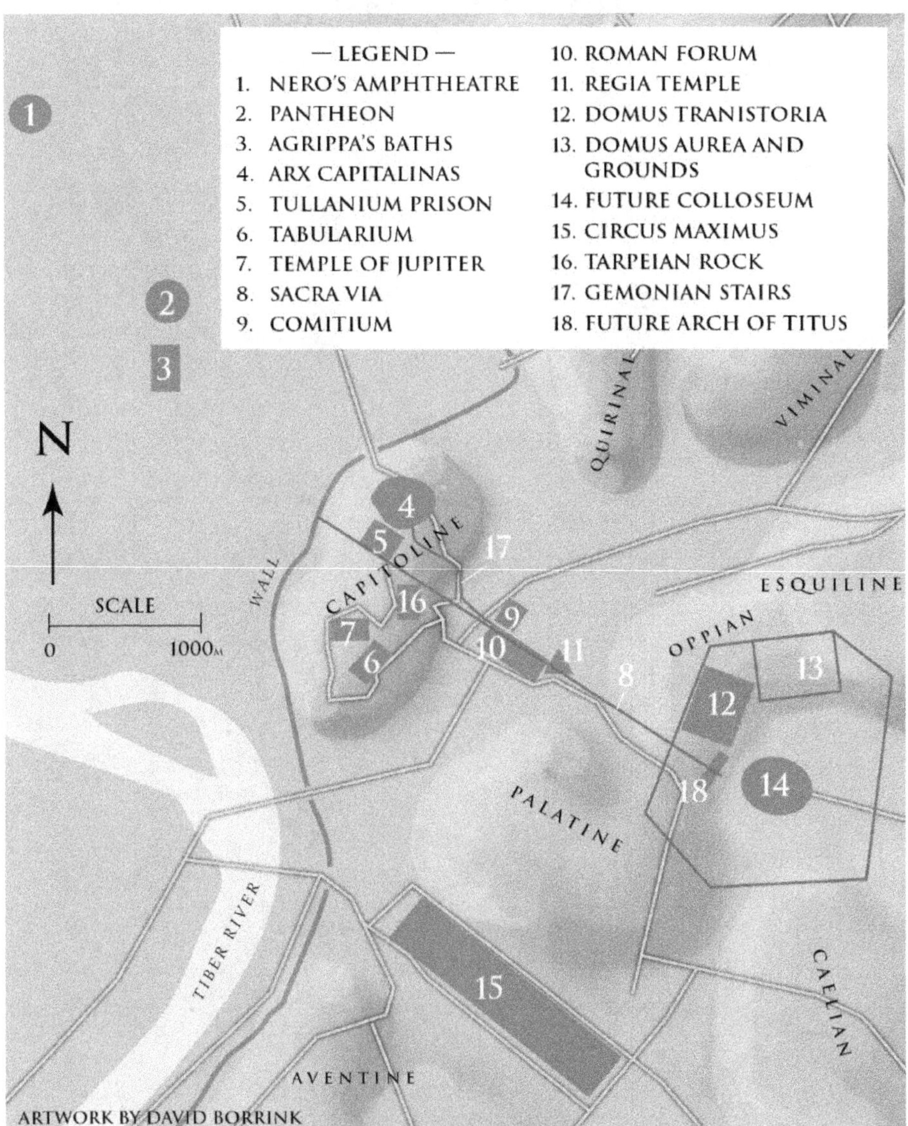

MAJOR FEATURES IN THE FIRST CENTURY CE

MAP 8 – THE WESTERN PART OF THE ROMAN EMPIRE

THE WESTERN PART OF THE ROMAN EMPIRE
IN THE FIRST CENTURY CE

"A VOICE FROM THE EAST, A VOICE FROM THE WEST, A VOICE FROM THE FOUR WINDS, A VOICE AGAINST JERUSALEM AND THE HOLY HOUSE, A VOICE AGAINST THE BRIDEGROOMS AND THE BRIDES, AND A VOICE AGAINST THIS WHOLE PEOPLE! WOE, WOE TO JERUSALEM!"

YESHUA BEN ANANIAS 64-70 CE

ACT I

I

September 67 CE

Between Ptolemais and Caesarea

Yosef studied the expanse of the sea in the late summer sun. The green of shoal water near the shore swirled around a cluster of discarded building stones. It turned blue as the water deepened and rippled toward the horizon. The wind flecked white the edges and tops of the waves. He had not seen a body of water of any size since fleeing Tiberias, where Yohanan of Gischala had attempted to assassinate him. The fisherman Nathan and his two sons had saved him. Nathan's wife, Imma—bless her memory, had tended to his wounds but then died horribly soon after in yet another attack by the Gischalan. Yosef wondered if Nathan and his boys still lived.

He was glad this stretch of the Roman road south of Shikmona, which the Romans called Sycaminum, closely followed the coast. But soon, it would bend inland, Titus had told him. Caesarea was a Roman port, and the city sat upon the edge of the sea, but he doubted they would confine him where he could see it. Being out of sight might be best for his safety. Local Greeks had trailed the oxcart in which Yosef was shackled, demanding his death. But their shouts had faded as the Romans trundled him behind the first infantry cohort of the 5th Legion. The rest of that legion and all the 10th spread out behind and inland, formed up by units.

As the road curved away from the sea, cavalry elements would shift to straddle both sides of the way they traveled. He had observed the reverse of that on the march from Ptolemais as the road narrowed and hugged the coast—they constantly maneuvered the larger number of units toward the source of any possible threat. But two full Roman legions alert and ready for battle would dissuade any rebel force that might still be large enough and near enough to try.

For a good portion of the morning, Vespasian and Titus had ridden alongside his cart and talked freely. Vespasian had wanted to move Yosef and travel by coastal galley, only a half day's sail from Ptolemais to Caesarea. But reports had come in that rebels fleeing Galilee had gathered in Joppa just south of Caesarea. Many had commandeered boats to raid the coast and harass Roman ships. So, Vespasian had joined Titus and the legions for the two-day march to Caesarea.

Yosef was relieved at the decision. He had barely survived one shipwreck as a free man. If the rebels took or sank a galley he was on, he would not last long in the water wearing chains. The thought made him conscious of them, and he tugged at the iron collar around his neck. Wincing at the chafing made worse by the rough rattling of the cart, he found his fingertips smeared with blood. The flesh where the links and cuffs bound him at the waist, arms, and legs was also raw. It would grow worse until they reached their destination. Ahead, the first arcing of the ranks of marching men showed that the road had begun its turn... and he now had to look over his shoulder to see the sea. In a half-mile, it would be out of sight, and tomorrow they would enter Caesarea.

* * *

CAESAREA

Despite his present circumstances, Yosef still marveled at the artificial harbor created by King Herod. Two immense submerged barriers made of cement blocks on a bed of rubble and stone extended west from the shore. They then bent north to form a northern channel into the harbor. The two breakwaters were topped with a promenade nearly 200 feet wide. As the road moved closer to the sea again, he could see—tiny in the distance—the six giant statues and the great lighthouse on the wall of the western side that greeted ships entering the harbor.

Climbing some 40 feet from the wharf, an enormous east-west staircase led from the dockside up to the area constructed for the dozen vast warehouses of goods entering the port or to be loaded on outbound ships. The extended foundation that capped and leveled the dirt and stone beneath also formed the highland for an immense complex enclosed on the north, east, and south by columned porticoes marking the *temenos*, sacred to the gods. In its center was the temple that Herod had dedicated to the goddess Roma, the embodiment of imperial Rome, and the god-king Augustus.

There, four years ago, before boarding the *Salacia* for Rome, Yosef had seen their colossal statues, carved from local *kurkar* stone and covered with white stucco that shone in the sun. Sailors could see them through the porticoes even from far offshore. The figure of Emperor Augustus, Yosef had been told, equaled the massive statue of Zeus at Olympia. And that of Roma was said to be comparable to the statue of Hera at Argos.

During his previous brief visit, four years before, the freeman Yosef had not gone down the stairs from this plateau to the south and into the city's center. He had stood at their top and looked around and then down at the ships along the quay, wondering which of those vessels would take him to Rome.

What had happened to him since would have been unimaginable to his younger self. He had left Caesarea a free man, fired with the anticipation of seeing Rome and doing what he could to gain the release of the Jewish priests imprisoned there and with hopes to establish a peaceful resolution to Judea's issues with Roman rule. Now he returned a defeated Jewish general, blood-streaked and in the chains he had worn since his capture, his country at war with Rome. He looked up as Vespasian and Titus slowed their horses at the side of his oxcart and matched its pace.

"There is your King Herod's Hippodrome," Titus said, pointing at the stadium where athletic contests, gladiatorial combats, hunting spectacles, and horse-and-chariot races were held. "It is one of the largest outside Rome, and it holds 13,000 spectators."

As they reached the midpoint in passing it, Yosef calculated it must be nearly 1000 feet long. From inside, he heard the echoes of hooves from teams of horses. It did not seem any Games were on—the only crowd around the stadium was now facing them—so someone within must be practicing or breaking in new horses and chariots.

"And just beyond is the procurator's palace," Titus said. He turned to his father, who was staring at the men now lining the road. "And on the other side of it is the villa for your command headquarters, General."

"Who are these men?" Vespasian asked as he waved his cudgel at the thickening rank of onlookers; perhaps a hundred had pushed forward onto the road.

"I don't know, sir," Titus answered and called to a nearby cavalry officer. "Ride ahead with your men and see what those people are about. Clear them from the road."

Yosef watched as they drew closer, and the groups, pressed by Roman horsemen, moved out of the road. The men began shouting vulgarities in three different languages he understood: Greek, Latin, and Aramaic. The variety of phrasings and crudity called for General Vespasian to have Yosef executed or taken to the stadium pens and held for the next gladiatorial Games. On the march, Yosef had heard some of the soldiers talking about the Games with hopes of gambling on their outcome. There was mention of how a thousand Jewish rebel prisoners had already died at the stadium.

* * *

Yosef's cell had no view of the sea, though it was close enough to hear. But then, horses and donkeys cared little for the view. All they needed was shelter from the elements, food, and water. And that is what Yosef was given in his stall in the stable alongside the villa Vespasian had moved into. The stall's original outswing door bracket and bar drop had been replaced with heavier brackets and crossbeams. And inside, Yosef found two bowls—water and gruel—and hay for his bedding.

Titus waved away the slave who had brought these items and then spoke to Yosef. "You must remain chained for now, but General Vespasian promised your friend, Centurion Nicanor, that we would keep you safe and cared for." He removed a small container from a satchel, slung over his shoulder, and tossed it to Yosef, who awkwardly caught it, his hands slowed by the weight of the chain attached to the cuffs at each wrist. They joined to the broad circlet of iron at his waist. "That's *sebum*—tallow," Titus said. "It works beneath armor and the *subarmalis*, the underpadding to help prevent chafing. Coat your skin beneath the metal you wear. I'll send more water for you to wash and clean clothing, too. Tonight, General Vespasian dines with the Procurator Marcus Antonius Julianus, but tomorrow morning he will send for you."

* * *

Now somewhat clean, Yosef was thankful for the clothing and the balm of the sebum, which had eased the rubbing of rough iron against his skin. Though his stall was windowless, he could smell the scents carried on the sea breeze... the Procurator must have feted General Vespasian with a grand meal. His stomach growled as he looked into his empty bowl; his wishes had still not refilled it.

The tang of salt-laden air made Yosef think of Cleo and Nicanor, who were well gone from Judea and on the sea somewhere closer to Rome with each passing day. He was thankful Cleo had escaped the brutalities of her husband, Gessius Florus, and was under the protection of Nicanor to find a life far from the tragedy and devastation awaiting his country. His own fate, his family's, and Judea's were sealed. He had last entered Caesarea on the eve of a journey that had forever changed his life. His return would likely begin its end.

II

SEPTEMBER 67 CE

JERUSALEM

THE LOWER CITY

Hananiah limped to his workbench. The focus needed to work an unblemished edge on the metal would lessen his awareness of the pain he still felt in his knee and groin. The swelling in both had gone down, though he could still taste the coppery blood from his tongue, reminding him of how hard he'd bitten it when he had been kicked in the crotch. That blow had riled him to a wave of anger he found hard to control. But he had done as he must. Dazed, he had pursued whoever it was that had killed Esau ben Beor, intent on retaliating before they disappeared into the dark labyrinth of galleries and tunnels in Solomon's Quarry. He had gone back to where Esau ben Beor's body lay and found the message his killer had dropped. It was a note from Beor himself, intended for Gessius Florus. Hananiah had left the body, limped nearly the length of the city to his shop, and prepared to forward the message to Florus along with the news of his spy's death... presumably by the Sicarii's deadly assassin, "The Hand."

He lighted the lantern and pulled the sharpening stone wheel from beneath the bench. With a sigh of relief at getting off his feet but careful of the tender spots, Hananiah settled on the stool. The vertical back of the bench above the work surface was a honeycomb spread of openings, receptacles for his rasps, files, and burnishing tools to smooth and polish metal. From the bottom right slot, deep back from within its shadows, he took out his bag with its *reliquiae.* The souvenir of the remains of each person he had taken for pay or pleasure. The contents of the bag had become so dried and cured that only he could detect their scent. He had replaced the stained bag through the years, and the aroma was more a fragrant and pleasing memory than reality. He moved the bag, feeling them shift inside. With a smile, he picked up the flat bar of metal he was transforming into a blade and spun the sharpening wheel.

The sputtering wick marked the passage of more time than what had seemed to him only minutes. The blade revealed itself from within the Iberian iron, the metal's quality valued by Roman armorers. He had bought it in Alexandria from the man who had taught him cold-hammering, which produced the finest double-edged daggers, the *parazonium* preferred by higher-rank soldiers. The blade he worked on was in that style, leaf-shaped and about 19 inches long. He would affix a bone hilt, grip, and pommel once the metalwork was done. It was a lethal work of art in his hands.

The sound of the door opening disturbed him, and he was irritated by the sound of footsteps the appearance of someone in the pool of light from the lamp on his workbench. He scowled at the man who had interrupted him. "Yes?"

"Your name is Hananiah, right?" The man was not intimidated by the glare and did not wait for a reply. "You know my sister, Miriam?"

Now recognizing him, Hananiah slowly nodded and brought the blade away from the sharpening stone; a ripple of light glinted along its length.

"Have you seen her lately?" Matthew asked.

Hananiah shook his head, set the blade on the bench, and stood, stepping closer to the counter. "No, why?"

"She's missing. If you see her, please tell her to come home." The two men stared at one another. "I'm Matthew. My mother, father, and I are worried."

"If she comes in, I will tell her." He watched as Matthew nodded and left. He thought of the young woman. Almost as quiet as he, Miriam had enjoyed handling the knives and daggers he had shown her. Something within her had brushed fingertips with the person he was before he had become what he was now. Hananiah blinked, then reached into a woven basket hung out of sight below the countertop. He pulled out a blade sheathed and strapped it to his waist. Turning to quench the lantern on his bench, he grabbed his cloak and left. He would search for her.

III

SEPTEMBER 67 CE

BETWEEN PTOLEMAIS AND JERUSALEM

Sayid had heard the other travelers in the countryside talking about the two Roman legions leaving Ptolemais and heading south toward Caesarea. That and word about a third legion moving toward Scythopolis meant that Roman patrols would be fewer in a day or two, and they could move more freely. The 12th Legion would remain in Ptolemais. He felt a twinge of guilt yet again at leaving the legion behind. He had once had a duty to the 12th's former commander—Cestius Gallus—to part from the legion and deliver the commander's letters and copied reports to his wife, Lady Octavia, in Antioch.

Now Sayid must save Cleo and the young boy she had taken in before he could return to the legion. Gessius Florus had ruined her plans to meet Nicanor, who was to sneak her out of Judea and away from the danger he posed, so now he was all the hope she had. Yosef had the crazy idea that she should go to Jerusalem, where his family would take her in. She had taken a letter from Yosef and a means to prove she went to them at his prompting, and they all hoped that would work. It would work, assuming he could get her there without getting them all killed. Roman patrols were one concern, but bandits and rebels posed a more significant threat. The former tended to be on the open road; the latter liked to wait behind bushes.

The sweep of land on his left now had a strip of gray tinging orange—growing against the darkness. The ground leveled between hillocks and mounds dotted with patches of scrub brush and stunted, twisted trees. He had found a trough for them to camp in the lee of a knoll. Three days before, he had used the last of his money to buy food and two skins of water from a traveling merchant on a cart trail connected to one of the main paths to Ptolemais. This morning they would eat the last of that food.

Lady Cleo stirred, half-waking, on her side and wrapped in a blanket; Elian huddled asleep next to her. A puff of wind swirled loose dirt around a large clump of brush, and the same current teased the locks of hair that had escaped Cleo's headdress beneath the hood of her cloak as she slept. Despite the clothing he had gotten her, she did not look like a Jewish woman. He hoped she was more clearheaded when she awoke. Each day since fleeing Ptolemais, she had gotten a little better. But the beating from Gessius Florus—gods curse him—that had knocked her out had left her confused, with a headache, and it was painful for her eyes during the day's brightest sunlight. A fluttering of wings in the shadow of Cleo's shoulder made him frown. Cicero—Cleo's pet parrot—worried him more than anything. Still, so far, the ill-tempered bird, seeming to understand the danger, had kept quiet and not strayed from Cleo and the boy.

Sayid had told Cleo about how he'd set fire to Florus's villa to save her. And in the blaze, he had struggled with a man—Florus, he hoped—and kicked them back into a flaming room. He prayed to the gods the man was dead. Cleo did not remember what had happened but cried that she was glad to be free, no matter what they faced.

* * *

"I've eaten already," Sayid said as he served Cleo and Elian the last of the food and willed his grumbling stomach to be silent. The sough of the wind was just loud enough to cover it.

"So, what should we do now?" she asked. He had told her their present circumstances and been relieved she had grasped and understood on her waking.

"We must have money," he replied. "Some good people will help us... but too many we may meet now, between here and Jerusalem, will not be good people. The frightened will not acknowledge us. Others will take what we have... and more..." Sayid looked away from Cleo's steady gaze; she knew what he meant. The boy, Elian, was white-faced and trembled, but Sayid must be truthful. "Then, they will kill us."

Cleo replied and smoothed Elian's hair, which stood up in every direction after his sleep. Tears coursed down his face. "Shh shh, Elian... don't cry," Cleo said. She held the boy and looked up at Sayid. "We must sell what we have for the money we need."

"Sell what, Lady Cleo?" Sayid worried he had overestimated her recovery from the fog of confusion after her beating. "We have nothing."

"I have one thing," Cleo lifted the *lunula*, the silver and moonstone pendant that Poppaea had given her long before. An aching pang pierced her when she thought of her best friend, who had married Emperor Nero... the man who also killed her. "Are we still close to Ptolemais?"

"We cannot return there, Lady Cleo!" Sayid was alarmed. "That would stick our hand into a hornet's nest!"

8

"Not me, Sayid... I'm afraid it will have to be you. I know a merchant who will buy this... with no questions asked."

* * *

Two days later...

"What is this?" Cleo studied the bundle Sayid handed her as Elian tore into the wrapped bricks of pressed dates from the packet of food Sayid had set upon the ground next to him. The boy's mouth was already full with a handful of dried olives from another bag.

"It's clothing—a new robe and cloak for you," Sayid replied and grinned at the boy who was chewing and trying to smile at the same time.

"Why?" Cleo's fingers plucked at the robe she wore.

"I'm sorry, Lady Cleo, but you do not look Judean. Near where my mother lives, in Antioch, there are many Greeks and Greek Jews. My mother knew several—some of the women looked more Greek than anything, closer to your looks—who came from Tarsus, north of Antioch. In Ptolemais, next to the shopkeeper I sold your necklace to, I spotted clothing that seemed like what I had seen those women wear. I know there was some disagreement between them and other Jews... but being one of them is better than being seen as a Roman. But from now on, we must speak only Greek." He kneeled beside the boy next to her, who since his return had resumed his chattering ways, judging by how he had greeted him that morning. "And Elian, you must be silent around anyone other than Lady Cleo and me."

IV

TAENARUM, ROMAN PROVINCE OF ACHAEAN MACEDONIA

The old navarch, Marinus, owner and sailing master of the *Delphina* and the two accompanying cargo vessels, *Pistris* and *Xiphias,* had taken a liking to Nicanor. Since leaving Ptolemais, he had tried to convince the centurion he was better off not bringing some provincial woman to Rome, where there were plenty of women to be had. With a lewd wink, he'd said, "There are brothels... or if you've enough coin, then buy one or two women... the slave markets always have at least a few comely maidens you'll find to your liking." The man had plied the trade routes of the *mare internum* for a decade and more since he had retired from the army. The mariner seemingly knew every brothel and slave market along the coasts of the great sea.

Marinus had spent much of their time explaining the merits of every port. Nicanor let him chatter on; it helped pass the time, and perhaps some useful information would come forth with all the chaff. After events of the last few years, Nicanor was convinced that once he left the army, he wanted a quiet place with no fighting. Maybe one of the places the captain spoke of could become his home.

For a fleeting handful of hours in Ptolemais, he thought of living there with Lady Cleo, in a place where they could hide and hope to be forgotten. Even if her brother Marcus Otho, governor of Hispania Lusitania, provided protection or safety for Cleo. Gessius Florus would never stop searching for her to punish her for running from him. And it seemed the man had the support of Emperor Nero.

When Cestius Gallus had been commander of the 12th Legion, he had made uncharacteristic mistakes that Nicanor thought resulted from the manipulation of a hidden hand. It had all led to the embarrassing defeat of the 12th Legion and the deaths of thousands of Roman soldiers. Once also the governor of Syria, Gallus had been found dead in Antioch, apparently by his own hand. Nicanor doubted that. The common thread was the arrival of Gessius Florus as the Roman procurator in Judea. The man had lost that position, only to gain one of lower stature. Still, he seemed more powerful now, which could have come only from Emperor Nero's favor. Nicanor was sure the two greed-driven men had formed an alliance of some sort.

Nicanor leaned on the ship's rail and watched the men rolling casks of water up the gangway and onto the boat. For the past two days, they had been in the port of Taenarum at the tip of the Peloponnese to repair a cracked—then broken—mast spar that tangled the rigging and loosened deck planks with its fall. Marinus had cursed at the delay: "Here we sit. I break my record time to reach this point—ten days out, mind you—from Ptolemais, and now nearly two of the three days gained are gone."

Nicanor had already seen what there was to see in the small port. He had little to do while the men worked on the repairs. Marinus had told him of the green marble quarried nearby, saying it was much esteemed by the rich for their homes and edifices. He told of the snails they harvested that yielded the prized Lacedaemonian purple dye—it sold at high prices to clothe Roman nobles. Nicanor had watched the merchants of those commodities busy haggling with traders from most points of the empire. But that held little entertainment for him.

He had enjoyed seeing the remnants of temples erected by the Spartans. He had heard many stories of those fighting men from a man he respected, his mother's father. *Men who returned either with their shield or upon it*, he thought as he had stood among the structures. The stories said Spartan women quoted this instruction to their men as they went off to war. He mused, one day, he would leave his shield behind and find somewhere to spend his days drinking good beer and sweet wine... and eating good food prepared by a woman he loved.

"Nicanor...."

He turned at Marinus's call and hoped, now that the captain's anger had faded with the completion of repairs, that he did not plan to tell him stories of the local women.

"We're almost ready and will sail just before sunset. I want to clear the harbor before nightfall." He stood beside Nicanor and rested his thick forearms on the rail. "They say Emperor Nero and his entourage are in Greece. They will be holding special events for him at the Games in Corinth." Marinus shook his head, spat over the side, and cast his eyes around. "The summer must be too hot for him in Rome."

Ever cautious, as he had learned to be in that city, Nicanor did not reply in kind. "Well, at least you are still a day ahead of your record." He clasped the old sailor on the shoulder. To himself, he thought, *Good... that means the Praetorians are with Nero and likely the Praetorian Prefect, Tigellinus, is among them.* Though Vespasian had given him written orders to Rome and had sent copies to Tigellinus and the emperor, informing them, Nicanor had no desire to run into the prefect in Rome. After arrival in Ostia, he would do as General Vespasian directed and carry his letters directly to Antonia Caenis in Falacrine. He would then go to Rome.

* * *

SYRACUSAE, IN THE ROMAN PROVINCE OF SICILIA

Marinus was livid—not fit for any man, even Nicanor, to be around—as they slowly came into the harbor at Syracusae on the eastern end of the island of Sicilia. "*Futio*—more time lost!" he fumed. The spar and rigging repaired at Taenarum had not held, and the work must be redone before the next sea leg to Ostia. They could not sail until the next day, and he would not be able to break his personal record.

Nicanor nodded to the angry captain as he stepped from the gangplank onto a long, wooden dock still bustling even at day's end with the work of three vessels the size of the *Delphina* that were docked on either side. He headed toward an equally busy *taberna* on the stone-paved road fronting the wharf and its warehouses. Inside he found only a single table with an open seat. The man sitting there looked up at him and nodded. Even wearing only plan field garb, a centurion got a response from civilians. Nicanor slid the chair out and sighed, enjoying the steadiness of land. He had never gotten accustomed to standing, working, or sleeping on a ship's deck—no matter how solid—that moved beneath his feet. He studied the man across from him, a workman, judging by his thick-muscled shoulders and calloused hands. "What's better here," he asked, "the beer or the wine?"

A grin flashed across the man's seamed face. "It depends on the coin you carry, centurion."

Nicanor took a silver *denarius* from the pouch at his belt and set it on the table.

The man nodded. "Then it's the wine for you...." He frowned at the cup in his own scarred hand and raised it to his lips.

The man's long sleeve hiked up to reveal the lighter, hairless skin of his inner forearm. Tattooed there were two fish, one on each side of an anchor. The *Ichthys*es were like what he had seen on Christians in Rome. "Will you join me, then?" Nicanor asked.

The man caught Nicanor's gaze and tugged his sleeve down. "Thank you but, no." He gulped his drink and rose.

"I mean you no harm," Nicanor said, glancing again at the man's arm, then at his eyes. "I know the symbol... don't worry. I knew a man in Rome who was a Christian, and some I served with listened to his teachings."

The workman settled back in his chair. "What man?"

"Paul of Tarsus... have you heard of him?"

The man nodded. "Ten years ago, I heard him speak here, and it took not long for his words to fill my heart. That's when I..." he tapped his forearm.

"What does the anchor mean?" Nicanor asked.

"It's a symbol that most reassures me in my faith. When I see it, I'm reminded that the Christos is my anchor." For a moment, the man studied Nicanor, waiting, no doubt, for denouncing or capture. Nicanor himself had witnessed the burnings, the death before wild beasts. All for sport.

The man risks all that, Nicanor marveled, and he could not help a little laugh when the man asked, "Do you still wish me to drink with you?"

"Yes," Nicanor said with good cheer, then waved the tavern keeper to them. "When I'm back in Rome, I hope to visit Paul in prison and speak with him again."

"He is no longer a prisoner," the man whispered, his eyes down, staring into an empty cup.

Nicanor turned from ordering a pitcher of wine, surprised but relieved at the news. "Good... but I still hope to find him if I can. Do you know if he is still in Rome?"

"Yes." The man's voice remained low, but his lifted eyes glistened. "But you misunderstand me. The Romans executed him... his body remains there, but he is now in the arms of our Lord."

The stab of regret and sadness Nicanor felt changed to worry for his friend Yosef. Would he remain a prisoner? Was that the best he could hope for, and might he end up being executed, too?

"I was afraid I might discover that," Nicanor said, shaking his head. He stood, his thirst for wine now gone. Without looking at the man, he left the denarius on the table and returned to the *Delphina*.

V

SEPTEMBER 67 CE

JERUSALEM

THE LOWER CITY, KING DAVID'S TOMB

It was her only hope. Using the next-to-last partially burned torch, with its sputtering flame, Miriam had discovered what appeared to be a passage sealed with a slab of stone. Its top, bottom, and sides were covered with clay that had dried to a hard packing. She had no idea why it had been fashioned and sealed in place like that, or whether a way out lay behind it, or anything at all. But it was the only other opening in the large chamber she had tumbled into. The one she had entered through was blocked with the collapse of tons of stone.

Miriam took out the dagger she had managed to keep hold of after the fight in Solomon's Quarry. Regretting the damage to its blade, she scraped out the mortar used to seal the slab. She had gotten one side free at the edge, and the bottom layer cracked and fell away. She smelled an increasing foulness that burned her nose and eyes as the slab sagged an inch, then two.... widening the new gap. She raised the torch held low at her side, and it was at waist height when the wisp of air from inside ignited as a whooshing tongue of fire. The slab blew out, crashing into her with a punch of blue flame that licked around its edges and then washed over her. With the left side of her tunic enveloped in the blaze, Miriam tumbled to one side. She frantically rolled to put out the burning sleeve and the cloth over her chest.

Miriam lay in the darkness, tunic scorched and smoldering, trying to catch her breath and gingerly checking her singed breast and shoulder. Her hand reached out for the staff she had leaned against the jamb of the doorway. She could not find it and, despite the pain in her chest and back, scrambled onto her hands and knees. Crawling from side to side along the wall, she felt for the staff. It was the only thing she had left that gave her comfort in the dark.

Zechariah—her mentor—had lived in the darkness most of his adult life, and that staff had helped him navigate it. He had used it to kill the two Roman soldiers who had raped her and then taught her how to fight and defend herself with staff and blade. Before being killed by a Roman mercenary, his last act was to save her—yet again—

with the staff. During the years of dark memories since then, Zechariah's staff was what meant most to her. With it, she felt safe. Without it… she was lost.

Her hands touched something she recognized by its feel. It was the now-empty message pouch carried by Esau ben Beor. She had cut it from his waist with the thrust of her counterattack and then snatched it up. She must have kicked it to one side as she fell backward. She picked it up and slung it over her head by the new cord she had attached to it. She shifted around to keep searching, and her knee pressed painfully down on a round shaft. Her heart surged… it must be the staff. But no, it was the short haft of the nearly spent torch she had dropped. She pulled it to her, her hand sliding up to feel for its head. There was still a wad of the old material wrapping it. She sniffed the air. The rank odor was gone, and her eyes and nose no longer stung. Was it that odor that had caught fire?

Zechariah had once mentioned the unseen dangers of some of the old tunnels and natural chambers buried deep below Jerusalem. They were threats one could detect only by senses other than sight. If she ever encountered a choking, stinging smell, she was to extinguish any lamp and not relight it until the smell was gone or she had moved far away from it. And he had urged her not to be frightened by the dark: "Be still in the dark when you must… but do not let anything that happens make you fail to act. Fear that immobilizes you is only conquered by your will to move and do what must be done. Even in the darkness."

Miriam settled the torch across her lap and took out the sparking stones she kept in a small pouch secured at her waist. She had checked them countless times since running from the man who attacked and wounded her after she killed Esau ben Beor in Solomon's Quarry. She struck sparks, but the torch did not catch. She tried again. Nothing. Her deep, shuddering breath drew a dart of pain from her left breast and a sharper one from the slash across her back. The back of her tunic tugged at the wound, where there was a new stickiness from fresh blood. Tears ran down her face and loosened the crust of blood from the gash on her cheek. The pain of more than the injuries, the pain of everything else—the past, the present, and what she faced for a future—was too much. She was too tired to try again. Her hand, still holding the stones, lowered to her lap, and soon the sobs quieted.

* * *

Miriam jerked awake as something crawled over her leg. She heard a skittering echo in the dark, and fear gripped her. The torch was still across her lap, the stones still in her hands. She held the sparking stones close over the head of the torch and struck them again. A long runner of sparks landed on the ancient once oil-soaked fabric. One caught within it, and a spot glowed. She struck again, and the rivulets flashed and joined it. An ember spread, and she bent over it, pursed her dry lips, and breathed. The slight current of air fed it, and the cinder flared into a flame that flickered then steadied to eat into the remnant of the thick wad of cloth.

She carefully raised the torch, slowing if the fire dimmed and moving once it strengthened, and walked toward the opening she had discovered. Near it and rolled up against the wall was Zechariah's staff. She gripped the long rod and felt a surge of hope at its weight in her hand. At that moment, she understood something she'd read in Zechariah's letters to his wife and daughter, letters she had found in his shop after his death. They had been hidden with the maps of the Masada tunnels that Elazar ben Yair, the Sicarii leader, had searched for unsuccessfully.

In the letters, Zechariah had often mentioned how his staff was what he counted on, how it was always faithful and good. Reliable. It was his comfort in the darkness he had lived within since he had been blinded. She had read the letters in a literal way, so she took him to mean his staff was the length of wood she held in her hands. But with this last troubled sleep, her fears had turned into dreams of her family. She loved her father, mother, and brothers, who were important to her. Now she realized most of Zechariah's reference to the staff that gave him strength was really about his love for his wife and daughter. Even after they had been tragically killed, they were still his strength. They were what kept him going, and his life had a purpose in honoring their memory.

Miriam stepped closer to the opening—where the stone slab had been—and heard the echo of claws on stone far within, beyond the opening and moving further away. She had not heard the scratches so loudly before, and those slight activities had seemed random foraging. But this was movement in a purposeful direction. *Too big for a mouse. A rat, perhaps?* Raising the torch, she thought of her family she wanted to see again... and of Ehud, who was a lost love unexpectedly returned. Maybe there could be a second chance for them. She stepped into what seemed a long dark passageway.

VI

SEPTEMBER 67 CE

PTOLEMAIS

GESSIUS FLORUS'S RESIDENCE

Drusus's stature had once made him the butt of jokes in the legion until the fools realized his strength pound-for-pound was greater than that of many men much larger than he. Some witnessing him atop a horse thought him a youth until they got closer and saw his leathery visage. But his out-sized sinewy hands, wrists, arms, and shoulders bunched with muscle, and his shrewdness made him master of even the most headstrong horse. "Stranglers...." A *lanista* had called his hands, and the man had hoped to recruit and train him to fight as a paid freeman gladiator or make him a public executioner between events at the Games.

Drusus had learned his slightness gave the deep-chested and long-legged horse he rode even greater stamina. So he now made more money than he had as a legionary. He sold customers on his speed, reliability, and disposition to ask no questions about what he carried for them. His sole purpose was to transport on horseback whatever they gave him wherever they wanted. It did not matter to him what was in the cured and waterproofed courier pouch he sometimes found in its well-hidden spot on a trail north of Jerusalem. Without looking around for the one who had left it there, he would take it to the nobleman outside Ptolemais. The noble's major domus—a sour persimmon of a man—would have the coins for his pay and a similar pouch to return to that hidden spot outside of Jerusalem. Drusus looked forward to seeing the vinegary man shortly and collecting his money.

The wind brought the smell of a recent burning before he turned from the road onto the graveled grade with its slight climb to the nobleman's domus. As the grade leveled, he saw the now smoke-stained porticoed front, the stucco of the columns charred, and half the building's roof burned away or collapsed in with the butts of blackened beams canted at angles and askew. The covered entrance that jutted from the main building was intact, though it showed the marking of the fire that had consumed much of the back—the seaward side of the domus.

He reined in and called out. Before, there had always been a slave or servant nearby attending to the entrance. With such a fire destroying much of the building, perhaps all were gone. He called out again. The breeze stilled, and he heard a faint cry from around the side. Hooking a thumb into the strap of the pouch, he dismounted and, holding the reins, followed the sound. He reached the corner where a peristyle colonnade began its run toward the rear. The wooden shutters of the inner walls along its length had burned away.

"Help us!"

The call turned him from searching the openings for movement inside. A woman lurched from the end of the colonnade, leaning on a charred length of wood.

"Help!" she beckoned to him.

He approached her, still leading his horse. "Who are you? Where's Glaucio, the major domus?"

"Glaucio's gone... before all this happened," she waved an arm at the building and staggered, leaning heavily on the piece of a small beam. The woman's hair was a tangle and her face smeared with soot... although her mouth and chin were cleaner than the rest of it. She reeked of wine and had the red-veined eyes and puffy face of men he knew who drank themselves to sleep every night and started the next day with a drink. It was only because she was drunk that she could weave and sway despite the swollen ankle and mottled bruising around it that, from his experience, meant a broken bone.

"I'm Eris... follow me." With a grunt, she swung toward the back of the villa. "The master, Lord Florus, is hurt."

The walkway at the rear of the building had been lined with wooden columns, and several had burned completely through. At the center point of the span was a shallow-stepped terrace that changed from stone to well-tended greenery that extended to a high hedge and piled-stone wall. Beyond that, an expanse of scrub brush and stunted trees covered rolling dunes that led down toward the sea.

On the edge of where the portico ended and the open terrace began, a man was trapped beneath two large beams that had collapsed when the columns gave way. The beams were fire-marked, and from what he could see, the man's legs were red and blistered from burns. Drusus kneeled next to him, noting the scorched hair, blistered arms, and singed and soot-blackened toga trimmed with purple. This must be the nobleman who had paid him, but he would no more. He looked at the still body and shook his head with regret.

Then the man opened his eyes and gasped, "Eris...."

* * *

It had seemed a pain-addled, fever-filled dream, thought Gessius Florus as he watched the man mount a horse that seemed too large for him. Florus was still drunk on the wine Eris had steadily given him since finding him beneath collapsing beams as he tried to escape the fire. The wine had lessened the pain in his legs, and she had not stinted on medicating herself, though he doubted she needed her own hurt leg to justify it.

The messenger, Drusus, would go to Ptolemais and return with a *medicus* and cart to take him to the town. Though startled at first, the man had found that though Florus was pinned down and smashed between timber and stone, the crushing weight of the heavy beams had been borne mainly by chunks of wood from one of the collapsed columns. He would likely have died had the messenger not come from his spy in Jerusalem. And a lucky thing it was that the man was so strong for his size. It was almost unbelievable how he was able to lift the massive beams from Florus's legs.

Gessius Florus read the messages Drusus had brought him. So, Esau ben Beor was dead. The gods-cursed Sicarii assassin, The Hand, had killed the man as he had others working for him in Jerusalem. Florus would order Hananiah, a hired killer, his man in Jerusalem, to put more pressure on Ehud, his one remaining spy with some level of access to those making decisions in the city. And Hananiah must hunt down that cursed Sicarii as he had been hired to do. Whoever that assassin was, his talent seemed to match that of any he could counter with. The last letter from Tigellinus in Rome also had him concerned about developments there. What if Nero lost power and was ousted? Florus had heard the rumblings against Nero from men he knew in Alexandria. The two-sided game he had been forced to play, diverting tax revenue for his own use, was becoming riskier. He did it to ultimately benefit Nero, too. But that would not matter if he failed to accomplish his objective, the greater theft of the Jews' temple treasure in Jerusalem.

Short term, Florus needed the taxes the allied and regained cities were paying to the empire. They needed to pass through him, so he could siphon off money to hire men loyal to his coin. If Nero were removed, he must have a secure place to hide with enough money to control those who could help his efforts. Galerius Senna and Tyrannius Priseus of the 12th Legion still had a part to play.

The night that had ended with fire, Quintus had left on his mission to raise a private mercenary force for Florus. Perhaps this Drusus could continue to serve him, too, only more directly. The man was strong, and Florus detected in him a degree of brutal greed he could bend to his use. He would have him spread the word of the bounty he offered to anyone who could either bring Cleo back to him or tell him where she hid. She must be punished for her betrayal.

VII

Between Ptolemais and Jerusalem

Sayid's arms ached as they never had, even during his days working the docks in Laodicea Ad Mare. He had stayed with that backbreaking job until his mother had become well enough for him to leave her and return to the legion. But now, another duty had fallen to him—to get the Lady Cleo safely to Jerusalem, along with the boy he had now carried for miles. Elian had fallen ill two days before with a stomach sickness that would not even allow him to keep water down, and then a fever racked him. The boy was so hot that Sayid felt it baking him, too, and he had to grip the boy all the firmer in his sweat-slick arms.

He looked over his shoulder at Lady Cleo near faltering with exhaustion, her face caked with trail dust and dirt. Each night since Ptolemais, he had heard her softly crying until dawn, trying not to disturb him nor alarm Elian. But she never uttered a cry in the day and never a complaint or claim that she could not go on. She was so much more durable than he had first thought when he had met her four years before when he was assigned to be in her escort for her tour of the empire's southern and eastern provinces. She had seemed a beautiful—yet fragile—young maiden come to life from one of the stories his mother had told him when he was a child. She was highborn, regal, but she had also proved to be kind. And she was strong, though he had not grasped that until the shipwreck of the *Salacia* when they drifted for days and thought they would all die. Now, after all that had happened to her... and what was happening now... she still showed her strength.

The day before, they passed a man who told them of a village ahead where several paths crossed. Sayid would have planned to go around it—they had to avoid any attention—but would camp close enough so he could circle back alone and pick up more food and water. Now, with Elian far sicker, they must head for the village and hope they had a doctor or healer and medicine to help the boy. With a groan he could not hide, he lifted Elian higher and clasped him to his chest. He felt they were now near the place, but the late-afternoon sun was fading, and they must find the village before nightfall. The boy seemed afire, and Sayid doubted he would live another night.

* * *

"I've given him ground bark from the willow," said the old woman as she stiffly rose from kneeling beside Elian, who had swallowed the mixture of water and medicine without waking. "Before I returned home to marry, I worked for a time in Damascus for a lady whose son suffered from fevers. I come from the Hula valley—north of the Sea of Galilee—where willows grow along the smaller lakes, and the remedy we used for fevers there gave him some relief. With the Romans in control of Galilee, many of us came south to get away from the fighting, but I brought a supply with me."

Sayid noted her eyes watching his hands and scanned the village that even in the dusk did not seem permanent. It existed only because of the well with good water and the trails that converged there. "Will you continue to Jerusalem?" he asked.

A look of scorn crossed the old woman's face. "No... my people do not trust any in Jerusalem. We'll abide here for now. We have little the Romans want unless something brings them down upon us in these hard times. But a trader from Ptolemais came through and told me of a bounty placed on a Roman noblewoman who had fled that city. She's wanted, and there's a tidy reward for anyone who returns her."

Sayid wasn't sure if it was the shifting light of the fire he had just built with nightfall upon them or whether the woman's eyes had flicked toward Cleo, who lay quietly, her back toward them. Cleo was exhausted and, as Sayid had explained to the woman, sleeping. But he was sure she was awake. "Well, thank you for your help." He gave her the coin he had promised and that her eyes kept watching for.

She handed him a small packet made from folded parchment. "Add some of this powder in the boy's drink each morning and night until it's all gone, and keep bathing him with cool water. Both will help stop his fever, and he should get better."

A flapping sound drew both their eyes back to Cleo's sleeping form. Between her and the restless boy was Cicero. One of the parrot's feet had a slender cord tied to it and was attached to Cleo's wrist. The bird was awake, and his eyes agleam as he watched them. Sayid had tried and failed to get Cleo to turn that bird loose, but she would not.

"I've seen birds kept in the rich households of Damascus... but never one that traveled." The woman's eyes sank deep into her folds of flesh and glittered at Sayid. "Or traveled with a lady. Where did you say you are going?"

"Like you and your people... we hope to stay away from the fighting." Sayid took the woman's arm and guided her to the edge of the growing light from the several fires now blooming around the center of the village. "Thank you again." She walked away and gave him a last glance over her shoulder. He returned to the camp he had set up on the outskirts of the village. He prayed the boy was soon better and knew he would not sleep until they were away from these people. Alone, they were safer. At least until they got close to Jerusalem and tried to enter the city.

* * *

The clatter of armed men woke Sayid. He jolted up and remembered that at daybreak, Cleo had convinced him to rest for a while. He went to rub his eyes and found Cicero was tied to his wrist. He and the bird blinked at each other. Thankfully the parrot hardly squawked anymore... barely at all since the first hours after the fire in Ptolemais. Maybe the creature understood how precarious their situation was. Sayid stood and looked around the camp for Cleo. The noise of men and animals turned him again to the village center. He could now see the crude structures, some of wood, some half-built of mud brick, that had been erected near the well, leaving an open area around it.

Several men—four on horses, two on donkeys—had dismounted and were watering the animals in a long trough next to the well Cleo had recently visited. All were heavily armed with an assortment of weapons that appeared to have been taken or stolen from Romans. He did not like their look and whipped around, searching again for Cleo. Elian—his hair still wet from Cleo's hand cloth used to tend to him and swept back away from his face—seemed to sleep more easily. An empty cup and the packet of willow bark were near his head.

The sound of loud talk at the well drew him. As he walked nearer, he saw the old woman talking with one of the men, who glanced at a woman kneeling to fill a water skin from a leather bucket drawn from the well. Cleo! Her hood had slipped back upon her shoulders, and the morning light was full upon her face. She finished filling the skin and set the bucket back on the broad stone lip of the well. Holding the full waterskin carefully in her arms, she began to walk toward him. The old woman's eyes followed her.

* * *

Sayid had tensely waited throughout the day, but none of the men had come near them, and he had not seen the old woman since that morning. At sunset, he relaxed. Elian had awakened and been

23

hungry. He drank a bowl of broth and vegetables, his medicine mixed within, and had fallen back into a gentle sleep. The fever flush had faded, and he felt cooler to the touch. If he slept well and was fever-free in the morning, they would quietly leave before dawn.

* * *

Cleo's scream brought Sayid to his feet, and before he knew it, the wooden dockworker's spike he always carried in a loop at his waist was ready in his hand. The fire had burned low, but he could see a burly man—a Roman bow and quiver of arrows strapped across his broad back—with a large dagger in one hand and a fistful of Cleo's hair in the other. She fought as he dragged her. The knife flashed and cut Cicero's cord from Cleo's wrist, but the parrot did not fly off. Instead, in a squawking rage, he launched himself at the man's face just as Elian came up from his bedroll to pull at the man's back. The man whirled, slapping Elian away so that the boy crumpled to one side, and the assailant batted and slashed at the bird scratching at his face.

Sayid leaped across the fire, forcing the man to let Cleo go and face him. He stumbled as Cleo crawled away, and the man's fist crashed into the side of his head. Sayid's knees buckled, and he twisted to fall on his back and felt a crunch and snap of wood beneath him. The man was atop him with the dagger raised. It was a legionary's *pugio,* and its long blade glinted in the firelight. The cords of the big man's neck stood out as he bore down on Sayid, bringing the knife closer to his chest. There was more snapping beneath Sayid, and he felt something sharp pierce his back. Then an arrow transfixed the man's thick neck. His eyes bulged, showing all white, and his mouth frothed with blood. The man gasped and rolled off Sayid, who scrambled to his feet half-bent over and saw the shafts of broken arrows and their points on the ground where he had been pinned.

Cleo stood there, still holding the bow Elian had stripped from her attacker, and the boy held the smashed quiver. Cleo's shot had been the only whole arrow remaining in the bunch. Sayid shakily straightened, his head still ringing from the blow of the man's hard fist. Where were the other men? He stopped over the dead man, stripped the sheath from his belt, and pried the dagger from his hand. He recognized him from that morning and knew why the man had come alone. The old woman, thinking to earn the bounty but not wanting to share with others, had convinced him it was worth trying to take them by himself.

"We must go now before the others discover this." Sayid went to Elian and kneeled to say, "They will come after us... we must move fast... can you make it?" The boy nodded. Sayid thought Cleo would still be shaken, but she had already rolled their blankets and slung them on her back. She took a thick piece of cloth, wrapped her right forearm, and called to Cicero, who fluttered from the dark and landed on her arm. Sayid took the water skin and food bag, and they ran into the night.

VIII

OCTOBER 67 CE

GISCHALA, GALILEE

Titus reined in before the palisade-style main gate of Gischala. He reached down to pat the glossy black coat of Tempestas, the horse he had promised to look after for Nicanor. She had become his favorite to ride. The mare stamped her hooves, then settled down, faint tendrils of vapor gathering around her muzzle. Her head came up at an angle that told him she watched as shrewdly as he for any threat from the city.

Sections of the wall had been strengthened, and new-made wood and stone watchtowers reduced the intervals of the former reinforcements. Two men stood in each—an archer with arrow ready-nocked and presumably a slinger at his side, gripping the cords of his sling and loaded with a shoulder-slung bag of projectiles at the ready. These were likely the best men with their respective weapons, and dozens of other men—archers, slingers, swordsmen, and spearmen—lined the wall and parapets.

"Why do they not fire upon us?" asked Iulius Placidus, now beside him. The senior tribune and *praefectus alae* was the officer in command of the 1,000 horsemen encircling the city. He and his men had sealed it just as they had done at Yotapta while they waited for the infantry and heavier siege equipment necessary to begin an assault. They had tested the defenses by coming near enough to see what arms men on the wall were equipped with and how they responded to the approach.

Not taking his eyes off the walls and gate before them, Titus replied, "This city, though fortified, is not as well situated as Yotapta or even Gamala. You've seen both. They were built upon steep hills with limited and difficult approaches—they proved quite challenging. As General Vespasian expected, news of those two cities falling has weakened the spirit of any forces that remain to defy Rome in Galilee—for those were the best defended of them all. The defenders of Gischala know they cannot stand against us. I don't think they want to fi—"

A shout came from one of the largest towers at the gate and made him look toward it.

Placidus waved his hand, and a unit of cavalrymen came forward. Six positioned themselves in front of them, shields out and set before the pommels of their saddles. The *parma* each carried was about 36 inches across. Its center boss, a round conical piece, was made of thick metal and designed to deflect blows and projectiles. Inside, it also provided a solid grip for a man to handle the heavy shield. The design and the iron in its frame made it a very effective piece of defensive armor. As the shield-men formed in front, the *eques sapsarius*, a mounted medic, moved next to Titus and would not leave his side until he fell back from the line of any attack. General Vespasian had made this order explicit after his own wounding at Yotapta. Six more cavalrymen, the mounted archers called *sagittarii*, formed up three on either side. They guided their mounts with their knees, bows ready, arrows nocked, and aimed at the two watchtowers.

Once all had formed up, Titus ordered them nearer the man in the tower who had drawn his attention. He wanted to be close enough to shout distinctly but far enough away to react to any attack. He stopped there and called, "Open your gates and surrender your city... do not suffer the same fate as Gamala and Yotapta. I have a legion of infantry only a day's march away, and they transport siege engines that will bring your walls down upon you."

"I'm Yohanan ben Levi!" the man shouted back. "I am the leader of this city. We have heard of your destruction of our cities and know the number of your foot soldiers. We do not wish to die at your hands... but I ask you not to enter the city today. Tomorrow the gates will open for you."

"Open them now and order your men to lay down their weapons."

"It is our *shabbat*, lord—"

"I am Titus Flavius Vespasianus, rebel. What matters a day? Unless you wish to make this the day you and your people die."

"It is a holy day for us... Let us have it, Lord Vespasianus, then the city is yours."

* * *

Next morning...

"How did they get out of the city?" Titus slammed the flat of his sword on the folding table that held a rough map of the area. He glared at Placidus. At dawn, they had found the walls and watchtowers unmanned and the gate open. The townspeople were all in their homes, none on the streets, and Yohanan ben Levi and his personal unit of men were nowhere to be found.

"We discovered a network of secret passages under many of the homes... We had to press the townspeople to find out—but they lead to caves all over the area."

"Send men to follow the deserters to those caves and set patrols to search the area."

"I have, Lord Titus, but there are dozens... and we're not sure how many others we don't know about. I have patrols out, but the people say they must have left at sundown... the last time they say this Yohanan ben Levi and his close followers were seen was shortly before then."

"After convincing me to let them have their holy day..." Titus muttered. "Then he skulks way and leaves his city open to us." He picked up the sword and sheathed it at his hip; a grim expression hardened his features, making him look even more like his father.

"Yes, lord." Placidus was just as angry at having been lied to and fooled by the rebel leader.

"When the infantry arrives, tell them to strip the city of anything of value. Then burn it down and kill any who resist... Send to Ptolemais for the slave masters to be ready for the rest. I'll leave now with my escort to report to General Vespasian, who will not be pleased. That bastard rebel and his followers are likely fleeing to Jerusalem for security."

IX

October 67 CE

Caesarea

Vespasian's Villa and Command Headquarters

General Vespasian's personal guard, a centurion, did not come alone to escort Yosef to his routine discussion with the general. This morning, he brought a blacksmith wearing a work belt of tools and carrying an iron block with a slightly concave surface.

"Down on the ground," the centurion ordered. When Yosef hesitated, he took a step toward him, repeated the command, and pointed at the floor. "Down. Now!"

Yosef kneeled and then stretched prone on the floor. The blacksmith kneeled beside him and said, "Lift your head." Then he slipped the block so that Yosef rested his cheek upon it. The link ring on Yosef's collar lay flat on the metal, exposing the linchpin of the chain running to Yosef's waist. Taking a sledgehammer and chisel from loops at his belt, the blacksmith set the chisel's sharp edge across the linchpin. "Do not move," he warned, and with several blows that made Yosef's head ring, he sheared the pin and pulled the chain free. He then repeated the process on the opposite side and rose.

"You're done," the centurion said, and the blacksmith hurriedly left.

The leg shackles chained to the iron band at his waist remained, and the collar and wrist cuffs were still in place, but at least Yosef could raise his arms over his head. He lowered them, clasped his arms behind him, and twisted his torso, feeling a couple of snapping pops as he eased his back for the first time in seemingly forever.

The centurion gripped his bared *gladius*, the short sword's razor tip inclined toward Yosef's stomach. "General Vespasian has ordered this… do not do something stupid you'll regret. I'll gut you before you can blink." He gestured toward the door.

While the meetings had become expected, having his arms freed was not, and Yosef was grateful. He had begun to look forward to the sessions. His writing materials had not yet been returned. The time in his cell left him with little to do but dwell on the past and wonder about the future. If there was to be a future for him at all.

Vespasian sat at his campaign desk with a map of Judea spread across it. The map was studded with numbered wooden blocks along the coast and inland at what seemed to be Sythopolis. The general pointed with the ferrule end of his cudgel in northern Galilee. "Titus is there with a force to deal with one of your leaders... Yohanan ben Levi of Gischala. Do you know him?"

Yosef did not reply but took the seat Vespasian offered him with a gesture.

The general waved at another older man who had remained near the entry. "Gaheris, have wine brought... and two cups."

The wine came and Vespasian, again with a motion, offered one of the full cups. Yosef took it but did not drink.

"I have heard of this Yohanan of Gischala," Vespasian said. "He claims to be quite a leader, though I've also heard he is like our god, Janus, in that he has two faces, two mouths. And at times, he changes what he says or promises... and maybe what he believes in, too. Perhaps he goes with whichever wind blows fairest for him." Vespasian chuckled. "The Romans have a few leaders like that too." He poked the wooden marker positioned at Gischala. "How do you think this Yohanan ben Levi responded to General Titus surrounding his city... much as we surrounded you at Yotapta?"

Vespasian paused a moment and studied Yosef, who did not reply. Then he continued. "The man chose not to fight but stalled my son, Titus, asking that he not enter the city on your day of worship. The next morning, he learned Yohanan ben Levi had fled with many of his followers. Unlike you, he chose to escape but left his people behind. You shake your head... you mean you don't believe he would do such a thing?"

Yosef felt a qualm at the memory of what had happened at Yotapta. When the Romans appeared, his first thought was to escape and raise a larger army and come back to fight the Romans or surrender himself if that would save the city. Neither option had been supported by those at Yotapta, so they had all stayed and fought. Many thousands died, and over a thousand were captured and sold into slavery. And here he was in shackles but wanting to hold onto a dream he had for this man across the table from him. If that dream should come true, it might enable him to live. So, he thought he had done many things for the good of his people, but the last was a selfish concern. Was this nothing more than what Yohanan of Gischala had done to save his own life? Yosef shook his head again. "That's not it, general."

"Then, you're not surprised?"

Yosef decided that answering him truthfully would cause no harm. "No, sir... I'm not."

Vespasian took a deep drink from his cup and settled back, studying Yosef over the brim. "Nicanor told me about your meeting in Jerusalem. Cestius Gallus halted his attack and arranged a talk, hoping to resolve the issues peacefully despite the bloodshed on both sides. Nicanor said you claimed both Roman and Jewish factions had created the circumstances that escalated the conflict." Vespasian stood and tapped the four corners of the map with the cudgel. "Soon, all of Judea will be secure, and I will move against your city, but it will not end as it did with Cestius Gallus. Jerusalem will either surrender or be destroyed. Do you think these factions will agree to surrender... to save your people?"

X

PTOLEMAIS

The shirt's sleeves beneath his toga covered the burned patches on Gessius Florus's forearms. And the toga covered the discoloration of the dark-blue and brownish-yellow bruises that spread over his thighs. Yet his lower legs still revealed the reddened flesh where blisters had burst, and a layer of skin had sloughed off. But the ache of the deep contusions was worse than the stinging of the healing burned flesh. Gessius Florus took a cloak from a peg near the door and slipped it on, cinching it with a belt at the waist so it would stay closed over his lower legs. He could do nothing to cover the raw, inflamed skin on one side of his face, from hair to jaw. Thankfully the medicus said his arms and face would heal—without much scarring—quicker than his legs.

"Drusus, you may leave," he said, "but stay nearby. See Eris about the room arranged for you. I'll call for you later." Gessius Florus eased himself onto the high couch he had requested be set behind the table he would use as a desk. He looked up at the other man in the room. "Tell me what's been done, Quintus."

Quintus studied the short, broad-shouldered Drusus, who eyed him in return as he left the suite of rooms. Drusus had arranged the best available rooms at the largest taberna in Ptolemais—on a second floor. Then, when Florus arrived, Drusus had carried the injured former procurator up to the rooms and then waited beside him until dismissed. "Lord Florus, Lady Cleo's description and news of the bounty on her has been spread throughout the city. Riders already carry the announcement to other towns up and down the coast. The men I brought from Alexandria have been scouring the area and have talked with every ship captain, merchant, and dealer in information I know at the port. There is talk of a ship, the *Delphina*, headed to Rome with two passengers. A centurion had orders from General Vespasian, and, curiously, he had booked passage for a local woman, too. I guess he could not leave her behind. That's not a usual thing among the legionaries; the men who loaded the chest sent by the centurion were told it was held women's clothing and other items."

"What was the centurion's name?"

Quintus checked a scrap of parchment in his hand." Nicanor, from Vespasian's staff...."

"May the gods curse him and her..." Florus slammed his hand on the table.

"You know him?"

"Yes. Nicanor's a friend of hers from before she married me. She must have run to him at the legion encampment. But would he really try to take her all the way to Rome?" Florus winced as he shifted his legs to recline on the couch. "Why would General Vespasian send a common centurion to Rome? No,"—Florus shook his head, "there is no reason for him to go to Rome for Vespasian. He must be taking her to Antioch or Alexandria, using Vespasian's orders to get there."

"The man said the *Delphina* usually made port calls along the coast, but the end destination was Rome. I immediately sent men on fast galleys to check. They boarded every vessel they could."

"You'll bring Vespasian down on my head," Florus snapped. "He won't stand for that.

"I had the men dressed as Judeans and their vessels rigged out as the Joppa pirates I've heard about."

"Good... good..." Florus nodded.

"But they've not found any centurion or woman on board the ships they could catch. One captain they questioned said he had seen the *Delphina* off the coast and making great speed. As they neared them to call out and exchange messages, the captain told him Governor Mucianus had ordered—and paid for—as fast a transit to Rome as he could make. He said a centurion stood next to the captain during the brief time they matched course and speed and could talk. So at least the man himself is on that ship... and they must really be headed to Rome."

"Then you must go, too."

"What?" Quintus squinted, not happy at that thought; there was money to be made in Judea.

"You're a sea captain; take the fastest vessel you can find—leave today—and go to Rome."

"Lord Florus," Quintus said, unable to mask the exasperated tone that had crept into his voice, "how will I find them?"

"They'll go to Cleo's friend, Octavia."

"The wife of the—"

"The man you killed in Antioch, yes." Florus sat up, biting his lip as he swung his legs under the table. He picked up a pen and parchment. "I received a report that Lady Octavia was back in Rome.

Here is where she lives." He wrote quickly and handed the note to the mariner. "Question her, Quintus. Find Cleo and Nicanor."

"And when I do?"

"Kill them both—bring me proof—and I will triple the bounty I've offered and increase your pay."

XI

OCTOBER 67 CE

NORTH OF OSTIA, WEST OF ROME

Nicanor wrapped his cloak more tightly around him, tucking the edges around his thighs to keep out the draft. Though he welcomed the coming of fall—a relief from the hot summer—his breeches were not enough for the morning chill. He did miss the trees and their changing color he had enjoyed in Italia the two times he had been here before. As sunrise broke through and lighted the leaves, he was glad of his decision to make an early start. The silence of the morning and the sights of the scenery were much better than the tedium he would have had with Marinus's offer to stay a day in Ostia and make the rounds with him. The captain of the *Delphina* had different ideas of enjoyment—his 'rounds' of drink and prostitutes did not appeal to Nicanor. He did not care for the falseness of the blonde hair the *meretrices* were required to have, whether dyed or as a wig. One woman, alone, was on his mind, and he must begin to do what could be done to protect Lady Cleo, wherever she was in Judea.

It was a two days' ride to Falacrine, and he would not press too hard the gelding he had purchased at the horse market in Ostia for the little he could afford. He did not yet know the animal's abilities or heart, and horses had taught him the heart was the most important quality—for people, too. You must discover it, so you know whether the individual can be counted on.

Despite the aches of his old wounds the damp chill had brought on, especially in his leg, Nicanor was glad to be doing something other than staring at the sea, worrying about what he had left behind in Judea.

Vespasian had assured him that Falacrine was his first destination, to take the general's letters to Antonia Caenis at his home. "She is wise and will counsel you," he had told Nicanor, "on how best you can learn more for us about Nero's vulnerabilities. And about the likely outcome if unrest increases." Nicanor hoped something in that counsel would also aid him in his goal of helping Cleo.

He and the horse had settled into a rhythm by the time the sun had climbed over the trees lining the road that narrowed as it led away from Ostia. The sun shone upon him, and he loosened the cloak to sweep back from his legs. He sighed and wished his work done, his wishes and wants achieved, and that he was instead headed toward where he had just come. That he was at the end and not the beginning of what he must do before he could return to Judea with a hope to find Cleo, Yosef, and Sayid safe.

* * *

FALACRINE

Since morning the road had twisted through a valley and found its way among hillocks, hills, and mountains. The dense forest seemed to be thinning, the underbrush not as thick. The way ahead descended onto a broad plain between the mountains.

Nicanor slowed as five mounted men came onto the path from the last copse of woods ahead of him. The nearest man looked his way and spoke to the others, then all turned their horses to face him, waiting. He heeled his horse forward. Beyond the men was the first of cultivated fields. In the distance, a village became visible though shrouded by the sinking twilight fog. One of the riders was a lean youth taller in the saddle than the others, who looked like household men. As he got closer, he observed their drawn swords—though the young man kept his sheathed—and he noted that their weapons showed little wear.

Without drawing their attention to the movement, he loosened the dagger sheathed at his hip. He shifted the gladius that hung from the pommel so the short sword's scabbard would not catch on the saddle if he needed to pull it out quickly.

He called out a greeting: "Am I close to the estate of Titus Flavius Vespasianus?" He reined in several feet from the nearest rider.

"Why do you seek it?" asked the youth.

"I look for Antonia Caenis." Nicanor saw the flash of recognition on the boy's face but wondered why it seemed one of disdain.

"Why?"

The youth was not more than 15 or 16 years old, Nicanor judged. He replied, "Before I answer that... who are you?"

"I am Titus Flavius Domitianus... son of Lord Vespasian."

Nicanor could see the similarities now, but the boy was more like his older brother Titus.

"My name is Nicanor, and I have letters from General Vespasian."

"A centurion as a courier?" The boy's eyebrow quirked in the same way Nicanor had seen in the father.

"I serve your father, and I come here at his command."

"Give me the letters." The boy pointed at the legionary's satchel hung crossways over Nicanor's chest.

"Your father's orders are to give them to Antonia Caenis."

The boy stiffened, and his four men bristled, too. The horses shifted as the riders clenched their knees into their sides.

Nicanor smiled and released the reins to drape across the saddle pommel. He doubted this horse would follow knee and heel commands as had Abigieus, his warhorse killed at the defeat at Beth Horon. Or Tempestas, who he had had to leave behind in Judea. But he wanted both hands free in case there was trouble. "I serve your father and will hand his letters to her."

The boy studied him, a gauging look in his eye that Nicanor also recognized, then relaxed as did his men. "Follow me," the boy replied, "I'll take you to her."

* * *

Next morning...

VESPASIAN'S VILLA

"I've read what you brought me." Antonia Caenis's tone was warmer than had been her greeting the evening before. "Lord Vespasian thinks highly of you."

He watched the woman as she walked from the house onto the terrace. A servant had brought him there after daybreak and served him tart fruit, pungent cheese, and thin wine. "She will join you shortly," the servant had said.

Antonia Caenis was not a beautiful woman. Her hair was arranged in what must be the current fashion he had observed among the Roman women as he passed through Ostia's marketplace. Though others dyed theirs, her once-raven-black hair—judging by the color of her eyebrows—was now streaked with thick coils of gray. She had a presence to her, a commanding air that impressed him.

"Thank you for saying so, my lady. I think highly of your husband as well."

She shot him a piercing look from the eyes beneath those brows. "I am not his wife."

"I'm sorry I misspoke, my lady."

"No apology necessary, centurion." She sat down across from him at the table, with the still-rising sun at her back. It gave her hair a silvery sheen. A servant brought another amphora and a cup for her. "Vespasian and I—because I was a slave,"—she paused to watch for

Nicanor's reaction, "were joined in a *conturbernium*. The civil union was not a true marriage, and it ended when he married a Roman noblewoman. When she died, a little more than two years ago, Vespasian and I chose to rejoin our relationship, and now we are partners in all things." She paused to watch the boy Domitian cross the terrace and head toward the stables. He did not acknowledge them. Antonia shook her head and continued. "Some are not happy about that." She poured a cup of wine and brushed loose strands of hair from her face as she settled back in her chair. "Where is the lady that Vespasian mentioned in his letter, the one who would accompany you?"

Nicanor did not know what he could tell this woman about Lady Cleo, so he must be careful. "I'm afraid she remained in Judea."

Antonia searched the centurion's face. "I see that sorrows you."

Nicanor bowed his head but stayed silent. Vespasian had told him Antonia was the most discerning person he had ever met, that she could see into people.

She let the silence last for a handful of heartbeats. "Vespasian wants me to educate you on some of the political intrigues of Rome and of Roman politicians. But first I must know more about you... something I read in his letters. Tell me how you became friends with both Lady Cleo—I know of her family—and a Jewish rebel general."

* * *

Two days later...

"I know you must go, as Vespasian hinted at urgency, but you are welcome here at any time. Remember. To my knowledge, Cleo's brother Marcus Otho was not part of Gaius Calpurnius Piso's plot against Nero. Piso had already died when it was carried out by his close friend Galba, who was well-shielded so that his name never came out. But I believe he and others still work to overthrow Nero and take the throne. Nero has given them and many other Romans reasons to want the same," she said with a sigh. "The emperor has nearly bankrupted the empire... and it still teeters on that edge. You must report to my husband everything you hear or can discern from your meeting with Marcus Otho. Some men, like Galba, are as concerned about the allegiance of Rome's generals as is the emperor. I do not doubt some will seek to remove any competent commander backed by loyal legions. To eliminate any commander who could pose a threat to their attempts to take the throne."

A loud whinny interrupted her and turned them both. A servant was leading a horse to the edge of the terrace.

Antonia clapped her hands and beamed. "I have a gift for you!"

She rose from the bench where they had been sitting and said, "Come with me." She beckoned Nicanor to follow her down the steps to the grass. The mare was silver-gray with a black mane and dark gray hocks from hooves to knees. "She is young but born wise... I have ridden her, and she never makes a misstep and always anticipates what the rider wants. I named her Carmenta after the nymph of divination."

"She's beautiful, my lady, but I cannot accept her...."

"In his letter, Vespasian said you saved his life during the siege of a Galilean town... Yotapta. For that, I cannot just say thank you. I must show you how much his life means to me. And even this," she stroked Carmenta's neck, "is not enough."

"But I have a horse."

"Yes, you had the horse you arrived on, but—if I judge you right—you need more than an animal to ride. You miss having a companion you can trust. They can be hard to find, and you have a long journey... a long road ahead of you."

XII

OCTOBER 67 CE

JERUSALEM

THE LOWER CITY, KING DAVID'S TOMB

The passage had seemed unending, and her travel was not in a straight line. Miriam's sense of direction had never failed her in her tunnel excursions with Zechariah. And she knew she had not gotten turned around because she had not yet passed into the open chamber from which she had escaped. How long ago that was, she didn't know. The darkness gave her no sense of the passing of time. But she sensed that the passage was almost maze-like in its turns that seemed to double it back on itself. The parallel leg after alternating corners was slightly longer made her believe she was getting farther from the vast chamber she had found herself in. The path must lead somewhere, so she must keep going until... what? The end... if there was one, or until she could go no further.

Time to move, Miriam thought as she rose with the stiffness and ache of too long sleep on a hard, unyielding surface. She could not help herself and greedily drank the last water she carried in a small amphora. After partially slaking her thirst, she had filled it excruciatingly slowly, drop by drop, before leaving the chamber to explore the passageway, hoping to find a way out. She had had to force herself to not lift the amphora to her lips as soon as she had collected a mouthful. Never had anything been so hard, but she could not count on finding more water and must carry what she could.

During the time she spent in the darkness, to save what was left of the old torch, her mind had been filled with as many thoughts as there were drops of water in the amphora. Who had attacked her in Solomon's Quarry and chased her deep into Zedekiah's Cave? Was Yosef alive, or had he fallen to the Romans he had so admired at one time? And she thought it likely, knowing her brother, that he still respected the Romans at some level. And what of Matthew and her parents? She knew they must be worried and would mourn her if she never found a way out. But would they forgive her for the questions she had not answered, the things she had not told them? Would they forgive her hateful secrets? But she must keep her own counsel, or she could never continue to hold her new identity. There was no going back to the old Miriam; years ago, that young woman had been lost in that tunnel she had followed the Romans into on that terrible day. What they had done to her had set her on the path to where and who she was now.

Yet Ehud's return had made her hope she could somehow go back to her former self, her old life. Part of her wanted to love Ehud as she had before his father moved their family to Alexandria. When he was around her, she had seen in his eyes, in his gestures, that he still loved her. But he, too, had seemed guarded, as if he had reservations. He had also changed in some way that seemed to mean they could not be together. Ever.

That trail of thought led her to Ya'akov, a man who—after Ehud left Jerusalem—had claimed his love for her, and she thought she could feel the same for him. He had done nothing wrong and had been confused and hurt at the breaking of their betrothal. But how could she marry any man after what the Romans had done to her? After what they had torn from her? No man would ever accept her if he knew. She had stood firm, first before her mother, then her father. Uncrying but crumbling inside, knowing she could never reveal why she would not marry Ya'akov. She had a newfound determination to conceal her reason for refusing.

The cut across the arc of both breasts from a Roman soldier's blade had healed. The deep bruises made by Roman hands on her inner thighs had been hidden by the robe clenched tightly around her as she faced her parents. Secrets. Those secrets, those memories beat on her just as brutally as the brutal Yonatan beat his wife, poor Leah. She was Yosef's lost first love, and so she and her brother shared similar pain. Yonatan deserved punishment just as surely as did the Romans.

Since she'd entered Solomon's Quarry, those thoughts had filled her mind as she tapped through interminable darkness. It was more exhausting than Zechariah had ever told her it might be. The trek took total concentration... the constant forcing down of any fear of what was ahead in the dark... or that she would die in the darkness. While the experience extended her senses of hearing and smell, the two sentinels that would warn her of trouble or threats, keeping such constant alert, drained her.

Miriam came to a stop. The sound of small creatures was not as frequent, just one or two every so often moving past her in the dark. That told her something—that ahead must be an exit out of the depths she had reached. But she must rest again. The hunger she had at first contained had become as sharp-edged as her thirst.

Miriam felt a sniffing and brush of whiskers at her ankles and flinched. When they were younger, Yosef and Matthew, hoping to frighten her into not following them on their explorations of the old tunnels and caves of the valleys surrounding the city, had told her of the bones of rats found in once-sealed caves. Those rats had died when they ran out of food or other rats to eat. But the remains of long-dead rats had not stopped her then. She wondered if she could catch a live one in this darkness. Maybe, but could she bring herself to kill and eat it... eat it raw? Her gut wrenched again, and she pressed a hand against her side. Yet, in the last few years, she had done other things she would never have dreamed of. There was nothing she could, or would, not do if she must. But not that... not yet.

She sat against the passage wall with Zechariah's staff across her lap. After a moment to make sure she was oriented, she lay down with her back against the wall, head pointing in the direction to continue in when she awoke. Her stomach cramped again, but soon even that didn't stop her from slipping into sleep marred by a final thought that at some point, she might lie down in the eternal night and never awake.

* * *

The dark was timeless and made progress slow, and she had no idea how long she had been walking since her awakening in the maze-like passageway. Unless she had missed it, which was very possible, there had been no side exits or entries to other passages or chambers. But her sandaled feet and calves felt the passageway she trod was inclining and climbing to a higher level.

Ahead she heard a whisper of squeaks and twitters. Then the scraping and scrabbling of claws on stone and a shuffling, digging sound that grew louder as her feet encountered a cluster of creatures. And in that second, the ferrule-tip of her staff hit something unmoving, and the impact nearly jarred it from her hand. She leaned into the dark before her and reached out a hand. Stone. The passage had ended or was blocked. She carefully set the staff against the wall on her right and ran her hands over the obstruction. No... it wasn't the rough stone of a collapse like she had encountered before, a blockage or dead end. This stone was smooth and in a single piece, just as the slab had been at the other end of the passage.

It felt like the cluster of rats milling at her feet had grown smaller. She stooped to probe where she had heard most of the scurrying and scraping and touched the rump of the last rat as it squirmed through an opening at the bottom left corner of the slab. Rising vertically from there, she traced her fingers along the mortar used to fix the piece in place.

Carefully, not wanting to repeat what had happened at the entrance to this passage, she sniffed and checked for any smell. Still, she would not light what would be the last of her only torch unless she absolutely had to. Working by feel with her knife—starting at the bottom, then the sides, then the top, she loosened the slab. She stopped to check... and there was still no odor. She pushed the slab, and it fell away from her. By touch, she determined it had settled against something in front of it. Pushing forward, she felt it shift, and the piece of stone, as tall as she, slid down and crashed to one side. Putting her shoulder against what had momentarily held the slab up, she shoved. It took all the strength of her arms and thighs to move it out. She checked the edges to see if there was an opening. Yes! But not enough, even for her to squirm through. With a grunt, she pushed harder, and whatever the object was, it scraped along the stone floor, and she felt an increased current of air.

As she stepped around it, a sensation of a change in space washed over her. No longer within the confines of walls she could touch with either hand with just one or two steps. She found herself in a chamber that was smaller, judging by its echoes, than the one she had left behind her.

Cautiously, she went further in, tapping with the staff and moving her feet carefully—not lifting them, but shuffling forward to nudge out of her path any stone or debris she could have stumbled over. She kept to what she thought was a straight line from her entry. Soon the floor felt clear, but then her tapping staff—finding the frame of a doorway—told her she had come upon an alcove or the entrance to an antechamber. Stepping carefully closer, she felt something that draped from above grazing her head, and she jerked back until it no longer touched her. She used her staff to hold off what must be the tattered remnants of a curtain and stepped through the opening and fell over something just inside. With a squeal and skitter of claws, the lingering rats raced off and away.

On her hands and knees, Miriam groped to discover what she had fallen over. Her fingers brushed something, and she got her feet under her to squat and warily reach for it. She felt the roughness of hobnails, the sole of a sandal, and then what must be a foot... the toes of shrunken skin and bone. With a cry she could not suppress, she rocked back on her heels.

XIII

OCTOBER 67 CE

JERUSALEM

THE LOWER CITY, KING DAVID'S TOMB

Even in the sputtering light of her pitiful, nearly spent torch, Miriam could see the body had been gnawed. But she could also tell that the man had first died from the blow that had caved in his skull. He had not gone down without fighting back. His hand still gripped the *pugio* he had buried in his killer's chest.

The man with the dagger in his chest held an iron-clad cudgel in one hand. That had likely dealt a death blow to the other's head even as his free hand tried to stop the counterthrust of the blade into his heart. His tunic and cloak were finer than those of the man he had killed.

Both were Roman soldiers, and on the floor between them was a slashed and bloody legionary's satchel. She had seen one before, and Matthew had once used a similar one. Within its open flap, something glinted. She stooped and looked closer. Small gold bars! Beneath them was a piece of parchment that, when she tugged, slid out to show it was a flattened scroll. Spreading it out, she could see it was a diagram of the layout of an enormous structure. A large room in the bottom right corner was connected to a smaller space in the top left-hand corner by a passageway with myriad turns.

The guttering light hastened her rolling the parchment to set it aside and see what else the men had carried. Hidden by the folds of the cloak worn by the man with the crushed skull, she found a true treasure—four torches in loops at his waist and a small sealed-skin bladder of lantern oil. Relieved, she put them aside to search the other man.

Shifting the stiff body, she found twisted beneath his centurion's cloak a small sealed and waxed bag tied to his belt, and—she tasted the blood as she smiled and her dried, cracked lips split—a water skin. It sloshed half-full as she worked free the waxed stopper, raised and gulped a mouthful of stale water that tasted better than any she had drunk in her life.

* * *

Miriam sat upon a long bench with the diagram parchment spread over her knees. A crack in the stucco wall behind her served well enough to hold the torch she'd wedged in place. From the small bag beside her, she took another of the *bucellatum*. The hardtack biscuits were like what Matthew had once brought back from visiting the Roman garrison at Antonia Fortress. He had laughed at the face she made after he convinced her to taste one. These were bitter and even harder with age—almost rocks—but once they were moistened with water, she could choke them down. At least they had filled her stomach and eased the pangs, though she had to admit the irony of two dead Romans providing the food and water that had saved her life.

She realized the diagram depicted where she was and where she had come from. It had been meticulously annotated with information about direction and distance. She found a *sarcina*—the pack she knew Roman soldiers usually carried on a forked pole, called a *furca*, braced over a shoulder. Within it were writing and measuring tools. They must have belonged to the brown-cloaked soldier since a centurion was unlikely to carry such implements. The man had numbered their path of exploration with a pace count between points and notes on the orientation. Yosef—who marveled at the Romans' engineering and attention to detailed documentation—had told her of the Roman army's surveyors, *bematisai*, who used such methods to make field maps. The bars in the satchel must have been all they could manage to carry out. They must have planned to return to empty the full chests Miriam had seen in the enormous chamber she had first been in.

But Romans had not walked the streets of Jerusalem freely since the Passover massacre of the year before. This Roman engineer or surveyor, along with the centurion, must have heard rumors of Jewish treasure before that and entered what she now thought must be King David's tomb. Just where the glow from the torch faded, she could see the two bodies. Yosef had told her a story once long ago, about two men who stole a treasure but then greed had set in... and he had ended the tale with a wink she always remembered as he told her: "Thieves fall out...."

She looked down at the chart. There was another passageway with turns and step count detail in the top left corner and marked leading to the chamber she was in. Nodding her head—that must show her the way out—she rolled it and put the scroll into the bag she had taken from Esau ben Beor after her attack. The bag now also held some of the small gold bars, called *mina*, she now remembered. They each were worth 60 silver shekels. Their weight oddly made her recall sitting with Yosef and Matthew years before, listening to their father talk of Solomon's and King David's time. Back then, coins with stamped images did not exist and were only uninscribed tokens of gold and silver of prescribed weight. *I wish I could be that little girl again*, she thought with a sigh and raised her head.

She stood. Fixing her dagger at her hip, and on the opposite, the Roman pugio taken from the Roman surveyor's chest, she slung the waterskin over her shoulder. She was ready.

* * *

Miriam squeezed past blocks of cut stone and rough rocks and followed the broadening shafts of light with their swirls of dust caught within that danced on a strengthening current of air. She drew in her chest and stomach—holding her breath—and ignored the roughness of stone as it scraped her flesh. She staggered into the morning sun from a slender crevice in an outcropping of rocks used to form part of what she recognized as the eastern wall above the Kidron Valley, near to Gihon Spring. Blinking in the bright sun, she gasped and stood still, breathing in the fresh air in deep draughts. She felt the weight of Beor's bag with the gold bars as she straightened. The Roman surveyor's map was—to her—the more valuable.

Wrapping closer around her the tattered brown cloak she had taken to replace her far more stained one, she tottered along the path at the base of the city wall until she reached the Water Gate and was thankful there were so many people entering the Lower City. They would bear more scrutiny at the northern gates next to the Upper City. Even so, most were not as bedraggled as she, and many cast doubtful looks at her appearance, though she did her best to hide her grimy, blood-streaked face. She must make her way to Zechariah's first to bathe, and since she was still weak, she must eat and drink something more than years-old water and soldiers' food. She could also put on the clothes she kept there.

It was not much further to Zechariah's, but the streets kept tilting under her feet like what Yosef had described as the feeling of being at sea. She stopped to lean against the wall of a merchant's stall. The sight of fresh fruit arrayed in trays, and the smell of breakfast being prepared nearby, nearly made her open Beor's bag to take out a *mina* and buy food to eat right there. But that would create a stir... and lead to questions she could not answer. The dizziness made her close her eyes.

"Miriam... is that you?"

She opened her eyes and looked up at Hananiah. The lean, tall bladesmith stood before her, expressionless, dark-eyed, staring. Then he started sliding from her view as she sank to the ground. His eyes followed her all the way down, and then all was dark.

* * *

Miriam had awakened in her filthy clothes with Beor's bag under her arm. She remembered her last thoughts when Hananiah had half-carried her into his shop. He had not questioned when she brought it with her to the screened area, where he had brought in a tub and heated water for her to bathe before leaving.

"I will be only a moment," Miriam told Hananiah. "Please wait out here." She wished for the clean clothes she kept at Zechariah's but did not want to show Hananiah she frequented a dead man's shop and stored personal things there. Something he would surely question. Minutes later, she came out dressed in her soiled tunic and robe to find him holding a cloak for her and watching the door. "Thank you." Miriam took her hamsa from the worn cloak from the tombs and clasped it to the clean one Hananiah handed her. "I must go home now."

He had insisted he would walk her all the way. They were silent as they walked. She had explained to Hananiah that she had hurt herself—been knocked unconscious in a fall—while exploring, which her family frowned upon. And she asked him to help her prevent even more questions. He should only mention that he had helped attend to her until she could return home. "I understand," he had told her, and she wondered that he asked no questions of his own.

* * *

THE UPPER CITY

Miriam knew she could not just enter with Hananiah, and he had not turned to leave her at her door. She was about to ask him to wait there so her parents could thank him when the door opened.

"Miriam!" Ehud exclaimed. Then behind him, now crowding through the doorway, was Matthew.

Just as the door opened, her eyes had been on Hananiah— debating what to do—and she saw something flash in his eyes at seeing Ehud. She had no time to wonder at it, as she heard Ehud's exclamation, and Matthew called back into the house, "Father, Mother... it's Miriam!" Her brother's eyes on her that had been alight with relief and joy now shifted to Hananiah, and his expression hardened.

XIV

OCTOBER 67 CE

JERUSALEM

THE UPPER CITY

Hananiah didn't move from her side. Miriam felt him stiffen as Ehud took a step closer and unthinkingly took her hand to draw her nearer, a flash of happiness on his face. Ehud's eyes locked on hers and filled with concern.

"I'm fine, Ehud...." she gently pulled her hand away.

Matthew inserted himself on her other side, thinking Hananiah would step aside to make way for him. But he didn't. Miriam had watched the bladesmith's expression lighten and ease as they walked from his shop in the Lower City to her home. It was a subtle difference from his usually taut face and deep-set dark eyes. As he stared at Matthew for a heartbeat before moving, he hardened again as if he had never softened.

Matthew took her arm. "Let's go inside," he said as he tugged her elbow and shot a glance, then a curt nod, at Hananiah.

Miriam caught the look from Hananiah, who was watching her expectantly. It was not right to ignore or dismiss him. "Hananiah must come in, too," she said. "I owe him my thanks for his help." She glanced at Ehud, who had a puzzled, downcast expression as his gaze shifted from her to inspect Hananiah. She had always been able to read most people's feelings and knew she had hurt him by pulling her hand away.

Matthew protested the invitation, but Miriam had already gestured for Hananiah to follow her as she stepped inside the house.

* * *

The atmosphere of home was refreshing sunlight and cool breezes laden with the fragrance of the courtyard's fruit trees, with the thread of an aroma of lamb roasting over a brazier of coals in the neighborhood. Now in fresh clothing, with a shudder, Miriam remembered where she had recently spent days. That bleak, murky darkness underground, with the smell and taste of dusty shut-in air whose staleness was broken only by wafts of sooty smoke from her torch. That fading to sleep and awakening to the same realm of shadows and worry that its inky nothingness would be her last sight.

Tonight, she would go to bed knowing dawn would welcome her with its dependable light. Miriam's gaze swept the table. Around her were those who cared most for her. Only Yosef was missing. They had all told her of their worry and their search for her. That had touched her so much she almost regretted the lies she had just told them to explain what had happened.

Miriam shivered at the thought, and Rebecca noticed, rose from the table, and fetched a shawl for her daughter, lovingly draping it over her shoulders.

Ehud and Matthew sat on Miriam's right. Across from them sat Hananiah. Matthew's expression had settled into concern from his earlier irritation, but he was still watching the bladesmith. He turned to his sister. "We're all glad you're home, Miriam... but you should know better than to explore on your own..." He darted a look at his father at the end of the table, who had been mostly silent. "You should not roam about in those old tunnels without someone with you." He shook his head and half-turned to his mother, who had also been quiet so far. "It's not safe. Striking your head hard enough to knock yourself out... you could have died down there." He pointed at the bandage their mother had replaced for the healing gash on her cheek. His eyes cut to Hananiah. "And it's not proper for a young woman."

Hananiah had stiffly sat watching Miriam as the others talked, and he lowered his eyes. He quietly commented, "I only helped her home."

"Yes, but when I came to your shop—when Ehud and I were searching the city—you told me you had not seen her... and acted as if you did not know where she was." Matthew's tone was accusing as he leaned across the table toward Hananiah.

"He hadn't seen me, Matthew, and didn't know." Miriam cut off what might have led to Hananiah being forced to explain more than he already had. If he said what she had asked him to say, he might slip up and say too much. "He didn't know where I was... and had not seen me until he came upon me dazed and trying to make my way home. I fainted at his feet in the street, and he let me recover at his shop."

"Why didn't you bring her home right then?" demanded Matthew.

"I did not know where she—and you—lived. And I did not want her to awake and be alone..." Hananiah, still not looking at Matthew, continued to study Miriam. "To waken like that, bruised... hurt...

alone... is frightening. And once she awoke, I gave her food and water. She bathed, and when she fell asleep again after, I thought it best to let her rest."

Miriam shifted in her seat and lowered her eyes. The way Hananiah said 'alone' came close to bringing her to tears. He must know what it was like to be a frightened person lost in the darkness.

"Any more discussion on this is for family only," Mathias said to Hananiah as he took Rebecca's hand. "We thank you for helping our daughter." A knocking at the door turned him to Matthew. "Go see who is calling on us."

With Matthew's seat between them vacant, Miriam found herself trapped between Ehud's sideways glances and Hananiah's stare. Ehud seemed poised to speak but kept quiet. She tried to rouse herself from the sadness that had returned.

Voices broke her reverie. Matthew came into the courtyard with Yohanan ben Zaccai, who answered Matthew's question the rest of the family had not heard: "Yes, they are ready. Nahum and I even visited several of the proposed locations, and his men have done an admirable job. Whatever portions are placed there will be safe, impossible to find without precise directions."

Yohanan stopped at the table and, seeing Ehud and a stranger, he switched to a greeting: "Mathias, I hope you are well. After entering the city, I stopped at the Hall of Hewn Stone and spoke briefly with Shimon ben Gamliel... he told me of the killing of Esau ben Beor." His eyes swept the table, lingering on Ehud and Hananiah. "I must speak to you about that... and other things... You too, Matthew."

Mathias stood. "Hananiah, I thank you again for helping Miriam and to you, too, Ehud, for searching for her."

* * *

Ehud and Hananiah had taken the same way until they reached the market and terrace of the Xystus near the Temple Enclosure. Neither man had spoken, and the distance between them made clear to both that they were not walking together.

Ehud stopped at a small *pundaq*, taking an outside table under a striped awning, and watched as Hananiah was lost in the crowd. He had selected the tavern because it was near a scribe's stall where he could buy a pen, ink, and a sheet of parchment. He was worried that he had not heard from his father, Meshulam, and had yet been unable to discover much that would be of value to Gessius Florus. But maybe now he had. Taking the writing materials back to the tavern table, he ordered wine and wrote quickly:

> I have learned that a priest named Yohanan ben Zaccai has met with the Essenes in Qumran. They have established the locations, I believe, where they plan to move the Temple treasure. From what I heard, that will require precise directions to find, so they must be planning to create some map or chart showing the locations. As soon as I know more, I will share it with you. Please, I beg, do not harm my family.

He folded the four corners of the sheet to the center. Draining his cup, he stood and walked to the scribe's stall for sealing wax.

* * *

Hananiah followed Ehud as he left the Xystus and headed back toward the Upper City, passed through it, and continued north, descending a staircase cut into the bedrock stone, then passed open cisterns to cross a broad courtyard of massive flagstones. Along the courtyard ran a frieze that decorated the tomb complex Queen Helena of Adiabene, who had converted to Judaism and was sent to Jerusalem for burial on her death. Hananiah was a purveyor of mortality going back to the Alexandrian merchant who abused him as a child. Since his father's death, crushed beneath the rock he worked upon, he had always been drawn to stone markers of death. When he came near... he often stopped to study Queen Helena's.

Ahead of him, Ehud approached the *Sha'ar Shechem* gate in the middle of the northern wall. The road from that gate led to Shechem and on to the greater city of Damascus. Now Hananiah knew where Ehud was headed. It was no longer necessary to heel him, but there was a pleasure in trailing closely someone who would later become his prey.

* * *

The eastern path off the Damascus Road had eventually brought Ehud south again to *Gat Shmaním*, at the base of the Mount of Olives, *Har ha-Zeitim*. For a thousand years, Gethsemane had been a burial site for Jews, including the most prominent Jerusalemites brought to rest upon its southern slope. From there, the souls of the dead could look down upon their Temple over 200 feet below.

Ehud was deep into the grove of olive trees before he stopped at the base of what had—centuries ago—been three trees twined and grown together as one to form a massive bole. Many of the largest tree trunks were hollow inside. Hidden nearby behind another ancient tree, Hananiah watched as Ehud fumbled within the space and placed a document there.

Once the Alexandrian was well on his way back toward Jerusalem, Hananiah went to the triple tree and stooped to see that within the space was a large stone pot with a fitted lid and within that a stiff hide pouch. He opened it and found the wax-sealed document Ehud had placed there.

The small package secure within his clothing, Hananiah returned to the city, thinking of Ehud's looks with Miriam; the two had some feelings for each other. And that he would not allow. *Yes,* he thought, *the moment Ehud is no longer of use, he will become prey.*

∗ ∗ ∗

THE UPPER CITY

Once Ehud and Hananiah were gone, Matthew left Miriam talking with their parents and Yohanan ben Zaccai, retelling for him her story of what had happened to her. Matthew told them he would be right back to talk as Yohanan wished, and then he had come to Miriam's room. The murmur of voices came thru the wooden shutter overlooking the courtyard. *Her story doesn't sound right,* he thought. *She seems even more determined to keep secrets from us.* And the account from that man—Hananiah—who had backed up what she said... it did not ring true.

He didn't know what had prompted him to enter his sister's room. *To do what... to find what?* At the foot of Miriam's bed was the pile of clothing she had changed out of when she returned. Her hamsa— one of her prized possessions—glinted, the clasp still pinned to her cloak. He shook his head and touched the hamsa as he prepared to leave. He felt something odd on its surface. He picked up the mantle and carried it over to the window, where he held it under a beam of sunlight through the slats of the shutter. The hamsa was deeply scored as if it had been slashed by a keen blade. As Miriam had

53

described her accident, no fall onto rocks would have made such a deep cut in the metal. *What really happened?*

"What are you doing in my room, Matthew?" asked Miriam from the doorway.

XV

OCTOBER 67 CE

CAESAREA

VESPASIAN'S VILLA

"Back in Falacrine, I have many fine horses," Vespasian said to Yosef, who sat across from him. "Mine are better than most I have seen here so far, though your friend Nicanor has a good eye and found himself an excellent mount. Titus tends to it now for him and has grown fond of the horse. Nicanor may have trouble getting the horse back when he returns."

Yosef, still shackled, had been allowed to eat at the general's table for the first time this day. Vespasian had started their morning conversation as he had in days past: discussing the politics of their countries. He stayed away from any commentary on the emperor and steered it more toward news of Judea. Yosef's intelligence and his fluent Latin and Greek had impressed the general. The young man easily switched between the two languages. His extensive reading and understanding of history—its importance—made for interesting discussions.

But this morning, Yosef was silent, even more somber. Vespasian had thought a personal touch—talking about his friend Nicanor— might draw him out to speak freely again. So far, it had not. If other Judean leaders had intellect similar to Yosef's, why was there so much disorder among them? Yosef's past comments had suggested turmoil plagued the Judean government. Others' reports had made that disarray even more evident.

"A group of local men, Greeks, called on me," Vespasian began, looking for another direction for the conversation. But Yosef's eyes stayed on the blue horizon of the sea beyond where their terrace ended, and the hillside descended to a stretch of beach. "They were fairly well-to-do traders who asked again for your execution." Vespasian paused. "They also brought news of the ongoing dissent among your leaders in Jerusalem and how the rebel commander, Simon bar Giora, is wreaking havoc in Idumea to the south. I recognize the name from Cestius Gallus's reports. He's the rebel commander who led your forces at Beth Horon and took the 12th

OCTOBER 67 CE

Legion's *aquila* and parades around with it. We will hunt him down to get that legion's standard back."

The general waved an attending servant forward to pour more wine. Yosef had not touched his but had devoured the plate of fruit set before him. Vespasian tried yet another topic: "I think we will remove your heavier chains today."

"That would be appreciated, Lord Vespasian." Yosef finally looked away from the sea and at the general.

"But you will always be guarded and remain locked in when you are not in my presence or that of my son. When you are with Titus or me, your guards," he gestured at the two burly legionaries behind Yosef's chair, "will accompany you. Do you give me your guarantee you will not try to escape? The locals seem to want you dead... Only here—with your enemy—are you safe from your own people."

Yosef shook his head. "Only some of them, lord... the Greeks of Caesarea have long had issues with Jews and Jerusalem."

"They claim you are a coward... a traitor to them and others in Judea." Vespasian tested Yosef. "I know your men at Yotapta fought valiantly. I saw your Jewish Hercules—you told me his name was Dov—and he fought like a Roman champion. I would not have believed how well he died if I had not seen it myself. Your friend Nicanor saved my life that day."

"Will Nicanor return to serve you, general?"

Vespasian noted the wistfulness of Yosef's tone. "You and he really were friends?"

"Yes. Nicanor's a good man."

"He said the same of you... and how you disagreed with your leaders... your government's decisions to persist in resisting Rome."

"They believe—as I and most do—that any proud people will resist tyranny and persecution, lord. There was a pattern of that before Gessius Florus became procurator, but after he assumed that position, things became far worse. I witnessed it myself. The slaughter during the final days of the siege of Yotapta was much like during last year's Passover massacre, allowed by Gessius Florus when we were at peace with Rome."

"Could this war have been prevented?"

"Perhaps... I like to think so, general, but the opportunity to avoid war with Rome is gone."

* * *

Yosef shifted in his chair, wincing as the ankle cuff of his right leg rode upon the open wound formed by the chafing, no matter how much of the salve he applied. He shook his head at sitting across from the man who had defeated him at Yotapta, killing thousands of his people and yet not hating him. There had been hints from Vespasian that there was a possibility of his willingness to negotiate Jerusalem's surrender, which would save tens, maybe hundreds of thousands of Jewish lives. He had to explore that prospect.

"But maybe it could be stopped, lord," he ventured. "It would take some delicate discussion... and an understanding of the Judean factions."

"General..." came the voice of the man Yosef knew was Gaheris Clineas. The general's personal aide was on the gravel path leading to the terrace. "I have the scout reports on the Joppa pirates... where their leader—or at least one of the leaders—has anchored his ship for repairs."

"You're sure it's the rebel captain?"

"Yes, general. A former Galilean fisherman. He and others from Galilee have re-fortified Joppa and will not yield."

"Then we will make them. Send for the commander of the 5th Legion; Joppa and its pirates will become his task. That will end their disruption of grain shipments from Alexandria to Rome."

As Gaheris Clineas hurried away, Yosef thought of his friend Nathan; who else could it be? When he last saw the man, he was burning with rage at the death of his wife, Imma. Though Nathan knew that death came at the hands of Yohanan of Gischala, Nathan and most Galileans believed the Romans ultimately caused most of the evils done in Galilee. It might be too late to save Nathan, who had once saved him. But perhaps he could convince Vespasian to let him speak to his people in Jerusalem.

"General, I give you my word—my guarantee—I will not try to escape if you remove my chains."

Vespasian, whose thoughts seemed already turning toward the attack on Joppa, motioned for the legionaries escorting Yosef. "Take him and have his ankle chains removed. But leave his wrist cuffs and chains attached around his waist with enough slack for him to eat and write with ease. Two men are to be with him—never to leave his side— when he is out of his cell."

XVI

November 67 CE

Jerusalem

The Upper City

Matthew sat with his father and Yohanan ben Zaccai. The after-dinner discussion was about the two older men's meeting with the Sanhedrin president, Shimon ben Gamliel. The meeting should have included Eleasar ben Ananias, the Temple Guard captain, and himself. But it would not have happened at all if Mathias and Yohanan had not seen Shimon scurrying from the Temple and caught up with him. The Sanhedrin leader had not met privately with anyone since Esau ben Beor's death, and the strain of some new tension showed in his face in public meetings. They were glad to have caught him because they needed answers and a decision about moving and hiding much of the Temple's treasury.

"He is frightened someone plans to kill all the Sanhedrin leadership," Mathias told Matthew. "It's still unknown who killed Esau ben Beor. Although the Sicarii are suspected. And I think Shimon's worried most about his close association with the man and how he might now be a prime target."

"Surely things haven't come to that, Father. That after the bloodshed the last couple of years, there are still some within Jerusalem willing to kill our own people over internal disagreements. With the fall of most of Galilee and the Romans now securing the rest of Judea, I thought the Moderates and Zealots would finally stop the infighting, and we would stand together to protect Jerusalem."

"There is still much going on that is not in the open, Matthew... at least not yet." Mathias exchanged a look with Yohanan ben Zaccai that suggested there was more to say—that they feared what was to come. But they had moved on to the pressing matter of protecting the Temple treasury.

Nahum, the Essene in Qumran, had given Yohanan information about which locations could handle specific parts of the Temple treasure. Sacred items—those not needed for worship or display—had to be packed properly to not be damaged in transport. Their locations had been selected to prevent discovery and to provide the best protection from the weather. Once securely hidden in the places best suited for them, they must be sealed to survive the elements. Then the locations would be documented on something more durable than parchment, because no one knew how long the treasure must remain hidden.

Gold, silver, and jewels were easier to handle. Still, the quantities were so large it would require scheduling a steady flow of loads by horse, mule, or even hand carts if necessary to disperse those portions of the treasure. Regrettably, a fair amount must remain so as not to raise questions and alarm the city government and the public about where the treasure had gone. They knew that if the Romans pressed a siege, the walls could not hold them out. To not make the Romans suspicious, they wanted more treasure to be found than just in the Temple. They must leave enough to satisfy Roman greed. That meant leaving not just gold and silver but also valuable items like the massive golden menorah that stood five feet tall and stood in the antechamber of the Temple sanctuary against its southernmost wall. Even the Romans knew it was cherished and venerated. They could not remove it without notice, and they hoped its presence in the Temple would convince the Romans that what was there for them to take... was all there was.

Matthew heard Miriam's voice and looked up from the scroll of vellum Yohanan had unrolled before them: "I'm done, Mother...." He knew that meant she was done cleaning up from dinner and was headed upstairs. Since her fall that injured her while exploring, about which she would not say more, that had been her routine. But at least she had been spending her time during the day at home with mother and father. Not as she had before, walking the streets of Jerusalem or at some shop in the Lower City. She had talked to their parents more about what had happened, and he had heard her tell them she appreciated the freedom and independence they granted her. That had been the talk at meals and other moments when he had been home.

But not once had Miriam spoken to him since she found him in her room, and he had asked her how her hamsa had been damaged. Their conversation had been short and heated: "I told you, it happened when I fell," she had replied, and her face had gone white with fury at his going through her things. That anger and something else had flitted across her expression as it tightened. The bandage on her cheek had loosened and slipped, and he saw the wound there for the first time. It, too—like the cut on the hamsa—appeared to have been made by a sharp blade and not a rock. A stone's edge would have caused an abrasion or ragged tear. Miriam had covered the healing wound with her hand and demanded he get out of her room. Those were the last words exchanged between them.

He turned back to his father, who had said something to him. "Sorry, what was that, Father?"

"I said Shimon has agreed the Temple Guard shall move the treasure. They're armed and trained well enough to defend it, though we must see that they do not draw attention nor seem to transport anything of value. But—and Shimon made a good point—the guardsmen's absence might be noticed. So, you and Eleasar must also recruit and train auxiliary guards—enough for all watches—to serve the Temple. You can have the excuse that the regular guards are in special training elsewhere for Jerusalem's defense."

Matthew sighed and nodded. "Eleasar and I can do that. Bring in new men—for more enter Jerusalem every day. We can at least train them enough to relieve the regular guards."

Yohanan cleared his throat: "Shimon says he may have a body of men who could serve in the Temple Guard."

"Who? I don't know of any other than the workmen busy on defense improvements. We could use some of them, but mostly we must find men one or two at a time and teach them their duties." He saw consternation harden on his father's face. "What is it, Father?"

"Shimon told us that Yohanan of Gischala will enter the city tomorrow morning, and he brings with him many of his men." Mathias rubbed his eyes with the heels of his hands, and when he lowered his hands, his eyes were full of doubt. "Those are the men Shimon wants you and Eleasar to use to replace the Temple Guard."

XVII

Between Falacrine and Fortuna Primigenia

The road had been empty for miles, the silence broken only by the clopping of Carmenta's hooves and an occasional snort. The quiet suited Nicanor's reflection on the past days spent with Antonia Caenis. Just as Vespasian had told him, she knew a great deal for someone without a position in Rome nor proximity to it.

That first morning in Falacrine, Antonia had had asked him how he had come to be friends with Lady Cleo and how he had come to serve Vespasian. He felt at ease and told her of the shipwreck of the *Salacia*, the great fire in Rome, the return to Antioch and Judea, the defeat at Beth Horon, then his return to Rome as a Praetorian Guard and assignment to Vespasian in his new role of commander of the Judean campaign. Vespasian had replaced Cestius Gallus, whose death—likely suicide—had surprised Nicanor.

They had been enjoying the villa's interior courtyard warmed by large bronze bowls of burning wood. Antonia settled more comfortably on a couch and shared with him what she knew of Cleo's family and how it was entangled with the current intrigue in Rome. "I learned early on I could cultivate connections with people who wielded power and could yield valuable information. And I learned how to use wisely what I had learned. That's what brought me out of slavery. I became secretary to the mother of Emperor Claudius. Then as a freedwoman, I carried out business on that emperor's behalf. Thus, I came to know Claudia Acte, another freedwoman and Nero's mistress at the time. Marcus Otho, Cleo's brother, had helped keep the mistress a secret from Nero's then-wife Octavia."

She held up her fingers to count off the names. "No one—not Otho, Galba, Gaius Calpurnius Piso, nor any others—wanted to jeopardize Nero's politically helpful marriage to Octavia. For she was Claudius's daughter and Nero's stepsister. Many of them would later sour on Nero as the senators grew angry at the young emperor. But they thought it prudent at the time. Joining with Octavia ensured Nero as the heir-apparent... and so it was. He became emperor upon Claudius's death, which all suspected was caused by poisoning. The new emperor, increasingly annoyed with Octavia, continued to see Claudia Acte, then had an affair with Poppaea, Marcus Otho's wife.

Finally, Nero divorced and then banished her. Octavia's banishment was so unpopular with the people that Nero, both offended and worried, ordered her death."

Antonia held out her hands as if to sum things up. "That series of self-indulgent acts is how I became acquainted with Marcus Otho, through Claudia Acte. I knew something of his young sister, Cleo, and her friendship with Poppaea. Nero desired Poppaea so much he had her divorced from Otho so he could then marry her. As it had for Octavia, being with Nero led to Poppaea's death, but that time it was by Nero's own hand." She sighed deeply, shaking her head.

"Claudia Acte benefited by doing what I had decided not to do: seduce and ensnare a young man who would become the emperor. As a result, she has been rewarded with considerable wealth. I still correspond with her at her estate in Velitrae, southeast of Rome. And she still has a connection to Nero and others in power—she and I share what we hear that might serve our mutual interests."

As Nicanor had listened to her story of the empire's noblemen and noblewomen—many 'noble' in name but not in deeds—he wished for the honesty of battle. He did not want to wade into the foul waters Antonia had portrayed for him with its eddies of shifting loyalties and currents of constant maneuvering based on lust or greed. But he must do as Vespasian asked and hoped to find a way to help Lady Cleo to safety.

Antonia had learned from Claudia Acte that Cestius Gallus's widow, Lady Octavia, had purchased a country villa just south of the Temple of *Fortuna Primigenia*. That was where Nicanor was headed now. It was just 50 miles from Falacrine by a direct route. Still, Antonia had recommended he use the longer, more traveled road toward Rome. Then, he turned east for the 15 miles to the temple at the city's northern outskirts. Antonia's major domus had given him directions to find Lady Octavia's villa from there.

The ride had given him and Carmenta time to get familiar with each other. At the end of the first day, he realized a comfort he had not had in years. In the provinces, even in peaceful Roman-controlled towns and camps, he was always on edge when he marched or rode cross-country. He or his mount trod upon land that had once belonged to others, and he always sensed they wanted it back. But in Italia, at least on the stretch of road he traveled, once he got a sense of Carmenta's walking, trotting, or even full gallop, he had settled into daydreams not had since he'd been a very young man.

At the end of the first day, on the part of the road that wound through a series of hillocks, each with a dense growth of trees,

Carmenta had nickered. With a quick shake of her head and forward cant of ears, she was warning him something or someone was ahead. As the path arced over the curve of one hill and followed the downslope of its shoulder, he spotted the gleam of eyes in the growing twilight and then the dim shape of their bodies. A pack of wolves, he thought at first. Then he could tell it was a male, female, and four adolescent pups, and they were not afraid of a man on horseback as they might have been of hunters on foot. Carmenta's intuition that they were not at a threat passed on to him, and he relaxed as she came to a stop. In the quiet, he felt their eyes on him and heard running water nearby. He scanned the area and saw a cluster of rocks holding back the dense forest to frame a small clearing suitable to camp in for the night. The wolves watched as he dismounted and led Carmenta toward it.

That night Nicanor had dreamed of a family of his own... perhaps one day. And that had made him think of Cleo. He prayed to the gods she was somewhere safe. As he closed his eyes, he saw the huddled shapes of the wolves in a hollow between rocks and hill—their home. Family.

* * *

PRAENESTE

Nicanor had been in and among the monumental buildings in Rome. Still, the temple of *Fortuna Primigenia* was the most impressive structure he had ever seen. The sanctuary complex and temple dedicated to the Goddess of Happiness were five vast terraces built upon massive masonry foundations connected by majestic staircases. Rising one above the other as they climbed the hill, the terraces formed a complex capped at its highest by a circular temple and the statue of Fortuna inside it. He could see even from the ground that they had carved the sculpture from white and gray marble that shone in the slanting sun.

Praeneste was a small town built on a spur of the *Monti Prenestini* mountain range. It spread around the base of the hill complex, and its central square had stairs leading to the two lower terraces. Nicanor stopped there for the night to make sure he took the correct road the following day. At the taberna, while one of the attendants saw to Carmenta, he satisfied his thirst with warm mulled wine. Above where he sat, the temple shone in the late-afternoon autumn sun. *Fortuna...* happiness... it made him think of his dream and of the wolves.

The next morning, after a two-hour ride, he arrived at the villa and reined Carmenta in before going closer. The villa was nestled between hills that were smaller versions of those in Rome. This was more rustic than many of the nobles' country estates he had passed outside Rome. According to the men he had overheard in the taberna, the terraced expanse of now-empty trellises surrounding the villa had recently yielded a fine harvest of grapes.

From the dirt road, a gravel path led to a broad flagstone area before a large central structure with smaller wings, one on each side. Nicanor kneed Carmenta forward, and the crunching of her hooves on the stones was loud in the stillness. The morning was chill enough that he could see puffs of vapor from his mouth and Carmenta's muzzle. He had barely dismounted and gathered his cloak about him when a man came from the front entrance.

"What do you want?"

The man's voice—a snappish bark—matched his look. He was undoubtedly a retired legionary, possibly a centurion, to judge from his sharp-edged tone of command. The man was shorter than Nicanor but equally burly. He stomped to a stop before him. Nicanor felt the scrutiny as his eyes inspected him, pausing a half-heartbeat on Nicanor's face with a slight nod of recognition for how his scars had likely been earned. The man's visage had its own marks of combat, and a glint of respect now showed with the alertness in his expression.

"I'm under the command of General Vespasian and ask to meet with Lady Octavia. Before serving under him, I served under the lady's husband in the 12th Legion. I'm Nicanor, a centurion, and I have met Lady Octavia before. She may remember me."

"Wait here." The man tramped back into the villa.

Nicanor waited long enough to feel the morning was growing chillier, not warmer. The lead-gray clouds above seemed to be lowering even as he studied them. He sniffed—wondering if his weather sense-memory was accurate; it had been years, but his nose gathered hints that early snow might be in the air.

"Centurion."

The woman's voice turned him back toward the house, and he beheld her bundled in a heavy mantle, but its cowl laid back to rest on her shoulders. Lady Octavia looked thinner, even in the thick cloak, and much older than he had last seen her. He knew that she and her husband, Cestius Gallus, had truly loved each other, and his loss was a tragedy that marked her face. The stout veteran had returned with her, his eyes steady on Nicanor and hand on the dagger at his belt.

"I'm very sorry about Lord Gallus's death, my lady."

"Thank you, centurion... it was..." She stopped, shook her head, and spoke to the man beside her. "Magnus, please see that the centurion's horse is taken care of." She gestured at Nicanor to follow. "Come with me. My husband told me of you, and we'll speak as you wish."

* * *

LADY OCTAVIA'S VILLA

The day had passed in talking before a massive stone hearth, Magnus periodically feeding pieces of wood to the fire. Nicanor had learned the man had formerly been the First Centurion of Legio III Gallica in Gaul. Cestius Gallus had known the man's last commander, who had recommended the recently retired centurion to serve a suitable household if an opportunity arose. When Lady Octavia arrived from Antioch, she contacted him. He had joined her as an unusual major domus overseeing the vineyards and workers and the handful of servants she brought from Antioch.

Before them, the broad table held a spread of documents Lady Octavia had brought out at Nicanor's request: flat sheets of vellum, smaller half-sheets, and scrolls of parchment. Nicanor gestured at them. "Except for your personal letters, the rest looks like the reports and official messages your husband had me deliver to the emperor."

"Are you sure he received them, centurion?"

"Yes, Lady... personally. I was there with Emperor Nero when the Praetorian Prefect Tigellinus put them directly into the emperor's hands."

"They have done nothing with that information that I'm aware of, and they did not look into what my husband reported. Neither the emperor nor any imperial representative even reported his death to me. After my husband's last words in Antioch and then the silence afterward, my fears proved warranted. I learned the news from a note of condolence from General Vespasian right after I settled here."

"My lady, I must also tell you something else, something I did only because of my concern."

"What concern?"

"I had copies made of Lord Gallus's reports and letter to the emperor." At the widening of her eyes and her stern expression, he hurried to explain. "My fear was that Lord Gallus's reports about Gessius Florus's actions as Judean Procurator—about his meddling—

65

might somehow become 'lost' or 'misplaced.' I agreed with your husband's suspicions that Florus influenced events. Including leading to Lord Gallus's decision to pull back from Jerusalem, and that contributed to our defeat at Beth Horon."

Lady Octavia settled back in her chair and nodded. "Cleo wrote me that she felt her husband"—a flash of distaste crossed her face—"was doing all he could to provoke the war. She felt it would somehow serve his purpose."

Nicanor leaned forward and rested his thick forearms on his knees. "Just before I left Ptolemais, I also discovered that Gessius Florus was beating Lady Cleo."

"What?" The woman half stood from her chair in alarm.

"Lady Cleo told me so herself. Sayid—the Syrian auxiliary who brought Lord Gallus's reports and letter to you—got her away from Florus and brought her to me for safety."

Lady Octavia stiffened, and the stern look returned. Magnus shifted, and Nicanor noted a hardness come over the old veteran's face as the lady stood and paced in front of the fire. "She must not return to that man! If he knows that she warned me, he will surely kill her."

"I had a plan to bring her to Rome with me," he added, "to do just as you say, to save her. But the night I sailed, she did not show up as we had arranged."

"Where did she go, then?"

"I don't know, Lady. I'm sure that Sayid will do what he can to keep her safe. But from here, I must return to Rome and go to Lady Cleo's brother Marcus Otho in Hispania Lusitania to see if there is some way... if he has the power... to save her."

"What can I do to help?"

"I had sent my copies of these," he waved a hand at the documents on the table, "to Marcus Otho. He is the only person with some level of power that I have a slight connection. I had the documents hand-carried to him by Lady Cleo's retired major domus, Graius. I asked him to tell Otho of his sister's worries. Can you make copies of yours and extra copies of Lady Cleo's letters with her suspicions, so I can also show them to Lord Otho?"

"Magnus, send someone to Praeneste to return with a scribe," Lady Octavia said. She turned to Nicanor as the old centurion walked from the room. "When you leave, you'll have copies of everything. We must help Lady Cleo. And, Nicanor," a fierce expression took hold of her as she waited for his full attention, "I do not believe my husband killed himself."

Using his name had touched Nicanor. "Neither do I, Lady, and along with saving Lady Cleo, I hope to find whoever had a hand in killing a man I respected... and I will see them punished."

XVIII

November 67 CE

Ptolemais

Galerius Senna entered the taberna, concerned that it seemed he'd been summoned. The commander of a Roman legion should be the one doing the summoning. And Gessius Florus, the summoner, no longer held a prominent title such as Procurator of Judea. But he now seemed to wield more power by not being bound by politics or Rome's monolithic provincial administration. Florus apparently continued to have the emperor's ear and support, so he might be able to deliver on the promised reward for Senna's ongoing help.

The armed man outside the door did not move aside as he approached. Instead, he held up a large hand for him to stop. "Your name, lord?"

Senna had served in Alexandria and recognized the accent. Florus must have hired this mercenary to serve as his personal force. At least the man knew enough to note he was of some noble standing and to act respectfully.

"Galerius Senna," he replied, "commander of the 12th Legion, to see Lord Florus."

The man did not question why he was there and merely said, "Please wait here, sir," and went inside. A minute later, he was back, holding the door open. "Lord Florus will see you."

The legion commander entered the room to find Gessius Florus stretched on a divan, attended by a sturdy man standing beside him, with a low table before the lord holding only a large earthenware flagon with a ribbed strap handle and a goblet. Florus reached for the cup and drank deeply, then set it back on the table. Immediately a sallow woman Senna had not noticed limped across the room, lifted the flagon with practiced ease, and refilled the cup. She slid it closer, within reach of the jeweled hand that raised the cup to his lips again. In Florus's other hand, he held a creased sheet of parchment he looked up from as he drank.

The imperial tax collector followed Senna's stare, set the parchment on his lap, and flipped the long robe over his lower legs. They were healing but unsightly, and Senna supposed they still hurt.

"What did you need to meet with me about, Galerius?" asked Florus. He looked over his shoulder at the short, thickset man and raised the parchment. "Thank you, Drusus. See me later. I'll have a reply for you to deliver." The man nodded and left without looking at the legion commander.

"Lord Florus," Senna reported, "the 12th Legion's patrols will not cover the Sycaminum port area as you requested. There will be no concern about potential issues between your Alexandrians and the legionaries." Florus had not asked him to sit, and Senna was relieved; he wished to finish and go.

"Good, and what else?"

"My man in Caesarea reports Lord Vespasian meets daily with the Jewish prisoner, Yosef ben Mathias, and recently removed some of his chains to give him more freedom."

A grimace spread over Florus's features. "The general," he sneered, "pampers an enemy of Rome."

"I know that you prefer the Jew dead," Senna said. Vespasian's high-ranking Jewish prisoner was only part of what stoked Florus's anger, but Senna was wise enough not to mention Lady Cleo's desertion, the details of which he had no desire to know. He had been surprised at the size of the reward offered to find her. "I may have a solution... or a resolution to achieve that for you."

"What is your solution?" snapped Florus.

"The prisoners taken in the fall of Yotapta have been held in a temporary camp near Ptolemais. The 12th has provided a cohort of guards for them. One officer came to me reporting that his men overheard one prisoner—a woman—spreading stories. She said that this Yosef, the commander at Yotapta, the man held by Lord Vespasian, was a traitor to his people and should be killed."

"Really... she interests me..." Florus drank more and waved the woman away when she moved to refill his cup. "Why does she call him a traitor? And why would she want one of her own people killed?"

"I don't know, Lord Florus. I did not want to draw attention to her by having her questioned. She will need to be taken from the camp for that. But I'm sure there is a way to use her for your purpose."

"Send her to me... I'll find a means." Florus dismissed the legion commander with a wave and lifted the flagon to pour for himself, but it was empty. As Senna walked out, he heard Florus call, "Eris bring more wine."

XIX

November 67 CE

Jerusalem

The Temple Enclosure, Hall of Hewn Stone

Just beyond the Court of Women, at the entrance of the Priest's Court, the meeting hall and chambers for the Sanhedrin were built into a wall of the Temple. Half-inside and half-outside the sanctuary and constructed from hewn stones, unlike according to ritual and tradition altar rooms built from stones untouched by iron. The Hall of Hewn Stone was the sovereign court and the center of political and religious leadership in Judea.

The chamber was packed. For the first time in months, every member—71 venerated priest-judges—was in attendance and had brought guests. Matthew scanned the room. Some members had brought many, for they lined the walls behind the benches and along the sides.

"Of course, Yohanan ben Levi would command the 'stage'..." Mathias scoffed at the man standing with Shimon ben Gamliel in front of the arced ranks of the members of the Sanhedrin.

"Yes, the Gischalan preens, does he not?" Yohanan ben Zaccai whispered as Shimon ben Gamliel stepped forward to hush the buzzing of the crowd.

"Your attention please... please, all of you, sit... and listen. We have important news to hear and discuss." The Sanhedrin president waited for all to settle and the hall to quiet. He turned to beckon the man a step forward. "Yohanan ben Levi of Gischala will now speak to you." The Sanhedrin president stepped aside.

"Some of you know me, some may know of me...." The man's voice was distinct and forceful.

Matthew felt Yohanan ben Zaccai shift around next to him and snort. Faint as it was, it caught the Gischalan's ear, and he squinted at them before continuing.

"Some may think you know me... but you do not. I come from Galilee, but what I have to say is important to all Judeans, including the men who have followed me to Jerusalem. We are all Jews."

Matthew watched the man who had caused his brother so much trouble—had even tried to kill him, according to the old priest sitting next to him—as the Gischalan's gaze panned the chamber. There was a rustling among the men who lined the walls, and Matthew realized they must be some of those loyal to Yohanan ben Levi. He searched for Eleasar ben Ananias, who would usually be in front in his role as commander of the Temple Guard. He spotted him standing off to one side, eyes locked on the Gischalan and full of the fury he was capable of. Matthew looked around again and realized who was *not* there. The usual detachment of Levite Temple Guards attendant for meetings in the hall had been ousted or removed to make room for Yohanan ben Levi's lackeys. Matthew's attention returned to the Gischalan.

"I come to you from my city, which, like all of Galilee, has fallen or bowed to the Romans. They had no trouble taking Galilee's many villages and small towns. But were it not for treason and traitorous leadership, they would not have taken cities such as Yotapta. And that emboldened them to seize mine. Now they come for yours."

Matthew shot a glance at his father, who was sitting white-faced, eyes blazing, on the other side of Yohanan ben Zaccai, whose own expression was of consternation and contempt. The Gischalan again implied Yosef was a traitor and the losses in Galilee were Yosef's fault. The old priest had a firm hand on his father's forearm, and that might be the only thing keeping him seated.

"Many," the Gischalan leader's eyes flicked to Shimon ben Gamliel beside him, "doubted the wisdom of giving command of Galilee to one so inexperienced and whose admiration for Rome was so well known."

Matthew felt the tremble of terrible anger shake him and started to stand. The old priest put his other hand out to restrain him. Matthew knew he was right. Better to speak when the time and place suited, confronting the Sanhedrin with facts and truth. Not now, in what would become a raucous crossfire argument fueled by the man's fearmongering and hearsay. But to sit still and listen to the Gischalan spread lies about Yosef took all his willpower.

"Yotapta and Galilee fell because of leadership weakness... or their fondness for the Romans. But Jerusalem will not fall. The Romans will not take this city. But that outcome is only certain if you listen to me and not those who have divided us. Many believe that members of this body have been killed because of their factional beliefs—Yehuda ish Krioth and recently Esau ben Beor. And not long ago, sect leaders such as Menahem ben Judah of the Sicarii were murdered, to be replaced by Elazar ben Yair, who chooses not to help Jerusalem and confines himself to readying Masada to stand against the Romans. With strong leadership, law and order will be restored, and Jerusalem can stand against Rome. My men and I have the full endorsement of the Sanhedrin president to help make that happen, and we will yield to his commands." The Gischalan half-turned to clasp Shimon ben Gamliel on the shoulder. "Together, we will bring order and make Jerusalem strong." Yohanan ben Levi left the chamber with a last nod to the Sanhedrin president, and the rows of standing men followed him out.

Matthew was quickly on his feet to confront Shimon ben Gamliel, who still stood before them; the man did not look entirely happy. He turned to his father and Yohanan ben Zaccai, who had also risen but now faced Eleasar been Ananias, who had joined them. With him was a man Matthew knew as Yoshua ben Gamla, one of the Moderate leaders.

Eleasar nodded in understanding at the expressions on the faces of Matthew, Mathias, and Yohanan ben Zaccai. "I'm angry too," he said, "but it will do no good to shout at Shimon. Or to debate the true intentions of that deceitful Gischalan, who speaks far better than he acts."

"He's a liar!" sputtered Yohanan ben Zaccai. "I was with Yosef in Galilee and Yotapta, and that man lies. That Gischalan did more to hurt Galilee than help. Yosef fought and fell with his chosen city... Did this cowardly man fight to save the city he was born in?" Zaccai turned to Mathias. "I am sorry for my words about Yosef, Mathias. We still can hope he survived."

Mathias closed his eyes and shook his head. "You're right, my friend... Yosef did what he felt he must do. He would lead even if it meant dying in the city he commanded. I have no hope he lives. We cannot change what has happened with words or arguments, even though what Yohanan ben Levi claims is untrue."

"But," Eleasar interjected, "we must not let him come here—having abandoned his own city—and use fear and distortion to bluff his way to power. We must work together to prevent a liar and coward from assuming a leadership role in Jerusalem."

"And make him pay for the things he implies about Yosef," swore Matthew.

XX

November 67 CE

Near Beth Horon

"But I thought we decided to avoid people until we reached Jerusalem?" said Cleo. She added to the fire the last piece of brushwood from the pile they had gathered when they made camp earlier in the day. Cicero, perched on a pad of cloth draped over her shoulder, softly clucked as she straightened.

Sayid nodded, likely understanding how frightened Cleo had been by what happened at the crossroads village days before. It must have scared him, too. The man nearly killed him and then would have taken her back to Gessius Florus. "Yes," he said, "but we will soon be close to Jerusalem. There are so many people headed there, too, it will be difficult to not encounter them as they bunch together near the city. So we should attach ourselves, if we can, to a group entering the city... but before they get there."

"That trader's caravan you spotted—it had families headed to the city?"

"Yes," Sayid nodded. "This morning, I spoke with one of the livestock drovers trailing the caravan with their herd. He told me they are camped a little ahead of us. We'll join them tomorrow morning, and then it's another couple of days to Jerusalem."

"If we must, we must," Cleo said, rising and dusting the dirt from her knees. "I'll go settle Cicero for the night and see that Elian is ready for early tomorrow morning. I'm glad the medicine worked—he no longer has any fever."

When she returned, she saw that Sayid had not moved and still stared into the fire. "Sayid..." He did not look up as she sat next to him and noticed the glistening of his eyes. "Sayid, what is wrong?" The youth she had considered a boy when she first met him, though he was still of slight build, was no longer so young. He had the harried expression of a man with too many worries... too many unpleasant memories.

Sayid shrugged and shook his head. "It's nothing..."

Cleo leaned forward into the light of the small fire. "It cannot be 'nothing'... tell me what's bothering you, Sayid."

His eyes lifted and scanned the shadowed hills. "We are near the pass at Beth Horon. You've heard of the battle, but you do not understand how terrible it was. The rebels rained arrows and javelins down upon us until the ground at our feet was soaked with our blood. Thousands died; thousands more were wounded and dying. Their screams echoed off the hills surrounding the pass." He paused and looked at Cleo silently for a moment, then continued.

"I was struck—wounded, Nicanor, too, though he never went down as I did. Our only hope to escape was to leave Nicanor and a cohort of men—nearly 500—to pretend the legion remained. To sacrifice themselves so the rest of us could retreat in the night. Nicanor had strapped me to his dying horse—good Abigieus—and that horse carried me from there with the rest of the legion, else I would have died. Near Antipatris, where Lord Gallus halted the retreat to reorganize, I remember the sadness as I buried Abigieus. I could not let him be dumped with the other dead horses. I mourned him and Nicanor, who I was sure I would never see again. Oh, how happy I was to see him later! I don't know how any man could have made it from the pass with such awful wounds, but he did.

"In my life, only Nicanor, Yosef, and you have become my true friends... and I only have my mother, an aunt, and a father I do not know for family." He wiped his eyes with a sleeve. "I'm sorry, my lady.... you have had an even crueler time these past years at the hands of Gessius Florus... and you face a greater unknown than I do. I have my legion to return to."

"I'm no longer a lady, Sayid, no longer Cleo of Rome. I'm Ya'el of Judea." She squeezed his shoulder. "And you can cry for what has happened... but we—your friends—are still alive. And we must do what we must.... no matter how hard that is."

* * *

Sayid had awakened long before the others and readied to leave camp, setting an armload of wood next to the blackened-stone circled remnants of their campfire. It was a good spot that other travelers might come upon, and the ready stack of firewood would be helpful to them. He watched as Cleo—no, Ya'el—with the parrot on her shoulder again, and Elian beside her raised a blanket oddly shaped by its contents. He knew what it was and had seen her keeping it near since the incident at the crossroads village.

"Lady?" At her look, he corrected himself. "Ya'el... it's best if I carry that for you... and in the open."

She reluctantly unrolled the blanket to reveal a Roman bow to the grinning Elian. He ran his hands along its curve and carried it to Sayid.

The Syrian remembered how bravely Cleo had shot the remaining arrow from her attacker's smashed quiver and saved his life. She had formed a new quiver from plaited strips of bark Elian had gathered for her. The shape of a simple cylinder with a roughly circular piece of thicker bark for its bottom. It now held three crude arrows she had fashioned as well. They had simple whittled-and-smoothed shafts made from somewhat straight long sticks shaved to a sharp point. But without fletching—there'd been no time—they would not fly far and could only be deadly up close.

"I'll need my bow back once we're in Jerusalem," she said.

"You cannot carry it there... you must not draw any attention!"

"I won't carry it... it'll be hidden again, but it stays with me."

Sayid sighed and nodded, "Yes... Ya'el." He slipped bow and quiver over his shoulder. He stooped and smiled at the boy, tousling his hair: "Remember what we've told you, Elian. You must do as I do... don't call the lady "lady," or Cleo. You must call her Ya'el."

The boy's usually smiling face turned thoughtful, and he looked from Sayid to the one he must now call Ya'el. "May I call her mother? I have never had one in all my life."

Cleo knew the boy's story: his mother had died in childbirth, and his father had raised him, but only until he was old enough to sell to the slave market. Then the father disappeared. "Come here," she said, beckoning the boy to her, then hugged him. "Yes, you can call me Mother."

* * *

They entered the caravan's camp just as they were forming up. Sayid saw the drover he had spoken with the day before. "Stay right here," he told Ya'el and Elian and went to the man and talked briefly, then waved to them to join him. "He will take us to the trader who leads the caravan." The man nodded, and they followed him past a line of mule-drawn carts and clusters of people that must be families seeking the safety of traveling with others. The driver stopped at a large wagon with a heavy-set man standing beside it studying the sky, his red face shining above a jutting gray beard that reached mid-chest.

"Jonas, this is the traveler I told you about... who wishes to join us and go to Jerusalem."

"See to your animals, Yitzhak. We leave as soon as everyone is ready." The caravan's leader shifted a full wine or water skin from his shoulder to set under the wagon driver's bench. He turned back to

75

Sayid. "Yitzhak told me you are escorting this woman and child who have family in Jerusalem."

"Yes, sir."

"Where from?" The man's eyes passed from Sayid to Ya'el, who had donned a headdress and veil, to the bird perched on her forearm.

"Tarsus, sir. That's northwest of Antioch." Sayid took a half-side-step to get more between them.

"I know Antioch; it is far from here... but I don't know Tarsus." His eyes shifted from Ya'el back to Sayid. "Do you come from there, too?"

"No, sir, I'm from Laodicea, which is just south of Antioch."

"Are you a fighter then?" The man's smile split the beard to show uneven but strong-looking teeth. "A fighter who escorts women for a living?"

Sayid knew the man was gauging him, as anyone on the roads would do who had sense. "I have fought... but my last work was on the docks of Laodicea. I do this—I'm escorting this woman and boy—as a favor to my mother's friend, who knew of the women's situation."

The caravan leader turned to Ya'el with another glance at the bird who stared back at him. "Who is your family in Jerusalem?"

"She is Greek, sir." Sayid started to translate, and the man repeated his question in that language.

"My husband's father is a cousin to Mathias ben Yosef, sir."

"I know the name," the man nodded, "but where is your husband... why is he not with you?"

"He is dead, sir, killed by Romans. His parents and mine are dead, too, though they died because of illness and old age." Ya'el took in a shuddering breath that came out a sob. "My husband's family is all I have left... it is terrible to be so alone with no one to help you. So, we go to Jerusalem."

The trader nodded; his face now solemn. "These are hard times for many... and harder days to come, I fear." He spread his hands and gestured at the groups behind each wagon, draped with bags and carrying baskets of all they possessed. He looked down at Elian, who had remained slightly behind Ya'el but now peeked from behind a fold in her robe.

"Is this your boy?" The man bent down and smiled again.

"Yes," Ya'el drew him around to beside her, "this is Elian... my son." The boy hugged her waist tighter, and a broad grin spread over his face as he looked up at her.

"And I see he loves his mother!" The man laughed and turned to Sayid. "Can you help us load the wagons and unload them if it is needed?"

* * *

JERUSALEM

The long line for people on foot to enter the city gave Sayid ample time to see that the gate and walls had been strengthened impressively and well-fortified as far as he could see. *If all are now like this,* he thought, *it will be even harder to take these walls. I know the legions will come here again... but I hope I never find myself in the attack on them.*

Ya'el had overheard the people ahead of them reply to the questions from sentries at the gate and whispered to Sayid, "They are asking everyone their purpose for entering the city."

He shook his head. "We just tell them our story... Yosef's family is known."

Minutes later, they discovered that alone—saying they were coming to be with Yosef's family—would not be enough to let them enter the city.

The sentry looked first at the bird on Ya'el's shoulder, head tucked down and seemingly asleep, and told them: "Please step to the side of the gate, and we will send for them to come for you. It will be a while; so many are coming into the city, and our men are busy with others. You must wait."

Sayid asked, "Can I go for them and return, so they can vouch for her and the boy? I was once with Ya'el at Yosef ben Mathias's home for *Seder* two years ago; I can find the way and will return with someone from the family."

The sentry eyed Sayid from head to toe, pausing at the Roman dagger belted at his waist and the Roman bow on his back... not uncommon since many armed themselves with what they could find or get. Still, it was not a point in his favor. "No, you cannot."

"Then let me go," Ya'el said. The longer this took, the more risk of something going wrong or someone becoming suspicious of them.

The sentry, increasingly irritated at the press of people growing around the gate, replied, "You can't go, but you can send your boy."

Ya'el quickly bent down to Elian, awakening Cicero who let out a low squawk of protest. The boy was awed by Jerusalem's walls and size, far greater than he had ever seen, and he had not stopped gawking. "Elian... Elian," she spoke quietly, "listen to me and do not forget. Once you are inside the gate, speak only Greek and ask how to get to the Upper City and the home of Mathias ben Josephus or his son, Yosef ben Mathias. Yosef's parents are Rebecca and Mathias... and his brother is... Matthew and he has a sister." She could not remember Yosef's sister's name. She took the letter Yosef had written for her from the pouch at her waist. "If anyone asks, tell them we— you and I—are their family from Tarsus and waiting at the gate to be allowed to enter the city. Do not lose this letter—it is very important— and give it only to Yosef's family. Do you understand?" The boy nodded. "Then hurry!"

* * *

More than an hour had passed, and Sayid and Ya'el had gone from fretful patience to anxiety. The sentry's treatment had changed from a man just doing his duty to glaring scrutiny. It would soon become an accusation that they were liars and would be turned away from the gate and into the coming night outside Jerusalem's walls.

"Mother... Sayid!"

Ya'el and Sayid heard the cry and struggled to their feet, stiff from sitting on the hard ground. Elian came running through the gate with two young women hurrying behind him. They stopped in front of Ya'el.

"Where did you get this letter?" asked the one in front with a healing cut on her cheek. "It's in my brother's handwriting." She waved the message in her hand. "Where did you get it!?"

Ya'el was surprised at the difference in Yosef's sister and almost did not recognize her. At the Seder, she had been a puffy-eyed, heavier, sullen, much younger woman.

"I got lost... Mother... I'm sorry I took so long. I got lost." Elian whimpered.

Ya'el looked down at him. "Shh... shh, Elian. Everything is fine now." She straightened and met the woman's glare. "I got it from Yosef, who wrote it for me."

The woman with the scar stepped closer and dropped her voice. "Who are you? You look familiar to me somehow." Her eyes cut to the sentry who had momentarily turned away to speak to another guard.

"I'm Ya'el... just as Yosef's message to you says."

The woman—Yosef's sister—shook her head. "You could have found this letter. How do I know you got it from Yossi!? He is dead. Did you escape from Yotapta?"

"Yosef is not dead." Ya'el reached into her robe and drew out the small coin on its cord. It spun and caught a ray of the setting sun.

The second woman who had returned with Elian and had yet to say anything came forward to study it.

"Miriam," she whispered, "that's the *kinyan* Leah gave Yosef... he would never part with it unless he had good reason to... she must have come from him!"

XXI

DECEMBER 67 CE

OUTSIDE ROME

The road into Rome from Praeneste was dotted on either side by tombs and cenotaphs, more of them closer to the city, but none within that sacred boundary. Many of the memorials of the wealthy dead had benches designed to invite travelers to stop and rest, for which Nicanor was grateful. The ache of his old wounds in leg and hip had increased with each mile on horseback.

Sitting, he shared with Carmenta the dried apples Octavia had given him as he departed. The *cestine* variety he had discovered and enjoyed during his last duty in Rome in the Praetorian Guard. The plaque on the bench where he rested asked those who stopped there to respect and pity the dead. Another one was inscribed *tempus edax rerum*—time is the devourer of things.

He drew his cloak closer around him and studied the scudding clouds, black-edged and swiftly filling a once-blue morning sky that now matched Carmenta's silver-gray coat and dark mane. Time did devour everything, including the seasons, and winter would soon be upon them. That thought brought thoughts of Cleo. Was she safe? Was Sayid still with her to help and to protect her? Surely, he would. That boy had grown to become a man in the few years he had known him and would stand by their friend no matter what. With all that had happened since the shipwreck of the *Salacia*... he, Cleo, and Yosef had all changed. It seemed each had matured in unexpected ways.

Carmenta's nose brushed his shoulder.

"Yes," he said. "We must get moving again." He gave the mare the last slice of dried apple and lifted the reins to mount.

* * *

ROME

Nicanor entered the city and reached the familiar *sacra via*, the broad avenue used for important ceremonies, where the Roman Triumphs were held. General Vespasian had experienced some of these and promised Nicanor would join him in the one held for their victory against the rebels in Judea. That avenue would lead him to the forum square and the Capitoline Hill, upon which loomed the Temple of Jupiter Optimus Maximus. But his route would turn before he reached that impressive structure that watched over the heart of Rome.

Nicanor had first planned to go where he would have typically expected to see Graius to simply wait for him, as he had before in his last time in Rome. After all, Graius had told him the city was his birthplace, and he expected to die there. The old major domus would assuredly have not moved and could give him exact directions to Marcus Otho and counsel on how best to get to him.

But Lady Octavia had thought that unwise. "Roman hands, not the hands of a foreign enemy... and not his own... killed my husband." Nicanor must learn to be discreet. She had sent Magnus's son on her best horse, days before Nicanor's departure, to find Graius at his *insula* and arrange a meeting place away from the apartment building.

Antonia Caenis had also told him to be careful in Rome. Nicanor must mind who he spoke with and where he met with them, for all public places—the streets and tabernae—had eyes and ears. Many were willing and able to find buyers for the content of overheard conversations. Antonia had stressed Rome was a battlefield for politicians and just as dangerous as any field he had fought upon. "Wits and will are your offense and defense," she had said, "not sword and shield."

Nicanor knew that every day, as had been reported by Magnus's son when he returned from speaking to Graius in Rome, Cleo's retired major domus would be at the Temple of Hercules near the *Forum Boarium* close to the Tiber River at the hour before sunset. Nicanor rode through the city's center to one of the oldest sections, the centuries-old area of the city's original cattle market. He had heard about it but never been and had never seen the Temple of Hercules. There were not as many people as he would have expected this close to the *Forum Romanum*, a half-mile east and the city's major political, ritual, and civic center.

He judged it to be about 50 feet in diameter and 35 feet high as he rounded the temple. His first time in Rome—after rescue from the wreck of the *Salacia* and before the great fire—Yosef had told him about the different building designs as they walked the city. This was a *tholos*, a round temple of Greek design with walls constructed of travertine upon marble blocks and encircled by a colonnade of 20 marble columns.

Carmenta's ears pricked forward, and she gave a soft nicker. Through the columns, Nicanor saw the circular *cella*, the inner chamber, and within it stood a man with his back turned. He was wrapped in a heavy, fur-trimmed mantle, the plume of vapor from his breathing matching those of Nicanor and Carmenta in the chill air of the coming evening.

Nicanor shifted the oversized satchel Lady Octavia had given him, one that had belonged to her husband. It contained his copied report and letters, including those from Cleo to Octavia. He dismounted and rested the bag more easily on the hip opposite his sword arm, beneath his cloak. The figure inside—profiled by the slanting rays of a setting sun—held what looked like a gladius in one hand at his side. He tapped it against his leg as he studied something above him.

"Graius?" Nicanor asked once he was a dozen feet from the man. He must have heard the clop of hooves but had not turned. He saw now the temple had an *oculus,* a circular opening in the middle of the roof.

The man brought the sword up, arm extended, and pointed to the sky above in a salute. *Odd, there is no glint of metal even in the waning sun*, thought Nicanor. The man lowered his arm, turned to face Nicanor, and stepped toward him. "Yes, centurion."

His face was gaunter than when Nicanor had seen him last. But the grip was still firm as he grasped his forearm. He released Graius's free hand and noted what he held in the other. It was a *rudis*, the wooden sword he knew was given to gladiators whose success has earned them their freedom.

Graius had followed his eyes. "I was never the largest, strongest, or fastest... but I still live, and that means I must be the luckiest. My owner allowed me to come here with an offering, before and after the Games." He swept the circuit of the temple with the *rudis*. "*Hercules Invictus,* Hercules the victor."

Nicanor studied the man, who seemed lost for a moment in the past. "How long?"

"I fought for 10 years before earning enough for my freedom.... and received this." He lifted the *rudis* again toward the opening above, now rimmed with the fading goldish-red light of the day's ending. "I poured much blood here," he said, pointing down between their feet at the massive carved marble face set in the floor beneath him. Its mouth was a lipped drain that still showed the stains of centuries of use. "Though I've often come to stand outside the temple and consider my past, it has been many years since I last stood right here, within."

Nicanor was surprised at the revelation and curious. "Why did you choose this place?"

"The note Magnus's son carried said that Cleo is in danger." He glanced up at the darkening oculus and around at the growing shadows. "Soon, the lone attendant for this almost-forgotten temple will come to light a single lantern, so I must be brief. I have known Lady Octavia all her life.... when I became a freedman, her father recommended me to Lady Cleo's father. I left the arena with many lasting wounds—a low trident thrust rendered me unable to father children... and I never married. Without a family of my own, I watched Lady Cleo grow up as if she were my child. If she is in danger, this," he shook the wooden sword, "will be replaced by a real one. So, I came in here to pray for the luck that never abandoned me when I fought and bled on the sand and dirt of the Circus Maximus and countless smaller stadiums."

"You won't need to fight anyone, Graius... I just need you to tell me how to find and get to Marcus Otho. I want his help to protect Cleo in Judea or, better yet, his help to find her and get her out of Judea and away from Gessius Florus, no matter the cost."

The old gladiator shook his head. "The Rome you left, Nicanor, is ever more unsteady. Provinces other than Judea are rumbling, and I hear some desire a change. All are tired of higher taxes with less to show for them. They grow weary of having an emperor they cannot respect, much less worship as he seems to demand. But enough of that, the things we cannot affect. To get to Otho in Hispania Lusitania is two weeks or more on a coastal vessel from Ostia to Tarraco, and then 16 days on horseback to his capital, Emerita Augusta. Nearly a year ago—when I went to Otho with what you gave me from Cestius Gallus—the bandits on the road and winter weather made the travel difficult. It will probably be riskier now, with more questioning the empire's ability to punish those who break its laws. You know from your own experience that declaring *Civis Romanus Sum*, Roman citizenship, has never truly protected all Romans. So, I will go with you and with a real sword in hand, though you think I cannot be of help." Graius gave Nicanor a stern look. "When do we leave?"

Nicanor sighed at the thought of another person to watch over and protect. "Soon, I must do something for General Vespasian before I leave Rome."

XXII

DECEMBER 67 CE

CAESAREA

Gessius Florus waited to speak until Vespasian's aide, Gaheris Clineas, had left them, refusing to wince as the brisk wind slapped the tail of his cloak against his legs. "So, general... you'll be here in Caesarea long enough to require a permanent headquarters? When will you move on to Jerusalem?" He waved a jeweled hand at the men completing the construction of the *praetorium.*

"Yes," answered Vespasian. "This is better suited for my needs than the private residence I've worked from since my arrival." He studied the man who was so close to Emperor Nero in his position as an imperial tax collector. *I must be cautious in my dealings with him,* he thought. There was something about Florus he disliked, but he could not risk disregarding a man who had the emperor's ear. Nicanor did not trust the man and had not hesitated to tell him so. But the duties of a centurion were more straightforward. As a general, especially under Nero, the less circumspect could find themselves exiled at best. At worst? Killed—by their own hand or assassination. He feared little for himself, but if he made a foolish step, Antonia Caenis and his sons would suffer, not just himself. So, he would listen to Gessius Florus and consider anything that did not conflict with his need to finish this campaign successfully.

The general squinted into the brisk wind, admiring the building, and continued. "When Galerius Senna asked for this meeting on your behalf, he said you have the means to ensure my prisoner's full cooperation and prevent any thoughts of escape. But I think his escape is unlikely—I have his word."

Florus scrutinized Vespasian before replying. "It is one thing that he promises not to escape, general. But to get his complete cooperation is another. The rebel commander has valuable knowledge about the leaders in Jerusalem. You must do what can be done to ensure success here—right?"

"Of course, Lord Florus." Vespasian turned to enter the tent erected next to the construction site. "Give us this space," he said to the two legion engineers inside. *It is good the headquarters will be ready for use by the end of the day,* he thought. Then there would be more privacy, more security. He beckoned: "Join me in here, Lord

Florus." He sat on one of the vacated folding camp stools and studied the imperial tax collector's stiff gait as he followed him inside and sat awkwardly on the other stool. "You seem to be healing well."

"Yes, general." Florus drew the long cloak closer over his legs to cover them.

Vespasian could not restrain the harshness that came out with the question he must ask: "What's this I've heard about you placing a bounty on Lady Cleo? I don't understand why you would do such a thing against your wife."

"General, that's a private matter." Florus met his stare with a steady look of his own.

"She's a Roman citizen in a country at war with Rome. I am the general commanding the campaign to win that war and have a duty to protect any Roman citizens who remain here. So I have a concern when I hear word has been spread throughout the area offering a bounty for her capture."

"Lady Cleo... is not well, general. I fear she could harm herself and others," Florus glanced down at his legs, "I search for her only to help her. I have offered a *reward*, not a bounty, for her safe return."

"How is she a danger?"

"She set the fire that did this"—Florus's hand passed over his legs. "I do not know what else she might be capable of... but I fear for her."

Or fear her, Vespasian thought. "Why did she do it?" He knew it was not uncommon for a man to be harsh with his wife and sometimes for her to retaliate. But he could never imagine a man mistreating his wife in such a way that she might find it better to run away, alone and into a region at war.

"Lady Cleo's mind is unsteady and has been since we arrived in Judea.

"What do you mean?"

"She—um—has some affinity for Jews. She even befriended your prisoner after the shipwreck of the *Salacia*. She thinks I—in my actions as procurator—bear some of the fault for this war."

Indeed, Vespasian had heard some rumors through Cestius Gallus—his wife Octavia had contact with Lady Cleo... He lowered his head in slight acknowledgment, and Florus sat forward, seemingly eager to continue and dispel the rumors.

"After her shipwreck and days at sea believing she would die... Lady Cleo changed, and when I went to her in Rome, she was not the same woman I had planned to marry. Her condition worsened when we arrived in Judea."

Vespasian nodded. He had known many soldiers who survived battles and were forever changed. Their nights were frequently a fitful sleep if they slept at all and often were full of anger. Surely, a woman who had suffered a shipwreck could be different afterward. "What will you do when you find her?"

Florus's mouth smiled warmly, yet his eyes had a harsh glint as he replied. "Why, I'll take care of her... general." Then he sat back. "May we now talk about my idea? Anything I can do to end this war and return the flow of taxes and tribute to the emperor is good for the empire. Perhaps I can then return to Rome after, the gods willing, I find Lady Cleo."

"What do you propose?"

"Galerius Senna mentioned to me that one of his officers reported a problem with a female prisoner from Yotapta. She had fought back before being knocked unconscious and captured."

"Yes," Vespasian nodded, "I had reports of at least two women who fought capture... just before my soldiers discovered their men, who were hiding in a cave. All were led by my prisoner. One woman was killed in the attack, and the other was brought before me with the shepherd's crook she had used as her weapon."

"This woman, I was told... was betrothed or married to a man who has become one of the Jews' heroes of Yotapta. He was a fierce warrior and mighty giant, one of the leaders, and sacrificed himself to save others."

As he spoke, Florus's manner reminded Vespasian of actors portraying selfish liars, the *parasitus* on stage, preparing to weave the truth with lies. *I must watch him closely,* the general thought. "The Jewish Hercules?" Vespasian asked—*but it must be.* "I saw him fall, and he died bravely." He glanced down at his foot, wounded by the Jewish hulk's last spear cast as he died. "Explain what you have in mind with all this, Lord Florus. What are you suggesting?"

"As a condition of Yosef ben Mathias's captivity, force him to marry this woman, and she becomes leverage you can use against him. For his cooperation or lack of it, will then have ramifications not only for himself but for another one close to him."

"What if he refuses... why would he agree to this marriage?"

"Tell him the woman is the beloved of one who died valiantly under his command at Yotapta. Surely even a Jewish rebel, especially a leader and military commander, should assume some responsibility for caring for a hero's woman. If he does not marry her, she will go to the slave market with the others that were captured."

Vespasian considered it. Yosef was both intelligent and principled. Titus thought so and suggested Yosef would prove of great value to them at some point. While Yosef would not try to escape—the animosity of the local Greeks being one reason—he also had no reason to provide information that could help Vespasian deal with the leadership in Jerusalem. If Vespasian could not get them to surrender, he could at least further fracture the rebel leadership, turning them against each other. That would weaken that city's defenses.

"Where is this woman?" Vespasian asked.

"In Ptolemais, general."

"Send for her."

XXIII

DECEMBER 67 CE

JERUSALEM

THE UPPER CITY

Kislev was the time of year, and Chanukah the holiday Miriam had always loved most. Even in the recent years of her season of darkness and regret, the Festival of Lights always brightened her spirits for a few days. The story of the Maccabees and the Hasmoneans, her mother's people, reminded Miriam that their blood ran in her veins, too, and that inspired her.

When Jerusalem was ruled by Antiochus IV, civil war erupted between those who had adopted Syrian and Greek customs and those determined to maintain Jewish laws and traditions. The traditionalists led by her ancestors wrested control of Israel to create a Jewish kingdom that lasted for more than a century. That liberty beyond our ancestors' hopes appeared as if a fresh-born light had shined upon them. So began the Festival of Lights celebrated for us to remember gaining freedom. Now, so long after that time, Jews and Judeans fought again for sovereignty.

Miriam watched as her mother handed a burning taper to her father. As he lighted the first wick of the menorah, she studied Ya'el, who had left her annoying bird in her room, and Sayid across from her. A purported Greek and a Syrian... but both really Romans. It rankled her to have to go along with the story that Ya'el was the wife of a relative the Romans had killed and had no other family.

She shook her head. The anger she felt at them being there and at her mother and father for honoring Yosef's request burned inside her. How could he even ask they take in Ya'el and her boy and protect them? They had all been overjoyed to hear Yosef was alive, but still... how could they allow this Roman into their home?! Miriam had finally recognized her as the Lady Cleo who had visited at Passover, and that brought back nightmares of the massacre and the first man she had killed. Yosef's message claimed that this Cleo had been responsible for the Roman withdrawal from Jerusalem. How could that be? Regardless, she had barely spoken with them since enabling their entrance to the city and bringing them from the gate. Their presence extinguished the moment of lightness this holiday always had brought her.

Her eyes slid to Matthew sitting next to Ya'el, who now slept in Yosef's room, while Yosef was held in chains by a Roman general. Matthew had accepted her and the boy as their mother and father had. That added to the anger she still felt at Matthew for entering her room and going through her things. She noted his suspicions and the way he watched her. But then they all watched her with questioning eyes. Even Ya'el and Sayid now sensed it; she saw the looks they exchanged. How could they judge her... how could her family be more at ease and trusting of two Romans than of their daughter—or sister!

She watched as her mother covered the wick's sputtering, nurturing the feeble flame, cupping the light in her hand as it grew. Then she pulled away to reveal its illumination.

After dinner, as they had each evening since their arrival, Ya'el and Sayid in their clear Greek had thanked them for dinner and their protection then gone upstairs to where the tired boy and bird were already asleep.

Miriam felt her father's and Matthew's eyes upon her as she helped her mother, who had again refused both Ya'el and Sayid's offers to clean up after dinner. And she wondered again at her mother's insistence that her father not keep regular servants for such chores. But then it was also unusual that her mother insisted—and her father had agreed—that Miriam learn to read and write Greek. A sign of culture and education not offered to many women. She would be even more irritated at 'guests' who spoke only Greek were it not for that.

"I'm done, Mother," she announced and went upstairs, slowing at the mutter of soft voices within Yosef's room. She wondered what Ya'el and Sayid talked about. Her mother and father—Matthew too— were worried about hiding them. Everyone in Jerusalem seemed on edge, and hiding Romans would be considered treason. She did not want to think what would happen if Elazar ben Yair and the Sicarii discovered that. Rachel had been with her that day, meeting them at the gate. Afterward, Miriam made her swear not to say anything to anyone about them, not even telling Leah that Yosef was alive. But it worried her the way her eyes had brightened at that news. She had doubts Rachel's silence would last for long.

Miriam entered her bedroom and stood in the dark for a moment again, trying to hear what was said in Yosef's room. By feel, she found and lighted Zechariah's lamp, his gift to her against the darkness he knew she feared. In its glow, her eyes caught her reflection in the small polished bronze mirror—Roman-made, to her regret. Yosef had given it to her on his return from Rome. Her fingertip traced the ridge of the scar on her cheek. It would have been much worse if she was not as quick as Zechariah had often boasted to the Sicarii.

Stooping, she pulled a packet from beneath the chaff-filled mat she slept upon, held there above the floor by the web of rope stretched over a wooden frame that made her bed. The packet held Zechariah's letters to his wife, Bayla, whose name meant "beauty," and to his daughter, Meira, "one who gives light." With them, but separate, was the folded note she had found slipped under her door just a day ago. She had read it a dozen times. Her fingers tingled each time she unfolded it.

Please meet with me alone. You are in the Lower City often, so leave a message at my glassworks. Tell me when and where to meet you. -Ehud

XXIV

OUTSIDE ROME

Graius's story had surprised Nicanor. The man he had known little in previous years had seemed a studious and mild household administrator who had retired into a quiet life. Standing there with that rudis in his hand, he was much different. And the look in his eye as he brandished his wooden sword was a look Nicanor knew. He had met men with that same expression—no fear, no remorse. That, not luck, was what had made him a successful survivor of the Games.

Even the strongest or most skilled men come to a point—perhaps when facing a metal one—when they will flinch at pain, at the thought of pain to come, or in the face of death. Regrets flash like lightning strikes in those seconds, and momentary hesitation leads to the final, fatal slip in that onslaught. That moment of mortality reveals the man, leaving an opening for his opponent in a physical contest or his enemy in combat. If you hesitate too often or for too long, what's left of you is cast in the meat cart used to clean up the floor of a stadium or arena. Or, on the battlefield, the scavengers feed on your carcass.

Nicanor had seen that look in his own eyes—upon a polished bronze mirror or in a chance reflection in still water. But since Beth Horon and Yotapta, he did not view things as he once had. He was no coward and would fight if he must. But his heart had been changing since meeting Yosef, Sayid, and most of all, Cleo. Cestius Gallus, too, a compassionate man out of his element commanding a legion in battle, had affected him. And so had Paul the Christian, imprisoned at the Tullianum when Nicanor was a Praetorian watch captain. Now, sadly, Paul had been executed, but the many hours they'd spent talking during the long watches stirred thoughts and made him ask himself questions. All of these had changed him.

Nicanor felt Carmenta's gait stiffen as her mane bristled, and she flourished her tail in an arc behind them. The mare was not just the most alert and aware of any horse he had ever known. She also had some show and carried herself regally around other horses. He heard just over the rise of the hill the sound Carmenta had picked up moments before. It was the thud and thunder of dozens of horses in formation. The cavalry must be wheeling and charging across the turf of the vast training fields he recalled in that location. He remembered teaching his friend Yosef some of the things Roman soldiers practiced endlessly. That had been under the blistering summer sun. Today was just as bright, but a cold blue sky with a cutting wind swept over and between the hills above him.

He reached the crest and paused only a moment to look down upon the plain to the left at the charging horses and hundreds of men practicing infantry attack and defense formations. The clang of blades on shields echoed as the might of Rome honed the deadly skill of beating a man's defense down or aside, so the thrust would strike home and end their existence as an enemy of Rome.

Carmenta watched with interest; her ears twitched. He had become aware of that subtle sign indicating she would rather follow her own will than accept his neck rein to turn her in the opposite direction. That way was his destination. The *castra stative* was a massive permanent camp. Its extensive main street, the *via principalis*, ran through the center in a north-south direction. The central portion of the camp was used as a parade ground and headquarters area, its praetorium housing the praetor or camp commander and his staff. To one side was the *quaestorium*, the supply officer's building. But this camp lacked a forum, the small duplicate of a city's forum, where public business could be conducted. This close to Rome, it was not needed. Along the main street were the homes or tents of the several tribunes arranged in front of the barracks of the units they commanded. Sprawling beyond them were materials storage yards and the shops of woodworkers, metalworkers, and rope-makers. Those skilled craftsmen and others produced the weapons and the engines of war for the empire. Nicanor had seen many permanent camps. Each province with a permanent legion presence had one. But none of them was on the scale of this one here at the heart of the empire.

Minutes later, he was at the *porta praetoria*, handing Vespasian's orders to the sentries at the main gate. He was to meet with the senior *armamentarii*, weapons engineers to discuss siege engine improvements. Jerusalem's walls were far greater than Yotapta's and far better defended. In any attempt to breach them, they could not have a ram fail as had happened at Yotapta. Even given the size of the rocks that the Jewish giant had hurled down upon it, the ram's head should not have broken so easily. He had some ideas for better sheathing the ram's neck and wanted to discuss the hardness of the wood.

The guards waved him through.

* * *

Nicanor had talked to engineers in the field, but the conversations usually came in times of demand or stress. This time he had enjoyed speaking with these engineers, who were not under pressure. It was good to see the shops that produced the weapons he had wielded for decades, never thinking of when or where they were created. Hours later, he approached the main gate to leave, satisfied they would build what was needed for the assault on Jerusalem. He had a sudden flashing vision of Yosef's face. It made him regret his professional pleasure at improving what would be used for a future assault on his friend's city.

"Centurion...."

The voice had a familiar eerie quality, a questioning lilt. But with an undertone of threat... of danger that prickled the hair on the back of his neck. He looked around.

"Imagine meeting you here, centurion," rasped Tigellinus as he and several mounted men came around the guard post. "You are far from the Tarpeian Rock." It was the same tone he had used that day Nicanor had reported to the Arx Capitolina in Rome for duty as a Praetorian Guard. Within the man's tone was the implied warning the Praetorian Prefect had given him that day: *arx tarpeia capitoli proxima*. The Tarpeian Rock is not far... and one's fall from grace can come swiftly.

"Lord Tigellinus, I thought you were in Greece with Emperor Nero." Nicanor cursed silently to himself. He had counted on not having to deal with the prefect of the Praetorian Guard, his former commander before Vespasian requested that he join his staff for the Judean campaign.

"No, we've returned." The prefect, bracketed by his personal escort, stopped only a few feet away. "There is much to see to in Rome. And the emperor takes his duty seriously to ensure peace and prosperity in the empire." He lifted his hand from the saddle pommel... his index finger waved left and right, and the four Praetorians—two on either side of him—began to move. "Tell me why you are here... and why your reports on General Vespasian, from when you were with him, tell me little more than do his official reports."

Nicanor felt Carmenta tense as the men—hands on the hilts of short swords unsheathed on their thighs—came within arm's reach on either side of him. Beneath him, Carmenta shivered, and her chest and belly expanded, bracing for what Nicanor might be forced to do. Her head canted back and forth, and her eyes rolled as she tried to watch all four of the Praetorians at the same time. "Lord," he began to explain, but the movement of someone behind him—close—stopped him. Carmenta's tail lashed, but not as she would whisk away flies. It snapped out like a short-corded flail, a warning she was poised to kick on his command.

"Once you answer the prefect's questions, centurion... I have some of my own."

Nicanor turned in his saddle to look over his shoulder. The mounted man behind him had one milky eye in a scarred countenance. Tall in the saddle, he sat awkwardly astride a horse that nervously shifted its feet. The man gripped the reins too tightly in both hands, and his heels clenched, digging hard into the horse's ribs. The horse did not like its uncertain and inexperienced rider, and Nicanor felt the same way. The man's sneer made him instantly dislike him. "Who are you?"

"I'm looking for Lady Cleo... the wife of Gessius Florus."

XXV

December 67 CE

Caesarea

Yosef heard the grating slide of the door's crossbar and rattle of the lock as it was removed. Four guards, instead of the usual two, entered his cell without speaking. But then the guards never did talk to him. They either ordered him... or insulted him.

"On your feet," said the largest and most senior, with the jerk of an upturned thumb.

Yosef rose from his cot and wondered, *Why the extra two guards*? They led him from his cell in the opposite direction from the customary route to meet with Vespasian. Perhaps the general's new headquarters were ready, and they were going there. They did not go far from the stable he had been held in since Vespasian brought him to Caesarea. He knew the building and workshop where the two large doors swung open.

"Bring him in." The blacksmith motioned with his hand and went to the block and anvil next to the forge, where a brazier full of cherry-red embers was tended to by his apprentice.

Yosef had learned the Greek blacksmith would not respond to questions or talk to him except to give orders. So, he did not ask why he had been brought there. That the apprentice was arranging chains, chisels, and a hammer on the workbench said enough.

The early morning dimness was lightened by the apprentice applying handheld bellows to the embers to hasten the heating of the metal pins sitting atop them. The flame flared behind the Greek blacksmith and backlighted his bald and gleaming head framed by a fringe of hair. He stood there expectantly, hammer in hand.

"Hephaestus awaits me," Yosef muttered. He shook his head and quoted from an often-read favorite, Aeschylus's *Promētheús Desmótēs, Prometheus Unbound*. "The man who can free Prometheus has not been born." He readied himself, already feeling the burning pain that could not be avoided.

The blacksmith pointed at the block as the apprentice opened the side and back doors so light could pour in. Yosef knew what was happening, but he did not know why. He hesitated, but the hand of the enormous guard always behind him shoved him forward.

* * *

VESPASIAN'S PRAETORIUM

The Praetorium of plaster-covered brick was constructed around two open courts, similar to the atrium and peristyle of the Roman buildings Yosef had seen in Rome. Judging by the number of legionaries he saw, the area surrounding it seemed delegated for the legion's exercise and drills. Behind that, the ground was filled with tents that housed the officers and men of the legion.

Slowed by his additional shackles and chains, Yosef passed through a public area brightened by a row of open windows. He entered an inner chamber set up as both an expansive office and a meeting place. A long, broad table centered in the room had a half-dozen stools around it and was lighted by a large lantern hanging above. On the side facing him was a heavy wooden chair with a padded leather back.

Vespasian's familiar desk filled one corner of the room, lighted by lamp sconces on the wall, and was covered by an unfurled map and a mound of scrolls and parchments. Behind it, on a stone pedestal, was the water-clock Vespasian had told him was a gift from the woman he referred to as his wife, Antonia Caenis. All was quiet, but for his breathing and that of the four guards, and he thought he could hear the clock's movement, the drip of each moment passing.

From a curtained entrance to the right of Vespasian's desk, Gaheris Clineas brought a tray holding an amphora and three cups. The man did not look at him but returned to the curtain and spoke: "He is here, general."

Vespasian swept the curtain aside on its wooden runner, it remained open, and he walked to the long table and sat in the chair. He waved Yosef forward but did not gesture to sit across from him as had become routine with their meetings. With all the chains reattached, that would have proven difficult to manage, anyway.

Yosef had increasingly felt his dreams and visions meant he still had important work to do for his people. That mission was somehow linked to this man who silently studied him. But it worried him that he had been brought before Vespasian bound in all the chains used during his early captivity. Something had changed or was about to change. And not for the good.

"You are shackled because you are an enemy of Rome," Vespasian said. "Some of your restraints were removed for a time, but I ordered them restored to make the point that whether you live or die depends on the will of Rome... and of the emperor's representative. Me. My forces have secured all of Judea, and next, we will take Jerusalem.

You have told me that you will not betray your people. But you indicated that you might speak to them about a surrender that would save that city from its destruction. To get that commitment from you, to ensure it is sincere, I must—" he stopped and looked to his right.

Though Yosef had not seen him since he had occupied Herod's palace at Passover over a year before, he recognized the man who came from the curtained antechamber. Gessius Florus had let loose the soldiers who killed many of his people in Jerusalem and threatened his family. He looked back at Vespasian. Yosef caught the flash of consternation on the general's face as Florus stiffly lowered himself to the stool next to the general, then reached for the amphora and filled two goblets. Without waiting for Vespasian, Florus lifted a goblet to his lips and drank deeply. His eyes glinted over the rim as he stared at Yosef.

"Lord Vespasian," said Yosef, "I believe this man is largely responsible for the war that made me an enemy of Rome." He could not keep the disdain from his voice. "A war I do not think was necessary." He lifted his arms, and the iron links rattled loudly in the room. "He ordered a massacre of my people without provocation. That led to many tragic events, to my command in Galilee and the death of thousands of my countrymen. That is why I wear these chains."

Vespasian's eyes flicked to Gessius Florus, but the man—his eyes on Yosef—did not speak or look at him. "The chains, some of them, will come off again if you do as I order."

"What order is that, lord?

"To marry a Jewish woman who has been chosen for you. She lost her husband or betrothed, one of your men at Yotapta, one your people honor as a hero of that siege. I saw in that man the kind of bravery in battle that any people would be proud of. This woman has courage too; she fought my men with a shepherd's crook before she was taken."

"Lord Vespasian, you cannot order me to marry any woman, nor should she be forced to marry me."

"You just mentioned all the tragedy and death, rebel," Florus finally spoke. "Would you not do what you can to stop one death? Or possibly to stop many?"

Yosef understood Florus's implication but did not reply and kept his eyes on Vespasian, who spoke.

"Do as I order, and when I ask for your knowledge and experience in certain matters, you must comply."

"Or she dies," Yosef said bitterly.

"Yosef..." Vespasian leaned forward and spoke more personally, as he had come to do in their routine conversations. "I trust your word that you will not try to harm me or to escape if some of your chains are removed again and if I allow you certain freedoms."

"But you want me to betray my people, general." Yosef felt the anger building.

"You have told me you believe this war to be the fault of not just Romans," Vespasian said, his eyes cutting to Florus again, then back. "You also name factions in your own government. What I require is that you—at my direction, at the proper time—speak to your people and possibly save your city."

Yosef let out a deep sigh, releasing a breath he had not realized he held, stirring the iron links that ran from neck collar to waist cuff as he lowered his head. "May I have some time to think about this, lord?"

"Yes." Vespasian waved the four guards forward. "Return the prisoner to me this hour tomorrow."

Yosef's heart and mind were far heavier than all the chains as he left. Still, he noticed the cloaked and veiled woman, covered with the dust and with the wafting smell of the road. A tribune and two centurions escorted her into Vespasian's presence.

XXVI

Jerusalem

The Upper City

"Some do not like that Ya'el's Greek, even if she claims to be a Jew," said Yohanan ben Zaccai as he sat at the table with Mathias, Rebecca, and Matthew. "But everyone I've spoken to thinks we all must take in any family fleeing the Romans, so they understand about Ya'el. I think the story has been accepted, and her presence in your home with the boy should not raise any concern. But Ya'el must never be out in the city without one of you—Matthew or, even better, Rebecca—escorting her. Some are curious, and too many questions would be asked of her. Someone must be there to deflect them." He stopped talking as he heard the heavy tread of steps coming closer.

Sayid, wrapped in a heavy cloak, appeared in the entry with a large, soot-smudged canvas bag that hid him from the waist up. He leaned his head around, chinning the bag to one side to speak. "My lady, where should I—"

"This way, Sayid." Rebecca rose from the table to show him where to store the charcoal from Shammai the Tannaim. The rabbinic sage, also a collier, had been introduced to them by Yohanan ben Zaccai years ago. The charcoal he made was of good quality and fair price.

"The young man seems helpful," Yohanan said as he watched Sayid re-grip the large bag and follow Rebecca. "It's some distance to Shammai's kiln outside the northern wall."

"The nights and mornings have grown cold, and Matthew has been busy and not able to go pick up more. Sayid offered to go. But he must stop calling Rebecca 'lady'... though I think it pleases her." Mathias shared a smile with his oldest friend, who grinned in return.

"Yosef's letter asked you to take Ya'el in and protect her," Yohanan continued. "But Sayid told Matthew and me something I believe is another reason to care for Ya'el. It answers some questions you and I both had at the time. Something you should know."

"Know what?" Rebecca sat back down.

"That Cleo... that Ya'el sent Sayid with letters to Octavia, Cestius Gallus's wife, in Antioch.

"Cestius Gallus, the Roman commander of the legion that attacked us?"

"Former commander. Octavia read the letters and then had Sayid take them to her husband. On his way to do that, he was captured by Yohanan ben Levi of Gischala and held but then released.

"What was in them that was so important?" Matthew asked. "Wait. Why did the Gischalan let a Roman auxiliary go?"

"Something in the letters made him release Sayid so he could get them to Cestius Gallus." Yohanan ben Zaccai put his hands on the table, palms down. "Once he did, Gallus stopped his attack here. Somehow, Ya'el—something she shared with him—convinced him to pull the 12th Legion back."

Mathias turned to his wife. "Miriam should hear this. No matter what Yosef said in his letter about... Ya'el... I've heard Miriam's comments about how she can only think of her... and the boy and Sayid, too, as Romans—our enemies."

"Clearly, they're not," said Yohanan.

Rebecca squeezed her husband's shoulder, then leaned back tiredly. "I asked Miriam to join us, but she said she must go to the Lower City."

"Tell her she cannot go... go and bring her down."

"She's already gone, Mathias."

Yohanan looked from Mathias to Rebecca and back to Mathias again. "There are many people—strangers—flooding Jerusalem. The Lower City streets especially are becoming less safe, Mathias. You must speak with her... for her own good."

"*We,*" Rebecca emphasized, "will talk to her."

"Lady Rebecca..." Sayid interrupted them. "Excuse me, but I'm done. The charcoal is unbagged and stored in the bins you showed me. And I went ahead and fixed the cover that needed repair."

"Thank you, Sayid," Rebecca said with a smile. "Please tell Ya'el that she and Elian do not need to stay out in the cold. Come inside."

"I'll tell her, Lady... but they have a fire I started for them before I left. We do not wish to intrude on your family discussions. And I'm afraid Elian has found one of your trees he can climb."

* * *

It was cold but not unbearable, especially around the fire pit that blazed and smoked. Sayid joined Ya'el, where she sat on the stone bench wrapped in a heavy mantle and her thoughts. Above her in the courtyard's largest tree, Elian clambered among the branches, laughing, and occasionally showing his red face. Cicero perched at the fork of two lower limbs above the adults, his colors vivid against the bark.

"What do they talk about?" Ya'el asked as Sayid settled next to her and drew his own cloak more closely around him.

"I overheard a little of it... they talk about you—good things—and something about Miriam."

"She hates me," said Ya'el.

"No, she hates Romans."

"How can I change that? We depend on these people for our lives. Without them, we are lost."

"All you can do is continue as you always have, Lady... Ya'el. You are a good person who tries to do what is right. That is all that really matters—not whether you're a Roman, a Jew, or a Syrian. Just continue being a good person. If Miriam has the same heart as the rest of Yosef's family, then she will see who you are."

Sayid hesitated, hating to say what he must while she felt so dependent on others. "It is time I go, Lady... I believe you are safe here, as safe as you can be. I care for you and Elian and could come to care for Yosef's family as I do for him. But there are things I must do. I hope to find my father, and to do that, I must return to the legion." Sayid did not add that he had heard that Yohanan ben Levi of Gischala and many of his men now roamed the city. The rebel leader's men had killed the *tesserarius* Arruns Vulso, the gruff sergeant near retirement who had died saving him. The Gischalan leader had held him captive for days before releasing him to get to Lord Gallus and try to stop the attack on Jerusalem. What if he came across the Gischalan and his men and was identified? That would lead them to Ya'el and Elian... and to the realization that Yosef's family had harbored a Roman noblewoman... and soldier. He could not risk that happening to them.

Sayid could not look at her, and the silence grew, broken only by the crackling and snap of burning wood, a clear sound in the crisp air. He felt a cold hand grip him, and then he looked at her. Tears glistened on her cheeks. Behind her, Elian, who must have heard him, dropped from the lowest branch and ran to her.

"Then you must go, Sayid... you must go," she said. "And I hope you—as a soldier—never return to Jerusalem."

ACT II

XXVII

JANUARIUS 68 CE

JERUSALEM

THE LOWER CITY

Miriam stepped out of Zechariah's shop into sheets of rain that swept the street. Within seconds she was soaked and shivering and about to turn back. Nearing Hananiah's shop, she felt a pang of regret that she had not been to see him since he had helped her home after he found her staggering along the street. It was dark when she passed, but then it often was, even when Hananiah was inside. They both shared something about darkness, though he seemed to embrace it while she endured it. Somehow that formed a kinship between them. Still, not wanting to see nor speak with anyone, she kept moving.

At Zechariah's, she had run through her training exercises and read Elazar's message Kefa had brought her. She and Elazar had managed to meet only once since she had killed Esau ben Beor. Elazar had been pleased but concerned that they still had not identified who else in the Sanhedrin was treasonous and must be held to account. The message said he would soon meet with her about what the Sicarii had found out about other suspected Roman collaborators or agents.

The exercise that tired her body had not settled the thoughts that whirled and spun in her mind. Hananiah's growing interest in her was one thing. She owed him a debt for helping her and not revealing anything to her family. Still, she kept moving and did not stop at his door. Just past, she heard the splash of steps behind her coming closer, and a voice called out: "Miriam... wait!"

Thinking it was Hananiah, she turned, resolved to greet him. Instead, it was someone else, the subject of the most nagging of her thoughts.

"Miriam..." Ehud sloshed to a stop in a puddle before her, the rain coursing down his face. "I must talk with you."

She stared at him without answering and could not stop the shiver that wracked her as the rain coursed down her sodden cloak. Jerusalem had not known a winter this cold since, as children, she, Yosef, and Matthew had been delighted with a rare dusting of snowfall. That evening they had watched it drift down at sundown, the flakes catching the colors until it faded as they dropped on shadowed streets. A dart of worry flashed as the memory made her think of Yosef in a Roman prison cell. She shivered again.

"I must get you inside to warm up." Ehud took her arm, and the touch through the cold, wet wool... felt warm, though it could not be.

She followed him into the taberna at the next corner. She had never been in one of these places near evening, much less after nightfall. Large braziers of charcoal in the four corners and one in the center warmed the large room. Ehud guided her to a small table—one of the few not occupied and in a quiet corner near the heat. He took her cloak and hung it on a peg. A gust of wind-driven rain rattled and splattered on the shutters of the window facing the street. The sound prickled the flesh on her arms and made her glad to be out of the weather and inside near a fire.

Ehud had not stopped staring at her. "What do you want to talk about, Ehud?" she asked.

"Did you get my note? I was with Matthew, caught him briefly at your home, and snuck upstairs to put it under your door."

"You're fortunate my mother or father did not find it," she said, all she *could* say. She had wrestled with doing as he asked. But it was at this moment that she realized what had made her hesitate was how she felt. She had loved him before, lost him when he moved away, and after that had tried to recover by liking Ya'akov. She had been set to marry him, though she did not love him. Then the chance for that small measure of happiness—not real love, but acceptable— had been torn from her. She was no longer the girl who had loved Ehud or the one who had been willing to marry Ya'akov. If any knew of her rape by the Romans, she would be shunned by all. She had been soiled. And now... despite the hurt... despite what had happened to her and the things she had done, somehow that flicker of love for Ehud had reignited and grown since his return to Jerusalem.

Miriam could tell by how he sat and waited that Ehud wanted to know more about why she had not sought him out to arrange a meeting. The moment turned into minutes. Then he stood, and she thought he had had enough waiting and was leaving her. Her heart ached as she watched him. At the serving counter, he spoke with a man wiping the surface with a towel. The man turned and lifted a bronze pitcher blackened at the bottom from sitting atop a small brazier and filled two large cups. Ehud dropped a coin on the counter and carried them back to the table.

"Mulled wine... it will warm you."

Miriam felt that warmth seep through the sides of the cup as she raised to her lips. She never had drunk wine in public, and really not much at home. The first sip was much more potent than the watered wine her mother and father drank. She blinked at its bite on her tongue; the fragrant spice tickled her nose. "It's good... thank you." Ehud's expectant look had returned, and she deflected it. "I do not want to talk about our past, Ehud." She shook her head and sipped again.

"Then, let's not... not about the past and not about the future."

The smile on his face was one she remembered, and she could not help but return it. "Then what do we talk about?"

"How about now... this moment?" Ehud reached his hand out to cover hers, and she panicked, darting her eyes in a quick search of the room for someone watching them.

"In these times, Miriam... no one will notice us."

Miriam felt her pulse quicken, but time slowed just as Zechariah had taught her to cultivate it when readying a strike or counterstrike. But this was not fighting... this was... she didn't know, as it had been so long. Her chilled hand warmed beneath his. The feeling spread up her arm and settled in her chest where the ache had dwelled for so long it seemed it would be there forever. She felt it ebb... lessen and loosen, and something that reminded her of hope replaced it.

"When will your family come to Jerusalem?" Miriam whispered, looking for something to lighten the moment. "It must be soon... before the Romans get here." But what she said did the opposite. She saw the light in his eyes dim, and by an inch... then another... his face dropped, and he looked away. "Or are they not coming at all?" The hope faded, and the ache returned.

"I don't know. That's a future I can't contemplate right now." Ehud stood and took her cup; she had not realized it was empty. He returned with two full cups, sat, and drank half of his in one swallow.

She matched him, though the taste brought tears to her eyes, and she felt her mind spin. Ehud's expression shifted, and she thought he must be trying to think of something... anything to say. But the moment was broken, and its pieces would not come together.

"How is your brother?" Ehud finally said. "Since your return, I barely see Matthew, mostly when he is going to and from the Temple and meetings. I came across him and Yohanan ben Zaccai poring over some list and map with Eleasar ben Ananias." He looked questioningly at her, though he had not asked a question.

"He is... very busy." Zechariah, being blind, had relied on people's voices, how they talked to some people, and spoke differently to others. The changes in tone and inflection were his gauge of people's words... and often their true meaning or intent. She had tried to become more discerning herself, and Ehud's tone seemed off to her. He was not trying to make general conversation and was more probing than personally curious. He was after something specific.

"And I've heard you have relatives who've come to Jerusalem... from Tarsus. And that they escaped from the Romans in Galilee."

It wasn't a question, and she would not reply. Though she felt the warmth from the nearby brazier, the chill had returned with the shift in Ehud's interest. "It's late, and I must go," she said. She took her cloak from the peg on the wall.

"I'll walk you home." Ehud rose and pulled on his own cloak.

* * *

THE UPPER CITY

Night had fallen, still blustery, and the moon rising behind breaks in the clouds shot silver beams through them. The rain had stopped, and all was still. They had walked companionably close, despite the abrupt end of their uncomfortable conversation. But neither had said a word.

At the street entry gate to Miriam's home, a gust of wind revisited them and caught the cowl of her robe, lifted the scarf, and freed her hair. As unexpected as that sudden wind, Ehud took her arm and pulled her close. His fingers were cold at first but then warmed as they traced the scar on her cheek. He leaned in and kissed her on the lips. It lingered, and she tasted a faint vestige of spiced wine. The heart-yearning that earlier had pushed her ache aside rose again, and she responded, kissing him back. Ehud pulled away, surprised, and his eyes widened in the gloom cast by the half-hidden moon. Without a word, he turned into another rush of wind and walked into the darkness.

She opened the door, careful of noise. Were it not for the shock of Ehud kissing her, she would have thought to go around the house and come in through the back courtyard gate as she usually did.

"Miriam!" Mathias met her as the door opened, and his voice sharpened when he saw her, hair wind-blown and awry and with a reddened face. "This has gone on for too long. I have been too forgiving... too lenient. We must talk now!"

Despite his anger... all she could see was her father's frailty. The loss of Yosef, the chaos of Jerusalem's leadership... the dread of the Romans arrival at their walls, and what would happen once they were here—it all had worn him down. And that on top of the illness, he still had not fully recovered from. Remorse washed over her at how she had become someone who added to his woe. "Tomorrow, Father...

Please let me by... We... we will talk tomorrow." She hurried upstairs, bumping into Matthew as he came out of his room.

"Look at you," Matthew said with a smile. "The color in your cheeks suits you... you've grown so pale lately."

"I'm still mad at you," she said as she started to push by him. "Did you talk to Ehud... tell him to find me?"

"Talk to him about what? You? No, and I didn't tell him to find you. I mean, not since he helped look for you when you went missing."

Miriam's eyes flinched away. "No... it's just that he..."

"So that's where you've been... with Ehud." Matthew sniffed. "You smell of wine."

"Shhh... lower your voice. Father and now probably mother are downstairs. They already want to talk to me. I've put that off until tomorrow." Miriam swept the hair from her face. "No, I was not 'with' Ehud... well, yes, I was... but...."

"He likes you, Miriam... he more than likes you. He always has, even before he left."

"I..." She shook her head, and hair swung over her eyes that she brushed away again. "No." She hesitated, then asked: "Do you talk to him about your meetings? With Yohanan and Eleasar ben Ananias... on... on the thing you are working on?"

"What do you know of what I am 'working' on?"

"Don't accuse me of spying, Matthew. I hear conversations in this house. I'm not stupid, and I pay attention to what's happening... though you all think I don't."

"No one thinks you're stupid, Miriam, but we all worry about you. That scar..." He pointed at her cheek. "And the slash on your hamsa you no longer wear... those did not come from a fall." He backed off as she glared at him and sighed. "The only thing I do with Ehud is talk about hopes for the future." The stern look faded, and he smiled. "And I answer his questions about you."

She told herself she didn't care, but she did. "What questions?"

"What's your favorite color. Your favorite food... what stories or poetry you like. Things like that." The grin broadened. "He really does like you, Miriam."

"He seems to notice what you do... are doing." She moved past him to her door.

"What do you mean?"

"He mentioned how busy you are and that he saw you, Yohanan, and Eleasar working on some map."

XXVIII

It must be near the time for them to come for me, thought Yosef. It was hard to tell the passage of time without a window and with only the periodic refilling of a ceiling lantern in the guard vestibule. The corridor leading in from outside was beyond his sight. His new cell was a single-entry structure attached to the back of the Praetorium. It projected out toward the ranks and rows of the tents of the legion's officers and soldiers. When he had been brought from his meeting with Vespasian and Gessius Florus, he had seen the posting of second-watch sentries in the watchtower that overlooked the Praetorium and camp. The two-guard watch on his cell—likely matching that rotation—had changed five times since. Judging by what he could see through the bars of the two men shifting around, he thought they must expect their relief soon. Eight shifts per day and that timing would meet Vespasian's orders for the time when he was to be brought back to him.

Yosef had not slept, though the cot in this new cell was broader than the one in the stable, and he discovered when he sat upon it that the bedding was thicker and more comfortable. There was enough room that two people could share it. Two. *A man and a woman?* But he had never heard of Roman prisoners with such privileges.

He rubbed his eyes, and the manacles clinked and chafed his skin. He wished he had some of the salve Titus had given him his first day after arriving from Ptolemais. But mostly, he wanted his journals. Writing settled his mind, allowed him to focus on something other than the physicality and discomfort of being chained and imprisoned. Detailing and documenting the moments and experiences, the observations of his day made him focus on his thoughts and not on where he was or his present circumstances. What he wrote gave him something concrete to review in retrospection, too. He had promised Levi ben Altheus that he would get it all down and tell their story, lest it be lost.

Yosef studied the bed again. It must be intended as a prod—a very pointed one—from General Vespasian that he must accept the forced marriage or face serious consequences.

Vespasian had more than once mentioned Nicanor's encounter with Dov—one he was thankful his friend had survived—and talked of Dov's last battle. He told of how the giant had wounded him as he died; that had impressed the general. Yosef's glimpse of the woman the day before had confirmed what he had thought when he heard the description of her. The woman captured fighting with a shepherd's crook... she must be Dalit, who went nowhere without it. Yosef had last seen her leaving the refuge cave in Yotapta, going after water with Ariella.

Dalit did not love him, and he did not love her, but she deserved to live. If he did not marry her, Vespasian might keep Yosef as some asset or send him to Rome as Nero's gift. But after the attention on Dalit waned, Gessius Florus would punish her out of spite. He would find the cruelest slave owner to sell her to, ensuring years of suffering. He shuddered in remembrance of the account Cleo had given him of how Florus abused her; the brute enjoyed hitting women. He could take Dalit, beat her to death, or have her killed for his enjoyment.

Yosef had loved Leah and, because of circumstances, lost her to another man. He felt his hand go to his neck for the kinyan she had given him, but it was no longer there. Cleo now had that small coin suspended around her neck. Yosef had married Ruth and lost her to death. Then he had fallen in love with Cleo, a Roman noblewoman. The spark of his love for Cleo had been struck while the two of them floated on debris from a shipwreck before she was married to Gessius Florus.

Yosef shook his head several times, but that did not rid him of thoughts of the lost loves. Cleo could never be his, but Gessius Florus likely intended to wound her further by having revenge upon him. He was not sure how a forced marriage punished him or achieved anything for the former Judean Procurator. Still, he was certain the man had not suggested it for the good of the empire alone. Gessius Florus had no doubt brought the idea to Vespasian, and there was more to it than what at first appeared. But no matter... to save Dalit, he must marry her. He wished he had his journals; writing had always steadied his mind.

* * *

The four guards were the same as had been the day before, and the blacksmith stood stoically next to the anvil block he used to attach pins or to shear them to release chains or cuffs. Vespasian and Gessius Florus were already waiting. Next to them, standing uneasily with a perplexed expression and eyes that twitched back and forth from Yosef to the Romans, was a rabbi with the vestments for performing a marriage ceremony.

"Your decision, Yosef?" Vespasian motioned toward the blacksmith and priest. "Do we need these two men, or shall I send them away?"

Yosef saw then that the rabbi was shackled hand and foot... and terrified. He nodded at him, but the man only blinked. Yosef looked at Vespasian's stern visage for a moment, then at Gessius Florus. The former Judean Procurator's lips had a curl to them, a sardonic grin but a fixed cold-eyed glare. Yosef almost asked him about Lady Cleo... hoping she had gotten away, that she was free of his cruelty and that it had caused him pain. But he did not; Florus had enough reasons to harm him and the people he cared for and did not need more incentive.

He turned to Vespasian. "I will marry the woman you've chosen, General Vespasian. Do I have your word she shall not be harmed?"

"A Roman need not give his word to a rebel Jew," scoffed Gessius Florus.

Vespasian glanced sideways at the man he must try to accommodate for now but still answered as he must. "Do as I wish, and you both will be treated well," he called to his aide positioned at the curtained antechamber. "Gaheris have her brought in."

Two centurions brought the still-veiled woman into the room. She wore a clean robe, but her forearms were still streaked with dirt. Her hands were bound in front of her by a winding of leather cords. He could see the raw flesh bleeding a little around her wrists. Still, she did not wince when they positioned her in front of the rabbi. One of the centurions pulled out his pugio and used the razor-sharp dagger to cut her restraints and roughly pull the cords away. She did not rub her bloody wrists and lowered her hands to her sides.

"Your chains will be removed when the ceremony is done," said Gessius Florus with an undercurrent of menace. "Then you can unveil your... bride."

Yosef wondered again about his real purpose. He watched the rabbi's hands tremble... the man was still quaking. "General Vespasian, I ask one more thing."

"What, Yosef?"

"Afterward, please free this rabbi. I doubt he has harmed any Romans, and he is not a threat to anyone. Please let him go."

"Lord Vespasian, you can't listen to a—"

The general cut him off. "Lord Florus, I see no harm in that. I agree, Yosef. The priest will be freed as soon as he is done."

"Thank you, general." Yosef went to stand before the rabbi and the woman who had remained still and quiet. Dalit would agree to anything that could save her from the slave market. Now was not the time to fight back. Now was the time to live.

Minutes later, the rabbi was speedily done, and the blacksmith cut off Yosef's shackles. "Thank you," the rabbi whispered to Yosef as a guard took the man's arm to lead him from the room.

Yosef kneeled beside the blacksmith and bent forward to position his head so the pin could be sheared away from the chain attached to his neck collar. He looked up at the woman he had just married. "I will see that you are taken care of..." he said. "Do not worry...."

"Steady, do not move," the blacksmith warned, "or my chisel will go through your neck, or my hammer will crush your skull."

As the man lifted his massive hammer, the woman took a step toward them, bent down, and lifted her veil. "I swore you would pay for letting Levi die," she whispered in Aramaic, her eyes blazing balefully. "And you will."

XXIX

Januarius 68 CE

Rome

Office of the Praetorian Prefect

Ophonius Tigellinus stood on his office balcony at the *Tabularium*, looking out from the Capitoline Hill. He glanced to his right and squinted into the afternoon sun. Below him, to the left, was the center of the city. The *Comitium*—part of the Forum Romanum—between the Capitoline and Palatine hills was just now falling into the shadow cast by the Capitoline and her buildings. This was where he felt most secure, or at least where he could do the most to benefit himself.

The Greece trip had seemed a good idea. Even if the fawning of the Greeks was not sincere, it had assuaged some of Nero's self-doubt that he would never admit but nevertheless dwelled on. If the Greeks loved him... then how could the people of Rome not love him? But the emperor's perception did not always match reality. The people of Rome—when not entertained—were not happy. Men with power were not happy. And being away from the city for a while had made that reality seem even starker upon Nero's return.

It did not help that an advisor like Phaon, the empire's secretary of finance, his *rationibus* in charge of the imperial treasure, told Nero one thing: 'all is well.' And then that freedman and confidant of the emperor turned around to give more ominous warnings to the powerful Romans concerned about the empire's financial condition. Some tribute and taxes had begun to flow again from Judea. But that trickle had been taken by force and did not flow from fealty and routine commerce. The unrest in Gaul and Africa was also of concern... instability always affected income.

Tigellinus scanned the skies and listened to the wind, but unlike his emperor, he could find no inspiration from them, neither from nature nor from idle abstract contemplation. He was not the artist that Nero believed himself to be. His world was one of facts and numbers. And the tribute and taxes from the entire empire—amounts that had once helped him secretly and carefully gain power and wealth—were falling, and costs were not. A once-profitable arrangement with Nero now seemed at risk.

Nero and Gessius Florus had agreed on one avenue of lucrative exploitation. Yet, Tigellinus's part in that agreement seemed to have stalled. Glaucio, his inside man to spy on Florus while serving as his major domus in Judea, had fallen silent. This crude sea captain Quintus had appeared straight from a ship at Ostia seeking help for his mission for Gessius Florus. He said all he knew was that Glaucio was 'gone.' It seemed Quintus needed help so that Florus could achieve his—and Nero's—aims in Judea. But how could it matter that he find the simple, unimportant centurion he knew Nicanor to be— and Florus's runaway wife? Yet, Florus's letter insisted these things were important. So he would help the man. He had sent word out to all commands: send runners or dispatch riders immediately to his office if Nicanor reported in. Or if anyone should while carrying orders from General Vespasian in Judea. When he had been alerted of Nicanor's arrival at the engineers' camp, Tigellinus had wasted no time gathering Quintus and his personal guard to hurry there and confront the centurion.

Nicanor had provided his orders from Vespasian and denied knowing anything of the whereabouts of Lady Cleo. There was no cause to carry matters further at that time. But Quintus believed the centurion lied and wanted resources to follow Nicanor every minute of every day.

A horseback interrogation was not the best setting in which to judge men. After that first heated exchange with Quintus, he had let the centurion continue with his business for General Vespasian. When he returned, he learned from his clerk that General Vespasian had reported that Nicanor would come to Rome to meet with siege engineers. To discuss design improvements and check on weapons supply shipments for the Judean campaign. The more he thought about it, how Nicanor had reacted, he could not help but believe Nicanor had been skilled enough to lie in such a way. And so forcefully as to ensure they became suspicious of him. Why invite a man like this Quintus to bear down on him? There seemed an ulterior motive Tigellinus could not discern... It felt odd to be suspicious of such a dull, blunt soldier as Nicanor.

Tigellinus went to the antechamber and ordered his aide, "Send in Captain Quintus now." Gessius Florus needed help, so he would give it to him. And in doing that, maybe he could swing Quintus to his side. He must have someone to monitor Florus. That man's plan... if it could be pulled off... would make him fabulously wealthy just from skimming part of the Jewish Temple's treasure as it flowed to the emperor. He must not jeopardize that.

"Lord Tigellinus," the sea captain said as he entered.

"I'll give you all the men you need to find what you want... to find the Lady Cleo for Gessius Florus. But I also want you to find out whether Nicanor is up to something else here in Rome."

"And when I do, Lord Tigellinus?"

"Report to me what you found and then kill him. I'll reward you well."

The sea captain smiled.

XXX

JANUARIUS 68 CE

JERUSALEM

THE WESTERN HILL, THE HOUSE OF CAIAPHAS

"So, the young Syrian—Sayid, you said his name was—has left the city?" Eleasar ben Ananias looked closely at Matthew for an answer as they entered the lower courtyard of the House of Caiaphas.

"Yes. Sayid returns to his people." Matthew did not want to talk about Sayid, who he really was, or what might come in the future. He hurried past the outer *mikveh*, the ritual bath still filled with water despite the cold temperature and the fact that the mansion was no longer used as a residence. Lifting the hem of his heavy cloak, Matthew took the steps up and into the upper courtyard with its large charcoal brazier offering warmth he regretfully had to pass by. He hoped that someone had lighted the one inside the reception hall, too.

Eleasar turned from where he had paused for a quick glance at the city sprawling below the hill and followed Matthew. "I wonder if he will be safe," he said. "With Roman authority now gone, there are increasing reports that Syrian towns have killed the Jews living there. And anger against Syrians is spreading. Against the Greeks, too. In Caesarea, they have embraced the Roman General Vespasian and openly lash out at Jews, even murdering any Greeks who have adopted our faith. It's good your cousin Ya'el made it here where she's safe, but the Syrian who helped her might not be." He caught up with Matthew as he slowed to enter the vestibule entrance in the courtyard corner. An angry voice came from the chamber.

"What did you expect, Shimon?"

Matthew recognized his father's biting tone used only when he was angriest. He and Eleasar entered to find him with the Sanhedrin president.

"Mathias, all I said was Yohanan of Gischala wishes to become more involved. And he asks me what is being done and how he can help to prepare Jerusalem." Shimon ben Gamliel glanced at the two younger men joining them. "He is curious, too, about the Temple's defenses and what is planned for that."

"He does so with a plan to stir up some trouble we won't discover until it's upon us."

Matthew saw the lines tighten in his father's face, and the furrows deepened on his brow as he frowned. Neither father nor son would forget and would not forgive the Gischalan's harsh words and condemnation of Yosef before the Sanhedrin. Yosef was alive, but that could not be announced, or they would have to reveal how they came to hear that news, and that would turn eyes upon Ya'el. Matthew doubted it had occurred to his father or mother that since Yosef had survived the destruction and killing of thousands at Yotapta, men such as Yohanan ben Levi would point to that as proof Yosef had surrendered to the Romans to save his own life.

"You have allowed a serpent into Jerusalem, Shimon." Mathias turned away, his steps echoing on the stone floor. His condemning words led him to recall other potential rival leaders, such as Yeshua ish Natzrat, who had once stood in this room, to be judged and condemned. He moved closer to a burning brazier in a corner and held his hands out to warm them.

"We need more men to help defend against the Romans. Yohanan ben Levi supports the Zealots and can attract thousands of Galilean fighters. He is with us and not with the fanatical Sicarii." Shimon turned to Eleasar ben Ananias and said, "You hate the Sicarii who killed your father, and you rightly distrust them. Should we not trust Yohanan ben Levi, who is also against them?"

"But I don't trust *him*, Shimon," replied Eleasar. "Some who have come from northern Galilee to take refuge tell a different story about Yotapta and how ben Levi fled his own city in the night. He and his men ran from the Romans and left his people behind to face them."

"That Gischalan is interested only in himself and his own survival," Matthew said with the same bitter tone as his father's.

"If we must use him and his men, could we send them to Herodium? It's only a few miles south of here and already fortified to serve as a southern outpost for Jerusalem. He and his men can serve there," Eleasar suggested. "Better he be there than here, skulking about the city trying to learn what we who care for Jerusalem plan for its defense."

Shimon walked to Mathias and put a hand on his shoulder. "Is that why you wanted to meet here and not the Hall of Hewn Stone?" he lifted the hand and waved it around at the expanse of the long-ago high priest's former mansion. "Two of the provisional government's leaders have asked that all meetings be held formally in the Hall of Hewn Stone. Since Esau ben Beor's death, a place such as this is not a lawful place for Sanhedrin business."

"Perhaps, according to them... but I sent the attendants away, and it is more private," Mathias said. "Hanan ben Hanan is becoming more vocal about his displeasure with those who disagree with him. He has begun making claims the Zealots are robbing or are planning to rob from the people, then abandon Jerusalem to the Romans." He turned toward his son. "He says the Temple Guard captain here"—his gaze shifted to Eleasar—"in command of those guards and controlled by the Zealots... plans to steal the Temple treasure."

Mathias's stern expression hardened on Shimon ben Gamliel. "You know that is not so and must begin to speak out against Hanan and that wild allegation." He shook his head. "But more important is that he is friends with Yosef ben Gurion, whose wealthy brother, Nikadimon is the main supplier of food and wood for Jerusalem. If Nikadimon believes as his Hanan does, it could disrupt our supplies and affect how long we can hold out against the Romans."

Shimon paced the room as he said, "If we cannot rely on them— the men chosen for the government—then who do we rely on?"

"Ourselves and those we can truly trust. Judea has splintered, and the Romans have secured all the pieces. Only Jerusalem remains. Just as you began to have misgivings about Esau ben Beor... you must be careful of others with you in the Sanhedrin and in the provisional government. Egotism rules among many, Shimon... and perhaps some have wished you to remain closer to your lineage... the blood of King David you believe is within you. Yohanan ben Levi manipulates men's egos, pulling the strings he thinks he has found for them. Hanan ben Hanan is arrogant and bold—we both know his family. Both men can be heartless and could give up on a cause that no longer serves them."

Mathias's eyes went to the two younger men, pausing to offer a grim nod to his youngest son. "We must work together... and against any who wish to weaken Jerusalem through their own self-interest."

* * *

Matthew steadied his father as they went down the steps from the top of the hill to the street that wound around the base and branched toward the Temple Enclosure and the Upper City market area. Eleasar ben Ananias and Shimon ben Gamliel, moving more surely and quickly, had already turned toward the Temple, where both had duties awaiting them.

"Yohanan ben Zaccai left early this morning to meet with Nahum in Qumran," Mathias commented. "He has copies of the list and map that you have both worked on, and he plans to have the Essenes create a more durable version than parchment. Who knows how long the Temple treasure must be hidden before we have our country back? We must be prepared to leave a lasting record."

"Yes, Father..." Matthew hesitated, wanting to talk more to him, but decided to remain quiet. He had heard him confronting Miriam and asking questions that she had deflected. He needed to speak to his father about his own concerns about his sister, but maybe he should wait. Right now, what Miriam had said about Ehud's curiosity in what he 'was working on' alarmed him more. He hated that he must now worry about someone he thought of as a friend, almost a brother, along with handling the fear that filled him about his real brother's fate. That morning, he had come upon Ya'el crying. He knew Yosef cared for the woman... so he must try to help her, but he did not understand how he could and had little time to try to find out.

XXXI

JANUARIUS 68 CE

PTOLEMAIS

12TH LEGION ENCAMPMENT

Sayid shivered, hugging his arms tight against his chest. He had not been warm since leaving Jerusalem. Armed rebels, some in groups of a dozen or more, roamed the countryside between Jerusalem and the outskirts of Ptolemais. He was afraid of the attention he might draw with a smoking fire. So he was protected from the chill of winter by only his tunic, breeches, cloak, and a blanket... all dampened by spells of rain.

Near Ptolemais, the rebels disappeared or were well hidden as they watched for any movements of the Romans. But Sayid worried that if the legion patrols found him, they would strike first, not giving him a chance to present his orders and its attachment. Nicanor had gotten General Vespasian to write additional proof he was not a deserter. But if the patrols acted too quickly, they might execute him without asking any questions and leave his body to the carrion-eaters. Only the buzzards, beetles, and ants would appreciate his death. At least his exposure to the weather had disguised him. Mud-daubed, mud-stained, with patches of brush stuck to his hair, his cloak, his clothing... he blended with the earth. Even alert Roman horsemen had cantered by him only a few steps from where he hugged the ground.

Sayid bypassed two smaller entrances into the camp because the more senior-ranked legionaries were assigned to the main gate. An *optio custodiarum,* the officer in charge of the guard posts, or a *tesserarius,* the watch sergeant stationed at the main gate, would hear him out. Less experienced sentries—the *milites,* basic infantrymen, or even *tirones,* new recruits—might run him through with their spears at the secondary gates. They would find Vespasian's order only later when they searched his body.

He had reached the main entrance an hour before and waited to see a senior rank soldier appear before he rose from the ground and approached him.

"Halt!" The command was accompanied by an iron-shafted pilum striking before him with such force that the spear sank deep into the still-moist, traffic-churned earth. Sayid saw the officer who cast it wave forward a half-dozen armored legionaries posted along the entrance. The gateway was blocked by a string of *valli*, hardwood stakes joined into symmetrical crosses lashed in pairs at intervals along a beam hewn from a large tree.

The high-ranking soldier ordered the legionaries, "Search him."

The men slipped through the partially opened barrier that closed behind them. They quickly stripped Sayid of the small sack that held his few remaining rations, the wooden spike he had used when he worked on the docks of Laodicea, and the packet strapped to his chest containing Vespasian's orders. "He has no weapons, centurion," called one soldier.

"Bring him here." The guard captain waved them forward as two men swung the barricade open again to let them enter.

Sayid tried to move closer to promised warmth, a large bronze bowl filled with flaming chunks of wood and set in a hole in the hard-packed earth. Next to the thick pillar securing one end of the gate beam, the fire warmed a rough lean-to of wood and hide that served as a windbreak for the sentries.

"Stand still!" the centurion barked. Sayid halted.

The guard captain accepted from the legionary the wooden spike and the stained packet. Turning the spike over in his hands, he thumbed its ferruled tip, then tucked it—tapered end first—into his belt and unwrapped the stained packet. The centurion wiped dirty hands on his *fascia*, smearing his wrapped leggings. He peered at what was written on the sheet of vellum folded inside.

"That is from General Vespasian," explained Sayid. "He orders that I return to duty as an auxiliary with the 12th Legion." He shuffled closer to the fire.

The centurion finished reading the parchment. "General Vespasian has moved his command to Caesarea... and I do not know this centurion mentioned here," he tapped the sheet. "Whether or not this Nicanor is here, I can't say." He jerked a thumb at the camp runner next to him. "Take this to the commander and ask what to do with this man." He handed the parchment to the runner, turned back to Sayid, and put his hand on the gladius at his hip, gripping the hilt of the short sword, "I told you to stand still where you are."

The cold that climbed Sayid's legs and bit through his clothing had forced him to fidget, for after more than an hour of hiding and now standing in the wind, his feet were numb. He swayed and shook as they waited. The sun that seemed to hold no warmth for him had moved higher by the time the runner returned. The man held his spear high, diagonally in front of his chest as he puffed to a stop next to the centurion. More vapor spilled from his lips as he reported. Sayid, clenching teeth to keep from chattering and focused on steadying his stance, did not hear what he said.

The centurion nodded and waved a hand at four of the legionaries who had searched him and remained alert nearby. "Take this man to the commander's quarters."

* * *

Once inside the camp, Sayid saw that it had grown extensively and had a more permanent look. Many wooden and fired-mud-brick structures had replaced the hide and canvas tents he remembered. And the 12th Legion's commander's quarters now were far different from the simple one occupied by Cestius Gallus, the last 12th Legion commander he had served under. The four legionaries, swords out— one in front, one behind, and one on either side of him—led him inside. Tapestries shrouded the rough walls, and servants attended the man he had known before as Lord Gallus's senior military tribune, Galerius Senna.

One legionary escorting Sayid approached the nobleman, waited to be acknowledged by him, and then announced, "This is the man you asked to be brought to you, commander."

"So, you claim you are not a deserter...." The Roman nobleman waved the legionary away and took a brimming goblet from one servant. In his other hand, he held the discolored sheet of vellum Sayid had protected for all the days and miles he had traveled since receiving it. He flapped the pages. "This is your proof... why we should allow you to return to duty. This also mentions a centurion named Nicanor, who I know is... or was... on Vespasian's staff. He has gone to Rome, I believe. But I also know," he glared at Sayid, "most Syrians are liars and cowards... and most of them look better than you."

The legion commander's comments brought snickers of laughter from almost all the senior officers standing with him, each with full cups of what must be wine. They smacked their lips as they drank. Sayid recognized one of them—Tyrannius Priseus, the legion's camp-prefect. He was the man Nicanor had disliked and distrusted most... one he had warned Cestius Gallus about. Nicanor, Sayid recalled now, also had his doubts about Galerius Senna.

The legion commander's contempt and the sneer on the camp-prefect's face kindled a flame in Sayid's stomach that replaced the shivering. Sayid had wanted only two things all his life: to serve in a

Roman legion and prove his worth to the father who had left him and his mother. A third desire formed a burning ember he would not let dwindle but would soon fan to a white heat. He would show he was as brave as any man in any legion of the empire. And he would find his father to witness it, too. "My father, Marcus Sabinus, is a legionary. And he serves—"

"Silence!" Galerius Senna cut off Sayid and rose from the comfort of his chair to walk to a small desk. He set down the orders from Vespasian and quickly wrote something on a parchment square that he folded and sealed. He picked up Sayid's orders, rolled the sheet of vellum, and tied it with a leather cord, then sealed. Beckoning the camp-prefect closer, he handed both the message and the orders to him. He muttered something too low for others to hear, then straightened: "Priseus, take this to General Vespasian in Caesarea and ask that he confirm its legitimacy."

The camp-prefect sniggered again and gave a side-eyed smirk at Sayid as he strode from the room. Galerius Senna turned to Sayid's escort: "Hold him with the Jewish prisoners until we have word from General Vespasian." He fluttered a dismissive hand and walked out of the room, followed by his entourage.

The one centurion who had not laughed and had not followed the others called to the legion commander. "Lord Senna... the Jews could kill him if they believe he is a Roman soldier."

Senna stopped but did not turn. "Then, if we find out he proves to be one—a soldier of Rome—we will kill the Jews."

XXXII

Januarius 68 CE

Rome

The Temple of Hercules

"So, since the engineers' camp, the men continue to follow you?" Graius asked as he ran the sharpening stone along the edge of the short sword he had brought to their regular meetings at the Temple of Hercules. Seemingly unfrequented, there was never anyone around to wonder about the gray-haired man handling a blade within the temple with a centurion idly watching. "Do they work for Tigellinus or this Quintus you told me of?"

"Yes, they watch me openly, and I think they work for both men... or maybe one man who pays them all. But it's the ones I cannot see I worry about. When I go out to places other than the camp, I do my best to throw off any who follow me."

"Do you think they follow you here?" Graius stood and stretched. Setting the stone down, he gripped the sword righthanded, stepped a few paces away, and made several passes. The blade arced out and back with increasingly fluid grace. He repeated the weaving slash and thrust with his left hand—the metal flickering under rays of the day's last sunlight.

Nicanor watched as Graius, with a flourish that ended with an upthrust salute, sheathed the sword between his gaunt shoulders. Though he was no longer thick with muscle from fighting and training, the man's shoulders were still broad enough for the blade to rest comfortably there. Its hilt at the nape of his neck, easily hidden by the collar of a cloak. A shorter armed man could not reach back and pull such a sword free quickly enough to bring it to bear in defense or attack. But Nicanor had seen the old man perform the exercise many times now, each movement more smoothly and with controlled power. *I would not wish to face Graius in his prime*, Nicanor thought. But even though the man had found his ease with a sword after so many years, Nicanor knew he could wear the old gladiator down and then strike through the slowed defense of age.

"I have seen no one around here but would not be surprised if they are," Nicanor said, settling his mantle across his shoulders and drawing it close. Graius sat on the bench next to Nicanor and rubbed his wrists and gnarled hands. They still ached, he said, though not as much as a month before, when he had met Nicanor again and picked up a real sword for the first time in more than a decade.

"What are they waiting for?" Graius asked.

"I guess for me to lead them to Lady Cleo. I made sure when they were done with their questioning to leave them with their suspicion that I knew where she was."

"You purposely draw danger to yourself." Graius nodded with a grim smile.

Nicanor shrugged. "If they think Cleo fled to Rome with me... then maybe they will not search as hard for her in Judea."

"Octavia has had no word from her?"

Nicanor shook his head. "No... I received the latest message from her this morning. Neither has Antonia Caenis... that is, she has not received anything from General Vespasian. I doubt he knows anything about Cleo's disappearance from Gessius Florus. That man—Florus—is devious... and quiet about his pursuits and real interests. But Antonia Caenis had other news. It seems Gaius Julius Vindex, governor of Gallia Lugdunensis, has rebelled against Emperor Nero. Antonia believes he and some other senators are beginning their first real efforts to replace the emperor. Vindex hopes to gather more men to his side by declaring support to Servius Galba, who seems to have drawn a following. Antonia believes him to be one of the hidden figures behind Piso and his conspiracy a few years ago."

"Galba is the governor of Hispania Tarraconensis... and Marcus Otho is his closest friend."

Nicanor rubbed his chin. "What Vespasian and Governor Mucianus were concerned about seems to be happening. Along with helping Cleo, perhaps Otho can tell us more that I can share with the general."

"When can we leave? The coastal waters have already seen winter storms, and they will worsen before spring."

"There have been delays—something to do with supplying the northern legions. But tomorrow, the engineers will have finished their work. And that completes what my orders call for... at least officially. Then they will ready the siege equipment for shipment to Caesarea for the legions that will assault Jerusalem."

"Then we can go to Hispania..." Graius said. "To Otho in Emerita Augusta?"

"Yes. I will meet you at dawn the next day, and we can be in Ostia that night. We must both be careful to misdirect anyone watching us. I hope to be long gone before Tigellinus or Quintus realizes it."

* * *

The Thracian had followed the old man as the sea captain with the dead eye had ordered: "Bring him to me... there's no worry he'll resist you," the captain had said. "The old man is the retired major domus of a lady sought by the man who pays us—a Lady Cleopatra." The Thracian drew his *sica*, a short, curved sword longer than a large dagger and nearly the length of a Roman gladius. The sica had been his companion for years and earned him many coins he almost regretted he had then reveled away. But he was young and strong... there were always more coins to hire a man willing to do anything or kill anyone.

The moon waned yet still shed some light. As he neared the temple, the glow from the large lantern within gleamed upon his well-tended blade. The light caught the craftsman's work—an eagle and snake engraved when he had a rare moment with extra money that the drink and prostitutes in the *lupanars* did not require from his purse. He always made the girls earn their money... and this bit of work would pay enough for a month's worth of whores and wine at a fine brothel.

The old man, wrapped in a heavy mantle, stood within the temple, his back to him, staring up through the opening in the temple's roof. He did not turn until the sound of the hobnailed sandals on the stone broke the stillness.

"Who are you... what do you want?"

"A man has questions to ask you... I am to take you to him."

"Why does he not come himself?"

"Because I'm paid to bring you to him."

"And do you think you can do so if I don't wish to go?"

The Thracian brought the blade up and caressed the metal's flat length with the palm of his hand. He came closer, stopping a blade's distance from the old man, who had not moved. "I know I can."

The old man smiled. "Are you a *thraex*? You Thracian fighters are so fond of your *sicae*." The old man closed his eyes.

"So, you know blades... and you've seen Thracian gladiators in the *ludi*, the Games? Then you know what can be done with this." The Thracian extended his sword until the blade tip touched the old man's chest. He put enough pressure on it for it to pierce the heavy cloak.

"Yes, I know blades... and the Games. What questions does this man you work for have for me?" The old man opened his clear, penetrating eyes.

The Thracian pressed harder, but the old man did not back away. "About what you know of a lady... Lady Cleopatra. You used to manage her household." He did not hold back his contempt for the meek who served others in such a manner. "Do you worry at the touch of my sica, old man? Come with me now and answer questions about her... or it will be more than a touch."

"Oh, I've felt more than that before... much... much... more." Graius pushed forward onto the tip. The remembrance of that bitter kiss filled him as an inch of metal pierced his flesh. He reached over his shoulder and pulled the sword into a scything arc that lopped off the Thracian's left ear, clipping his neck as well.

Staggering backward, the mercenary brought a hand up to hold back the blood spurting from the side of his head while still thrusting at Graius.

"Yes, I know blades...." Graius beat the Thracian's blade aside and cut the mercenary's throat with a sideway twist and slash. "And I know men like you," he gasped.

The Thracian dropped his sica and fell to his knees. His life poured between fingers that could not stop it from spilling onto his sword. A viscous scarlet thread ran along the grooves, filling the incisions in the metal, coating the design. Burbling blood, he watched the old man kneel before him on the massive circular drain beneath the temple's oculus. The Thracian's lips frothed as he choked out: "Who is this lady to you?"

"She is the daughter I could not have," Graius said, breathing heavily, "and I will kill any within reach who plan to harm her."

XXXIII

Januarius 68 CE

Rome

Media nox, Nicanor thought. *Midnight is far out of our ordinary routine for a ride.* Still, Carmenta welcomed Nicanor with a soft nicker as he entered the stable of the taberna he'd selected, away from the city center. Vespasian's orders allowed him to make his own arrangements instead of staying at one of the army barracks. That morning he had paid enough for two more days, though he did not plan to return. Should any of Tigellinus's or Quintus's men check on him, it served as a bit of misdirection. He had also told the engineers at the army encampment outside Rome that he would accompany the siege equipment for Vespasian's legions, bound for Ostia in two days. But that, too, was a ruse. Antonia Caenis had suggested both tactics.

He slipped a halter on Carmenta, draped two blankets on the horse's back and saddled her as she nuzzled him, then led her out a back entry. The exit was just big enough for a man and a single horse. It led to the alley behind the taberna. That setup was another reason he had selected this taberna since most city stables opened only onto the main street. The owner of the taberna and stable had struck Nicanor as a man with many enterprises. Some of which might require secrecy. Thus, he had asked few questions when Nicanor paid him enough coins in advance.

Nicanor smoothed the second, longer blanket he had placed on Carmenta. Beneath the saddle, it covered her from the base of her tail to drape over her neck. Providing her a little extra warmth on the road to Ostia. He studied the area, sweeping his eyes before exiting the alley. He paused to catch any movement among the street's shadows cast from the few lanterns that shed only low light. Nothing and no one he could detect. He held his breath and listened to the night for anyone or anything moving nearby. Nothing. He mounted. "Let's go, girl."

Now he and Carmenta would ride north some distance, alternating between a walk and gallop. Once Nicanor was sure they had not been followed, they would bend west and then follow the Tiber south to another stable between the river and the Forum Boarium near the Temple of Hercules. There he would meet Graius, who had arranged a horse for himself and a pack animal. Nicanor had not wanted a third packhorse or mule that might slow them, but Graius had convinced him it would be best to carry some supplies. Rations would be grim on the coastal livestock vessel they would take to Tarraco on the Hispanian coast. Nicanor could also bring the armor he had left with Graius. He was glad he did not have to leave it behind.

* * *

Nicanor and Carmenta had arrived at the stable at cockcrow just before dawn. But Graius was not there. As the eastern sky went from black to gray and brightened, Nicanor worried. *The old man should be here by now,* Nicanor thought as he paced. Behind him, he heard the stable attendant come out to take down the large lantern on its hook above the entry. *I must go find him.* Carmenta had been patient and as watchful as he, and now he picked up her reins. As he stepped up to mount and head toward the Temple of Hercules, where he would check first, the horse nickered and thrust her nose west toward the river. He followed her gesture. A shadowy figure approached, revealed by the sun's rise. Carmenta smelled it just before Nicanor did and blew through her lips and tossed her head. It was Graius, and he was covered with blood.

* * *

THE ROAD TO OSTIA

Nicanor glanced at the still silent older man. All Graius had said at the stable as he used cold trough water to cleanse his cloak as best he could was: "I'm sorry for being late. We must get the horses—mine are packed—and hurry." That had been a mile or more ago. They had just passed through a gate and onto the *Via Ostiensis*. Nicanor had gotten on the road from a different direction his last time in Rome, and he was stunned to see the pyramid they now approached in the open countryside. As they passed, he craned his neck, looking up at it. On a travertine foundation, the white marble slabs of its sides rose well over one hundred feet into the sky. The base must be close to 25 feet across each side.

Graius slowed with him, watching him studying the structure. "You have a connection to the man entombed within, Nicanor."

Glad his companion was ready to talk but confused by the statement, Nicanor turned in his saddle. "What makes you think I do? I've never seen this."

128

Graius angled his horse toward it. The pack mule in tow behind him, he stopped in the lee of the pyramid, out of the wind. He pointed at the words carved on the west flank of the impressive structure and recited: "'Gaius Cestius, son of Lucius, of the Pobilia, member of the College of Epulones, Praetor, Tribune of the Plebs, Septemvir of the Epulones.' Your former legion commander, Cestius Gallus—this is his father, buried here." Graius dismounted and removed a bundle from the pack mule. He took out a clean tunic from a blanket roll and set it aside. Shrugging out of his heavy cloak, he stripped off the blood-soaked shirt beneath it.

Nicanor saw the marks that crisscrossed the old man's torso. A long scar across his lower stomach disappeared below his wide leather belt and breeches. Some were the thin seams of slashes that had furrowed his flesh, but others were gouged out ravines of puckered skin. The skin of the old wounds seemed a dead gray in the chill air. His upper right arm was unmarked, the only scars on the forearm above the wrist. His left arm had been riven twice along its length and once across his shoulder. And there were four tears across the bicep. Nicanor had noticed before the deep trough that extended from elbow to wrist. Over his shoulders, along his upper back, was a cloth harness that affixed between his shoulder blades a length of flat leather that formed the sheath for his sword. The scars and sheath disappeared underneath the clean, heavy, long-sleeved tunic he soon covered with the thick mantle. As Graius rolled and stuffed the soiled cloth away within a blanket, Nicanor saw a glint of metal that was not Nicanor's armor Graius had shown him on the mule.

"What have you there?"

"Since you have yours," Graius poked at the bundle containing Nicanor's armor, "I thought to bring mine." He unwrapped the bundle to display the *manica*, a bronze metal-scaled arm guard, the *cassis crista*, a large bronze helmet with an ornate grill face visor, and a set of *ocrea*, metal-and-leather shin guards. "I lost my shield long ago; besides, it's too unwieldy to carry, and I thought we might get one for each of us in Tarraco if we feel the need of them."

"Will you now tell me what happened?"

Graius nodded. "Until this morning, I have not killed a man other than in the Games. And never as a freedman." He re-secured the mule's pack and mounted his horse. He looked up at the pyramid as he heeled the horse toward the road. "I wonder what happened to the body of Cestius Gallus?"

"I don't know. I hope he was buried with honor in Antioch." Nicanor shook his head and glanced over his shoulder at the pyramid as Carmenta moved them alongside Graius. "Why did you kill that man at the Temple of Hercules?"

"He wanted to take me to a man who had questions about Lady Cleo."

"Was it Quintus... a man as tall as you and me, with a scarred eye?"

"No, it was a Thracian... a mercenary, or one who earned his freedom from the Games as I did and turned mercenary. He had that manner to him. But he said he was paid to take me to a man for questioning... it must have been Quintus or Tigellinus. I killed him and dumped his body where they dispose of the offal from the slaughter of cattle—near the river."

They rode for a while, and Nicanor broke the silence. "We expected they would discover you through me, Graius. And I'm sorry I have dragged you into this."

"I will do what I must... to help you and to help Lady Cleo. She is the one I care for most in this world."

"But you sound like you regret killing the Thracian."

"No. The man needed killing." He paused and took a deep breath. "But long ago, I hoped to kill no one again... and it came back to me too easily."

* * *

Nicanor had been to only a few gladiatorial Games in the provinces. While he appreciated the combat skills of most of the men he had witnessed who fought in them, he had little interest in becoming a devout follower of what most Romans thought a sport. Still, he was curious. "What was it like?"

"To be a gladiator? Some think it's the pain of wounds that's hard to bear. But for me... it was the loneliness." Graius features hardened. "You have to be friendless. Else, one day, you may have to fight and kill someone who has come to have meaning for you. I knew men who formed friendships, whose hands hesitated... whose will failed them. They died at the hand of a 'friend' who wanted to live more than they did. It's better to face and kill a stranger... or be killed by one." He stretched and shifted the reins to his other hand. "One older man I knew—named Flamma—was admired for his skill. Though I was much younger, I was near his level with a sword. Flamma was a captured Syrian soldier who had fought as a *secutor* 34 times, winning 21 times and to a draw in nine other fights. In his four losses, he was spared because he fought so nobly. And four other times, he

130

was offered the *rudis*, the wooden sword that would mark his freedom from the Games. He refused each time."

"Why didn't he accept?"

"I didn't know why until I was matched against him, which was unusual. A *secutor* is armed similarly to a *murmillo*, like I once was, with a heavy short sword and shield, with the armor you saw. *Secutors* normally fought against a *retiarius* who was lightly armored and armed with a trident and net. The contest was to pit a more heavily armed—but slower—gladiator against a lightly armed and faster opponent who did not tire as quickly. But Flamma and I each had a reputation, which brought great demand for the match and raised betting to a fever pitch. There would be fortunes won... or lost. So, we fought...." Graius grew quiet again.

Nicanor gripped Carmenta with his knees and raised himself to see further up the road. "We near Ostia," he said, half-turned to the older man, who had slowed and seemed lost in thought. "What did Flamma tell you?"

"As I killed him, I asked why. Flamma looked up as the crowd yelled and jeered... as the brute beasts they become when other men's blood is spilled on the dirt and sand before them. This time the thumbs were against Flamma. With my foot on his throat and the blade tip over his heart, I asked him again." Graius raised his left arm and studied his hand. "Flamma knew what question I had to know the answer to and gripped this hand. He whispered... so I removed my helmet and heard him say: 'This is all I know... through it, I prove to the Romans the courage of my people. They think many of us— Syrians—as cowards. But I stand and fight... and do it well. But not today.' I then leaned on my sword, and so, Flamma died. I fought for years more, and the first time they offered me the *rudis*, I took it."

XXXIV

JERUSALEM

THE UPPER CITY

Miriam just could not do it. She could not shed her anger and help teach Ya'el and Elian Aramaic. And she would not help them learn how to practice and live by her faith. Ya'el, whom Miriam still thought of as Lady Cleo, was familiar with Judaism. She had even expressed appreciation for it when she joined them at Passover when Yosef invited her along with Sayid and that coarse centurion, Nicanor, to join his family. Learning how to be a Jew, speak and act as a Jew could be the difference between the woman and boy living and dying. Still, her anger prevented her from caring.

Her mother and father had spent hours each day with the pair, and they had worked hard to learn the language. She heard them practicing with each other in their room every evening. That morning she had heard them leave with her mother—for the market, surely—shortly after Matthew and her father left on their own business. So Miriam had slipped downstairs and passed into the courtyard to go through the back gate. She needed to check for Elazar ben Yair's messages and wanted to work on the chart she was making; she was merging one of Zechariah's with the map she had found on the dead Romans in the tomb. She planned to revisit soon.

"Why don't you like us?"

The voice came from above and behind Miriam before she reached the gate and was followed by a thud. She turned to see the boy, who had just dropped from a tree. Elian's cheeks bloomed red above Matthew's old cloak that had been cut short and hemmed, and though it was wrapped tight, it still draped overlarge on the boy. He seemed unaffected by the cold but hesitant to move. He asked again, "Why do you hate me and... and," he paused, "my mother?"

Miriam wanted to turn from him—were it anyone else, she would have—but she could not. She faced him... still, she could not answer the boy. How could he understand it was not personal? And that it was more about her than about him and Ya'el. Acknowledging to herself how unjust she had been, or especially admitting it to a mere boy... that now pained her.

Elian stepped closer and looked up at her. "We've done nothing to hurt you. The lady... Ya'el—she is my mother now... came here to keep from being hurt."

"What do you mean?" Miriam blinked. There had been no mention that she could recall from Yosef's message the one time she had read it in full. Her father and mother had told her Ya'el had done a great service for Jerusalem. They had told her, "There are things you must know about Ya'el." But admittedly, she had been unwilling to listen to them. However, she had apologized to her father, and that had mollified him. Her mother had not rejected the apology, but Miriam knew there was a foreboding look in her eyes that promised a less forgiving attitude. She blinked and saw the boy silently studying her, waiting for her to come back from her thoughts.

"She ran," Elian replied. "She had to get away from a man, her husband Lord Florus, who beat her terribly. Sayid was afraid he would kill her. And I was, too." The boy trembled a little, and Miriam dropped onto one knee to comfort him.

"Why would he kill his wife—a Roman noblewoman?" she asked. "For helping Jews?" A twinge of remorse and understanding flashed. She thought of what her parents had mentioned. "Or was it that she helped Jerusalem against the legion?"

"I don't know about any of that...." Elian shook his head. "But I saw how hard he beat her. More than once." The boy rubbed his hands together to warm them. "She likes your brother," too.

"Yosef?" she asked. He nodded.

"I heard her talk with Sayid about that, and he thinks your brother likes her, too." The boy met her gaze for a second longer. "I must go now and feed Cicero before he complains." He turned to go inside, and just before leaving the courtyard, looked back at her. "Your mother and father are nice... your brother Matthew, too. But it's lonesome here for us. I hope you stop hating us. Maybe we can be friends."

* * *

THE AGORA

"You spoke that well," Rebecca told Ya'el as they left the row of vendor stalls. "The merchants now know you are of our family, so remember if you come on your own—soon you'll be able to—just have your purchases sent to our home. But I can see that some of what we enjoy is getting harder to find and more costly."

Ya'el understood the concern on Rebecca's face but was pleased with the praise. Yosef's mother was a little intimidating but had proved patient and a good teacher. She was rapidly learning functional Aramaic. Simple phrases such as "How much is this?... I want to buy that... My husband's family is of the household of Mathias ben Mathieu."

And most importantly, she learned to follow that announcement with, "I was not raised in Judea, so please pardon my poor Aramaic." There were many new to Jerusalem, even on the Upper City streets. Several citizens wanted to help those seeking safety within the city walls and were courteous, tolerant, and compassionate. But some showed resentment borne in part by the demands of a suddenly growing population—and Rebecca had had to deal with a few of those, the kind who cast dark looks at Ya'el.

"Rebecca!" The strident tone came from one of two women marching toward them.

"Ya'el," Rebecca whispered quickly in Greek, "I'll introduce you, but then... can you find your way home?"

"Yes, of course," Ya'el replied and studied the two women, clearly well-to-do matrons, judging by their dress and manner.

"How pleasant to see you, ladies," Rebecca said in greeting.

* * *

Ya'el had often felt eyes upon her from women like the two who had called to Rebecca. They were affluent wives of men with power. It seemed Jewish society had similarities to Rome. The two women in the agora had assessed her from feet to head, and though that judgment seemed less than favorable, they still seemed curious. But thankfully, Rebecca had not allowed them to satisfy their snooping. After the introduction, she had sent her on her way: "I will see you at home later, Ya'el." And Ya'el had managed her goodbye to them in clear Aramaic.

Moving through a growing throng in the market despite the chill air, Ya'el soon passed out of the sight of Rebecca and the two women. She maneuvered around a cluster of shoppers before the silk merchant's offerings and spotted Miriam, who did not move like the other ladies idling through the lanes and stalls. Miriam was more purposeful. She started to call to her and stopped. Miriam had shown dislike and distaste for her. And she had overheard the discussion with Rebecca and Mathias that had turned into an argument about Miriam's treatment of the family's foreign guests. Also, there was something debated about what Miriam was hiding from her family. Ya'el cared little for what that secret might be—she had her own to keep—but it mattered a great deal if she could find a way to at least exist peacefully with Yosef's sister. They must talk and do so without others around them. Perhaps then she could clear the air and reach an understanding.

But Miriam was moving fast; Ya'el would need to run to catch up with her. That would draw attention, so she stayed near enough to follow until Miriam stopped. She could then approach her without causing alarm. They soon left the area she had learned well and from which she felt comfortable finding her way back to Yosef's home. Miriam crossed a large viaduct, and ahead were the walls of the grounds surrounding the Temple. *The walls and structure they enclose*, Ya'el thought, *are as impressive as many in Rome.*

Off to the north, she saw the tallest tower at a corner of Fortress Antonia that Matthew had pointed out and told her had once housed a garrison of Roman soldiers. Miriam turned right toward the south, then stepped onto a massive tier-like descent of steps leading into what she had been told was the Lower City. As she reached its bottom, she saw Miriam ahead pass into streets as busy as or busier than those in the Upper City. She hurried to catch up. Miriam's plain cloak and robe blended in with the crowd, but Ya'el's—once one of Rebecca's colorful garments—did not. Ya'el had already noticed a few rough men cast eyes on her. Theirs was a much different assessment than what she had experienced a short while ago.

At an intersection of two wide streets, she spotted Miriam and closed on her. Yosef's sister scurried down what appeared to be a craftsmen's street, pausing a moment at one shop to shake her head and move on. Miriam turned into an alley and stopped at a shop's side door, eyes searching it for something—she could not imagine what—then entered.

Lifting the hem of her robe, Ya'el crossed the street, entered the alley, and walked to the door. She knocked, but there was no answer. She knocked again. No answer. She pressed on the handle and felt the door swing in. Inside, the only light spilled in through the doorway. Just a step inside, the rest of the room was dark. *I know Miriam came in here*, she thought as she stepped further inside. *Where is she?* The dim light from the door abruptly ended with the sound of it slamming shut. Frightened now, she called into the darkness, "Hello... Miriam, are you there?" A hand pulled her head back, and she felt the tip of a knife at her throat.

"Why do you follow me!?"

XXXV

Februarius 68 CE

Caesarea

Vespasian's Praetorium

The guards entered with food for two and left. Yosef wondered how long they would leave him alone, not hover in the outer room. Still, he was not unguarded, and when escorted outside, he saw the unit of men permanently stationed at the only entrance to his two-room cell.

Florus's mocking final word at the marriage ceremony days ago had been, "Enjoy your wedding night...." Though the marriage was never to be consummated, Ariella had been allowed the entire first night with him. He was grateful she was not left with him overnight beyond that. At midnight the second night, she had been removed and returned at dawn when the guards brought the morning meal. If she had prepared his food, he would worry about eating it. When they were alone the first night, she had been clear she had meant what she said when the blacksmith removed his chains after their ceremony. Her sole purpose was to make him suffer and see him die.

He had not slept that first night for fear she might try to kill him with her bare hands. At least the talking he had done kept him awake. He had tried to convince her he had not let her husband die in the Roman surprise attack that finally breached Yotapta's walls. "Levi sacrificed himself to save us, Ariella. He was behind me and wounded when he shoved me away and triggered the deadfall in the passage that sealed it and buried the approaching Romans. I wish I had died, not him." He had told her just as he had in the refuge cave beneath Yotapta with the other survivors. She had not listened then and still did not.

Ariella had declared she would bide her time and seize the right moment. Adding that the best part of her had died with Levi and what was left was to die only when it brought the demise of the man she blamed. She had been willing to join with Yosef in marriage, but only so they could be sure they were united in death. So she came at dawn and remained with him until night, and the past several days had passed in watchfulness. He was not summoned by General Vespasian and instead was kept company by a woman set on seeing him dead.

His leg shackles and neck collar had been returned, and Ariella now wore her own restraints. A short length of chain attached to ankle cuffs let her walk but not run. He looked at her, sitting on the cot, staring at him as he sat in the corner with his back against the brick wall.

He tried again to break the silence that had lasted days. "What does Florus have to do with our forced marriage?"

The hatred in her eyes did not dim, but at least she answered him this time. "Only that I was brought before him when he heard of my hatred of you when I told what you did to others captured at Yotapta. The Roman you call Florus knew I believed you to be a traitor to your people."

"You know I'm not, Ariella."

"You live, but Levi, Dalit, and Dov—and so many others—died. And here... you have the favor of a Roman general." She spat a mouthful of barley gruel at him that splatted at his feet.

Yosef felt the stab of guilt that had frequented him since Yotapta. Were it not for his dream and its vision that he had survived for a reason, for a purpose to come... the guilt would have driven him to take his own life.

"Yes, I live... and so do you, Ariella. You breathe and eat... and hate. But do you blame yourself for remaining alive when your friends and loved ones are dead? Is their death your fault because you live? No, I can see you through your hate. You believe you bear no blame and are righteous in your loathing of me. I see the hurt and pain you carry."

He lowered his voice. "I carry my own burdens of what's past... and worry about what's ahead, but I would take your pain from you if I could." He studied her as she shifted on the bed and adjusted the two pieces she had torn from her robe to wrap around her ankles for protection from the rough metal. It seemed something he'd said had struck home for the first time and made her think, not just rely on raw emotion.

He leaned forward, his arms across his knees. "Ariella, I did not choose who would imprison me. But since I am here, I hope to sway General Vespasian to reach out to Jerusalem to surrender and resolve our differences peacefully without thousands more dying. And without that city—and my home and family—being destroyed. I wish I could have done that for Yotapta and all the towns of Galilee destroyed by the Romans. A terrible price has been paid for all the mistakes made by both Roman and Judean leadership. I failed to save

Yotapta... and Galilee. But still, I hope to save Jerusalem and many of our people."

"Why does that Roman, Gessius Florus, want you dead?" she asked. "I mean, other than you being a rebel military commander. When I was brought before him, and he talked of you, he seemed to wish you dead for a more important reason."

"I met him in Rome before he became the Judean Procurator," Yosef replied, "and I sensed his nature even then. But it was fully revealed once he reached Judea. Our government leaders—I was chosen to speak on their behalf—protested his abusive practices and actions. But he did not stop, and matters worsened. Then, in a heavy-handed effort to punish those he thought ridiculed him as they withheld tribute and tax payments, he ordered what became a massacre after Passover in Jerusalem. Our defense and retaliation to that slaughter triggered the 12th Legion and its Roman allies marching on Jerusalem. That response was incited by Florus."

"But why does he hate you personally? When I met with him, and he asked if I wanted your death... it was if he had that as one of his greatest desires."

"I think he identifies me as a representative of a people he hates. I cannot tell you why he hates Jews other than that we stood—and still stand—in his way." Yosef did not answer with all the truth. He could not tell her another reason, that Florus might know of his love for Cleo and—something she had never spoken of, but Yosef knew— her feelings for him. Jealousy could be part of Florus's hatred. Yosef was no traitor, but Yosef's having fallen in love with a Roman noblewoman married to a Roman official would not persuade Ariella. She believed worse. *And not just her?* He wondered if that belief had spread to others.

* * *

"General," said Gaheris Clineas as he stepped into the private office, "the camp-prefect for the 12th Legion in Ptolemais is here. He brings their latest requisitions, which after you review, I'll send to your *quaestores*, the chief of quartermasters. And he has a message for you from Lord Senna, commander of the 12th." Vespasian's aide glanced at the general's visitor. "He carries one for Lord Florus, too."

"Send him in."

Tyrannius Priseus entered with his helmet under one arm and two messages in hand. "General, here are the requisitions, and if you would, Commander Senna asks you to please look at this and confirm its authenticity... and that you still approve it."

Vespasian held out his hand and accepted the re-supply requirements and letter. He broke the seal and flattened the stained sheet of vellum. Squinting at the personal message to read it, he leafed through the accompanying pages and grunted, "Yes. Though I'm surprised the Syrian auxiliary returned despite Nicanor's trust in him." He took a pen, dipped it in a small inkpot, added a note, and signed. "Done. Return this to your commander." He looked up at the camp-prefect, who did not act as if he had been dismissed. "What else is there, centurion?"

"May I give Lord Florus his message, general? When it was known I was to come here, and that Lord Florus was still here, I was asked to deliver it to him."

"Yes." Vespasian flicked a hand and unrolled the scroll with a list of arms and supply requests, running a thick finger down the columns before handing it to his aide with a nod.

Gessius Florus took the message from Priseus, read it, and smiled. "Thank you, camp-prefect."

"Is that some good news, Lord Florus?" Vespasian watched the imperial tax collector's expression. "Has your wife been found?"

"No, general, she's not been found. But this is good news that might help." He looked up at Tyrannius Priseus. "I'll return to Ptolemais with you, camp-prefect."

XXXVI

Jerusalem

The Lower City

"I mean no harm; I just want to talk," Ya'el said, feeling the tip of the knife lift from her throat, but the pressure of what must be a forearm remained high on her chest, then slid to beneath her chin and pushed harder. And the strength of the sudden attack made her plead with the man: "I'm looking for the woman who just came in here. I mean no harm."

She knew she was speaking in Greek but didn't have the Aramaic to say it. She switched to what she could: "I am a family member of the household of Mathias ben Mathieu." The dark was silent, and still, there was no movement... but there was a familiar scent... a perfume she recognized. "Miriam, is that you?" she asked in Greek.

"Don't move," Miriam replied.

The pressure on Ya'el's throat was gone. After a heartbeat or two, she heard the sliding in place of a door-bar behind her. Then in front of her, a second later, a streamer of sparks flew, and a flame flowered and grew. Ya'el watched Miriam pick up the dagger she had set aside to light the large oil lamp set on what looked like a craftsman's bench along the wall. Miriam, wide-eyed with her recent action, or her eyes not yet adjusted to the light, slipped the dagger into a sheath on her forearm and tugged her sleeve down to cover it.

Ya'el was confused. "What are you doing here?" she asked.

"That's my question for you," Miriam crossed her arms and glared. "Answer me."

Ya'el looked around the room. In its center was a life-size straw figure dressed as a man wearing a tunic and robe and melon for a head. "What is all this?"

"Ya'el... or should I call you Lady Cleo in private?" The contempt rang clear. "What I do here is none of your concern. But what *you* do here is mine..."

Ya'el could not help but notice that Miriam's folded arms ended with her hands inside both sleeves of her robe. She wondered if Yosef's sister carried another hidden dagger. She shook her head at that thought. *This makes no sense.* "I mean you no harm," she said yet again. "I was with your mother in the market. Two women—her friends, I guess—called to her, and she told me to go to your home while she stayed to talk to them."

"Then why are you here?"

"I saw you as I was headed back. I know how you feel about Romans... about Elian and me. We have not talked about that... and I followed you. I thought I could—"

"What... convince me not to hate Romans?"

"No. To not hate the boy and me."

Miriam lowered her arms and went to the end of the bench where a clay pitcher and three cups sat. She filled a cup and sipped from it.

"May I have a drink?" Ya'el rubbed her chin and throat. "Please... I'm thirsty."

"It's only water... I've come to not trust wine." Miriam filled another cup and set it on the table.

"Water's fine." Ya'el moved from the wall. Her fingers brushed the straw man in the center of the room. She pressed a hand against its chest to find the figure heavily anchored on its cross-piece stand that supported the torso and thick straw legs. She had seen a piece of equipment like it once with her brother when visiting where gladiators trained, a *ludus gladiatorius* outside Rome. She never expected to find the same thing in a Judean shop where Yosef's sister clearly felt at ease.

* * *

"What friends of my mother stopped her in the market?" Miriam asked. Her father had told her about the growing curiosity of some women of the Upper City and their queries about her. The worry and tension of waiting for the Romans to attack had emboldened people to speak out and question many things they would have once remained silent about. They pried about when Miriam would marry, and that was one of her father's worries. She had tried to deflect it during his interrogation after that evening with Ehud, whose unexpected kiss had shaken her so. Still, she told him she was glad Ehud had returned... and that he had insisted on escorting her home in the rain. Despite that being inappropriate, the thought of an acceptable suitor... or the potential of one—even during a war—had satisfied him for the moment. Her mother's crossed arms and stern look showed she would not follow that lure but would not reject it in front of her father. *I must reckon with her soon,* Miriam knew and stared again at Yosef's friend.

Ya'el drank from the cup and set it down. "I didn't catch all the introduction your mother made, but think one woman was named Gamliel and the other Beor."

Miriam felt her eyes narrow at hearing those names, and though it was a fleeting expression, she knew Ya'el saw it.

"I cannot expect you to ever like me, Miriam. But I hope you can stop thinking of Elian and me as your enemies. We aren't and never will be. Rebecca, Mathias, and Matthew accept the boy and me. Yosef sent me to your family, knowing they would."

"Why here... Jerusalem?"

"I have nowhere else to go."

"Why do you run from your own people... what would make you feel unsafe among Romans?"

"Only the Romans in Judea... There was a plan for the centurion, Nicanor, to get me back to Rome where I have friends, and my brother, Marcus... but that failed."

"So, you run from your husband, Gessius Florus, who beats you?"

"How do you know that?"

"The boy told me... is that why Yosef wanted to help you?"

"Yes, that and... we—Yosef and I care for each other. That came to happen after our shipwreck."

"But you're married. Yosef would not involve himself with a married woman... especially a Roman woman."

"It happened before I was married."

"Is Yosef why your husband hit you?"

"And other things. When he began saying and doing things that seemed intended to hurt your people for no reason other than his own self-interest, I spied on him and gathered what proof I could. He suspected me, and that enraged him."

"Elian said he nearly killed you... and would have, had you not escaped with Sayid's help."

Ya'el nodded.

Miriam saw the ache form on Ya'el's face, the hollowing of her cheeks, and the tightening of her shoulders as they locked eyes.

"I mean you no harm, Miriam, and Elian is just a poor orphan slave boy who served me, and I could not abandon. We sought shelter from my personal storm here... for as long as it lasts. That's all we ask."

The haunted, hunted tone in Ya'el's voice pierced Miriam more than did the words the former Roman noblewoman spoke. She thought of Leah, abused and beaten by her husband, for she loved Yosef, too, but was trapped... she was a prisoner just as Yosef was now. The agony of her own brutalization by cruel men stirred awake, jolting her, as she considered what she had learned of Ya'el's own troubles. "My mother and father believe that you, as a highborn Roman, can somehow help Yosef be freed."

"I wish I could, but I have no power to change that. I have to hide and deny who I am just to save my own life." Ya'el's features sharpened more with the pain of that admission.

Miriam studied her and realized they had that, too, in common. "Maybe we will not be enemies... and I'll keep your secret. If you are found out, it will not be because of me."

"Thank you." Ya'el turned to look around the room. "And I will keep yours... is this—what you do here—the secret your family fears you keep from them?" She pointed at the training equipment. "I heard them asking you about how you go out on your own—"

"You need not know what I do here," Miriam said sharply. The iron came back into her heart. A clamor at the door meant someone was trying to enter. "Quiet..." she told Ya'el and went to see who it was. Pulling the bar aside, Miriam opened the door a crack. "Kefa, what do you need?" she asked the owner of the leatherworks across the alley.

"Elazar is in my shop now and asked me to see if you were in Zechariah's." His eyes darted past Miriam to peer into the shop. "I'll tell him you are here." He turned and dashed across the wide alley to his shop before she could stop him.

"Hurry, you must go!" Miriam said as she closed the door and spun toward Ya'el. "I'll show you out the front."

"But I don't remember how to get to your home from here."

Miriam grabbed her arm. "In here, then... hide!" She shoved her toward an open doorway that led to another room.

"Why... who is Elazar?"

"He is the leader of the Sicarii, and if he should suspect... you're a Roman, he'll either kill you... or tell me to kill you." Miriam pushed her inside the room and pulled the curtain closed.

Ya'el turned to look around in the dim light that leaked through a window covered with wooden shutters. There was a cot in the corner with a bundle of clothing. On a table in the center of the room, pen and inkpots sat next to a partially unrolled scroll that looked like a map. She wondered, *What does Miriam do here?* At the sound of a loud male voice in the outer room, she crawled under the cot.

XXXVII

At Sea

"Nearly 16 years ago was the one and only time I fought in a *naumachia* in the Games. It was a reenactment for Emperor Claudius of a naval battle against Rhodes. The enemy navy was hundreds of condemned prisoners. Before we 'sailed' they gave the expected *avē imperātor, moritūrī tē salūtant,* "Hail, Emperor. Those who are about to die salute you." They were nothing but fodder for our blades... slaughtered in the emperor's celebration. And they were, but in the doing of it, I was wounded." Graius spat and then dodged as a gust of wind caught the glob and cast it back at him.

"So," Nicanor said as he turned from the ship's rail, "you're on your feet finally, eh? You didn't tell me you had sea experience other than when you went to Hispania once before."

"Hah! That was only on a shallow barge rebuilt to look like a *bireme*—on a flat lake and with no wind." Working around the saliva that had built to excess with the first severe roll of the ship, he almost spat into the wind again but redirected to the deck. "But it was two fleets of 50 vessels each. We were told that was the number of ships based at Misenum and at Ravenna when they met for battle. Lake Fucino was large enough that we needed only part of it. There was room enough for the vessels to move about and even ram each other." Graius studied the ugly sky. "I'd rather be wounded than spend every minute spewing out my insides. My first time on this sea to Hispania on your behalf was smoother and quieter."

Nicanor had watched the old gladiator weave his way toward him. The pitch and yaw of ships always had taken him some time to get used to, also, and he did not envy the older man. Graius had been sick since the *Faustitas* had left port at Ostia the day before. The weather had steadily worsened, so there was no relief from the sickening motion that made Nicanor feel ill, too. He had reached out a hand to grip Graius's elbow and steady him until he could hold on to the rail near the backward curving stern. There reared the *chenisco*, the swan's neck design, he had been told gave the ship a more graceful appearance. *I don't think so...* had been his first thought after hearing that.

"Thanks. Despite the cold, I could not stay below any longer... the braying and lowing of the beasts... you'd think they would stop even for a little while. And the stench..." Graius breathed deeply.

"This is some bad weather... I've been through similar and don't care to relive it. And this ship wallows more than any I've been on." An *onerariae*, the ship was 180 feet long, had a roundish shape, and was pushed by its single large sail. There were no rowers, which surprised Nicanor, but he had been told it allowed for more cargo space.

"Your friend Marinus," Graius said, "cautioned about the weather headed west and was glad to be going south with his own ship. He said our captain trusted this ship's namesake too much—she's the goddess of fortune and protector of livestock... Before boarding, I'd never heard of *Faustitas*." Graius grabbed the rail with both hands as the ship rose and fell in a trough of gray-green water flecked with foam. "Your Marinus was interesting to dine with."

"That he is." It had surprised Nicanor when they had entered the taberna in Ostia, and soon after, he felt a hard, heavy hand clapping him on the back. He had reacted immediately and then apologized to Marinus for turning on him with his pugio in hand. But since Graius had told him of killing the mercenary at the Temple of Hercules, Nicanor had kept his dagger and sword loose in their sheaths.

"So, when we get to Tarraco, do you plan to visit one of these places he mentioned?" Graius asked. "He gave you quite a vivid recommendation for two of them."

Nicanor smiled. While Graius's face was still pale green, he must be feeling better, or at least the old man denied the sea its full effect upon him. He'd proven it could not keep him prone for more than a day. "No, there are things my energy and focus require once we get there. Marinus loves giving his tongue free rein to tell his stories. And I needed him in a good mood to persuade him to carry my letter and report to General Vespasian in Caesarea. It was lucky his ship was loaded for there. Otherwise, I would have had to use someone I don't know to carry them. I've written it as a report on routine matters that I was ordered to check on. But the general will understand the hidden meaning and references I make. Still, it's better to have someone take them I have some trust in."

"Well, you paid him well; that helped his mood, too." Graius spat again over the side and with the wind. "Did you tell General Vespasian about me?"

"No. I thought it best not to name you in case someone should see my letters who should not. You said the Thracian had just been told to follow you. So, maybe they have not connected you to me. Gessius Florus, knowing about your history with Cleo's family, likely told Quintus to see what you might know of her location."

"Then I should have gone with the Thracian and lied to this Quintus.... or Tigellinus if brought before the Praetorian Prefect." He shook his head, and the wind unfurled the thick scarf around his neck to stream like a cavalry pennant. "I would not have had to kill the man."

"Whether Quintus or Tigellinus... they would likely have had you killed afterward, Graius."

"I'm old... but not so easy to kill. You need not worry about me."

"If they had you, Graius, they'd strip you of weapons before they questioned you. And then...."

"I've killed barehanded before, Nicanor. Anyway, they are in Rome, and we are here." He turned around to look ahead and scan the horizon buried in a gray haze. "Where is this?"

"The captain says the steadying of the wind has helped our speed, and we'll enter the Straits of Sardinia and Corsica after daybreak. Come, let's go check our animals. I feel bad for Carmenta; she is used to much better conditions."

"So am I," Graius muttered, spitting again into the roiling sea, and followed the centurion. Above them, the strengthening gusts pulsed against an already taut sail and set quivering the lines that secured it.

* * *

The cracking noise, far louder than the creaking of wood that had lulled them both into an exhausted sleep, woke them.

"Is that normal?" Graius asked as he slid his sword into the sheath between his shoulders; he had slept with it in one hand. Steadying himself against a bulkhead, he pulled on his cloak.

"No. That does not sound good." Nicanor, too, had slept dressed and finished securing his weapons and the pouch at his waist: "I'll go on deck and see what's happening. You go check the horses, and I'll meet you up there."

Nicanor was drenched even before he got on deck to find it awash with a wall of water and not the usual spray that plumed over the brow and fell along the main deck. Sheets of rain driven by a slanting wind stung his skin. There was ice in it, too. He shivered and shielded his eyes, and he searched around him. To his left was a churned, white frothed sea mass with waves as high as the side rails—some much higher. One after another crashed over and onto the deck.

Above him, the sail with its edges torn and tattered capered and snapped in the gusts. He looked to his right. And up.

Futuo! The gray he had thought just more storm-tossed sea... was jumbled rocks at the base of a stone cliff. Seawater and rain coursed down them as the ship crashed against the jagged boulders and slid along them with tearing and rending, he felt more than heard.

A lone sailor staggered by, pushed by the wind more than propelled by his own legs. Nicanor grabbed and spun him around. "Where are we?"

The man's eyes were wide, staring, but he did not seem to see. "The winds picked up in the night and pushed us much faster than the captain—the drunken bastard—thought they would. It drove us into the straits in the dark. We should have lowered sail and set a sea anchor when he realized we couldn't see ahead... and then we lost our seaway. We're aground... on the rocks near Marianum."

"Where's the captain?"

"Overboard..."

"What can we do?"

"Nothing but abandon ship."

"What of the animals and your other passengers below?"

"It's every man for himself." The sailor pulled away and twisted off toward the forward part of the ship.

Nicanor staggered below. "Graius, we must abandon ship!" He untied Carmenta and the other two horses. "So much for the ship's name... it's foundered on the rocks, and we have little time before the ship breaks up and takes us down with it." He stroked Carmenta's forehead. "I'm so sorry, girl... I hate to—"

"Leave our horses? Can't we save them somehow?"

"The hold covers are still secured, and there's no way to open them and put ramps in place to get them out." Nicanor's eyes were not wet from rain alone. "We must go—"

Carmenta blared, nostrils flaring, and pushed the two men away from the hull.

"She panics!" Graius cried as he fell back.

"No, she—"

Nicanor felt the horse turn sideways to put her body between them and the hull's casing just as a splintered fang of rock broke through the wood and the sea poured in.

XXXVIII

Rome

"Beautiful, don't you think, Tigellinus?" Nero's call echoed within the vast porticoes of the atrium that divided the emperor's new villa from the rest of the city.

The Praetorian Prefect entered the enormous *vestibulum* of the *Domus Aurea* that spread over the Palatine Hill's north side and across the Velian ridge to the Esquiline Hill.

The emperor beckoned to him and pointed a finger at what he stood next to. "Walk with me and view it from all sides... then I'll show you the other splendors newly finished for my home."

"Yes, sire." Ophonius Tigellinus considered that this 'home' took up a vast tract of the city and included groves of trees, pastures with flocks, vineyards, and an artificial lake. He had heard Nero describe it as his *rus in urbe*, his countryside in the city. Tigellinus stared up at the *Colossus Neronis* towering above them and dwarfing all around it. The over 100-foot-tall bronze statue stood atop a *propylaea,* a massive square pedestal. The figure typified the imperial ego and was just one example of how the empire's wealth was disappearing. The extensive gold leaf that gave the villa its name was not the only extravagant element of its décor. Many of the stucco ceilings were faced with semi-precious stones and ivory veneers.

Tigellinus had heard the cries of those who protested that Nero spent too much on himself. He agreed with them. He cared little for their complaints about what they lacked, but the emperor's spending did leave less for him to divert to his own needs.

One of the emperor's personal guards stepped aside to let the prefect within the phalanx that surrounded the emperor. The escort had been bolstered by more men as many in Rome grew angrier at the excesses of the emperor when so much remained to be done to revive the city damaged in the great fire almost four years before. The soldiers surrounding Nero eyed Tigellinus stonily. Though they were Praetorians, they did not fall under his command—they obeyed only the emperor. Tigellinus did not care to be within their reach, especially since he had no good news to share with the emperor.

"Sire, I have news from the north about Vindex's rebellion in Gallia Lugdunensis. I have General Vespasian's latest report... and one from Gessius Florus."

"Do not spoil my mood, Tigellinus... I wish to contemplate my magnificent new home. It will be fully completed in the summer, in time for the Junius celebration... I'm told the harvest is great, and the Alexandrian ships should bear more grain than ever. In only a few months, the merchant vessels escorted by my warships will be off our shores. The *tabellariae* ships from Puteoli will herald their arrival, and the people will know they will not hunger. It will be a good time to mark my grand achievement." Nero's arms swept out as if he stood on one of the stages he enjoyed performing upon.

Not letting his thoughts show, Tigellinus followed the emperor further into the sprawling domus. Its rooms were sheathed in dazzling polished white marble; pools were inset in the floors, and fountains splashed in the corridors. After a few minutes of silence, he felt Nero's eyes on him. "Sire?" he ventured, then he realized the meaning of the emperor's questioning look. "Your home, Sire—is glorious," he studied the immense chamber they entered.

"This is one of the two main dining rooms. Celer and Severus have been most creative." The architects had designed the two dining rooms to flank an octagonal court surmounted by a dome with a giant central oculus to let in light. "Watch this." Nero motioned to a dozen slaves standing ready next to a massive spoked-wheel-and-pulley mechanism along a wall. They gripped the spokes and leaned into them. As they cranked, the ropes traveling into the wall drew taut, and the ceiling underneath the dome rotated—stiffly at first, then more smoothly.

"Ingenious, Sire. I've never seen or heard of anything like it."

"No one has." Two fingers—ringed and with their jewels flashing—drummed on the emperor's pursed lips. "Now they work on a canal to join my lake with Lake Avernus. It will be deep enough to sail upon." His eyes fixed on the Praetorian Prefect. "You may tell me your bad news later... leave me now. Come to dinner this evening."

Minutes later, Tigellinus hurried back through the vast vestibulum and glanced up at its giant occupant, which cast a long shadow.

* * *

NEAR PRAENESTE

Quintus almost envied the four men the Praetorian Prefect had sent with him. They rode easily, and their mounts seemed more agreeable than his. He did not ride well, and his horse detested him as much as he disliked the horse. But then, he had spent most of his life on ships and at sea. And his time ashore was spent on other things... things more important than horses. But he had to admit that riding yielded more time to think than he had as crew or captain of a ship. Vessels were mindless, and a captain and his sailors had to do everything to make them serve their purpose. Life at sea meant correcting course for wind and waves, set, and drift, commanding men to keep to their jobs to sail the ship to its destination. And the sea had more ways to kill you than did the land. Riding a horse was less demanding, and that was good since he had much to think about. "How far away are we?" he asked the oldest soldier, one of Lord Tigellinus's prized and loyal *evocati,* a seasoned legionary brought out of retirement and devoted to the prefect.

"We should reach Praeneste this evening."

"Good. Then tomorrow morning, we'll call on this Lady Octavia." Quintus settled back into the monotony of his ride, following the men ahead of him. He knew the lady had been in contact recently with that damned centurion, Nicanor. Then the man had disappeared... as had the Thracian hired to find and bring in Graius, that old major domus of Cleo's family, for questioning. He wondered again whether something connected the two disappearances.

"Tonight, let's find a good taberna in Praeneste," Quintus announced. "I'll buy the drinks." The man ahead of him turned with a grin that showed his rotten teeth. Nodding back, Quintus returned to his thoughts.

If he ruled out Nicanor hiding with Lady Cleo at Lady Octavia's, or his questioning yielded no answers or clues to their whereabouts, he would find and question the old man when he returned to Rome. Gessius Florus had 'retired' Graius from service to Lady Cleo's family once Florus married her and before he left Rome for Judea. The reward Gessius Florus offered for his wife's return, and the centurion's head was too substantial for Quintus not to turn over every stone. Lord Tigellinus had hinted at his interest in having Quintus report on the imperial tax collector on his return to Judea; he seemed concerned about Gessius Florus. A double game could be twice as profitable... but he would have to be twice as cautious.

* * *

ROME

DOMUS AUREA

Lord Tigellinus had spent the afternoon ordering a cavalry cohort of his Praetorian guards to the north and west. The uprising by Vindex and his declaration of support for Servius Galba had made Tigellinus think of all the threads of connection among what might be conspirators against the emperor. One of Galba's closest advocates was Marcus Otho, whom he had learned to be this Lady Cleo's brother. Nicanor might try to take Lady Cleo to her brother Otho in Hispania. So he had arranged more men and six ships to sail despite the weather to Tarraco, Dertosa, Saguntum, Dianium, Carthago Nova, and Malaca. These were the closest ports to Otho in Emerita Augusta. He had also sent a dozen riders out on the *cursus publicus*, the Roman 'public way' used to transport messages and tax revenues to and from most of the empire.

They would deliver his orders to all the waypoints and stations along the way to secure and hold the rogue centurion, Nicanor, should he be found or make himself known. Tigellinus had done what he could for now, and he brought his attention back to his surroundings as he entered the crowded grand dining room. Nero had invited 100 others to join him for dinner.

"Lord Tigellinus... how good for the leader of our magnificent Praetorians to join us."

The Praetorian Prefect recognized the honeyed voice but did not think much of the man behind it, Gaius Petronius. He turned to greet him. "Gaius, I'm pleased to see you. It's been too long. When you finish your *Satyricon*, I wish to read it."

As befitting the noble who had become Nero's *arbiter elegantarium*, the judge of elegance for the imperial court, Petronius wore the finest of togas beneath an indigo cloak trimmed in gold. "I'm nearly ready to share it. The work is a mixture of serious and comic—such are the times—but you might enjoy the more erotic and decadent passages." He waved a hand as bejeweled as Nero's. "Is this not the emperor's finest work?" He indicated the furnishings and tilework of the ceiling above them. "I'm told that Nero has received the last of the *silphium* from Cyrenaica and had them rendered to coax a rarity from its delicate blooms... ahhh... see." He gestured at the ceiling where clouds of mist formed and descended. "It revolves like the heavens," he said and pointed above as the perfume wafted down on them. "Are we not alive in wondrous times?"

Tigellinus nodded but pondered how long they would continue.

XXXIX

JERUSALEM

THE STEPS FROM THE LOWER CITY TO THE TEMPLE ENCLOSURE

"That man sounded angry," Ya'el said as she looked back down the steps toward the Lower City and then had to lift her robes to hurry and match Miriam's pace. She was thankful for the strength she's gained through walking on rough roads and across Judea from Ptolemais to Jerusalem, much of it on winding roads up and down mountains. Otherwise, she would have fallen behind, and she did not think Yosef's sister would wait to guide her. Ya'el wondered again at the change in Miriam—not just physically. Her finger brushed the small scab of dried blood at her throat, where Miriam's knife had nicked the flesh under her chin. "Who is this Yohanan ben Levi, and Simon bar Giora, I heard the man speak of?"

Miriam slowed on the steps as they approached the southwest corner of the Temple Enclosure and glanced at Ya'el. "Simon bar Giora has been harassing the Idumeans in the south as much as harrying the Romans. Elazar thinks he should focus solely on the Romans. The Gischalan, ben Levi, is a troublemaker who spreads dissent... and he hates Yosef."

Ya'el was surprised at the answer. Miriam had not spoken to her since they'd left the shop in the Lower City. "Why does he hate Yosef?" Ya'el did not understand some of what was said. Still, more than once, she had overheard Rebecca, Mathias, and Matthew talk as if there was a war within Jerusalem's walls that worried them as much as did the war with Rome. "That man, Elazar ben Yair, sounded like he believed this Yohanan ben Levi was a threat. But to whom?"

"Matthew or my father could explain it better to you, but we in Jerusalem are not unified. And now that you are among us, that should be of concern to you, too. He hates my brother because Yosef was chosen as Galilee's military commander and not him. And now Yohanan ben Levi thinks he should be the one to lead all Judeans. Elazar, the Sicarii leader, plans to remain at Masada, adding to its defenses and fighting the Romans from there. But he still wants Jerusalem to come together to stand against the Romans. He feels the Gischalan's prodding and stirring weakens the city."

"And they—we—won't work together against the Romans?" The sharp glance Miriam gave her made it clear Miriam still considered her Roman, but... that feeling of identity with the empire had been purged from her. She did not know where she belonged now. She wanted only to find a place of peace that it seemed she would never come to. They were at the top of the steps. Miriam halted for a moment before passing through a colonnade to enter the Temple Enclosure's outer courtyard, where she stopped at a bench. "Elazar ben Yair spoke as if you are one of his Sicarii," Ya'el said. "Will you then leave Jerusalem and go to Masada?"

"They'll light the Women's Court shortly," Miriam said, not answering her. "I like to watch the four lamp towers come alight and dispel some of the darkness."

Ya'el tugged the cloak closer around her and wished for a cup of wine. She missed the *vinum mareoticum,* a white, sweet wine from Alexandria that Gessius Florus had regularly brought from that city for his private stock. That was about the only thing he had introduced her to that was a pleasure and not pain. She doubted she would ever drink it again. "Why is Jerusalem not unified? And if it is not... why start a war with Rome?"

"We did not start it... you—Roman men did. Judea's men have done their part, too, to bring war upon us...." Miriam shook her head. "I once thought little about how emotions and greed can drive men to do things, things they might have once thought they would never do. But there are those whose ill intent has always been part of them—they seek power or money. Or both. I think that's why the men who are supposed to lead the city bicker and fight."

Ya'el knew the truth about which Roman mainly was responsible. She checked to make sure no one lingered nearby, then said, "The empire has gone through times like that... and will surely do so again. Some believe it is coming soon." She sat silent for a moment. "And Roman men—and women, both—have aspirations, but the pursuit of them can cause others pain." She could not help but think of her best friend... from when she had been Cleo. "My friend, Poppaea, had plans for what she wanted in life, and she ended up marrying an emperor." She felt Miriam stir and half-turn toward her, curious at the statement. "Only to die at his hands," Ya'el said. A northern wind spun down and tangled the flames of the nearby lamps that had just been lighted. She wondered if they would go out. "My father wed me to a man who could further his interests. He gave little thought to what kind of man would be revealed once married to his only daughter. A cruel man who needed me—my friendship with an emperor's wife—only to get what he wanted. To become a Judean Procurator."

* * *

THE TEMPLE ENCLOSURE, THE WOMEN'S COURT

The first twitch of empathy—which she resisted for her enemies—called to Miriam. The hands of men had hurt her and Ya'el... and they both could tell stories of others—friends—who had suffered, too. *Some still do.* Leah had been abused by her husband, Yonatan, and she realized that history was hers as well. The hands of the two Romans who had raped her still gripped her in her memories. They still hurt. She stood and went to the nearest of the four massive lamps, now lighted to illuminate the Women's Court. She looked up at its flickering, smoky flames as they grew against a darkening sky. Miriam scanned the area, a habit acquired under Zechariah's guidance; be aware of your surroundings, the coming and going of others. Ehud was coming into the arc of light. He reached a point where he was fully illuminated, then stopped. His eyes widened as Miriam, without thinking, took a step toward him. She had not seen him since the night of their kiss. He hesitated and then fled—his haste made it seem so—and was soon lost in a group of people moving toward the other end of the courtyard.

"Who was that man?" asked Ya'el.

Miriam was startled that Ya'el had joined her beneath the courtyard lamp. "No one..." And then she muttered under her breath, "And someone."

Ya'el was close enough to hear the whispering of her last words and detect the hurt and longing in them. It was a pain, she recognized. She started to ask about the man again, but Miriam turned away as if to escape him and her question. Something in the night—the sense of loss in Miriam's whisper—made her think of how she felt leaving Yosef behind. And of the loss, she felt when she could not make it to Nicanor for his help so she could escape to Rome.

"We must get home." Miriam had taken a few steps and paused at the edge of the lamp's glow long enough for Ya'el to join her. They passed through the shadows to lighted areas to shadows again, and soon they were beyond the Women's Court.

* * *

Neither woman saw the tall, lean man with a thin, pale face come out of the shadows to watch them go. He had seen Ehud too, and the look he had exchanged with Miriam. *Those two have some connection...*

154

and I must sever it, thought Hananiah as he stroked the stained pouch at his waist. His fingers rested there as he considered the other woman Miriam had brought with her from the Lower City. He had seen them leave a shop he thought had been abandoned; at least, it had been so as long as he had been in Jerusalem. In the Women's Court, he had watched as Miriam studied her surroundings without drawing attention. Much as he would do if he was concerned about being seen, which had prompted him to follow them. Miriam fit in in the Lower City... but the other woman did not. Then her eyes were filled with wonder just now, as if she were in the Women's Court, within the Temple Enclosure, for the first time. *There is something about her... she does not belong.* He moved into the night toward Miriam's home. He would watch for them there.

XL

Jerusalem

The Upper City

"Why did Eleasar do that?"

Miriam heard her father's voice and other muffled sounds come from the main room. Stepping aside to let Ya'el in, she motioned her to be quiet and carefully closed the front door. She hoped to slip upstairs without being seen. They had worked out an explanation of where they had been, and she would leave Ya'el to deliver it to her parents. She wondered at the Roman woman her family was protecting, a woman who had experienced some of the same heartaches she had lived through. Ya'el had made one comment before she became silent after leaving the Women's Court: "Maybe you'll share your secrets once I've told the truth of mine."

Miriam heard her father's voice rise. "Why did he ask the Idumeans to come to Jerusalem's aid?"

"We need more men, Father... anyone's aid from anywhere...." Matthew was getting exasperated. He was losing the respectful tone he almost always used with their father. She stood still to hear her father's reply, for she remembered Elazar ben Yair word's earlier about the Idumeans, too:

"Tomorrow, I must speak with him. Your Temple Guard captain is inviting more trouble to enter our city. When he was alive I never trusted Esau ben Beor, the Idumean representative in the Sanhedrin. We do not need Idumean soldiers in the city, no matter what Eleasar ben Ananias may think."

Miriam had heard her father speak of the Idumeans before. Though they were allied with Jerusalem, there was deep distrust. She had learned that Yohanan Hyrcanus, the Maccabean leader, had forced the Idumeans to become part of Judea nearly two centuries ago. Ordered to assimilate and accept the Jewish faith, many of them still bore ill will toward Jerusalem.

Mathias continued, "And Simon bar Giora worsens our relationship with Beor and his people by raiding their villages in Upper Idumea to supply his men. He has ravaged the areas surrounding Hebron, the towns of Halhul, Bethsura, Dura,

Caphethra, Bethletephon, and Tekoa. After that, does Eleasar... do you... think they will come to our aid?"

"Still, Father, Eleasar says they've agreed to help us and will send men."

"First thing in the morning, you and I will go talk to him."

With her father's last comment to Matthew, Miriam had taken the first step on the stairs to the second-floor bedrooms when a hand on her arm made her stop.

"Miriam, I have something to tell your family... I hope you will listen to me, too." Ya'el took Miriam's hand. "Please." She did not seem offended when Miriam yanked her hand away but smiled as Miriam reluctantly followed her.

"Where have you been?" Rebecca asked, rising from a couch as Ya'el and Miriam entered the sitting room. She looked first at Miriam—Rebecca's resolute glare promising a confrontation with her daughter. Then she added, to Ya'el, "I was becoming worried."

"When I left you in the market, Rebecca," Ya'el replied, "as I was returning here, I saw Miriam...." Her eyes slid sideways in a glance at Miriam. "We've been walking, and she showed me the Women's Court... and we've been talking."

Rebecca's features softened to delight. "That's good! I've hoped you two could become closer."

Mathias and Matthew were on their feet, too. Miriam saw the smile that eased the tautness of her father's face. He nodded to her as he commented, "Yosef would be most glad to hear that, Ya'el."

"Since you are all here...." Ya'el noticed Elian playing in the corner with a wooden spinning top Matthew had given to him. He'd told her Yosef had brought it from Tebtynis in Egypt on his return from Rome, teasing that his little brother needed a new toy. She could almost see Yosef's smile and feel his charm in the room. A deep sigh shook her as she faced them. "I must tell you my story, which is more than Yosef could share in his hastily-written note." She shrugged off her cloak and hung it on a peg on the wall near the entry to the courtyard. The warmth of the charcoal burning in large bronze braziers in the corners of the room was not as steady as the central heating she'd enjoyed at her family domus in Rome. But better than the cold and small campfires she, Sayid, and Elian had experienced since fleeing Ptolemais.

"Please sit." Without thinking, Ya'el gestured—a spreading of outthrust hands, palms up—at the chairs and divans, as if inviting guests in her own home in Rome. The sleeves of her robe pulled back to show forearms darkened by days of walking under the sun and weathering in the sun. Her skin was no longer the alabaster flesh desired by Roman noblewomen. Native Roman women weren't naturally fair-skinned. They spent their time outside with oils on their faces to protect them and require whitening makeup to better fit the ideal of beauty. Like her friend Poppaea, many noblewomen bathed in milk and used concoctions to keep their skin pale and unblemished. Or they applied chalk powder, white marl, and white lead to make it appear so. But Ya'el—who she was now—no longer had a *cosmetae*, a slave or servant to apply *cultus*, the makeup, perfume, and other beautifying treatments a Roman noblewoman enjoyed. That moment gave her a conscious jolt and hard realization she would never be that woman—Cleo—again. Even if it was possible, she did not think she could. Maybe in her heart of hearts, she had never been that Roman lady at all.

Ya'el stood facing them as Mathias and Rebecca took chairs, and Matthew sat on a long divan and called to Miriam, "Come sit next to me."

When Miriam did not move, Mathias, no longer smiling, ordered her: "Sit with us, Miriam—you do so little of that anymore. We have accepted Ya'el into our family. You dishonor Yosef if you continue to struggle with our welcome."

With a glare at Matthew, Miriam took off her cloak and sat next to him. She folded and draped the mantle across her lap and adjusted the leather pouch attached to a cord that looped over her shoulder.

One of the oil lamps on the small table between the two chairs sputtered several minutes later as Ya'el finished. "So, my husband, whom I and now a few others believe had a hand in Rome's great fire, came to Judea to stoke a war with your people. I do not know his purpose, but he has the power of the emperor behind him. I did what I could to stop the attack on your city and people. It worked but only briefly. Cestius Gallus, the 12th Legion's former commander, is dead, but Nicanor and I believe that death was not by his own hand. His wife, my friend, Octavia, has returned to Rome. And now Gessius Florus hunts for me and will kill me if I'm found.

"Nicanor has gone to Rome, and maybe... maybe he still plans to seek my brother Marcus Otho's help. Even then, I do not know what my brother can do. Yosef, Nicanor, and Sayid have saved my life twice, and I wish I could somehow help free Yosef. But I have no power to help... and I need yours for me and Elian to live. I have no one else... no place I can go."

The room was still as Rebecca refilled the lamp and lighted another larger one near the divan. The flare of light revealed the sadness that had come over Rebecca and Mathias. Seeing it, Ya'el's heart fell.

* * *

Miriam shifted on the divan, afraid that her family's eyes would turn to her, seeking answers to questions she'd rather not answer with lies. She stood, and the leather pouch swayed when she straightened. Its arc brought it close to the large lamp, and Matthew caught it before it struck. His fingers brushed an embossed section on its surface, revealed in the light.

"Where did you get this?" Matthew's eyes widened as he looked up at Miriam.

She pulled on the cord to free the pouch from his hand. "What do you mean?" Miriam tugged again, but Matthew's grip tightened. In her rush to get Ya'el out of Zechariah's, she had picked it up and secured it over her shoulder.

"This is—was—Esau ben Beor's..." Matthew's held it in one hand as his fingers traced the patterns on the leather. "That's his mark. I have seen him with this a dozen times." He tried to pull the bag from Miriam, and the pouch spilled a gold bar onto the floor. Matthew picked it up and held it under the light of the lamp.

Mathias was on his feet and took the bar from Matthew. "Miriam, how do you come by Esau's pouch? It was not found with his body." He shook the bar at her. "And where did you get this? Bars of this style are centuries old."

Miriam could not meet her father's eyes. Instead, she looked down at Matthew, who stared at the scar on her cheek.

XLI

Praeneste

The wine at the taberna had been fine, but then Quintus spent Tigellinus's coins to buy it. Still, the pounding head it gave him did not appreciate the jarring of the rough patches of the broad, uneven trail to Octavia's villa. The directions the innkeeper had given him had been clear enough. Her domus was set back from the more traveled road. He and his men had moved deep into a forest before the way cleared into an open area that ran up to the foothills covered with rows of trellises. The rustic domus was part stone and part brick under a roof of fired-clay tiles. Still, much of it was wooden, as were the surrounding out-buildings. Likely some were quarters for a small staff of permanent servants and the stables and equipment and gathering sheds for the seasonal vineyard workers.

Quintus and his men stopped on the broad flagstones near the front of the domus. He noted a youth at the stables carrying an armful of hay through a gate to a long, low, wooden latticework platform and piling it on top. He assumed that kept the fodder from lying on the damp ground. The boy brought two fingers to his mouth, and his sharp whistle cut through the cold air to echo just long enough for the vapor from the whistler to dissipate. A chorus of nickering preceded the six horses that trotted out of a defile hidden by a low layer of mist that still clung even in mid-morning. The gorge was likely excellent protection from the winter wind sweeping the pasture, but the promise of food brought them out. The boy, in his late teens at most, saw the visitors and crossed the broad yard.

"I must speak with Lady Octavia," Quintus called out to the boy before he reached them.

The boy looked at the other men dressed as legion centurions but with more elaborate helmets. Their tall *galeae* were crested with horsehair, and intricate detail had been worked into the metal. Their oval shields bore the gold figure of a winged woman, and the boy would not likely have seen the like of them before. "Why?" he replied, and then though he seemed uncertain, he followed that with, "my lord."

Quintus smirked at the boy's use of a title he would never claim, and he knew he was not attired in keeping with the honor of the address. But if he could find Nicanor and Cleo and share in whatever grand scheme Gessius Florus had planned, he would soon live as well as a noble. Someplace where he could not be found. "Just tell her... she has guests." He knew he leered, but so be it, and added, "With a message for her."

The boy nodded and entered the villa. He came out shortly, followed by a grizzled man who looked similar to the men beside Quintus, unlike most household administrators as he must be. "I must see Lady Octavia," Quintus told him.

"Felix, return to your work," the man ordered the boy, who turned back toward the stable. "Why do you *ask*... to see the lady?" He asked, tipping his head a little to study his visitor and his companions, suspicion clearly etched on the man's face and in his tone.

Quintus noted the man's emphasis on the word 'ask'... he chose to treat the demand as a request, and an appeal could be of no import and easily denied.

"It is about her husband, Lord Gallus." Tigellinus had told Quintus how to draw Lady Octavia out and not arouse any suspicions before he got his answers.

"Lord Gallus is long dead." The major domus put his hands on his hips, parting the thick mantle he wore to reveal a long dagger at his hip.

"I bring news about his death; she will wish to know it."

"What news?"

"That is only for the lady to hear. It will not take long."

The moment's silence grew until broken by his horses stamping on the flagstones as they grew impatient.

"Lady Octavia is not here."

Quintus steadied his mount: "Who are you, and when will she return?"

"I'm the lady's major domus... and administrator. Leave your news in a sealed message, and I'll see she gets it."

"I must give it to her personally."

"Who sends you here? The emperor?"

"No..." Tigellinus had thought that might be asked and had prepared him with a lie the woman might accept. "General Vespasian, who met Lord Gallus in Antioch." Quintus clamped his knees against the horse. He raised to look beyond the man and into the entrance to the domus. "When will Lady Octavia return?"

"It should be within the week... a week. You can return then and 'ask' again for the lady."

The *trecenarius*, the senior centurion and the largest of the four huge men—brought his horse alongside Quintus's and whispered: "Do not take that tone from this man; he is insulting. Will you let that stand?" The man's hand gripped the hilt of his gladius, a handsbreadth already pulled from its sheath.

Quintus noticed for the first time the finger missing from the legionary's hand and shook his head. "No, I won't. But that will come later after we've talked with Lady Octavia." He tugged the rein to turn his horse back the way they had come.

* * *

Quintus had grown tired of being on land... and even of the wine at the taberna. Waiting did not put coins in his purse... and the cost of feeding and boarding four burly men who loved to eat and drink was steadily emptying that purse of what he had brought with him. He pondered those men... Tigellinus had told him they had been loyal *speculatores augusti* recruited from the Roman cavalry. They were his operatives, enforcers... and killers of those judged to be an imminent threat to the emperor or his policies... And all that was decided by Tigellinus. A blast of icy wind accompanied the clatter of men entering the taberna. He looked up at the two—the most junior of the centurions—he had sent to Lady Octavia's every morning.

"She's returned, Quintus; got back last evening." Both men eyed the pitcher on the table and the cup of warm, mulled wine the scarred sea captain lowered from his lips.

Quintus waved two fingers at the innkeeper, who brought more cups. "One drink each, then go get the others out of the brothel. Then we go to call on Lady Octavia."

"It will be sundown before we get there, dark...." One man smacked his lips and eyed the pitcher, while the other offered, "Maybe we should wait until tomor—"

"Do as I say!" Quintus cut the man off and took the cups from both of them. "I don't care if it is black as Hades's gate. We still go... and now!"

* * *

The moon was rising over the tree line beyond the villa as they approached. Something—an animal—skittered in front of Quintus's horse and dashed for the trees across from the yard near the front portico. Close-reined, muzzle pulled down, the horse snorted and jerked its head. Another animal crossed at its feet, and the horse reared, dislodging its rider. Quintus got up cursing, rubbing the hip he had landed hard on, with his hand on the dagger sheathed at his waist. He grabbed for the reins.

"What is this... why are you here at this hour?" The major domus strode from the shadowed entry brandishing a lighted torch. His booted feet crunched on the gravel, and a heavy cloak billowed open to reveal he wore a cuirass, a breastwork of leather. The type used to protect the torso when sparring or training with a sword or spear. A short sword was sheathed on each hip, along with a pugio, the large dagger every centurion carried on their belt.

"You are oddly equipped, are you not... for a major domus?" Quintus commented. His men had already told him the man, Octavia's ill-seeming household administrator, had greeted him wearing such arms each day they checked on Lady Octavia's arrival.

"It's not... when you have unwelcome night visitors."

"You told me to come ask again... and it is not yet full night."

The man glanced up at the sky and the scudding of clouds over the face of the moon. "Close enough, I think."

"I'm here to speak with the lady."

"Come back tomorrow morning."

"No, it must be now. I have other matters to attend to elsewhere... but I must do this first. So, call Lady Octavia. Now." Quintus's voice cracked like the whip he had once used on the galleys.

"In the morning," the man replied calmly and moved his cloak to free the gladius at his right hip.

Quintus raised a hand, and the men behind him dismounted and came to his sides.

"Magnus," a woman's voice called from the entrance, "bring him in."

* * *

The hearth fire blazed and cast flickering shadows on the walls and on the people standing in the room.

"What does General Vespasian have to tell me of my husband's death?"

"Did you recently hear from a centurion named Nicanor?"

"What does that have to do with your news?" When the man had entered with the four soldiers and not alone, she had waved off Magnus, who had moved to block them. She now regretted it.

"It does, Lady, but please answer me."

"Yes. Nicanor served under my husband in the 12th Legion."

"What did he—this Nicanor—say to you?"

"He-he offered his condolences," Octavia stammered, then steadied. "He knew me slightly from Antioch... and respected my husband. And Cestius—Lord Gallus—thought Nicanor a hero for his bravery at Beth Horon in Judea."

Quintus shifted his gaze to the trecenarius across from him, standing next to Octavia's major domus. The man tugged at his belt and asked: "Lady Octavia... I'm sorry, but may I use the *latrinae*? It is cold out, and I would appreciate it."

Lady Octavia nodded. "Magnus, show him where it is."

The major domus hesitated, then bowed his head. "Yes, my lady. Follow me," he said, beckoning the man.

Quintus continued. "Did this Nicanor mention anything about a Lady Cleo?"

"No." Octavia moved away from the light of the fire. A spasm of alarm shook her; she hoped they would not notice it. She steadied her voice again: "Why would he speak of Gessius Florus's wife?"

"So, you know her." Quintus stepped toward her. "And your husband thought this Nicanor a hero? For Beth Horon?" He sneered. "It was an embarrassing defeat," he said and moved closer. "Where is Nicanor, and does he have Lady Cleo with him?"

"Stand away from her," Magnus ordered as he entered the room and drew his sword.

"Escort these men out, Magnus," Octavia quavered. "Now, please."

Magnus pointed his sword at Quintus. "You heard the lady... get out. Now!"

Quintus smiled at Octavia and turned around to reply. "No." He canted his head to one side and looked behind the man. "I'm not done yet... and I do not have an answer from the lady." He nodded. A sword thrust pierced the major domus's neck, and Magnus fell, choking on blood.

"Imagine, Quintus," the trecenarius said as he stabbed down into Magnus's chest. "Even out here, they have a sponge-stick and bucket of saltwater and vinegar to cleanse yourself when you're done."

Octavia bolted—trying to get out of the room—but did not get far.

Quintus grabbed the back of her head, pulling loose the coil of gray-streaked hair loose. Ivory hairpins fell out, and her hair flowed down her back. He took a fistful and dragged her to him. "Tell me where I can find Nicanor and if Lady Cleo is with him." His grip tightened as he yanked her to her knees. "Tell me where she is, and I will not harm you." He twisted and, with the other hand, not letting go, ripped a shank of hair from her head.

Octavia cried out, but with rage, not fear nor pain in her eyes. "Nicanor takes Cleo to her brother, Marcus Otho, in Hispania Lusitania. Now, let me go!"

"Do you still want to hear the news of your husband's death?" Quintus forced her to the floor, his knife out and at her throat. "I was paid well to kill him."

Octavia clawed at his good eye and missed, but she still scored gouges of flesh from his cheek.

Cursing, he shoved the blade in and, when she was still, wiped it clean on her breast. Standing, Quintus wiped his cheek with the palm of a hand. "Kill everyone... and burn it all down."

XLII

PTOLEMAIS

"So... being friendly with a centurion... and being an errand boy for Lord Cestius Gallus—none of that has served you well. Has it, Sayid?"

Sayid recognized the man from his previous legion auxiliary duty. He was a shirker who had received a minor wound at Beth Horon and boasted of his bravery afterward. But too many knew he was a liar and coward for any to believe him. Sayid was not surprised to find him now in the lowest auxiliary unit in the legion. Their unit was deemed useful only to do the scut work of the encampment. That kind of work was relegated to slaves in peacetime, but during war, the auxiliaries labored at it within a secured camp.

He ignored the man and continued unloading the wagon. It had been a great relief when the camp-prefect had returned with General Vespasian's validation allowing Sayid to return to duty and not be executed as a deserter. It wasn't a surprise he had then been assigned to the lowest of the low in the legion. Though it went unsaid, he knew his connection with Nicanor tainted him in the camp-prefect's eyes. Word had spread that Sayid had left the legion on a mission for its late commander, Cestius Gallus, who had also authorized his unprecedented absence. And then he'd been allowed by Vespasian to return to duty? It all raised too many eyebrows and questions.

Even those from his old unit who saw him in the camp shifted their eyes and turned from Sayid. He could not swear to it, but he thought some in the camp, even an *optio*, far senior to him, watched him with interest. That uncertainty and his worry over Cleo and Elian in Jerusalem kept him awake at night, so he was weary before his day had started.

Sayid sighed and bent to the day's task, full supply wagons from the port emptied and contents placed into their assigned storage areas. He would have to work his way out of this duty, and the only way was to show them he was too good to waste. They needed to know they could trust him. His goal now was to return to a regular unit. He did not belong in a company formed from the newest, least skilled, and least worthy. As soon as he proved that, perhaps he would not be watched as closely, and he could slip to where Yosef was being held.

He longed to check on his friend. He could also make inquiries about his father and confirm which legion he now served.

* * *

Gessius Florus looked up at Galerius Senna and kept to himself his satisfaction at the discomfort of the 12th Legion commander. Senna came from a long line of Roman patricians and hated being summoned to meet someone of lesser familial stature in an apartment over a taberna.

But where Senna had been given positions and enjoyed privilege passed on for generations, Florus had worked, manipulated, and maneuvered his way to powerful positions. He wanted finer dwellings and more refined things, such as he had had not that long ago. But he could forego them for now. His formerly urgent desire for wedding and bedding a highborn noblewoman had been burned away in the fire that enabled Cleo to escape. He wanted revenge on her but could not let such things distract him as he went after a greater prize. It was that prize—the promise of reaching it—that in Rome had caught the emperor's ear and given Florus the power even Senna recognized. He picked up the message Senna had brought him under the imperial seal. The letter had come directly from Nero and not Tigellinus, and that told him things must break his way soon, or he would face consequences of an unpleasant kind. The emperor pressed him, and there was the sharpness of a keen blade within Nero's message. There lurked a threat in the emperor's wording and the question about when the vast treasure from the Jewish Temple would be in Rome's— really in his— hands.

Florus did not have an answer, and that, most of all, stirred his anger and worry. Vespasian continued to bide his time, but soon the equipment he awaited would be here, and Vespasian must move his forces to an all-out attack on Jerusalem. Then the relentless pressure of the legions assaulting Jerusalem would crack that city, and the ensuing chaos would give Florus a path to the Temple and its riches. There was also the potential of taking the treasure from where the Jews were planning to hide it, should that come to pass. And that is what Florus hoped for most. With the correct information from his spies in Jerusalem, his men would take the treasure hidden in lesser amounts but easier to get to than within the Temple. Then a good part of it could be diverted and kept for himself. It would add up to be enough to make Florus a very wealthy man... rich enough to hide from the emperor.

If there was unrest in other provinces and Rome itself, Nero or a new emperor might become so distracted, he would forget about Florus. The discontent in the center and corners of the empire seemed to promise such imperial preoccupation. But Vespasian would not move on Jerusalem yet, and Florus's spies still worked to find out how and where the Jews planned to hide their treasure. He did not let his consternation show as he looked up at Galerius Senna.

"So, this Sayid has been assigned to the poorest duty. Good. Pay no attention if something happens to him." Florus returned the legion commander's nod as the man left. "Drusus," he called into the next room. "You followed and watched the camp-prefect when he ordered the Syrian auxiliary's release?"

"Yes, lord... I witnessed the Syrian leaving the holding cells. I'll know him at sight." The man's short, compact form did not intimidate until he got nearer, and his stance and bearing gave off a sense of restrained violence waiting to slip its chains.

"Wait for him to enter the town," Florus said. "He will come at some point. Then I want you to get him aside, out of eyesight, and question him about what he knows of my wife and the centurion, Nicanor. He was very close to them both and might know something of value to me."

"What if he doesn't wish to answer questions?"

"Make him."

"If he still won't?" The man smiled and rubbed his large sinewy hands together and loosened thick wrists that joined to his forearms of corded muscle.

"Then kill him."

Gessius Florus had yet to hear of the Jewish woman making any attempt on Yosef's life, but this Syrian, Sayid, was there for the taking. If he could not strike at Cleo and Nicanor, he would punish someone he knew was a friend to them. Then he would have someone call on Yosef's new wife to persuade her to act—kill her husband—or die. He might not dare to directly kill Yosef... but no one would care about the death of the woman if she would not do as she had sworn to him.

After a few moments, Drusus asked, "What if the Syrian answers your questions?"

"Once you have anything from him that can lead me to where Cleo has run... kill him. Make his body disappear. He was considered a deserter once, and he will be thought one again."

XLIII

Jerusalem

"I'll come with you," Ya'el called to Miriam as she swung a cloak around her shoulders and joined Miriam without asking permission. Miriam cast a narrow-eyed look over her shoulder as they went down the stairs.

"We must talk," Ya'el whispered as they reached the ground floor, where the sound of chatter came from the sitting room. Upstairs, she had heard these female voices and the male voices that echoed from the courtyard. The weather hinted at the coming of *Nisan*—she was learning the names of the seasons—spring was only a month away. Rebecca had opened the shutters and doors to let in a fresh breeze and to accommodate their visitors. A dozen women and men had called on Rebecca and Mathias to talk about Yosef's news that had spread throughout Jerusalem. The women had gathered inside, and the men sat at the table in the courtyard.

Ya'el had been shocked by what had happened the evening Matthew grabbed that pouch from Miriam. She had watched and heard Yosef's sister explain her possession of the bag Matthew recognized and of the gold bars. But even to Ya'el, Miriam's explanation did not sound right. Matthew, to judge from his disbelieving expression, must have felt the same way. This morning was the first time since that night Miriam had tried to leave the house on her own, and it was Ya'el's first opportunity to speak with her out of earshot of her family.

Ya'el followed Miriam out the door and matched her pace toward the agora. It was a beautiful morning. She had awakened to find it less chill, and the wild, heavy winds had become a pleasant breeze— the first sign of winter's passing. The wet weather had worn on her spirit, yet what the Judeans called the 'latter rains' smelled of summer and were welcome, for they nourished the barley and wheat crops. Earlier that morning, she had seen the first show of beauty in the apricot and almond trees in the courtyard and warned Elian to not disturb their fruit. The sky above was a cloudless blue, and the bright orb she shaded her eyes against shone down on them. Its rays warmed her upturned face. Confronting Miriam took some of her pleasure away, but she had to settle things with Yosef's sister. "We must talk," she said again to Miriam's back.

"We have nothing to talk about... please leave me alone and go back."

"Yes, we do... and you know it, Miriam." Ya'el scanned the area and noted the streets had only a few others headed to the market, but that would change soon. "At the shop in the Lower City, where you hid me from that man... I heard him talk about that man Matthew mentioned, Esau ben Beor. You talked as if you had been there at his death."

"You did not hear him correctly." The stern look shot again over Miriam's shoulder.

"I did... he spoke clearly. And I know what he said about Esau ben Beor, Simon bar Giora, your Sanhedrin president, Shimon ben Gamliel, and Yohanan ben Levi. He was angry at them all."

"What does that matter... especially to you?"

"I live here now, too. What you told your family about how you came to have that man's bag..." Ya'el hesitated, as she would not call Miriam a liar. "That does not match what I heard your Sicarii friend say."

Miriam stopped and spun around, checking to make sure no one was near to hear them. "What do you want, Ya'el? What I say to my family is between them and me. You—despite the lie, we must tell—are not family."

"Despite that lie... and I thank your family for it... I want us to be honest with each other." Ya'el stood her ground and did not flinch. "I've told you my true story... and I've heard and seen," she touched her fingertips to her throat, "what must be some of yours. The parts you hide from your family. I don't think you found that bag with its gold *mina* when you fell exploring a new tunnel on a whim. You're too serious for that. And I don't think Matthew believed you, either, even if your father and mother do.

"You're fortunate that young woman arrived with the news about Yosef," she added. Ya'el, too, was beyond relieved that he was alive, though a prisoner. "Matthew would have called you out on that, otherwise. Then they were all further occupied when that other man... Matthew's Temple Guard captain—your mother told me—showed up. Matthew has been distracted for days now, but I doubt he'll remain so."

As Miriam listened silently, Ya'el continued with a more personal note. "My father was dead to me once he married me to Gessius Florus. My brother is far away, and I'll never see him again. I cannot tell the few people I love, who love me... that I am alive. My life has fallen apart. I do not want to witness that happen to you and your family."

Miriam would not look at her and started walking again. Faster.

"Miriam!" Ya'el caught up with her and touched her shoulder; she saw the glint of tears in the young woman's eyes when she turned; a fleeting desperate sadness on her face.

"Miriam!"

At the call, Ya'el and Miriam both turned toward the young woman who waved for them to stop. Ya'el recognized her. She was the one who brought the good news about Yosef. Another woman, a little older, it seemed, though hard to tell because of her veil, was at her side as they approached.

"Good morning, Rachel," Miriam said, quickly wiping her eyes. "How are you, Leah?"

The woman nodded, and behind the veil, seemed to smile. A wince of some discomfort flashed in her eyes. "I'm so happy... for your family, Miriam. To hear that Yosef is alive brought joy to my heart."

* * *

Miriam saw Leah's eyes shift to Ya'el and said, "We're happy at the news and hope some way can be found to free him." She half-turned and said, "This is my cousin, Ya'el of Tarsus. The Romans killed her husband, and she has come to Jerusalem to stay with us." Miriam darted a warning look at Rachel, worried again she had said more than she should about Yosef being alive. Who else would have known that Ya'el's arrival in Jerusalem brought a note from him?

"Have you heard the news this morning?" Rachel asked.

"No... is there more, beyond that of Yosef?" Miriam saw Leah reach up to her veil as it loosened and came free in the brisk wind. A livid bruise covered her swollen left cheek, and her jaw was swollen. She felt Ya'el stiffen and heard her soft intake of breath.

Rachel did not notice their reaction at seeing Leah's face and rambled on. "They say Simon bar Giora, who harried the Romans so much they had to abandon their attack on Jerusalem... and then he beat them at Beth Horon... He and his men will be here soon. In a day or two. Isn't that wonderful?"

Leah, her hand still at the side of her face, turned to Rachel. "Stay and visit with Miriam... I must go. I cannot be gone long from home... He will be back to check—" She changed what she had planned to say.

171

"It was good to see you, Miriam... and to meet you, Ya'el." Leah's eyes beamed delight to Miriam. "I'm so happy Yosef is alive."

They watched as she turned and entered the crowd of people now filling the market.

"Rachel, you still must say nothing to anyone about knowing earlier about Yosef. If you do, it puts my family... and Ya'el... at risk." Miriam paused, and though she knew it already, asked. "What happened to Leah?"

The smile evaporated from Rachel's face. "After I went to your home to tell you the news was spreading, I was glad to finally tell Leah about Yosef. When she heard, it lightened her heart and face... she was smiling, though she hardly ever does anymore. I was with her when Yonatan came home. He told her something about meeting with Yohanan ben Levi, aligning with him, then he stopped and asked Leah why she was smiling. She told him, and he became angry and began calling Yosef a traitor. I said he was not, and Yonatan grew angrier and told me to leave. I did but went to see her this morning once he was gone. And she had been...." Rachel shook her head. "Though she's better, she is still unsteady, and I should go find her. Don't worry, Miriam... Ya'el, I won't say anything I should not." She turned and went in the direction Leah had gone.

"Leah's husband hits her?"

Miriam turned to Ya'el and saw her hand shakily stroking her own cheek. "Yes, he does." The bitter words soured on her tongue.

Ya'el's hand went to touch the small coin on the cord around her neck, hidden by her robe. She had heard Rachel whisper to Miriam the day she arrived at the gates of Jerusalem that Leah had given it to Yosef. In Ptolemais, he had given it to her to help convince his family she meant enough to him for them to take her in. "I feel her pain... I have felt it from my own husband's hand." The anguish in Ya'el's tone changed—hardened. She caught Miriam's eyes and locked on them. "We should make him feel what real pain is like."

Listening to Ya'el... to that indignation and desire to punish those who hurt women struck a chord within her. Miriam felt a need to loosen the hold on her own secret. It was already on the verge of slipping from her with her family. She ached to talk to someone—to confide in someone—who would understand. That twilight at the Women's Court, before she had seen Ehud and he had turned from her... she had sensed that Ya'el could be that someone. But she was afraid to try, to find out.

"Miriam..." Ya'el shifted to lean closer, a note of worry in her voice. "Who is that man staring at us?"

XLIV

MARIANUM

"How is she?" Graius groaned and tried to sit up in the low cot Nicanor had arranged next to a small brazier. The only window above him was still shuttered, though sunrise spilled light through the slats. The days had grown warmer, but the nights and mornings still carried a chill.

"Seems to be healing faster than you," Nicanor said. He was glad Graius's fever had passed, and the old gladiator seemed lucid as Nicanor entered the small room, took off his cloak, and hung it on a peg near the door. Since the wreck of the *Faustistas* and their staggering into the town, his morning routine had been to visit Carmenta. She was being tended to by a retired legion *medicus* who also had seen to the wounds of Graius and Nicanor.

"Well, I'm older than she is...." Graius grunted as he made it up, leaned back against the wall, and pressed the bandage across his chest that also wrapped his right shoulder. The fresh cloth applied the night before showed only a few new blood spots where his effort had broken the scabs. He had multiple puncture wounds in his upper chest and in the meat of his shoulder.

Nicanor's own injuries had also crusted over. He had a large patch of abraded skin on the plane of one cheek where a shard of rock had scored the flesh and nearly taken his eye. And the skin of his right forearm had been deeply scraped from elbow to wrist. He had removed its bandage just the day before.

"Will she be able to run again?" Graius asked. After the shipwreck, a battered Nicanor and Carmenta had found him splayed across a spur of rocks. The crash of waves had nearly swept him from the stone and back out to sea as Nicanor reached him. Before he passed out, Graius had seen the jagged tear on Carmenta's right flank that showed blood and white bone as she moved. Nicanor had told him how he had grabbed Carmenta's mane as they tumbled through the hole in the ship's hull. The backwash of sea yanked them away from the stricken vessel like an angry god's hand had snatched and slammed them into the rocks. But he had clung to the horse, and they had reached the beach, both bloody and injured.

"Craxa doesn't know yet if she'll be able to carry any weight. But he says he tended legionaries and their horses for two decades in the northern legions and has seen many wounds... in man and animal. He believes she'll heal; she's on her feet and walking more."

"What's wrong, then?" Graius knew Nicanor worried as much for his horse as he did about his human companion. The news about the horse was good, but the centurion's face was sadly stern.

Nicanor tossed his pouch onto the table next to the cot, and it made hardly a clink as it landed. "We're almost out of money... some coins were lost in the sea—thank the gods, not all. And now the costs...." He did not need to mention the retired legion medicus had not attended to their wounds out of the goodness of his heart. Nor had the taberna owner given them lodging and food freely. Nicanor sat and poured from the water pitcher; he saved the amphora of wine to help Graius with his pain. The man's upper chest and shoulder were a mess, but thankfully, no bones were broken, and the wounds were clean. The old gladiator also had a deep gash in his right thigh that Craxa had stitched up.

"I'm sorry, Nicanor... I have nothing left either." Graius reached for his cup, drank deep, and set it down empty.

Nicanor filled it again and handed it to him. "I know...." They had lost everything but the clothes on their backs, Nicanor's pouch of coins, and his waxed packet of orders from Vespasian. His pugio and Graius's sword, which the old man had sheathed between his shoulders just before being dashed into the sea, were their only weapons. "Now that the weather's clearing, they say there's a ship expected that routes to and from Massilia. There I can find an *argentarii,* and the banker can confirm I've money on deposit in Rome. I can draw enough to buy passage to Tarraco and from there on to Otho in Emerita Augusta."

"That's good, then!" Graius's eyes were bright as he smiled.

Nicanor shook his head. "But I don't have enough money," he nudged his pouch with the back of his hand, "for passage to Massilia, not to include Carmenta. I've barely enough for you and me. I can pay Craxa no more for her care. And no one will take an injured horse... she will probably be put down when we leave."

* * *

Nicanor kept an eye on Graius next to him as the man hobbled along with the help of a stout length of oak as a staff. The old gladiator was smiling. It was the first day on his feet for more than a few steps, and he was glad to be outside the small room and visiting Carmenta for the first time. *An aged, limping Hercules*, Nicanor thought with a smile as they approached the stable. His grin widened when he heard Carmenta's greeting nicker.

Craxa, the medicus, also greeted them with a smile. "She's up and moving about more this morning. Tight in that haunch, but then I had to cauterize and sew it twice to stop her bleeding. Her hindquarter on that side will never be as limber as the other; she'll favor it always from now on. But if you hadn't packed her wound with seaweed, she would have bled too much and died. I'm surprised she's able to remain on her feet this much. She bears her pain well." The man bowed approvingly at the horse.

Nicanor nodded in agreement. "She's a fine soldier... she'll not quit." Something in that made his thoughts flash to Cleo and Sayid. *Gods, please watch over them wherever they may be.* He saw Craxa turn from watching Carmenta to study him expectantly. Nicanor took a coin from his pouch to hand him but held it in his fist. If he gave it to the medicus, he would have to leave Graius behind, too. The old man was much better but could use the time to further heal, which would have a cost. But Graius had no money, either, if he could not reach an argentarii or make arrangements to move his retirement funds to where he could access them. Nicanor had considered going to the local legion camp, which was merely an outpost. He could prove he was a centurion. He still had his orders from Vespasian, including the part of them that verified his secondary mission authorized him to be outside of Rome. And as small as this garrison was, he could draw from the current pay owed to him. But he knew Tigellinus would have flagged all army posts to notify him of that activity. Then the Praetorian Prefect would know where they were and could easily trace them when they left. Likely he would send Quintus the sea captain, leading several men or more on the search.

Carmenta came toward them, and a slanting ray of sun showed clearly the ragged and raw scar, her large brown eyes shadowed with pain as she slowly moved closer. Her chest was now against the wooden rails, and she arched her neck over the fence's top rail and nuzzled his shoulder. He rested his forehead against hers, heard her breathe—felt her chest expand and contract—as he stroked her neck. "You're a good girl... I won't lose you, too. I owe you my life." He turned and gave the coin to the medicus.

* * *

Graius shuffled to the table, leaned his staff against it, and sat next to Nicanor in awkward silence. They had not been able to come up with

175

a solution to their predicament. Nicanor dreaded making the decision he feared was coming soon. Their tiny room was off the taberna's main room, and the sound from it increased as a girl brought in their meal.

"Seems you have more of a crowd this evening... louder than normal." The old gladiator smiled at her as she set the plates and a pitcher down on the table.

"The weather is better, and there'll be a *ludi*... they're all excited." She motioned over her shoulder back to the taberna's main room. "There have been no Games since winter began... and this one will be a special contest."

"What's special about it?"

The girl smiled and showed her own excitement at the coming entertainment. "Anyone can enter to fight... freedman or slave, or on behalf of a sponsor or owner. And there's a 1000-*denarii* reward!"

They watched her leave. Graius stood and went to his cot when the door was shut, stooped with a grunt of pain, and slid his sword out from beneath it. He raised it left-handed.

Nicanor saw the flash of pain cross his face as he brought his right hand up to press against his hunched chest and shoulder. "What are you doing? Put that down."

"That reward should get us all to Massilia. Right?"

"Yes. But with your injuries," Nicanor shook his head, "you can't fight." He left unsaid that he did not think the old gladiator could ever fight again, not as he had once been able to.

"I can fight well enough to beat some fisherman and some farmer locals." Graius's voice hardened.

Nicanor took the oak staff leaning against the table and approached the old gladiator. He spun the staff in a thrust that Graius awkwardly blocked and then backed away to the wall, chest heaving in pain. Nicanor brought the staff around and stopped short of another strike that would have gotten past Graius's weakened defense. "See? I'm sorry, Graius, but you cannot fight." Nicanor stepped back to the table and sat to eat. "So, I will."

XLV

Marianum

"The taberna owner smiled when I entered you into the Games," Graius said as he entered the room and leaned his staff against the wall near the door.

"He's probably pleased with all the business the Games will bring him."

"I don't think it's just that. I had to go find him down where they're building an arena next to the livestock corral. He's one of the chief promoters of the Games and hopes to make it a regular event. He thinks you look like a skilled fighter, and you'll make the bouts more exciting. But only if you don't kill your opponent too soon."

"I hope not to kill anyone. Did you confirm what we heard?"

Graius nodded and shrugged off his cloak. "No matches to the death... though I got the impression he thinks since it is combat, it's not a problem if an accident happens. The fighters can surrender or are beaten if they're wounded and unable to keep fighting. My opinion is that once you kill them... they cannot kill you."

"I have no desire to kill a man I have no quarrel with or anyone who is not an enemy of Rome. I'll fight to disable them as quickly as I can... no matter whether the taberna owner wants me to play with them instead."

Graius grunted his disagreement. "I checked, and there is no *lanista*, no facility nor formal training anywhere near... so you'll face self-trained locals, as I thought. The taberna owner said men from the garrison could not compete and asked if you were a soldier. I told him that though you look like a fighting man... you're passing through and plan to move on. If you survive."

Nicanor detected the teasing tone in Graius's voice with that last bit but held his smile and snorted. "I'll do my best." He opened the shuttered window and let in a warm breeze. It felt good on his face, and he drew in a deep breath. "I know how to fight."

"On a battlefield... but not in an arena." Graius sat at the table. "True, here you'll face only one man at a time. And I learned there will be at least three matches... if you win the first two."

Again, the teasing, but Nicanor chose not to respond. Fighting— to him—did not mean the same as it did to Graius, and he accepted the difference in philosophy. "What do you mean, at least three matches... if it's three... that's all, then, right?"

"I also heard from the taberna owner that he has sent word to his brother in Olbia, a town a half day's sail south, to arrange Games there under the same rules. Anyone can compete. Three matches determine the local champion. Then the two champions—from here and Olbia—will fight for the reward."

"That's not what we'd heard... but it means only one more fight. So, I must win four times to get the money we need. Did you hear anything about the men of this town, Olbia?"

"Only that it is much the same as here but without a legion garrison."

"So, likely the same quality of fighter, but maybe even lower since they do not have legionaries stationed in the area."

"I think so...." Graius replied, but he did not like the smile he'd seen on the taberna owner's face when he talked of Olbia's champion coming to Marianum. "The problem is that you have to use your own equipment. 'I provide nothing but the dirt to bleed upon,' is how the man put it. And all we have is your dagger and my *spatha*."

Nicanor went to the table where he had set the sword after honing its blade a fourth time. He had removed even the faintest vestige of a nick in the metal or a rolled edge that would catch and tear, not slice. More than one legionary had lost his sword by having it catch on something, get snagged, and wrenched from his hand. He picked up the weapon. Its weight, length, and balance differed from the short sword he had used all his years in the legions. Being a tall man had always given him enough reach so that his weapon's length had not mattered. "You've taken good care of this... it's a solid-made, fine sword."

"We have no armor for you. No helmet. No shield. No protection."

"Maybe I can get them from someone at the garrison." Nicanor noticed Graius shaking his head. "What?"

"I went and checked. The men there have been told to not let anyone have any army equipment."

"Perhaps if I talk to them."

"You would have to check in with the garrison commander, Nicanor. And you wanted to avoid being noticed and reported. I know you've not told anyone you're a centurion, nor have I. To the locals, you're merely a shipwrecked man who looks like he can fight."

"I think Craxa suspects, but he keeps his mouth shut and does not ask."

"Until you no longer pay him. Then he may think he can mention you to the garrison commander and pocket a coin or two if you prove to be wanted."

"Maybe," Nicanor nodded, "but if need be... I can prove I'm no deserter." That made him think of Sayid, and he wondered if he had returned to the legions. He hoped so since that would mean he had gotten Cleo somewhere he thought safe enough to leave her. He was glad he had persuaded General Vespasian to provide orders to allow Sayid to return to the 12th Legion. And if some in the legion had ill feelings toward Sayid... he had called in a favor that might help him.

"Back to the fighting you face," Graius interrupted his friend's thoughts, "it is different in the arena. It is deadly in a way unlike in battle when you have men around you who can come to your aid."

Nicanor understood. More than once, another legionary had blocked a thrust or throw that would have injured or even killed him. The shield arms and swords of the legion soldiers fighting together were the strength of Rome.

"With no men around you to block or hinder movement... use the sun to your advantage. Keep it behind you if you can. If the man is wearing a helmet... try to strike it off if you cannot get in a fatal blow... or enough to wound him and stop the fight. Feint to the body and quickly slash at the head. You might get an eye or slice the brow to bleed and blind him. That could give you an opening."

Nicanor listened and nodded, though Graius advised mostly the same things he had learned on more than a dozen battlefields and by killing more men than he cared to recall. He went to the window and craned his neck to look up and gauge the height of the sun. "It's near time. Help me get ready."

* * *

"Not quite the Circus Maximus, is it?" Graius commented as they approached the roughhewn wood and stone arena and its newly built gate near where Carmenta was stabled. She had healed well, and the day before—on seeing him—had managed a jerky half-trot to greet them at the fence.

Nicanor and Graius stopped before passing through the gate to give her two handfuls of salted grain. The horse nuzzled the centurion and nudged the hilt of the spatha he had set to ride high over his shoulder. Graius had rigged the sheath and drilled him to pull it and continue the motion in an overhand arcing slash. He never expected to use the move, but it made the old gladiator happy he had contributed something to the preparation other than words.

179

Craxa came out of a shed that stretched along the corral's fence and greeted them. "I've got her just about healed, Nicanor... so don't end this," he waved a hand at the arena, "with me having to stitch you back together, too."

"I intend to remain whole."

The medicus studied him. "That's all the armor you have?" Craxa waved his hand at Nicanor's crudely crafted leather greaves on his lower legs and the leather forearm cuffs that ran from wrists to just below his elbows. His chest and back were protected only by a thick, stiff canvas tunic, roughly made to fit his barrel chest. "Give me a minute...." He went inside the shed and came out with a cracked leather helmet and battered *scutum*. It was scored and nicked around its edges, but it seemed solid in the center, even if the shield had seen much better days.

Nicanor took the helmet and tried it. It would not go on, and he stopped tugging when Graius laughed at it, sitting half-cocked on his head. He handed it back to Craxa and took the shield. Its handle felt firm, with no wiggle to warn him of looseness. "Thanks—this will be of help." He rubbed Carmenta's chin, scratching where she loved it most, and rested his forehead on hers for a moment. "Let's go," he said, then turned and motioned at Graius.

Craxa picked up a satchel he had also brought from the shed. "I'm coming with you." He patted the bag and slung it over his shoulder. "Just in case."

* * *

Next morning...

"Was the man dissatisfied?" Nicanor looked up from daubing on his arm a paste of honey, vinegar, and some ground-up plant. Craxa had given him the medicine to slather over the ragged slash on his right upper arm below his shoulder and along the bicep. The wound was still raw, and Craxa's stitches not as well-sewn as those of his friend Aulus's, a medicus in the 12th Legion.

"Only a little... he hoped at least one bout would carry over to another day..."

"Another day of supplying food and drink. I bet he can't stop counting the coins filling his purse."

"The last man got a good one on you." Graius sat down to look at the wound. It was worse than the night before, with the swelling settled in and pulling at the stitches.

"Only by throwing a handful of sand in my eyes."

"Well, I warned you... whatever works. And in a place like this... there will not be the fine point of Games etiquette you might find in Rome. Too bad that shield came apart, but it was a good thing you were quick to drop it and parry the man's following thrust with your dagger. You deflected just enough to force his blade along your arm and not inches into your chest. I'm glad Craxa was generous enough to treat you without payment since his shield nearly got you killed."

The three men Nicanor had faced had been younger but equipped about the same as he. Though the last man had a visorless helmet and leather cuirass that protected his torso. "So, when will I face the champion from Oblia?" Nicanor asked.

"That's what finally pleased the promoter. Their champion arrived this morning, and you fight at *meridies*, with the sun directly above."

"Good. Afterward, we'll collect our money, and when the Massilia vessel gets here in a few days, we'll be on our way."

* * *

The sun was almost overhead, and there was no wind. The day had become more than warm. A trickle of sweat stung the slash on Nicanor's arm, though he had coated it liberally with Craxa's medicine and bound it tightly with a fresh bandage already growing damp from perspiration. He turned to Graius, who had joined him at the center of the arena. The crowd that filled every seat and place to stand and watch was restless and raucous with shouts to begin the match.

A *lorarius* with a leather-thong whip in one hand and a javelin in the other capered and paraded around them. The fool had irritated Nicanor at the matches the day before with his harangue and taunts. Graius had been surprised to see such in a rough-planned provincial gladiatorial game. He said, "In Rome, they're used to whip men or animals to fight better if they seemed reluctant."

"Do you miss this, Graius?" Nicanor asked. "The excitement of the crowd?"

A noise behind them—the sound of a mob now cheering—turned them toward the gate they had passed through only minutes before. Even at a distance... they saw the man clearly. His helmeted head with its crest, rim, and visor, and armored shoulders and chest rose above even the tallest of the people before him. They all quickly got out of his way. He moved closer, and soon they could see the sunlight dance off the carved amber breastplate. Gold cords—tassels, a dozen or more on each arm—draped moss-like from arms thick as an old tree's limbs when he raised them above his head. The scale armor plates of the *manica*, arm guards from wrist to shoulder, flashed in the sun. He brandished a short sword in one hand and a studded iron mace in the other. At his waist were two legion-style pugios, a dagger sheathed on each hip. Metal greaves protected his legs below the knees, and a full-sized legion shield hung across his back.

The sight stunned Nicanor. The man was bigger even than Dov, the Jewish Hercules at Yotapta—who until now had been the largest man he had ever seen. The armored colossus stomped to a stop a dozen feet away and loomed over them.

"Great Jupiter, it's a Samnite," Graius muttered and brought his staff up before him as if it were a weapon at the ready.

"What's a Samnite?" Nicanor asked but was drowned out by a trumpeting he had not heard in the previous day's matches.

"Welcome to Oblia's champion!" The taberna owner and promoter had climbed a small tower at the midpoint of the arena's seating and shouted down to them. "We are fortunate that weather forced a ship carrying the emperor's own gladiators to Leptis Magna to take refuge in a port near us. And fortunate that one of them wished to compete here. To stretch himself while they repair his ship. I give you Castor... twin brother to Emperor Nero's champion!"

The giant spread his arms and roared.

Nicanor felt it through the ground into his feet and legs as much as the ringing in his ears. Or maybe it was the din of a thousand voices screaming and the stomp of two thousand feet that shook the earth. As it subsided, he heard Graius again, barely loud enough for him to catch it.

"Great Jupiter..." Graius shot the centurion a worried glance. This was why the taberna owner had smiled.

"So..." Nicanor had absorbed the shock and began to settle his mind to what he had to do. He pivoted to scan the crowd and then returned to face the glowering behemoth who stood awaiting a signal. "Graius... do you miss this?" He wiped the sweat from his brow with the back of his left hand.

"No... not at all." The old gladiator had not taken his eyes off Castor.

"Now, tell me, what's a Samnite?"

"An ancient enemy of Rome. When they were finally beaten and brought into the empire, some of their soldiers became the earliest, fiercest, and most indomitable gladiators."

"What's the meaning of the gold cords hanging off him?" Nicanor pointed at them, which drew the massive man's glare.

"They are the number of men he has defeated in the Games in Rome... for the emperor."

XLVI

Martius 68 CE

Marianum

"If you fight him as you would any other man... you'll lose. He won't cripple you to make you surrender... it'll be worse."

"I know of no other way to fight." Nicanor shrugged, rolled his head, and his neck creaked as he loosened his shoulders and arms. The sweat had now gathered under the leather cuff on his right forearm, and it felt loose. He had tried to tighten it, but the bandage beneath helped it slip as he flexed his arm and rotated the wrist. Though most of the scab from the rocks damage had fallen away, the flesh was still tender, and the arm ached.

"He'll kill you. The emperor's gladiators always fight to the death. No quarter given... no mercy shown."

Nicanor kept his eyes on Castor. The giant had heard Graius and gave a curt nod... there would be no mercy.

Graius gripped Nicanor's elbow and lowered his voice. "Then fight as you best you can and as long as you can. Maybe you can tire this beast of a man, and he'll lower his guard, make a mistake. But if it comes to it, when all is lost, you have no more in you... try something you've never done before. Do it—if not for me... then for Cleo. My word alone won't sway Marcus Otho. She needs you."

"Clear the arena... unless you wish to fight Castor as well..." the promoter called down from his tower as the crowd jeered at Graius. Some began casting small stones.

The old gladiator limped away and joined Craxa behind the low wall on the arena floor that ran along the border, separating it from the stands. The retainer wall ran for a dozen feet on either side of the tower that held the taberna owner. Graius eyed the lorarius, who stood near them next to the opening onto the fighting area, ready to whip any slacker.

Craxa lifted the pack from his shoulder and patted it. "I should've brought more bandages; Nicanor's going to need them."

In the center of the arena, Nicanor circled Castor to study the man and his stance. The giant glared at him but did not move. When Nicanor had come around with his back to them, Graius watched Nicanor intently, but from the corner of his eye saw the lorarius shift back and forth on the balls of his feet. The fool danced out and flailed his whip at Nicanor's broad back, striking it with enough sting that the centurion spun to curse him as the man flitted back to the wall twirling his javelin.

Castor had not changed his position but turned with Nicanor as he arced around him, making another circuit. The mob's chant turned to screams: "Fight! Fight!" The lorarius moved again into the fighting area, the javelin extended to jab Nicanor from behind. This time the centurion spotted him and half-turned to fend the fool off. Then he stopped and smiled. Graius's staff connected with the side of the man's head, and the fool dropped unconscious. The old gladiator grabbed him by the scruff of his neck and dragged him back toward the wall while keeping his eyes on Nicanor and Castor.

Nicanor nodded his thanks to Graius, and that moment's distraction was enough. Without a roar or lesser sound, the pounding of the giant's mass through the ground gave Nicanor his only warning as Castor rushed him. The noise of the crowd vanished for Nicanor as he dropped and rolled. The heavy mace—its head larger than his own—shrieked over him and grazed his forearm, wrenching it aside as he tumbled to scramble out of the giant's reach.

Castor did not pursue him. He stopped and watched as Nicanor—wary of any movement toward him—used his dagger to cut a strip from his tunic to tie around his forehead to stanch the sweat stinging his eyes. The dart of pain in Nicanor's right arm told him the mace had glanced off the leather forearm cuff, catching it enough to twist and loosen its stays. The strike was not solid enough to break the bone, but the bruising reached deep. He felt the bandage underneath had slipped and wadded to rub off the scabbed remnants from the shipwreck's wounds. His arm was now slick with blood. Craxa's stitching had come undone, and the slash from his third match now gaped and bled.

Nicanor breathed heavily but in a sequence of deep drafts to charge his lungs and settle his mind. He must get to the place where everything and everyone around him slowed. That heightened state he had not needed to attain against the locals, but it had served him well on the battlefield. And this match—unlike combat on a battlefield—offered a single benefit. Graius, gods bless him, had taken out that distracting fool, and now he only needed to focus on the giant. He studied the colossus, who still had not moved. The man did not seem to mind the warmth of the day, and despite the amount of armor, he moved as if it were weightless. Nicanor looked up. The sun seemed directly above, but the shadow pooled at Castor's feet showed only a slight easterly spreading. The shifting of those massive feet alerted him.

Castor charged. His short sword glinted as it thrust and swung in a series of chopping attacks Nicanor met with Graius's spatha. Each block sent a shock up his arm and into his shoulder. Were it not for the quality of its metal and his deflecting twisting as he parried, the sword likely would have broken.

Castor breathed evenly and spoke for the first time. "You have some skill... not like those in Olbia I crushed so easily."

That word—the giant's emphasis on *crushed*—was a signal, and again Nicanor ducked and rolled from the sweep of the mace. He got to his feet and backed away, but not from the center of the arena. Getting pinned against the walls would be his death. He could not let the giant bull-rush him into them.

The giant closed on him. "You're unexpected for a fisher or farmer... but that matters little." Castor's blow with the mace knocked the sword from Nicanor's numbed hand.

The emperor's gladiator thrust with his sword as Nicanor spun to recover. He struck twice with his dagger in that second or two—while Castor's massive torso was half-turned from him. The blade punched into an opening in the scale armor where the plates had separated and bit deep into the giant's shoulder's meat. He tore it free, and the second thrust that missed his body caught and cut the strap securing the shield to Castor's back. It fell to the ground, and Nicanor scooped it up in time to block a roundhouse blow from the mace. The bone-jarring impact shot through him, and he felt the shield buckle as he bit his lip in pain. He gritted his teeth and spat blood. "I'm not a fisherman or farmer."

The giant gladiator pivoted on one heel. This time, the mace tore the shield from Nicanor's hands and knocked him backward onto the ground. As he hit on his back, the air forced from his lungs, the moment did not slow for Nicanor. It froze. He saw Castor, blood now coursing down his arm from the shoulder wound, with an animal's snarl on his face. Off to the side, he saw the shield close enough that he could scramble to get it. With a gasp, digging deep for breath, he found his movement returned but in slow motion. He watched Castor reach to his shoulder and then take the blood-covered palm of his hand and smear the head of the mace until it was coated crimson. But all was slow. So slow. Nicanor glanced at the shield again. He could reach it, but how long would it hold? He had placed trust just the day before in a shield that failed him. His belief in its false strength had nearly gotten him killed by one of the farmers or fishermen Castor had scorned. He had also dismissed them as worthless fighters and then learned amateurs can kill a professional, given the right circumstances.

Nicanor could grab the shield he had just lost... it was brand new and not worn down as the one Craxa had given him. Then with it, he could stand his ground and fight toe to toe as he would against any man. But Graius was right. Castor would break him. No... not break. Nero's gladiator would not allow him to surrender the fight. The giant would beat him to death just for the spectacle and the thrill.

And then Nicanor could never help Cleo.

Time's pace picked up. Nicanor saw the mace lift, and Castor's feet inch toward him. He got up and moved. But he circled away from the shield and toward where Graius's sword lay shining, where he had lost it in the dirt. He bent to pick it up.

"Yes!" Castor roared, and all the sounds from the throats of the bloodthirsty mob filled the arena. "Let me finish you as a man should die... with a weapon in his hand."

Nicanor gripped the sword and stepped toward the giant who waited for him. The blood streaming down his arm made the hilt slick, and he re-gripped it as he stopped just outside of Castor's weapon's reach. He raised the sword and, for a moment, admired the sunshine on the metal smeared with scarlet. With a nod at Castor, he rendered the salute Graius had taught him. Up and over, he sheathed the blade between his shoulders. He dropped his dagger and kicked it aside as he raised his arms and waited. The crowd had hushed, and he heard Craxa's cry but did not look where the former medicus and Graius watched from behind the low wall.

"Is he crazed?" Craxa turned to Graius to ask. "Call out to him to defend himself!"

"No." Graius shook his head. In the distance—from the corral direction—he heard a horse's scream. He wondered if it was Carmenta sensing Nicanor's peril. He studied his friend whose head was down, but the old gladiator knew the centurion's eyes were not. Graius looked up and gauged the sun.

"So, I was wrong. You are no more a fighter than the other locals... or maybe a little more, but not close to the men I've killed for the emperor." Castor stomped toward Nicanor, and within arm's reach, lifted his blood-glistened mace.

As the giant's arm came up, Nicanor took a half-step closer. His hand dropped to his shoulder to the hilt of the sword, and with a pull to clear it and sweeping slash, the tip sliced into Castor's visor opening. The spurt of blood and what was revealed as his sword tore the helmet from Castor's head showed the damage done. As the giant gladiator screamed and sagged, the man's hands went to eyes, and a curtain of blood spilled through them.

Nicanor spun and put all his weight and force into slamming the sword's thick pommel into the side of Castor's head. A crunching sound preceded the giant's slump to the ground. The centurion bent over him. "I'm not sure... but if I've left you one eye... you could join the cyclopes. They might welcome you." He straightened to see Graius limping toward him. He met the old gladiator just in front of the promoter's tower. The man, now speechless, gawked down at him as the crowd burst into a wild celebration of foot-stomping and cheers that rattled the wooden benches they sat upon. Nicanor held the sword out to Graius: "Thank you for the use of your sword."

Graius saluted him with his staff. "It's yours now... and well earned." he smiled and bowed.

"Let's get our money." Nicanor looked up at the promoter, who seemed in a hurry to get down from the tower. "If he doesn't pay, you must beat it out of him. I'm too tired."

XLVII

Martius 68 CE

Jerusalem

The Lower City

Miriam studied the leather worker's shop at the corner to make sure Kefa was not nearby. She crossed quickly into the alley, opened Zechariah's shop door, turned, and nodded.

Ya'el had waited on the other side of the street as instructed and did not move until she saw Miriam's nod. She gathered her robe and went swiftly to where Miriam waited to enter with her. Inside it was murkier than on a moonless night.

"Stay here," Miriam said and went further into the darkened room.

Ya'el heard her move unerringly, without a stumble or collision, and seconds later, a streamer of sparks flashed. The large lamp on a worktable along the wall bloomed with light as the wick caught.

Miriam turned toward Ya'el. "Why must we talk?"

Ya'el, still near the door, looked at Miriam. Other than a few short words, she had not spoken to her since leaving the strange man in the market and entering the Lower City. Miriam's stance and the angle of the light from the lamp cast half her face in shadow. Something in her expression made Ya'el remember a day nearly nine years earlier when she had watched as an *eclipsis* had swallowed the sun. Many in Rome, she included, had been frightened the gods were displeased and took the light from their world. Graius had held her hand as the shadow disgorged the sun and daylight returned.

Soon word spread throughout the city that Nero had taken it as a sign his reign was favored by the gods. Not long afterward, he had even had coins struck with his portrait on one side and a crescent sun on the other. But Nero was no god. Poppaea, her best friend and sister-in-law until Nero had made her brother, Marcus, divorce her, had told her of the emperor's inner dark. Her father and Gessius Florus had that darkness, too. The face men like them showed the world hid a creeping shadow—perhaps the *lemures*, shades, and malignant spirits many believed in—that either consumed them or, by its presence, revealed the men's true nature. The evil within. Nero, her father, and Gessius Florus all had that trait.

Ya'el looked at Miriam's half-illumined features and wondered at what had changed her from the girl Yosef had told her about as they drifted on the sea after the *Salacia's* wreck and thought death near. "We must talk," Ya'el said, "because whatever you hide from your family is eating away at you. I think you need to talk to someone about it before it consumes you entirely. I know how much Yosef loves you and his family. He and your family have saved me, and I want to help save you."

"You know nothing about me, and I don't need to be saved." Miriam shook her head as she picked up a hand lamp and held its wick with the flame of the larger one on the table. She turned toward the back room. "And I don't need to talk."

"It seemed you wanted to that evening at the Women's Court, that you wanted me to know something about you. I've told you my story, so you should know that I will not judge you."

Ya'el followed her into the room and watched as Miriam moved from a dim corner of the room, a tall mirror of highly polished brass framed in olive wood mounted over a shallow bronze basin. Miriam kneeled to open a concealed compartment in the floor beneath where it had been. "What are you doing?" Ya'el asked.

Miriam removed two rolled sheets of vellum, one larger than the other. She closed the compartment and pushed the mirror back over it. "I'm sorry for what's happened to you, Ya'el, but what you've gone through... is not my story." She took a large pack from a nearby table and slipped the vellum sheets inside. "Look, I have something to do. You can either stay here until I return or go back home."

"Let me come with you."

Miriam eyed Ya'el's clothing, the delicate fabric of her robe... the garments of a woman of the Upper City. "Where I'm going is not a place for a Roman lady."

"I've told you before, Miriam. I'm no longer a Roman... no longer a lady. Getting to Jerusalem from Ptolemais was difficult. I shed any trace of who I once was on that journey, and I have risked my old life to find a new one."

"You had Sayid to protect you."

"Yes, and I thank the gods for him and his help. But if not for me, he would have died before reaching here. And I would have been returned to my husband for more beatings or worse at his hands. Or raped and killed by the men who sought the reward he offered for catching me."

"What do you mean?"

"I killed a man to save Sayid's life... and I've learned there are other men who deserve to be killed."

* * *

Miriam could tell there was no regret in Ya'el's tone and saw the spirit that flashed in her eyes. She knew her brother, and it was likely that same spark had captured Yosef's heart... and had driven Gessius Florus to try to dominate her. It was a spark that Leah once possessed, but it had been beaten out of her by Yonatan. Zechariah had rekindled a desire to live in herself that she had thought extinguished. Perhaps she was wrong. Maybe she had judged Ya'el as a hapless victim and did not wish to be considered a victim herself. "I have some extra clothes here; I think they will fit you."

* * *

KING DAVID'S TOMB

They had reached the two desiccated bodies of the Romans. Miriam stopped to unroll the two vellum sheets and spread them upon the ground. Ya'el stood over her, holding a flickering hand lamp as Miriam took a large lantern and two torches from the pack she had prepared at Zechariah's.

"The small one is the map I found on them, and that's what showed me the way out. The way we just came in."

"What's the bigger map?"

"It's one Zechariah created...." Miriam traced several lines that spanned to the upper left-hand corner of the map. "This is what I've added to it."

"What is this place?"

"King David's tomb. My people sealed it long ago... and an earthquake did more to bury it."

"Is this where you found those gold bars and that bag?"

Miriam rolled the maps and stood, ignoring the question. "I want to explore more to see if there's an easier way in and out."

"You said there," Ya'el gestured at the passage behind them, "was how you got out. Then where did you come in, and how did that happen? Just exploring, like you told your family?"

Holding one torch to the lamp's flame until it blazed, Miriam raised it. She handed the other—unlit—to Ya'el, ignoring her question again. "But first, I want to see if there are any wells or a spring of water." She moved toward the passage entrance at the far side of the chamber without waiting for Ya'el to follow her.

* * *

The first torch had burned low before they lighted the one Ya'el carried and turned back. Miriam had answered no questions about why she wanted to explore this place, nor had she even spoken a word since they entered the passageways. Ya'el was glad to exit the central passage and see the chamber with the two bodies again. Her head was pounding. "Can we please stop here for a moment?"

Miriam picked up a skin of oil and refilled the large lantern they had left behind, and that had nearly sputtered out. She set it on a bench near one wall, and Ya'el sat next to it, rubbing her brow with the palms of her hands and wincing. "What's wrong?" Miriam asked, taking the waterskin from her shoulder and handing it to Ya'el. "Here...."

Ya'el took it, drank, then handed it back. "Since the last beating... sometimes my head hurts, and my eyes ache. Let me sit awhile, and it will go away."

Miriam sat on the ground and leaned against the end of the bench. She took out the large map and scratched a few marks with the tip of one of her daggers. They had found a side passage that led to a cistern and well. The cistern was dry, but the well held water. It was a little brackish but not foul. She would ink in the location when they were back at Zechariah's. Rolling the map and putting it away, she studied Ya'el, who had her eyes shut and grimaced. "I'm sorry your husband hurt you."

"He's hurt many... your people, too." Ya'el leaned forward and loosened her tunic from her throat, rolling her head and taking deep breaths. The kinyan around her neck swung free and the small coin twisted on its cord. She gripped it.

"You must mean a lot to Yosef for him to give that to you." Miriam touched Ya'el's hand, holding the kinyan. "Did he tell you about it?"

Ya'el shook her head and raised her eyes to Miriam's. "Only that it was special to him—that the one who gave it to him was someone he cared for—and it would prove to your family I came from him... and that I was important to him." Miriam thought Ya'el would say more, but she didn't; then Ya'el sighed and added, "In another place and another time... your brother and I could have found love. Now too much has happened to both of us."

Miriam thought of Leah, who had given the kinyan to Yosef, whose story had similarities to Ya'el's. She started to tell her of Yosef's love for Leah and what had never come to pass. But the sadness of it... and the despair in what Ya'el had just told her was too much. The weight of lost love was too hard to shift. It left no space to gather breath and speak of those things. "Do you think that when bad things happen... horrible things that change people... that they can no longer find understanding or love?"

"I don't know, but I hope they can," Ya'el said, sensing that Miriam was asking for herself. "That man in the market that stared at us, that you introduced me to... Hananiah. He seems to like you. Do you like him?" Ya'el hoped not. Something hidden behind the man's dark eyes had unsettled her. "Or is it Ehud, Matthew's friend?"

"Hananiah is just an acquaintance... a friend of sorts." Miriam seemed about to add something but did not.

"And Ehud?" Ya'el asked, and she was startled by the silent tears that now poured down Miriam's cheeks, cutting trails in the dust that had been kicked up as they walked the dry passages. "Miriam... what is it?"

Miriam gaped with her eyes clenched closed as if she were screaming at the top of her lungs, and Ya'el was shaken. But then she balled her fists and looked at Ya'el.

"You want to hear my story?" she asked as a challenge, "know what I hide from my family?" Miriam shook with emotion. "I was raped by two Roman soldiers. That's why I could not marry Ya'akov... and that's why no one will ever love me."

After a few moments of stunned silence, Ya'el slid from the bench and held Miriam as she shuddered with sobs that echoed with the flickering light that cast shadows on the wall.

XLVIII

Martius 68 CE

Jerusalem

The Lower City

"There's a basket for dirty clothes," Miriam said, pointing it out for Ya'el in Zechariah's back room. "And water and a clean cloth to wash up with."

Ya'el bathed her face, neck, and arms and put back on the finer clothes she had worn from the Upper City. When she left the back room, she found Miriam, her own face washed, in fresh garments as well, and as composed as she had been once her crying had stopped in King David's tomb. There, Ya'el's heart had broken for her. To have borne the unbearable silently for so long was unthinkable. At least with Florus's treatment of her, though she had spoken little of it, she had Poppaea to confide in until her death at Nero's hands. And even Octavia, Cestius Gallus's wife, was of a mind to listen to her troubles and offer sympathy and understanding. Miriam had no one until now.

Ya'el had not asked her in the tomb since that was too vulnerable a moment. But now seemed the right time, and she suspected the right place. "Were the two Romans, the bodies in the tomb, the ones who—"

"No," a pallid Miriam said as she shook her head. "I was attacked in a tunnel that runs beneath the Temple Enclosure and the *chanuyot*, the Temple shops near the Upper City. Zechariah moved throughout Jerusalem using the tunnels, and he came upon the Romans—and me—as they finished. He killed them both and then cared for me. He took me in and taught me how to defend myself, how to fight."

Ya'el nodded at the firmness and gratitude in Miriam's voice when she talked about Zechariah, the blind old man who had become Miriam's unexpected defender and mentor. In her own way, she felt the same for Graius. Despite his past success as a gladiator, he had not thought swordsmanship a skill to teach a girl. But he had approved of her interest in archery. He ensured her training with another retired gladiator who still performed feats of skill with bow and arrow in the arena. And she became better at archery than most men... even professional soldiers like Nicanor. She still remembered that day at her home in Rome and Nicanor's chagrin, and Yosef's, when she bested Nicanor's try at one of her targets.

That thought led her to think of Sayid, who had given her bow back without Yosef's family knowing of it. She kept it hidden beneath the bed in Yosef's room, which had become hers and Elian's. Cicero had begun his spring-time molt, and perhaps she could make some arrows. She had given the task of caring for the bird to Elian, who enjoyed Cicero's company, and it kept them both entertained. But the bird was not in the best of moods when molting. She should take him out more, and she wondered if she could find a secluded spot to practice with the weather growing nicer. Having her bow near was a comfort, and the thought nagged her that she might never use it again. Self-confidence grew as she'd developed a martial skill, but prowess required practice.

That ended her reverie as her thoughts came back to Miriam. "Who did Zechariah teach you to fight?" She had almost asked, *who do you want to fight?*

The clamor of shouting on the street outside interrupted Miriam, who had opened her mouth to answer. The outcry grew louder and became the sound of curses and fighting.

* * *

"Stay here," said Miriam, "and I'll see what's going on." She went to the alley door and stepped outside. Looking toward the corner, she saw a mass of people on the street—all shouting, many arguing face to face, and several men fighting. One huge man—a quarry worker fresh from his labors, with a covering of stone dust in his hair and on his clothing—swung a length of wood club-like at two men, either city militia or Temple guardsmen, who taunted him. A small knot of four men wrestling staggered into the alley, and she slipped her hand into her sleeve to grip the handle of a sheathed dagger. She kept it there until—not even noticing her—their struggles took them back onto the street.

"Miriam!"

She looked up and spotted Kefa standing just within the side door into his leather works. "What's happened... are the Romans here?" she called to him. As soon as she asked, she realized how foolish her question was. The people might run and hide from the Romans or race to the walls to help with defense. But why would they fight among themselves on the street?

"No, but a group of Zealots—ten men led by Yohanan ben Dorcas—arrested and executed three men. They were Moderates: Levias and Syphas ben Aregetes, and one of the Temple treasurers, Antipas. At the news, the streets filled with everyone who was angered about it and those pleased... everybody for or against the Zealots."

Miriam knew Antipas as someone her father and Matthew had spoken of recently. From what she could overhear of their courtyard discussions, it was about something to do with Matthew, Yohanan ben Zaccai, and the Essenes. They had spoken every day about the growing tension in the city, worried that it could end in violence that would bring chaos to Jerusalem. This, then, must be the start.

"Better stay off the streets until it's over," Kefa called to her and ducked inside, shutting his door.

But as Miriam watched, the shouting lessened, and the fighting turned to only shoving. The crowd on the street thinned as the clumps of angry men moved down the road. She turned and went back into Zechariah's for Ya'el. "Raise your cowl and affix your veil... we must leave now."

* * *

THE UPPER CITY

Avoiding the people taking the sloped path under the viaduct leading directly to and from the Lower City, Miriam and Ya'el went up the steps at the southwest corner of the Temple Enclosure. They crossed its colonnade to the Upper City viaduct.

Ya'el asked, "Why do some of them frown at you so, Miriam?"

Miriam had been quiet, thinking about her father and Matthew, two Moderates who had been long trying to bridge the fissure between what the Zealots believed and wanted and their own belief about what was right for Jerusalem. Matthew's good friend and captain of the Temple Guard, Eleasar ben Ananias, was a Zealot, and they had somehow gotten along. Why couldn't everyone agree, so they could stand together against the Romans? At Ya'el's question, she looked up and around. People were glaring at her, some muttering to each other between their sharp glances. "I don't know," she replied. But fear for her father and brother clutched at her chest, and she walked faster.

Minutes later, they entered through the courtyard's back gate and came upon the end of what seemed a heated argument. At the outside table sat her father and Yohanan ben Zaccai. Matthew and Eleasar ben Ananias were standing, both angry and red-faced. Miriam took

196

Ya'el by the arm and pulled her behind the trees that formed a row on either side of the gate. She held a warning finger to her lips and turned from her to listen.

"Perhaps I should not have confronted Yohanan ben Levi in the Sanhedrin meeting this morning," Mathias said. "And then he might not have retaliated so boldly. But I wonder where he heard this news of Yosef's marriage while he is still a prisoner of General Vespasian?" Mathias's beard bristled stiffly, jutting from his chin. "I doubt that it is true."

Yohan ben Zaccai patted his old friend's arm. "I'm afraid it is, Mathias. I heard it from the same source. I've known Jonah of Caesarea almost as long as I've known you. He is steady and would not lie."

Mathias shook his head. "That does not make true what he might have heard... and if true, it does not make Yosef a traitor; there must be a reason. Rebecca returned from the market in tears at how some treated her there. This Gischalan, who cowardly fled his people in the night without telling them, has no right to declare Yosef a traitor. And he has turned Yonatan into one of his rabble-rouser's that have been leading men through the streets to denounce Yosef." Mathias's eyes narrowed with anger.

"And that on top of Zealots killing those three men." Matthew frowned at Eleasar.

"I did not order that, Matthew," Eleasar replied. "I've said it many times now, but no more. Dorcas took it upon himself to have them killed."

"How did he gain such authority within the Zealots? And why did *you* vote to annul the position of our current high priest and bring in one that favors the Zealots and hinders open discussion?"

"Your high priest was ineffectual, Matthew..." Eleasar shifted his gaze and pointed at Mathias and Yohanan. "And Shimon ben Gamliel gives way to Yohanan ben Levi. You all know Jerusalem needs stronger leadership."

"True, ben Levi is a master at distracting any focus on his own shortcomings by pretending to be strong. His deceit must be stopped somehow. But Phannias ben Samuel, your choice for high priest, is an unlearned outsider and not even from Jerusalem. How is that strong leadership for our city? Or do you plan to do with him what that Gischalan has done to the Sanhedrin's president, Shimon ben Gamliel? Make him a puppet that will do what you want?"

"Mathias," Eleasar leaned to strike his hand on the table, "that choice was made by drawing lots to select a high priest not connected by lineage with a royal family or with those the Romans chose for Jerusalem. We have talked too long, trying to come to an agreement. Earlier today, I heard the speech Ananaus ben Hanan gave with Yoshua ben Gamla at his side. They have experience as high priests, and they're Moderates, and they condemn what Zealots believe. There must be no talk of peaceful resolution with Rome like they suggest. The Sicarii also believe... we will fight as long as we can and never surrender. I will no longer listen to any Moderate"—he turned to Matthew—"even you and your father."

They watched the Temple Guard captain leave through the house. Matthew pulled a chair out and sat. "I cannot change his mind."

"We've reached a point where no one sees reason, my son." Mathias turned to Yohanan ben Zaccai. "With Antipas dead, hiding the Temple treasure will become harder."

"Yes... and I hope Eleasar will not now choose to obstruct that work and make things more difficult."

"He won't," said Matthew. "He knows we must save what we can from the Romans. As much as he and the Zealots wish to fight the Romans... he knows we cannot win. As best he can, he will still help hide the treasure from them."

"Before we combat the Romans," Mathias said, "we may well have a battle within our walls. I listened to Ananaus's speech too. He exclaimed he would rather die than 'see the Temple taken over by blood-letting Zealot villains or see the people of Jerusalem do nothing about it.' Afterward, he immediately began recruiting men and arming them to fight the Zealots for control of the city. They will not let that stand... the Zealots will respond in kind."

Mathias looked at Yohanan. "You must leave today for Qumran. Tell Nahum to proceed. He must list the Temple treasure site locations on something durable and make copies we can secure. Who knows how long the treasure will have to remain hidden before the Jewish people can retrieve it?"

* * *

The two older men rose and went inside. Through open windows, Matthew saw Elian moving from room to room, helping his mother. The boy had begun to follow her everywhere, serving as he was able. The smile on her face at having a child in their home again—she longed for grandchildren—warmed his heart. Lessening for a moment some of his worries. A green feather drifted down, and an angry squawk followed. Matthew looked up at Ya'el's parrot on the broad sill of her bedroom window and thought, *Did that bird say,*

198

"Temple gold"? Cicero, in his new woven-reed cage, sat brooding and looked down at him.

XLIX

Aprilus 68 CE

Massilia

The city was built upon a rocky plateau on a promontory connected with the mainland by a narrow isthmus. Formed by a small sea inlet, the excellent harbor was about half a mile long and a quarter of a mile broad, with only a narrow opening. Three small islands sat nearly opposite the port entrance, and many ships were anchored at the largest. The port lay at the feet of the sprawling city, and both were well walled. At the town's heights stood a citadel, the Ephesium, and the temple of Delphinian Apollo, remnants of the town's Greek origins. A sailor had pointed it out to Nicanor as they entered the port.

"A pretty sight... and it can be well defended, judging by its look," Graius commented. He gripped the rail as a swell shifted his weight onto the leg that still pained him. The wound Craxa had stitched remained feverish and sore to the touch.

"I'm glad to see it," said Nicanor. "From here—soon, I hope—we can move on and get to Emerita Augusta and Otho." Nicanor caught the grimace on the old gladiator's face and his grip on the rail. "We'll get off... get Carmenta stabled and arrange a room for us. Then I'll find a medicus—one better than Craxa—to see to your leg." Graius did not object, which said more about his discomfort than any show of pain as the old man favored his leg. "Then I'll see one of the *argentarii* about the money we need."

"I've thought about that, and I should see him too."

"Why? I have enough for the passage for Carmenta and both of us to Tarraco and a horse for you once we get there to carry you on to Emerita Augusta."

"I should have paid my share of our expense from the beginning. And there's something important I must take care of. What money I have is largely from Cleo, my pension when I left her family's service."

"What do you mean?" The deck tilted slightly again as the wind shifted and the ship creaked. They had drawn near the busy mainland dock that ran along the water directly beneath the city, the dock one of the wide berths kept for livestock carriers. The town thrived as a significant Roman port that served the inland provinces' demand for Roman goods and wine. The vast vineyards near Massilia exported in great quantity, and commerce stemming from the region fed Rome's insatiable need for new products and slaves from the northern and western provinces.

"I'm old, not as strong as even when we left, and we still have far to go... better to give that money to you, Ni—"

Nicanor cut him off. "I'm not taking your money. You can pay your share of expenses. But that's all."

"You didn't let me finish. I want you to give that money to Cleo. Gessius Florus has surely seen that she is cut off from her family money and has access to none of his. So, she has nothing. I want her to have what's left of what she gave me."

"What if you live? And only the gods know if I'll ever see her again."

"Then you can take care of me in my even older age or give the money back if we find Cleo or she finds us, and I can then give it to her." Graius had caught something more in the centurion's words that was not about the money. "I know you care for Cleo, my friend." He clasped Nicanor's shoulder. "If we—if you—don't see her again... then use the money for yourself. Find peace somewhere."

Nicanor shook his head. "I won't take your money for myself."

"Then spend some of it to have a stone marker carved for me. Put it somewhere near the Temple of Hercules... and maybe one day, many years from now... someone will come upon it and say my name. And even if just at that moment, I'll not be forgotten."

"You will not be forgotten, Graius, I swear. Besides," Nicanor rubbed the scarred flesh of his forearm and tapped the hilt of the sword over his shoulder, "I remember when and where I got every scar I carry. This will remind me of who taught me something—when I thought there was no more for me to learn—and it saved my life."

* * *

Nicanor entered the *insulae's* ground floor room and wrapped the bundle of clothing in two cloaks on the second bed. The room was bare of anything but the simplest furnishings, and it was on the port's noisy main street, but it had been cheap.

"You just missed the medicus," said Graius, who lay on a bed against the wall, away from the street. His leg was bandaged from above the knee, nearly to his crotch. A blot of fresh blood had seeped to spread in the center of the clean linen bandage.

"*Futuo!*" Nicanor looked at the old gladiator's leg. "He had to cut it open?"

"Craxa neglected to get all the stone out." Graius flicked his hand at the three rough, red-smeared gray chips the size of the end of his thumb, sitting on a stained cloth on the table next to the bed. "He says I must not rip out his stitches, must keep it clean, and must use this salve." he pointed to a hand-sized pot also on the table. "It will heal, and I should have no more pain from it." Graius studied the centurion, whose brow remained clouded by a frown. "What's wrong? Several days waiting on the money's confirmation and then a few more on the vessel, and I should be well enough to ride once we reach Tarraco."

"That's the problem. I went to see the port master about a passage to Tarraco. Some pirate named Anicetus has been ravaging between here and the eastern coast of Hispania Lusitania. Survivors say he chases ships down, strips them of what he deems of value, and sinks any merchants who don't stop at his signal. Or he sinks those that do heave to but who raise his ire by not having anything worthwhile. So, few ships will sail that way right now until Rome sends army galleys to patrol the sea lanes."

Graius studied his leg. "I have no desire to end up in the sea again."

"Nor do I," said Nicanor. "But..." He pointed at the blood-splotched bandage. "You can't ride with that. So, we must wait, anyway."

"The money handler said the transfer request and return of its confirmation via the *cursus publicus* would take about eight days, right?"

"Yes."

"That will give time for me to mend, then I can drive a mule-cart, and that won't tear open the wound. And I'll tow a packhorse behind that I can ride once I'm fully healed or if the road becomes too bad for the cart. But with all the trade into and from this city, the road should be decent for some distance."

* * *

Nine days later...

"Where are the dispatches from Rome... those from the Praetorian Prefect's office?" asked the garrison paymaster of his clerk as he entered. A name had caught his ear. Boudilatis, Massilia's most prominent argentarii, had mentioned it at the taberna. The money handler had commented that the man he had recently met, Nicanor, was a senior centurion. It was odd that a centurion had not checked in with him for his pay nor reported to the garrison commander.

"Here, sir." The clerk set a large sheaf of parchment—some single sheets, several strapped together by a cord—on his table. The paymaster worked through the first dozen before he found it. He checked the routing, and it showed a copy of the dispatch was to be held at every stop on the empire's network of roads and stations west of Rome. So, Lord Tigellinus himself was to be notified of the appearance or word of a centurion named Nicanor or any centurion by another name that carried orders from General Vespasian. He set the prefect's dispatch aside.

"Call a courier to come here," he ordered the clerk and quickly wrote what Boudilatis had told him over their cups of wine. He quarter-folded the sheet, closed it with a blob of wax and stamped it with his seal, then placed it inside a waxed leather sheath and sealed that, too, just as the courier entered his office. "This goes out right now to Rome." He handed the packet to the messenger. "It goes to the Praetorian Prefect personally. The soonest it can reach him."

He watched the rider hurry from the room and hoped the prefect's promise of a reward would be kept.

L

APRILUS 68 CE

PTOLEMAIS

The men of the 12th Legion talked about a day when they would return to a real battle against the Jewish rebels. Yes, they had patrols and skirmishes and even destroyed a dozen poorly defended lesser towns... villages. But that was not enough for the veterans of Beth Horon, who wanted to wipe away that humiliating defeat. Their satisfaction had been denied too long. Even so, Vespasian waited, and the men speculated. Why?

Sayid heard them grumble every day and wondered, too, but he had no wish to be part of an attack on Jerusalem. He *was* tired of the duties he had been assigned, laborious tasks he had not done since his early days in the legion. Despite the shipwreck of the *Salacia* and all that had happened to him since ... he still thanked the random whims of the gods he had been assigned to travel with the Lady Cleo. That had made the difference and led to his meeting Nicanor. When they returned to Judea from Rome, the centurion had brought him into a more prominent position in the legion, as his orderly of sorts. Now those who had helped him, who had become his friends, were gone. Nicanor was off in Rome on a mission for General Vespasian. Cleo, pretending to be Jewish, was hiding from her husband's wrath—safely still, he hoped—in Jerusalem. And Yosef was a prisoner in chains. Sayid must try again to see him. If just to give his friend some comfort that he had seen Cleo safely into the care of Yosef's family in Jerusalem.

He guided the wagon loaded with bundles of arrows and *falarica*, ammunition for the ballistae, to the storage area. The six-foot-long, iron-shod, thick-shafted javelins rode upright in the bed of the wagon. They rippled like a harvest of sharp metal-tipped stalks that also rattled as he rolled along. The supply ships had brought a vast quantity. And they weren't just deadly in their sharpness and brute force. General Vespasian had seen them used as incendiary weapons in Germania and Britannia with much success and believed in their value. As Sayid unloaded the shafts, armorers took the heavy javelins to workshops for further preparations. They would wrap and secure a long, wadded cloth sheath below the sharp metal tip and then dip it in pitch and sulfur. Ignited at launch, the bolts would strike any wooden barrier, tower, or gate with enough force to lodge and spread their fire. Or they could be shot over walls—rain fire from the sky—to land within. A learned officer had explained. "Each will be hurled like a thunderbolt and cleave the furrowed air with a flickering flame, even as a fiery meteor speeding from heaven to earth dazzles men's eyes with its blood-red tail. And when it strikes, it will kindle a fire which burns until all the woodwork is utterly consumed."

Cestius Gallus had not had these weapons when he last took the 12th Legion against Jerusalem. This time Vespasian planned to make full use of them—whenever he finally attacked—and had ordered them from Rome along with dozens of reinforced rams.

Sayid's recent days had been spent moving arms from the supply ships at the docks to the encampment, then unloading them. It was not the work he wished to do, but the only thing that would change his assignment would be orders to form the legion to march against Jerusalem. Though he did not want to attack the home of his friend and the city where Cleo now hid, only an attack would allow him to show his worth. If only he could find his father and show him.

As he climbed back onto the wagon, he saw the man again watching him. He had no idea who he was, but sometimes he would look up and see him nearby. When Sayid looked his way, the man would casually turn and go. Sayid ignored him as he readied to return to the port for another load. At his next glance, the man was gone. *Tonight*, Sayid thought, *I'll go into town... and if he follows me, I'll not let him get away before I find out what he wants.*

* * *

THE PORT TABERNA

Sayid had passed the taberna a few times since returning to the legion but had not entered—he was not much of a drinker. He cared little for the company found in a room full of drunken legionaries and his fellow auxiliaries drowning their boredom in cheap wine or beer if they had only a few coins to spend. But on his return, he had been surprised to discover that his pay had continued while he was away from the legion. It seemed they considered he'd been performing duties under official orders legally issued by the legion commander. That was what the Roman army went by, and his money was accounted for in the legion's records. He had accumulated nearly 115 denarii, so he enjoyed a good meal and wine for a change instead of remaining at the camp for the usual rations. Fortune—or misfortune—had him sitting at the same table where he had last seen Nicanor. Sayid missed his friend. His last sight had been of the centurion's concerned expression as he and Lady Cleo left him, expecting to see Nicanor again soon so he could take Cleo to Rome and out of Gessius Florus's reach.

Thoughts of Nicanor and concern about what was to come for his role in the legion were replaced with worry about Cleo. Sayid assumed she was still safe in Jerusalem. Yet he had heard how the Judean leadership was at odds, full of suspicion of each other. The city seemed to face as much danger from its own people as it did from the Roman army. Unused to the drink, Sayid unsteadily rose from the table and staggered against the man who had been seated next to him for most of the evening.

"Steady there, soldier." The man reached out a large hand that gripped Sayid's arm.

He let go as Sayid straightened and rubbed where the man had squeezed hard. "Sorry," Sayid apologized and pushed through the crowd toward the door.

Outside, the night air had the smell of rank water and saltwater-soaked and rotting wooden pylons—and many other things seen or unseen that were usually awash in a port. He did not care to identify those. Sayid walked along the quay until it joined the street lined with shops to take him to the legion encampment road. His thoughts were on trying to see Yosef again when he heard steps behind him. A crossing breeze swept away the waterfront's fetid odor that seemed so much more pungent at night than in the day, and the steps behind him faded in the wind. It was not long before the stone beneath his heels turned to a graveled-bed road. Then he heard the crunch of steps again that stopped when he stopped. It must be that man watching him. Now he would find out. Sayid spun around. "What do you want?" he demanded.

A man stood in the moon-shadow of a tree along the road. "To ask a few questions," he said.

"Who are you?" This was not the man who had been watching him in the camp... this one was much shorter. "Wait... you were in the taberna."

"It's about your friends...." The man flexed his hands as he stepped into the moonlight and beckoned Sayid to join him off the road. "It's important we talk about them."

Sayid heard the snap and crackle as the man stretched his hands again and rotated his thick wrists. He seemed unarmed, but his corded arms hung at his side from the short sleeves of a tunic tight across broad shoulders and the trunk of his chest. The man took a few steps back further from the road as Sayid moved toward him.

Sayid stopped an arm's length away, blinked and weaved a bit, then straightened. "What do you mean... my friends?"

"Tell me about Lady Cleo... where is she?"

"I know no one by that name." Sayid turned from him, but an iron-grip on his shoulder stopped him halfway.

"Don't lie to me... you know her." Drusus's right hand shot up to grip Sayid by the throat to twist, turn, and shove him deeper into the shadows of the trees off the road. "And you know that centurion, Nicanor. Lord Florus wants to know more about him, too." He squeezed tighter.

"I..." Sayid used both hands to loosen the man's grip. He could not. "I do not know them," he gasped. His hits to the man's chest and stomach had no effect. He let his knees buckle, his weight fall, and as he dropped... he punched this tiny Hercules where there was no muscle to protect him. The man exhaled a grunt and grabbed his crotch with his free hand, but the one throttling Sayid did not let go. The man clung to him like a starving dog to a bone.

Sayid could not breathe, and the shadows grew darker around him. Between the limbs of the tree above, he could see the edges of a bright moon. He heard the crunch-crunch-crunch of someone running on the road and then that someone slammed into the man choking him.

With a gasp, clawing for breath, Sayid sank to the ground and watched as the larger shadow hit the smaller one again with a clubbed fist. The short man staggered, turned, and fled into the darkness away from the road. The taller man, still mostly in shadow, the gleam of a bronze forearm cuff on his brawny arm, reached down to offer a hand to Sayid to help him up. A ray of moonlight revealed his face as Sayid took it and struggled to his feet.

"You!" he cried. "The man from the camp... who are you?"

"A friend of your friend...."

LI

APRILUS 68 CE

ROME

"Since you have his ear," Gaius Sabinus said, shaking the sheets of vellum from Lucius Rufus, "will you tell him of this?" He leaned forward. "It's no longer a rumor when the emperor's governor of Germania Superior confirms it. Julius Vindex, governor of Gallia Lugdunensis, has openly rebelled. He calls for Servius Galba, governor of Hispania Tarraconensis, to become the new emperor."

Tigellinus studied the man who had overcome his lowborn position to become co-prefect of the Praetorian Guard. Sabinus was a quiet one who preferred that Tigellinus take the more prominent and public role of dealing with Emperor Nero. He was the son of an imperial freedwoman and the renowned gladiator Martianus, though he claimed a noble father. Sabinus was valuable because of his popularity with the Praetorians, though that usefulness came only when Tigellinus offered rewards. The man had been quick to take advantage of the same sorts of opportunities Tigellinus himself had taken. Both had roles in the Roman administration because the previous officeholders had been executed for involvement in the Pisonian conspiracy. He took the report Sabinus held out to him. "Yes, I'll tell Nero," he said, "and I'm sure he'll respond by ordering the northern legions to deal with Vindex. That will soon restore confidence in his rule."

"The empire's response must be swift and sure. There are other provinces also muttering their discontent. Something like this—someone like Vindex—could provoke a similar escalation elsewhere if they see any tolerance for disobedience."

The co-prefect's words were precisely the form of an imperial official's righteous demand to end a threat to the empire. Tigellinus knew the man who sat across from him was as shrewd politically as he, maybe more so, given his origin and harder climb. The throne of power Nero sat upon had uneven legs and had begun to totter. Both prefects knew that predators seek vulnerability in their prey.

"Here in the city," Sabinus said, "we have more he should be concerned about as well. The emperor was too quick to punish the two Christian women. Basilissa and Anastasia were Roman matrons of rank and wealth who made it known they followed the late

Christian leaders, Peter and Paul, and their voices were heard by many."

Tigellinus scoffed. "They would still be alive if the 'ladies' had quietly followed their newfound faith. And not gone around collecting the remains of executed Christians—martyrs as that religion's believers see them—and performing a public burial service for them. Since the great fire, the emperor has no lenience for Christians."

"Still, to torture them as the emperor ordered creates more unrest among the citizens, even some within the army who find that religion appealing. After all, their tongues were torn out, breasts and feet cut off, then they were burned and beheaded." Gaius Sabinus rose, shaking his head. "Even dead, their actions in life still speak for them... and others still listen."

Again, Sabinus's tone suggested to Tigellinus that the man was little bothered by the growing public displeasure with Nero. That was the sign of a man whose personal agenda and plans could alter to fit any circumstances. He watched the co-prefect leave and thought, *I have aligned my fortunes with Nero. Perhaps too much so.* He set aside Lucius Rufus's report on Vindex's rebellion and picked up another about the uprising in a different province. That was the people's response to the emperor's growing urgency to crush the rebels in Judea and free Gessius Florus to do what had long been planned. Once he stole the Jewish Temple treasure, it would help to replenish Rome's coffers. The continuing disruption in taxes and the new ones developing had reached a critical point, and Nero could not stop spending.

He took Vespasian's report over to the window to catch the late afternoon's waning sunlight and re-read it. The general was not as wordy as Lucius Rufus—his message was brief. His legions had received all of their supplies and equipment. But he continued to wait for the growing internal strife within the Judean leadership to weaken the will of Jerusalem's people and the city's defenses. He read aloud that part: *The rebels seem close to tearing their city apart from within. I can then more easily take the city, in less time and at a lower cost in men and materiel.*

Tigellinus sighed. He must now speak to an emperor who had grown less inclined to listen. And he must convey the unpleasant news of Vindex's now-public treason and Vespasian's decision to further delay his attack on Jerusalem. But before he called on Nero, there was another matter to attend to that might have more grave personal consequences. He must meet with Quintus to make further plans. The sea captain had returned to tell him that Lady Octavia had been killed, 'regrettably.' But had confirmed that Lady Cleo was traveling with that centurion, Nicanor.

He shuffled a stack of scrolls on his desk to find the dispatch he had received that morning. The garrison paymaster reported that Nicanor was in Massilia. There was no word whether he had Lady Cleo with him, but the report confirmed he was headed west, which could only mean he was meeting Otho. Tigellinus cared little for finding and capturing Gessius Florus's wife. He was unsure how that would hasten Florus's efforts, and their marital issues were of little import to any but themselves. But recent events in the provinces made him question Nicanor's real purpose for bringing Cleo to Rome. Vespasian had sent Nicanor to Rome with her and now announced a delay in attacking Jerusalem. Vindex rebels and openly declares his allegiance to Galba, pushing the man to depose Nero as emperor. And Galba's closest supporter is Marcus Otho, Cleo's brother. Nicanor was now headed west toward Otho. Once Lady Cleo was there, would Marcus Otho accompany Galba and his legions to Rome to oust Nero?

Was Nicanor using Cleo as his means to carry a message to Otho from Vespasian, possibly confirming the general's support, with his legions, of Galba? Tigellinus must send Quintus by sea, his preferred element—to head off Nicanor. He would put more men on the road after the centurion, too. But he wanted to take him alive and question him about whether Vespasian and Galba were colluding to overthrow Nero. If he could also capture Cleo, she would be a bargaining chip with Otho, giving Tigellinus some leverage to be included and benefit in what might transpire? Both Nicanor and Cleo could give him what he needed to maneuver around events and not suffer Nero's fate if what he feared brewing came to pass. And who knew—perhaps it could lead to even greater opportunities.

LII

ON THE ROAD TO CAESAREA

"You didn't answer me last night. Who was the man who attacked you?"

Sayid looked at the tall man riding next to him toward Caesarea. He had been relieved when the man who saved him introduced himself as Celsus Evander, telling Sayid to gather his things and come with him. Any change in duty was welcome. Still, his mind had wandered to regret he had not seen Yosef before leaving, and now he did not know when or if he would ever get to see his friend again.

"I don't know who he was... who he is." Sayid massaged his neck, where he knew purple bruises would soon be framed in sickly yellow. The little man who had choked him had been powerful, and it still hurt to swallow. "So, you're a friend of Nicanor's."

"I guess I am... in a way." Celsus shrugged.

"You said that you were his friend." Worried by the attack and the attacker's questions, Sayid had walked in silence to the encampment the night before. Celsus, dressed in a plain tunic, breeches, and cloak, but known to the sentries, had left him at the gate, telling him he would see him again and explain. Then in the morning, he had shown up in the uniform of an *optio*, second in command of a *centuria*, as he had seen him previously. "How do you know Nicanor?"

"Did he tell you about Yotapta?" Celsus asked.

Sayid lied to him. "I have not seen Nicanor since before he went to Rome to serve with the Praetorians and returned in service to General Vespasian." He had no idea of who this tall officer was other than his claim of friendship with Nicanor. Sayid had had little time to talk to Nicanor about anything other than the predicament Cleo and he was in after he saved her from Gessius Florus by setting their house afire.

Maybe this man, Celsus, was a friend... but perhaps he wasn't who he claimed to be.

"Right. You were gone for a while... off doing something for Cestius Gallus."

Sayid did not acknowledge that and instead asked, "What about Yotapta?"

"One night, the rebels attacked our siege engines and the ram battering their city gate. They were led by—I swear to the gods—the largest man I have ever seen. I'm not small, but he made me seem so, and he was a ferocious warrior. He crushed my shield, and I was torn open by just a second grazing blow. A little closer, and he would have gutted me. I lay there in a puddle of blood in the light of one of our burning siege towers and watched him kill the three men with me. That night Nicanor had had his own encounter with that giant and survived, too. Afterward, he found me and got me back to a medicus. Nicanor saved my life."

"That's how you became friends?"

"Not exactly. Nicanor—maybe you know this since you must be an actual friend—is not easy to talk to. Once I had healed enough to get back on my feet, I sought him out to thank him. He accepted my thanks for doing his duty... he had helped many others that night. Anyway, I saw him around the field camp more often, and we began to talk. Then there were issues with my wound." Celsus paused and pressed a hand to his stomach. "I was to be sent back to Ptolemais.

"I went to tell him goodbye... and to thank him again for my life. I found him a good distance away from the other centurions and staff... sitting and staring at the hill Yotapta sat upon. Before he saw me, he had the saddest expression. I told him I would be leaving and that I owed him a life. I said that if there was anything I could do for him...."

"That's when he told you about me."

"He muttered something about how he could not help all his friends... but maybe he could help one of them. That's when he talked of you and said that when you returned to the legion... you might find some there with ill will toward you." Celsus half-turned in his saddle to look questioningly at Sayid. "I guess you did. Like that man who attacked you."

"As Nicanor suspected," Yosef replied, "there are some who think I did something wrong by being gone so long."

"It's a good thing the man attacked you when he did."

"What?"

"I mean the timing. Because..." The optio waved a hand in the direction they were going. Ahead of them was the last wagon in a string of them with a cavalry unit patrolling around the group headed to Caesarea. "I would not have been there to help if it happened after I was gone."

Celsus looked at Sayid. "I see you do not understand. When I could not fight... not in the field, I had to find other ways to serve the legion. I discovered I have a talent for organizing the movement of supplies and equipment and managing their distribution."

"Is that why I saw you around where I worked in the supply areas?"

"Yes. That was fortunate, but I needed to talk with you privately. I was too late to catch up with you but followed when you left the camp. I had just received new orders and knew I must see you and explain who I was so you would not worry. I headed to the quay. At sundown, the captain of a ship just in insisted I see the cargo that had been damaged when they loaded at Ostia. He did not want to be blamed and lose his payment; someone might claim it had happened on board his ship. Shifting the load by torchlight took a few hours. Knowing I'd never find you after that, I headed back to camp and planned to see you this morning. Then I came across two men fighting in the road."

"Thank you again."

"I don't care for skulkers who attack in the night... It surprised me to find it was you, and I was glad. I owed Nicanor, and I'd promised to help you."

"But why am I going with you to Caesarea?" Sayid gestured at the road. "How did you manage that?"

"Someone mentioned my capability to General Titus, who mentioned it to his father. Now I'm to be in command of General Vespasian's quartermasters in all his legions. And I need an orderly... a clerk. It even states the requirement in my orders. Nicanor told me how smart you are... and reliable. 'Not a typical subservient auxiliary, mind you,' he warned me. So, I spoke with the *tesserarius* in charge of your unit, who checked with his officer. I showed him my orders and had you detached and assigned to me."

Sayid had caught the darted sideways glance Celsus gave him as he mentioned Nicanor's warning. And realized he had been talking to a superior officer freely and easily just as he had grown accustomed to when talking with Nicanor, who had not minded. "I'm sorry, sir... I don't mean to be disrespectful."

The optio looked down at him—the man was even taller than Nicanor—and nodded. "I came up through the ranks like Nicanor and think he and I have much in common. But in Caesarea, around others, you must be more careful. It seems you might still be in danger."

"I will be careful."

It occurred to Sayid that working with Celsus could help him find his father, and he smiled for the first time in a long time.

* * *

CAESAREA

VESPASIAN'S PRAETORIUM

The encampment at Caesarea was three times the size of the one at Ptolemais. Sayid had never seen so many legions in such close proximity. Celsus had requested that his orderly be quartered near him, within the array of tents that stretched for some distance behind the headquarters complex of new stone-and-wood buildings. Sayid had taken Celsus's belongings to his tent and now approached the rear of the headquarters to find him. Ahead, he saw four men escorting a shackled man and woman. The man, even from behind, looked familiar. As he turned to speak to the woman, Sayid saw his features.

"Yosef!" Without thinking, Sayid ran toward his friend and saw the startled look of recognition Yosef cast at him as two of the legionaries shoved him and the woman through a door. The other two guards turned to block Sayid. The largest brought his spear up as Sayid slid to a stop.

"Keep back!" The big legionary poked the spear tip into Sayid's chest.

LIII

Aprilus 68 CE

Jerusalem

The Lower City

"Your cousin... could have come in with you," Hananiah said to Miriam when she entered his shop, looking past her. Ya'el had paused at the door before walking up the street.

"She has things to do, and I'll join her in the agora." Hananiah had made Ya'el uncomfortable, but Miriam smiled for him. But her smile, rarely used anymore, felt awkward, and she let it fade. Though he had been kind to her in his own way, she did not think she had ever seen Hananiah smile. "I'm sorry I haven't come to see you," she said. "And thank you for helping me home and not saying anything to my family." Miriam left other things unsaid; he had respected her wish without asking questions.

"You're a grown woman," Hananiah said as he came from behind his counter, wiping his hands on a cloth rag. "Despite tradition... you're not a girl who must explain and be accountable to all of them."

"They're my family and were worried about me. You know how that can be." Miriam said it unthinkingly, then wished she could take her words back. She remembered Hananiah's father had been killed in a preventable accident when he was a boy. And then his mother, while dying from an illness, had apprenticed him to an abusive Alexandrian trader who had taken him from Jerusalem. His life as a child had been much harder than any she could relate to. "I'm sorry... I didn't mean...."

When she'd first come in, his eyes had softened from their usual cold dead stare. But now they hardened again, and he turned from her. He reached for something on the worktable next to the counter. When he faced her again, his eyes had lost some of their sharpness, and he held something wrapped in a rectangle of supple leather.

"You're not like others... Miriam." Her name, or maybe the shape of the words, seemed to catch at his lips. "You are not like the people I sell to from the Upper City... not like those I live among here in the Lower City." His speech and face stiffened again. "And you are not like any I knew in Alexandria." He tilted his head and beckoned her to follow him to an open window over a table lit by shafts of afternoon sunlight. He set the bundle in the light and unwrapped it.

"It's beautiful." Miriam studied the blade that lay gleaming on the soft leather. "It's like flowing water"—she ran a finger over the metal. The intricate pattern of banding had mottling like raindrops within the blade. Still, her fingers felt only the smoothness of polished metal. She started to thumb the edge.

"Careful"—Hananiah touched the back of her hand to stop her. "It is the sharpest blade I have ever created." His fingers lingered, and his eyes, softer but still penetrating, raised to hers. Those dark orbs would not let her look away.

Miriam worried about what he might say next. "I've seen nothing like this," she said. "How did you create it?" She stroked the flat of the blade again.

"It's a *dimasq* process I learned from my work with a bladesmith from Syria... who learned the skill and got the material from easterners. It gives the metal its elegant design without weakening it and makes the blade even more resilient... it will not snap. It's very tough. I think you are a lot like this blade."

"It's beautiful." Embarrassed, Miriam broke from his gaze and picked it up.

"Or it is a lot like you. It's yours... I made it for you."

Miriam lifted her eyes to Hananiah's. "I can't accept this." She shook her head. "It would not be appropriate."

The knife maker nodded his counter to her argument, and his expression shifted and showed concern. "Though you are a woman... you should carry something to defend yourself. Just the other day, there was fighting here," he gestured toward the street, "and each day Jerusalem becomes more dangerous... and soon the Romans will come."

Miriam set the dagger down. "But Hananiah, I can't..."

Hananiah picked it up and offered it to her hilt first. "I can teach you how to use this to protect yourself. Your family does not need to know."

"Thank you... but I must go. Ya'el is waiting for me."

"Wait!" He placed the dagger back on the leather square, quickly wrapped it, tied it with a cord. and pressed it into her hands. "Miriam, you are the only one I want to have this... I made it for you. Please accept this gift... from a friend."

Again, she thought he might say something that would force her to reject and hurt him. But he did not. She bowed her head and took the knife from him.

Hananiah followed her to the door and stood watching her as she melted into the busy crowd. She had walked up the street far enough toward the gate and steps that she was out of his sight. Then, using the side streets, she had doubled back to the long alley that ran along Zechariah's shop, where Ya'el had gone.

Miriam knocked with their prearranged signal at the alley door and waited but did not hear it unlock. She waited a little longer and then tried the door, which opened for her. The main room was empty, and she went to the back. That seemed vacant, too. On the table next to the window, she saw a scattering of sheets of parchment. They showed the crease marks of having been folded and refolded many times. "Ya'el...." she said as she turned to recheck the room.

Ya'el came from behind the mirror. "When I heard the door, I remembered not locking it, and I thought it best to hide." Ya'el held another sheet in her hand.

"Always lock the door. What are you doing?" Miriam walked to the table. "These are Zechariah's letters." She looked at the mirror and its base that hid the secret compartment. It was where it should be, but she was angry at the intrusion on her privacy, and she turned to Ya'el and could now see the tracks of tears on her face.

"I moved everything back in case someone else came in." Ya'el glanced at the letter in her hand. "I was curious about Zechariah... a blind man with skill enough to kill the two Romans...." She stopped when she saw Miriam's eyes. "Bayla and Meira were his wife and daughter... and they were killed by Romans?"

Miriam nodded. "Yes, many years ago. Zechariah kept writing letters to them after they died... that's how much he loved them."

"So, he was an educated man?"

"He was a craftsman—a warrior once—who could read and write... and still fight. He was the best man I ever knew, besides my father and brothers."

"And he taught you how to fight," Ya'el pointed to the sleeves of Miriam's robe, "with those knives?"

"Yes."

"Good." Ya'el nodded. "All women should learn how. I've learned I must defend myself... and even others when that's called for."

"Called for?" Miriam tipped her head to invite more explanation.

"I did it without thinking. A man was killing Sayid, and I had to do something. If it happens to you, or if someone you care for is in danger... you'll know what I mean, and you'll know what to do."

"You misunderstand, Ya'el... and you know little about me." Miriam studied her and decided for it to all come out. "I've killed four Romans or Roman agents... one of them Esau ben Beor."

The silence hung heavy in the room until sudden screams and shouts from outside startled them. From the main room came a banging on the door Miriam had barred on her return.

Miriam went to the door, followed by Ya'el, still trying to grasp what Yosef's sister had just told her. As Miriam withdrew the bar on the doer and cracked it open to peer out, Ehud pushed his way in.

"I saw Ya'el earlier... she came in here, I know, and I worried. Hurry—I must get you both home." More screams spilled through the door. "There's fighting in the streets." He took Miriam's arm.

"The same thing happened the other day... but it ended quickly," Miriam said and yanked her arm from him.

"You must understand... this is different. Ananaus ben Hanan's militia is battling the Zealots all over the city. It started at the Temple Enclosure against Eleasar ben Ananias and his men. It now spreads into the Upper and Lower City. Dozens... maybe hundreds are dead. It's a war inside the walls of the city."

LIV

Aprilus 68 CE

Jerusalem

The Lower City

A warm wind coursed through the city and brushed their faces as they exited the alley onto the street and turned toward the Upper City. The breeze would be welcome on any other early spring day, but this current brought the cry of a city's fabric beginning to tear apart.

"I was coming up from the Lower City and stopped a merchant fleeing down the steps from the Temple Enclosure. He told me groups of men had spread Ananaus's claims the Zealots were robbing the city. Helped by Eleasar bar Ananias, who plans to steal the Temple's treasure. When Eleasar heard that, he went to confront Ananaus with men from the Temple Guards. They clashed just outside the Court of the Gentiles. The fighting spread onto the viaduct and into the Upper City. So I came back to look for you." Ehud squinted into the darkness at Ya'el, who was right behind Miriam. "Both of you."

Miriam prayed Matthew was not with Eleasar. She heard metal striking metal, echoes coming from another alley as they passed. She knew that further on, it bent toward the base of the southern end of the Temple Enclosure. The alley ended at a street leading to the steps, and above, inside the enclosure wall, was the Court of Gentiles. The guard kept a strict watch over the Temple and all within the enclosure. And Matthew had been on duty when she had left that morning. The daily guard patrols, the *mishmarot*, was composed of three priest-officers and 21 Levites. The priest-officers were stationed one at the *Bet ha-Niẓoẓ,* Chamber of the Flame, one at *Bet ha-Moḳed,* the Chamber of the Hearth, and one at the Attic of Abṭinas at the southern courts of the Temple Enclosure.

Matthew usually had the southern section, and 21 Levite guardsmen were spread throughout the enclosure: one at each of the five gates and four corners within the Temple Enclosure, another nine positioned similarly around the court, and one each at the Chamber of Sacrifice, the Chamber of Curtains, and behind the *Kapporet*—the Holy of Holies. If Matthew had only the Levites to call upon, he would not have enough men to hold off a powerful attack, and the guards were not even intended for that purpose. The din of shouting men grew louder from that direction.

Miriam shook her arm from Ehud's hand, turned to Ya'el, and pressed the wrapped dagger into her hands, and whispered, "Use this if you have to." Ignoring the puzzled look on Ya'el's face, she reached into her sleeves and loosened the blades in their forearm sheaths. Someone bumped into her, and she half-spun. The wind caught the hood of her robe, flipping it back and twisting her hair into a tangle. Brushing the hair from her eyes, she looked at the receding back of the man who had struck her and shoved something into her hand. Kefa. She watched the leatherworker hurry toward his shop without looking back at her. Miriam cupped the scrap of parchment he had passed to her and tucked it into a pouch at her waist.

As they passed Hananiah's shop, slowly moving around a cluster of arguing men, Miriam saw him standing in its doorway, half in shadow. He seemed about to push the men away from his door for her to enter. Then his eyes locked on Ehud, who had retaken her arm. Hananiah's expression hardened to a scowl. Something flickered on his face as he glanced again at her and stepped back into the darkness, shutting his door.

The smell of fresh-baked unleavened bread grew stronger. Feast week had begun, and every family in Jerusalem had plenty of it. Still, the air became tainted with another odor. The acrid scent grew more pungent as they reached and walked along the western wall of the Temple Enclosure. They had seen several bodies of men in the Lower City streets, but now there were even more. Some were the fatally wounded who seemed to have been fleeing the fighting. Their bodies were sprawled, facing down toward the Lower City. Women were among the dead on the steps. Some men still held swords or gripped *hasta*, the short Roman spears legionaries used for thrusting, which they must have gotten from the Antonia Fortress armory. Some of those weapons were still embedded in the chests of the dead. No one could tell from their faces who was a Zealot and who was not.

As they reached the top of the steps at the colonnade porticoes, Miriam saw the shock on Ehud's face and felt the same gut-wrenching anguish. But it was Ya'el who said it: "Why do you kill each other?"

"Hurry!" Ehud waved Miriam and Ya'el to parallel him as they came off the steps. He moved to the inside of the walkway that bordered the Temple Enclosure, trying to shield them. Just within, a roiling mass of armed men pressed through the outer courts. Screams and the clash of weapons came from deeper within, where the gates led into the Inner Court.

They descended the lesser steps through the Kipunos gate, which brought them onto the Tyropoeon Valley viaduct and then down its steps leading to the Xystus, the Upper City market. The first street of shops mostly served Temple goers and was littered with many more bodies of both men and women. Some had been pierced with short spears or felled by the now-bloody stones lying near them. Fluttering in the breeze was a snagged veil half-torn from the still figure of a young woman sprawled atop an older woman holding a baby who had been crushed against the cobblestones. They lay there with a spilled armful of loaves around them. The still-fresh unleavened bread for feast week was meant to symbolize sincerity and trust. *After today, it will never again mean that for me*, Miriam thought.

Miriam looked at Ya'el, tears coursing down her face as they beheld the body of another woman, about their age, in the baker's shop doorway. Inside, a fire still burned along one wall, the opposite splashed with gore where a dead man slumped. It must have been the baker to judge by the flour that dusted the front of his tunic and his arms—and he had a woeful bread knife in his hand. "Fire and blood..." Ya'el moaned.

Miriam's own tears broke loose as she spotted two bodies in Temple Guards' uniforms, perhaps killed there or dragged from the Temple Enclosure above them. The one lying face down had the same build and hair like her brother. A fist squeezed her heart. Matthew!

"Miriam!" Ehud called to her as she bent to check the body... and she was relieved, as she turned it over, to see it was not Matthew. "We must hurry and get away from here," he said.

"Yes," a coarse voice boomed. A large man was coming down the street with a half-dozen others. As they got closer, their bloody blades and the crimson smears on their clothing showed they had been in the fight. Maybe they were even the men who had killed the baker, the women, and the two Temple guardsmen. Most of them showed minor wounds.

"You should get off the streets... especially any of your family, Miriam, or your friends." Yonatan sneered at Ehud as his men formed a half arc around them. He turned to Miriam: "Your brother Yosef is a traitor... and many now doubt your family's loyalty to Jerusalem. You should run and hide from justice." He lowered the spear he carried—reddened for half its length—and leveled its tip to touch lightly against Ehud's chest, who batted it away with the flat of his hand.

In the corner of her eye, Miriam saw Ya'el just behind her—with slight movements—carefully unwrap the leather bundle and reach in to grasp the hilt of Hananiah's gift. Miriam stepped forward beside Ehud and slipped her hands inside their opposite sleeves. She widened her stance with her left foot slightly ahead of the right. "My family... and my friend," Miriam said as she glanced at Ehud, "are not frightened women. We're not like Leah... we're not afraid of you, Yonatan. I see no wounds on you... nor little blood. Do these *men*"—she emphasized the word— "do *your* fighting?"

The burly man, surprised at first by such words from someone he had known as only a docile and spoiled girl, flushed an angry red. He took a step toward her and stopped.

Miriam darted a look to her left. Ya'el had come forward to stand beside her. Ya'el's hand was still inside the soft leather wrapping, but her eyes were locked on Yonatan. Ehud was unarmed but stooped to pick up a broken spear. He gripped the forearm-length piece with the iron tip intact. "Another step closer," he said, "and no matter how fast your men act, this will find your throat."

A rush of running footsteps on stone clattered behind them. Miriam turned to see a dozen men, heavily armed and carrying shields, trot toward them. The helmeted man in the front called to Yonatan: "What do you still here? We have most of the Zealot leaders pushed back, and they've taken refuge inside the inner courts. That's where you and your men should be. I go to report to Ananaus and Yoshua ben Gamla."

"Come," Ehud touched Miriam's arm and moved to go around Yonatan and his men.

"Yes," Miriam said as she took Ya'el's hand, "let's go home." The two women's eyes bored into Leah's husband as they passed him.

* * *

THE UPPER CITY

"How is Matthew?" Ya'el asked from where she stood at the open door into Miriam's room.

"Mother has bandaged the slash across his chest," Miriam answered, "and he's resting now. Eleasar ben Ananias released him from the guard and ordered him out—had him carried here—before they barricaded the gates." Miriam gestured at the wall to her left. "How is Elian... and the bird?"

They had reached home to find Matthew had just gotten there. That traumatic arrival and the chaos in the streets had brought the boy to tears, and the parrot was upset at the turmoil and Elian's distress.

"Cicero has calmed down, and Elian's a brave boy... but he's scared he will lose his new family. He's lost so much in his life..." Ya'el shook her head and thought, *We all have,* as she handed Miriam the re-wrapped dagger she had kept hidden after they arrived.

Miriam took it from her and set it on the bed beside her. "Come in and close the door." She waited, then said, "You did not flinch when facing Yonatan."

"After Gessius Florus, I won't let any man frighten... or hurt me again." Ya'el witnessed the first genuine smile she had seen bloom on Miriam's face. Finally, there was the bright, charming girl Yosef had told her of in stories of his family as they drifted at sea. He had expected to die and never see them again. "And I'll do what I must to protect my family." She was pleased that Miriam's smile held, and the young woman nodded at her words. It made Ya'el, at last, feel accepted. Some of the weight on her heart lifted. "What's that?" she asked, pointing at the scrap of parchment in Miriam's hand.

"Something Kefa shoved into my hand right after we left Zechariah's. I was about to read it." she unfolded and flattened the message on her leg. The smile faded, and her face paled.

"What's wrong?" Ya'el moved closer. "Miriam... what is it?"

Miriam rocked her head. "No... no... it cannot be," she crushed the message in her hand.

"What is it?" Ya'el sat on the bed next to her.

"Elazar ben Yair and the Sicarii say they've confirmed Ehud's family is collaborating with the Romans in Alexandria." Miriam stared at Ya'el without seeing her. "And... and they believe Ehud returned to Jerusalem to spy for the Romans."

LV

Aprilus 68 CE

Caesarea

Vespasian's Praetorium

The Roman general studied the sea as waves alternately crashed on and swirled around the jumbled piles of stone dumped decades before during the port's construction. But surf lapped gently, calmly along the shore. The view stirred him, for he was not often able to witness the power of the tides. He missed Falacrine, his home, and its groves... so far away. Most of all, he missed Antonia; she helped make sense of things.

Vespasian shook out the reports rolled into a scroll. Nicanor's had been delayed in reaching him, but it was like the report from Gaius Mucianus, except that the governor of Syria had been less circumspect. He considered the seascape again, almost a description of events in Rome. Nicanor and Mucianus reported the unrest and discontent of powerful men in Rome and in the provinces who wished to change the course of Rome currently dictated by Nero. The nobles were a steady beating of waves of discontent on the rock, Rome's narcissistic emperor. And the slow and slight pushes from Rome's common people Nero kept at a low level, like those waves on the beach, as Nero appeased the crowd and diverted its attention.

In Rome, just before Vespasian had left for Antioch, Mucianus had introduced him to a young man, a teacher who planned to build a school of rhetoric one day. Though Vespasian was no academic, he knew the three arts of discourse. Their conversation about Rome's circumstances and current events had intrigued him. The teacher, Marcus Quintilianus, had said, "If you give the people bread and circuses... the first for the stomach.... the second for their eyes and mind... they'll largely be content and care about little else." According to the letter from Mucianus, his contacts in Rome reported that Nero had soothed the mob with Games to the point that they were of little trouble. But the bedrock of the empire was shaking and shifting beneath the surface. Other forces, more powerful and focused, were at work.

Vespasian was an intelligent military leader and a skillful administrator, but Antonia better understood the never-ending

Roman political games. He wished he could talk with her and get her counsel.

"General..."

Vespasian turned from his view and his thoughts. "Yes, centurion?"

"The Jewish prisoner has asked if he might speak with you."

"Bring him to me." Vespasian stepped from the high flat rock onto a graveled path leading to a grassy area greening with the spring weather. Two benches, a chair, and a low table were set atop huge flagstones that created a gray-brown square within the larger green one. He sat in the chair facing the sea, and minutes passed as his thoughts returned to his family. He would soon send Titus into the field against the Judeans and bring this war to an end. Then he would return to Antonia and see his youngest son, Domitian. Titus had a clear path and vision for his future, but not so for Domitian; the boy was hot-headed and despised Antonia. The father would have to mend things with the youngest son when he returned, and he hoped to straighten the boy out.

At the crunch of many footsteps on gravel, Vespasian looked over his shoulder. Yosef and his four guards approached, leaving broad marks in the wet grass. The legionaries halted short of the flagstones and waited for orders. The prisoner was shackled at feet and hands and no danger to the general, but they would bring him no nearer unless directed.

Vespasian waved them forward with the short officer's staff—a vinewood rod— he had carried for years. He pointed at the bench opposite him, across the table. He tapped his palm with the cudgel as Yosef sat on the bench, and the guards stepped away from them, but not too far. Conscious of Yosef's bare feet and his effort to ease his ankles by shifting his shackles, he looked down at his own feet. The wetness of the grass had darkened the leather of his *caligae*, the thick-soled legionary sandals he wore.

"I'm surprised at the heavy dew this morning."

"It is typical along the coast," Yosef gestured at the glistening grass. "But this one's early for the time of year."

"Your guards report loud voices and many arguments between you and your wife. Is that what you wish to speak with me about? To protest, again, your marriage?" Vespasian shook his head. "The reasons for it have not changed."

Yosef blinked, not expecting that question. "No, general. I saw someone here that I know well. A Roman auxiliary, a young Syrian named Sayid, and wanted to know if I may speak with him."

"How do you know him?"

"He was with me, the centurion Nicanor, and Lady Cleo on the *Salacia*. We survived together and became friends and have remained so even in Rome and afterward. I have not seen him for a very long time."

"Why do you wish to see him?"

"When I saw him, he saw me, too..." Yosef looked up at the guards, who watched him closely. "There are no friendly faces around me... and no one to talk to who does not consider me an enemy. Even you, general."

"You and your people have rebelled against Rome. You are our enemy. Your need for companionship is not my concern. What about your wife? She is a Jewess... and was with you at Yotapta."

Yosef shrugged. "I get only accusations from her, general... and bitterness. I'll not say more about that." He lifted his hands and shook them. The metal of the chains rasped and clinked. "I don't know where things will end for me. I have no say or power, and my fate is up to you. But I have seen what the future holds for you, that you will become emperor... and I ask this as a favor."

"This auxiliary's name is Sayid?" Vespasian still had doubts about the Jew's prophecy and recalled Nicanor requesting special orders for the Syrian who had been off on a mission for Cestius Gallus. Recently, he had endorsed them for the Syrian's return to the 12th Legion in Ptolemais. "And you saw him here?"

"Yes, general, just outside your headquarters."

"I'll look into it. If he is stationed here... you cannot meet with him alone."

* * *

Yosef's guards stopped as previously ordered and let him enter the room alone. Vespasian sat at his large, unusually empty, campaign desk, resting his thick forearms upon it, pointing the bronze-tipped ferrule of his cudgel at Sayid, who sat across from him nervously shifting in his chair.

"Sit there, Yosef"—Vespasian indicated a chair two chairs away from Sayid's.

Yosef settled in the chair and arranged his shackles. He could not stop the spread of his smile as he looked at his friend, who had stopped fidgeting and grinned back at him. "I'm glad to see you, Sayid," he said.

"Wait." Vespasian raised a hand. "There are two more to join us." He crooked a finger and beckoned. "They, too, should hear of your

226

curious friendships." Titus entered with Ariella. To Sayid, Vespasian said, "This is General Titus... my son. And this," he directed the unshackled Ariella to sit next to Sayid, "is Yosef's wife."

Stunned, Sayid turned wide eyes upon Ariella and then to Yosef. "Who?"

LVI

Jerusalem

The Upper City

"Miriam…" Rebecca's voice came from downstairs. "Ya'el… I need your help."

Clenching the Sicarii leader's message in her fist, Miriam stood and tucked it back in her pouch and opened her bedroom door. "Coming, Mother." Ya'el followed her.

The sitting room was heavy with the odor of the streets. A wad of bloody cloth and the remnants of Matthew's torn and blood-soaked tunic lay in a pile beside the chair Matthew sat upon.

"Help me. I want to get him to where he can better rest." Rebecca steadied Matthew, who struggled to rise, his bare chest wrapped in an already reddening bandage. "Hand me that"—she pointed to a folded blanket.

Miriam picked it up, draped it across Matthew's shoulders, and got under his left arm to help him stand.

"You've gotten stronger, sister," he whispered as she leaned in. His eyes went to the now faint scar on her cheek and then locked on hers before they slid away and closed in pain.

Miriam caught the look and knew he still meant to question her and expected the truth. But not today. "Upstairs to his room, Mother?" She felt him shake his head.

"No, the courtyard," he said. "I want some fresh air, and I hope Ehud will be able to find Father soon. I must speak to him as soon as he comes."

Rebecca hesitated, then nodded. "Ya'el… please…" She tilted her head at the shuttered entrance to the courtyard. Ya'el opened the shutters and stepped aside.

"Ya'el—" Elian started, then stopped. "Mother, may I come down now?" But the boy was already at the foot of the stairs.

Matthew groaned as he settled on a couch next to the long table in the courtyard. "Ya'el, please let him… he can sit with me until my father comes."

"Yes, Elian," Ya'el called over her shoulder. "Come sit with Matthew for a while. But only until he says you must leave him."

"Bring my sword to me, Elian," he said. "It's by the chair... and oil and cloth and the sharpening stone. I'll show you how to clean and sharpen it." Matthew turned to Ya'el and said, "I know, Ya'el... you'd rather he didn't see the blood on it. But I fear this will not be the last of that he sees. And I will teach him how to handle a sword."

Miriam watched the boy bring the blade. The worry and fright on Elian's face had been replaced by the settling of his features. As if the weight of the sword he held by its hilt in both hands steadied him. "Jerusalem needs fighters to protect her," she told the boy, with a darted glance at Ya'el as he reached Matthew.

Matthew's grimace softened briefly into a smile as the boy sat on the ground next to him, the sword across his lap. With a tightening of his lips, he reached over and tousled the boy's hair. "So, we must all become fighters."

* * *

"Matthew is right," Ya'el said as she turned from the window. From below in the courtyard, the sounds filtered up—metal rasping on stone as Elian followed directions on removing the nicks in the sword's blade. "We must all become fighters... ready for what's coming. Those who come will not spare those who choose not to fight."

"That is what the Zealots believe—the Sicarii too—there should be no surrender to the Romans."

"You agree with them, the Zealots?" Ya'el asked. "Though your father and brother are what you call Moderates?"

"Yes." Miriam slipped the sheathed daggers from her forearms, bundled them with the knife from Hananiah, and slid the package under her bedding. She sat and faced Ya'el, who, arms crossed, remained at the window, leaning against its sill. "I love my family... but I do not believe we should lie down before the Romans, attempt to placate them, and accept any peace they dictate to us. Yet, we shouldn't fight among ourselves, either." She scowled. "Those who hurt Matthew and threaten my family should be punished."

"Why does Yonatan hate Yosef so much?" Ya'el's fingers found the kinyan suspended below her throat.

"Because he was Leah's first love... and she... his." Miriam pointed to Ya'el's hand. "She gave him that... as a remembrance of their love."

A cloud of regret passed over Ya'el, and she wished she had not spoken of the matter to Miriam. "I should return this to Leah then... it is not mine to keep." Ya'el had thought that many times since overhearing, at her arrival at the gates of Jerusalem with Sayid,

Rachel's whisper to Miriam that Leah had been who gave the kinyan to Yosef. She began to draw the cord from her neck.

"No. Yosef would not have given it to you if you did not have a place in his heart. His heart has been broken twice..." Ya'el felt Miriam studying her before she continued. "Leah was married to Yonatan—by her father's decision—while Yosef was with the Essenes. When he returned, I think he looked to fill that emptiness and soothe the hurt he felt by marrying Ruth. And I believe he loved her. Then she and his daughter, they had named Ya'el, died at the child's birth." Miriam paused at the resurrected jolt of pain she still felt for her brother's heartbreak and loss. She looked at Ya'el and could see the Roman woman felt it too. "It shows how important you are to him, Cleo, that he told you to go by that name."

Ya'el let go of the memory of floating upon the sea as Yosef told her about his broken heart. Her eyes flashed open. "Yet they say Yosef has married. Even as a prisoner, he found someone. So I must return this to Leah. It is not mine to keep."

"You can't, Ya'el. How could we explain why you have it? You must keep it and never show it to anyone.... better still... get rid of it. Give it to me, and I'll melt it down."

Ya'el shook her head, but her fingers let go of the coin on its cord. "Come with me, Miriam." They went to her room. She reached under her bed, careful not to make a noise and disturb Cicero, who, head tucked down on his chest, slept on his perch. She unwrapped the blanket-covered object she brought out. "I will teach you how to use this," she showed Miriam her bow, "if you will teach me how to fight with a dagger."

Before Miriam could reply, they heard voices from the courtyard. She hurried to her own room, for its window was directly above the courtyard table. Easing the shutter open, she motioned to Ya'el and held a finger to her lips.

Ya'el saw that Mathias and Ehud had returned. Miriam's father's voice was keen with anger.

"Ananaus had the effrontery to bring Yohanan ben Levi with him to our meeting... Shimon ben Gamliel, too, though he stood there mostly silent." Mathias pulled out the chair at the head of the table and moved it next to Matthew.

"Was it ben Levi who spawned the lies about Eleasar and the Zealots, about planning to steal the Temple treasure? Shimon ben Gamliel knows that Eleasar is helping to hide most of it, but that is to protect it from the Romans. Only he could have told anyone of that. And then the Gischalan turns and distorts it for his own use. Gamliel has deferred to that Gischalan since he got to Jerusalem." Matthew pressed a hand to his chest as he took a deep breath. "The man is a liar... he cares only for himself and what power he can gather for his own use. He'll abandon Jerusalem just as he did Gischala."

"I accused ben Levi of that to his face," said Mathias, "and of spreading lies about Yosef and Eleasar. Shimon defended him. The only time he spoke was to tell me the Gischalan had sworn an oath of 'goodwill' before the Moderates of the Sanhedrin. And that he was willing to speak to the Zealots on their behalf."

"He will not live up to that oath." Matthew shook his head and tried to sit up. "And they—we—will regret letting him become an emissary to the Zealots."

Mathias cautioned his son, "Lie back, Matthew. I agree with you, but I don't know what we can do here. But, we must warn Yohanan ben Zaccai to return now or wait with the Essenes and not return until this has been resolved. We cannot risk someone intercepting or harming him, revealing more of the plans to hide the treasure. That will turn the violence toward us."

"There's enough food and water for Eleasar and his men to hold out for a while within the Temple," Matthew replied. "But not long. Then the fighting will begin again. I must leave for Qumran—"

"You cannot go, my son... you're hurt." Mathias clasped Matthew's shoulder lightly, pressing him to lie back. "We'll find someone to go warn Yohanan and Nahum in Qumran."

"Who can we trust?" Matthew asked. Mathias remained silent. "See what I mean? Then I must—"

"I'll go." Ehud had been quiet, and at the moment, after all that had happened that day, Mathias and Matthew had forgotten to watch their words around him. "I can do it. I'll go."

Miriam's hand smothered her gasp as her other hand touched the pouch at her waist with its message from Elazar ben Yair.

Ya'el guessed what Miriam was thinking; *what should she do about Ehud?*

LVII

APRILUS 68 CE

NEAR NARBO, GAUL

"This is a good road," said Graius, the cart rocking as it passed over the worn, uneven stones. Most were hand- or head-sized. But some had fractured from a century of use, and the heavy rains over the years had carried away much of the dirt filling between them. The old gladiator's head swayed. His white beard had grown out considerably after 19 days on the road and showed patchiness in the afternoon's waning sunlight.

While the cart rattled along on the rutted road, Carmenta stayed as much as possible to the shoulder of dirt and grass. Stepping over or around the occasional rock loosened from the road and cast to one side, she moved with only a slight hitch to her stride but tirelessly on the long travel days. The horse's wounds suffered at the shipwreck of the *Faustistas* had healed well, but Nicanor had yet to test her at full gallop. Craxa—the retired semi-capable legion medicus—had treated her well but made mistakes when treating Graius that required a competent medicus's help in Massilia to save his leg.

Nicanor studied the road and glanced again at Graius; lately, the older man grew paler toward the end of each day. "The road needs work, but it will probably get better as we reach Narbo," Nicanor replied. "According to the merchants we've met, that port has grown to be almost as busy as Massilia. As Narbo prospers, they'll likely do more for this stretch of the road."

"No, I mean that this is a good road to be on," Graius said, waving a gnarled hand at it. Then he patted the cart bench he sat upon and added, "Even if the road and the cart together lurch like I'm back on a ship, it is a good road to be on. The via Domitia is told of in Greek stories before it got its Roman name when paved long ago. They believed it the road Hercules traveled on during his labors." Graius's head bobbed, and he spat to one side. "Lady Cleo, when she was young, loved to hear stories of heroes, and I read to her or told her the stories I knew of Hercules. And of the Greek goddess, Artemis—she preferred the name to the Roman 'Diana,'" he chuckled. "Cleo was so small then and I so much larger... she would pretend I was Hercules and she Artemis. I even made her a small bow, though we kept it hidden from her father. Lucius Salvius Otho might have been the sourest man I ever met. He wanted Cleo to become a refined Roman lady who would be desired by a man with power or one destined to attain it. That would further his own aims and rebuild his status and wealth." Graius spat again. "My master—when I was a gladiator—made money and achieved some fame from my success. And I think Cleo's father hoped the same for himself through his daughter's marriage. He cared little for Cleo other than that."

Nicanor readied to scratch the nub between Carmenta's ears. The horse pitched her head back with pleasure, and he could sense that she was happy. That comforted him, but that comfort dimmed as he thought about what Graius had just said. "So that's what led to her marriage to Gessius Florus."

"Yes. Florus's family, Roman citizens in Clazomenae, in the Asiana province, were moneylenders. And I think Cleo's father owed money to them—not being able to borrow in Rome. Or perhaps he owed someone else—and he needed them to pay his debt. By then, Marcus, Cleo's brother, had his own life plans. They had been very close during her childhood—their mother, Albia Terentia, died giving birth to Cleo. But Nero forced Marcus's wife, Poppaea, to divorce so she could marry him. He then exiled Marcus to Hispania Lusitania, and Marcus and Cleo drifted apart."

They rode in silence for a while. Nicanor shifted and half-turned to study Graius, lifting a leg to crook it across the saddle. The old man did not look well. "How did you come to learn how to read? That seems odd for a—"

"A gladiator?" Graius flashed a scant smile. "I taught my master's son to use a sword, and he got me interested. When I accepted the rudis and became a freedman, I placed that wooden sword on my mantle and left fighting behind me. I studied because I loved stories about heroes."

"That's why you went so often to the temple where I met you in Rome. And here we are on Hercules' road..." Nicanor pulled his leg down and looked ahead. "But we're not heroes." The ghosts of Beth Horon brought back a bitter memory. "I'm no hero."

"I know too much of men and myself to argue with you about that. But maybe we can be heroes for Cleo... I think we must become such," said Graius, "to save her."

Nicanor squared his shoulders and straightened. "Whether or not we have that in us, we'll do what we can for her. "Will Marcus help us?"

"I believe he will. Marcus did not discount any of it when I took him the information you gave me. All the material from Cestius

Gallus and the copies of Cleo's letters with her suspicions about her husband. He was not surprised about Florus's instigations of war with the rebels in Judea. He accepted the idea that Florus had much to do with the great fire. No one who knows Nero would be surprised that he had something to do with that, too. The near-destruction of his own city."

"But Lord Otho didn't act on it." Nicanor shook his head. "Why not?"

"We don't know that he has not acted," Graius said. "Marcus and Cleo's older brother, Titianus, is a member of the Arval Brethren. Some of its leaders were suspected collaborators who escaped punishment when Gaius Piso plotted to overthrow Emperor Nero. Some believe that plot still brews. And now we know of Vindex's rebellion and his support for Galba—someone who Marcus Otho also supports as emperor." Graius swept his hair from his eyes and shook the reins for the mule to pick up the pace and ignore the lateness of the day. "I think it must all be tied in together somehow. Men like the Othos fight differently than we do" scoffed Graius. "Their attacks, their thrust, and counterthrust... their moves are much slower, not made with blades. They play a long game and take their time. Men like us are mere *latrunculi* pieces on a gameboard. The likes of the Otho brothers, Galba, and so many others in Rome, move them where they want them."

"General Vespasian introduced me to men in the Arval Brethren before we left Rome," Nicanor said with a nod. "One of them is now the governor of Syria, Gaius Mucianus. Antonia Caenis, when I met with her in Falacrine, cautioned me about the intrigues of Rome. She worries that General Vespasian may already be caught up within them."

"She is wise." Graius reached back to check the knot on the rope to the packhorse trailing behind the cart. Then shifted, with a grimace, to stretch his legs out straight from the bench.

"Does your leg still pain you?" Nicanor asked, ready to shake off all the thinking of things past and things to come he could not control. "I thought it was better."

"I'm an old man, and how that has happened so quickly, I don't know. The years have been birds flying by, and they've taken my youth with them." Graius rubbed his leg, then pressed a hand to his stomach. "My leg aches, and other things. Since Massilia, we've bypassed the *mansiones* along the road and camped in the fields and woods. I know the roadside inns are costly to travelers, and we must save money, but can we stop at the next one for just a night? I'm not a legionary like you—I would welcome a good night's sleep on something other than the ground. And your camp cooking leaves much to be desired. I'd like fresh wine, not the stuff befouled by sloshing too long within a skin bag."

"You're a man born to live in a city," Nicanor said with a laugh and rubbed his face, his fingers catching in the tangle of his matted beard. "But a bath would be good, too." He eyed the lowering sun and judged their distance made since sunrise. The road had veered slightly further from the ridge of mountains on their right. The forested sections had become less dense, and some of the fields appeared cultivated. "We are nearing Narbo. The river beside it is the Atax, and the crossing must be just ahead, with the town on the other side. We should come upon a *mansio* soon. We'll stop, and both get a good meal and a sound night's sleep."

Ahead, the road arced more toward the southeast, and the seacoast and the shadows cast before them grew longer.

LVIII

Narbo

"I'm glad this place is on this side of the river, or we'd have had to camp anyway and wait for the morning to ferry the wagon across." Graius poured more wine into his cup and looked out of the open shutters of a broad window that let in a fresh breeze. The taberna and inn appeared to be newly built. The butt ends and planed bottoms of its wooden beams lighted by the flare of a large oil lantern showed the roughness and lighter coloring of recent sawing and shaping by an ax. The building sat upon a rise too modest to be called a hill but still looked down on the river. At the low end of the slope was the crossing. The spread of lights blooming on the other side as night fell and darkness grew was Narbo.

Scant baths were available, but both men looked more presentable after using them and trimming their beards. But the innkeeper—who also served as barman—had welcomed them warmly when Nicanor showed the coin in his hand. The centurion drained his mug of beer, and the barman was right there. "More *cerevisia*, or perhaps wine, good sir?"

Nicanor scanned the room; only two other men were drinking, shoulders hunched in conversation, in a far corner. He pushed his empty plate away to clink against Graius's at the center of the table. Though Graius had claimed to be hungry, pieces of beef roast and bread remained on his plate.

Graius turned from the window and glanced at Nicanor's empty cup. "Do you not want some wine, Nicanor?" he asked, and the barman looked hopeful.

"No... beer's fine." Nicanor shook his head, and the barman filled his cup from one of the pitchers in his hands, then retreated.

"This," Nicanor said as he raised the cup, "is a gift from Ceres... she gives us the 'wine of barley.'" *And it costs less too*, he thought. "Tell me more of Cleo. You mentioned that Otho discovered her bow... but kept her archery a secret."

A spreading smile added more lines that scored Graius's face. "She had crept out one night, and Marcus caught her shooting blunt arrows at the moon, pretending to be the huntress. He took the bow from her and walked her back to her room. But the next morning, he gave me the bow to return to her."

As Graius talked more about Cleo's girlhood, Nicanor looked forward to a night when he could sleep without worry. Camping along a road traveled by merchants and bandits who sought to relieve those merchants of their wares meant he and Graius had slept little the nights since leaving Massilia. From their place by the large window, he watched the moon sail above a scattering of clouds that did not block the gleam of moonbeams upon the river. The light was just enough for him to be able to see where the crossing had been constructed within a scalloped cleft in the river's bank. How many nights in faraway lands had he sat and watched this same moon? He'd never considered all that it had witnessed... the lives, loves, and deaths of men and women and children. And was there something beyond that life... something after? That thought made him recall his conversations with Paul of Tarsus imprisoned in Rome in the Tullianum. He felt again that pang of hurt at the Christian leader's execution.

The clatter of several men entering the inn broke his reverie. *It will get crowded in here*, he thought. *Best to avoid any more strangers.* "Let's go up now," he said with a motion to Graius and emptied his cup. "We've got an early start tomorrow."

* * *

"Wake up...."

Nicanor shook off the hand gripping his shoulder. "Graius... what is it?" His eyes opened to see the window with the rim of the moon he had been dreaming of in its top corner. He reached for the sheathed blade at his side and swung his legs off the cot.

"We must leave now." Graius straightened and turned to take the centurion's cloak from a peg on the wall.

"What? Why?" Nicanor's left fist knuckled sleep from his eyes.

"I went downstairs to get more wine... and saw the innkeeper speaking with a man—a *decurion*—if I have his rank right. I heard him tell the legionary something; I guess he was answering his question. He said, "I've seen no Roman noblewoman... but I have heard that name, Cleo. Two men, here earlier, were speaking about her.""

"*Futuo!*" Nicanor stood, belted his sword on, and took the cloak from Graius. "If he's a decurion... he'll likely have his ten men with him. Tigellinus has sent men on the road for us." He went to open the door.

237

"Don't... the barman is still serving them drink downstairs and has promised to point us out when we come down." Graius went to the window and leaned out, looked down, and sighed. "We must climb down the trellis."

* * *

Dripping wet, Nicanor and Graius clambered onto their horses. Carmenta snorted and shook a spray of drops from her mane and tail. Nicanor looked over his shoulder at the inn and did not see any activity outside. No men ran for their horses to pursue them. He regretted having to leave their mule, wagon, and supplies. The innkeeper would enjoy the benefit of their being abandoned. Wiping his face, he settled in the saddle as he kneed Carmenta forward. "Just the other side of town is the Via Aquitania... our way west. The sooner we reach it, the better time we'll make." Seeing Graius stiffly swing his leg over his mount, he said, "We must go fast. Can you stand such riding?" *And can Carmenta sustain it?* He wondered with worry.

"I'll have to. Away from here, there's no one to recognize us and point us out to them. They're still looking for Cleo traveling with a man... two men if they believe the barman. Maybe we can lose them."

"Maybe. But to do that, we must get far enough ahead and then try to stay out of their sight and reach. They are going to question everyone they see on the road." Nicanor heeled Carmenta into a run and prayed to the gods to give them enough time to escape.

LIX

Maius 68 CE

Jerusalem

The Hall of Hewn Stone

"You cannot be the one to speak to the Zealots," Shimon ben Gamliel said, though he would not look at Mathias. "Yohanan will meet with them to convince them to leave the Temple, and we'll work things out between us."

"This man," Mathias pointed, "can't speak for the Moderates, nor for Jerusalem. He did not even stand with the people of Gischala, his own town, his home. Why would the Zealots listen to him?"

"Why would they listen to you, Mathias?" Yohanan ben Levi snapped back. "You're the father of a traitor."

Mathias's beard bristled with fury, and he wished he were again a young man. "Yosef was captured by the Romans and is a prisoner—that does not make him a traitor. Nor do your words... your lies."

"I do not lie... and what I say comes from what's been reported by others."

"I want to hear it from their lips, then." Mathias glared at the Gischalan and demanded, "Bring them here."

"I have heard it myself, as have Ananaus ben Hanan and Yoshua ben Gamla, Mathias," replied Shimon ben Gamliel. "A rabbi arrived two days ago with others fleeing areas near Caesarea. Nearly four months ago, at the Roman army encampment, he performed Yosef's marriage to a woman forced to marry him. Two Romans were at the ceremony: General Vespasian and Gessius Florus. Yosef bargained for the rabbi to be freed after the ceremony. The rabbi was thankful for that, and he spoke with others in Caesarea about Yosef. One of them—a taberna owner—quickly told him something else. The Roman legionaries, camp guards, when they got drunk, talked of their prisoner that met regularly with Vespasian and his son Titus. All the other prisoners from Yotapta were held in Ptolemais until they could be sold into slavery." Shimon shook his head. "That raises many questions about why Yosef is in Caesarea, not with the other prisoners... and why Vespasian meets with him so often."

"Too many questions..." commented Yohan ben Levi with contempt.

Mathias scowled at the man he detested and turned to the Sanhedrin president. "Shimon, I can't explain the marriage if it really took place. But it does not seem to have been Yosef's choice any more than the woman's. But the meetings with Vespasian must be Yosef attempting to convince the Romans to contact us, leaders of Jerusalem, to discuss an offering of peace."

Shimon shook his head. "Yosef has been a prisoner for months... and we've yet to hear anything from Vespasian."

"But they've not attacked," Mathias pointed out, "which has given us more time to prepare."

"The Romans too prepare; they've received a vast quantity of supplies and equipment. They've taken all of Samaria and Galilee to the north of us and east to Jericho. Is Yosef giving them information they'll use when they do attack?"

"Yosef would never do that, Shimon."

Yohanan ben Levi scoffed. "Of course, you, his father, would say that."

"Others who know Yosef will say the same thing... you know that, Shimon," Mathias said, wagging his finger as he chided the man. "You must stop listening to this Gischalan... or any others he brings before you or the Sanhedrin. He plays his own game." Mathias smoothed his beard, prone to jutting out when he was angry.

"Some think Yosef's time in Rome changed him, making him admire the Romans even more than before he left. I've said as much before, Mathias." Shimon finally did not avert his eyes as he spoke. "I did not think him the right man to command in Galilee... and now— under his command—Galilee has been lost to the Romans."

"Did we really expect anything different? The Romans have mistreated us, done wrongs to our people, and brought many to death. None of our righteous indignation and anger, past or present, enables us to match the Roman army's power. We could never hope to change things by force. Yet others decided to not listen to reason, and they continue to provoke this war." Mathias tugged his beard, making it bob as if to show how the head could be manipulated by an errant hand. "It is not Yosef's fault that Galilee has been taken by the Romans. Don't listen to such talk." Mathias shot a glare at the Gischalan, who stood there with a smug expression and arms crossed. "Yosef has not and will not betray Jerusalem."

"The Zealots will not listen to you, Mathias," Yohanan ben Levi said as he uncrossed his arms. "Go home and see to your other son... and your daughter." He nodded at the Sanhedrin president, turned, and left.

"Shimon..." Mathias pleaded, but again the Sanhedrin president looked away.

"It's decided, Mathias... Yohanan is right. You should go home and be with your family."

* * *

THE UPPER CITY

"You just got home and no.... you must not go to the Lower City and visit your friend!" Rebecca repeated. "Go help Ya'el with Matthew. While *you* were gone, *she* changed his bandage, and he wants to go up to the rooftop terrace."

Miriam heard the sharp edge of an accusation in her mother's tone. "Mother, Ehud gave Matthew a message asking me to come to meet him at his market stall before he leaves today. He was packing up his wares and glassworks for while he's gone. The streets are safe now... I saw many people coming and going."

"What was so pressing that you had to rush out to speak with Ehud?" Miriam was silent, and Rebecca left that question to be asked again later, though they both knew it might remain unanswered. "I know the Upper City seems safe, Miriam, but we've seen how quickly that can change. Stay here and be of use. Help with your brother."

"Matthew is better, mother... he can—"

"Too many people now look at us differently, Miriam," Rebecca said as she wagged a finger. "This is not the time to argue with me. Just go sit with Matthew. He frets so, muttering about what he should do but can't until he heals." She disappeared into the kitchen with the brusque confidence of any mother sure she's made her point. Miriam reluctantly climbed the stairs to find the others.

The bright sun and blue skies above their home did not change Miriam's mood nor settle her thoughts as she sat on the rooftop, apart from Matthew, Ya'el, and Elian. She'd turned her face to the sun as if resting while her mind raced. *Be of use*, her mother had told her. She did not want to remain home and longed to explore more tunnels and King David's tomb. She had even thought she could take more of the gold bars from there. Maybe she'd have to melt them down so they could not be identified, or questioned. Or perhaps she could find someone who could exchange them for shekels and keep quiet about it. But having the gold on hand could make a difference if she and her family ever had to flee the city—if that was even possible once the Romans arrived. That was part of her hope in exploring the tunnels Zechariah had told her about, finding tunnels that led outside the city.

Some—her father and mother included—would consider it theft to take the gold or immoral to use it. And that had made her hesitate. Still, the *minae* had been there for a long time and were of no use to anyone. If they remained there and the Romans took the city and found the treasure... it would be as good as stolen.

Miriam also could not shake the feeling she should see Hananiah. He was the only person who accepted her and did not tell her how to behave. Hananiah seemed fine staying silent, which suited her. But the touch of his hand when she was last in his shop made her worry—something was stirring within him that could threaten their quiet friendship. And that morning, Ehud had jarred her thinking about the future. His words, most of them, had not been unexpected. She had not understood the meaning of some of his comments, but he had promised to explain when he returned from Qumran and had more time. Now she worried about the message from Elazar ben Yair. She must prove to the Sicarii that Ehud was not working for the Romans. But there was no way to do that if he was not in Jerusalem, where she could watch him and report that their suspicions were wrong. What if the Sicarii searched for Ehud and found him outside the city? They would kill him without hesitation... she knew they had done it to others they considered Roman collaborators.

"What's that?"

Miriam looked up at the sound of the boy's voice. Along the low wall that rimmed the roof to form the terrace, Ya'el and Elian sat on either side of Matthew, who was stretched on a couch between them. They all looked over the Upper City, facing south. The boy stood and pointed at something below. Miriam rose from where she sat near the steps down into the house, and as she drew closer to the others, she saw a smudge in the air over one street—smoke! The end of the cloud closer to them was thicker, the wafting trail behind... thinner and dissipating on the slight breeze. The path of the smoke followed the road it rose above.

Matthew struggled to stand, and Miriam reached down to help him.

"It's Yonatan..." The words were followed by a gasp, and they all turned to the stairs. Rachel stood there breathing heavily, with Rebecca behind her. The young woman continued. "Yonatan and some of his men are burning an effigy of Yosef!"

"And they march along the parade route we used to memorialize Yosef when we thought him dead at Yotapta." Matthew's voice cracked with anger and pain as he stared down at the approaching men.

"He boasted to Leah that he would bring the effigy right to your doorstep!" Rachel cried. "I ran to come and warn you."

243

LX

CAESAREA

THE ROMAN ENCAMPMENT, VESPASIAN'S PRAETORIUM

Vespasian brooded as he read a new report on the steady trickle of people deserting Jerusalem. It further reinforced his decision to wait a while longer before launching a full-scale attack on Jerusalem. The recent meeting between Yosef and the Syrian auxiliary had yielded little more than he already knew. He had been surprised, though he had not shown it at Yosef's wife's expression. After the men guarding him reported some of what they had heard from her, he had included the Jewess—Yosef's wife—to see for himself how she would act while Yosef talked with his friend... a Roman auxiliary. She had been silent, but what he had seen in her eyes was more than anger at Yosef.

The Jewess was intended as leverage against Yosef, to keep him from risking retaliation if he escaped, but word had spread that Yosef ben Mathias was a privileged prisoner and a traitor to his people. He had not been killed or sold as had other Judean rebels, so the stories grew that the captured Jewish general was a collaborator, which served Vespasian's purpose. Yosef was not likely to try to escape or even seek his release if the Judeans and Jews outside of Caesarea increasingly wanted to kill him.

Actually, Yosef had told him nothing he had not quickly learned from others about the factions within Jerusalem that vied for power. Their internal conflict would ultimately weaken the city and make it far easier to take, and it was happening already. Legion patrols found more and more bodies on the roads and scattered across the countryside between the coast and Jerusalem. Some were likely seeking to flee Judea on a ship or even to find refuge among Roman allies. Wounded survivors amid the dead had told of the Zealots' attacks or those of the Sicarii. That Jewish faction still held Masada and used it as their base for raids on Romans and anyone cooperating with them. Survivors had told of the recent fighting within Jerusalem's walls.

He still believed Yosef to be useful, but he no longer needed him to betray his people or provide him helpful information to aid the assault on Jerusalem. It seemed the Judean rebels were intent on fighting among themselves, and that would hasten their destruction.

But Vespasian had seen something pass between Yosef and Sayid when they mentioned Nicanor, Lady Cleo, and Gessius Florus; something unsaid but conveyed in the looks they exchanged. It had been a brief comment from Sayid about Gessius Florus and Cestius Gallus. Cestius Gallus had died in Antioch just before meeting with Vespasian, and the circumstances seemed odd. When he first arrived in Antioch, Nicanor had also expressed his feelings about the death of the former 12th Legion commander. The centurion had been concerned Gessius Florus was meddling in legion matters beyond his proper scope. Now Vespasian's own misgivings about Nero's tax collector were growing.

"General," Gaheris Clineas called from the entrance to his private office. "I have the auxiliary you sent for."

"Bring him in," Vespasian directed.

Sayid entered and stopped before the campaign desk. His expression showed he was surprised to be called back before the general. "You sent for me, sir?"

Vespasian did not signal for him to sit and instead stared at him silently long enough that the water-clock broke the silence.

"Nicanor thinks highly of you. When I spoke with Celsus Evander, he told me he brought you with him from Ptolemais because Nicanor had asked him to watch out for you when you returned. Nicanor also convinced me to endorse your orders to return to the legion." Vespasian stopped and watched Sayid, testing whether the young auxiliary might speak. When he didn't, he continued: "I want to know the nature of your mission for Lord Gallus and what it has to do with Gessius Florus and Lady Cleo." He paused again and studied the Syrian. "Nicanor told me he did not trust Gessius Florus and did not believe Cestius Gallus killed himself. Tell me what you know."

Sayid shifted his feet, then settled them and met Vespasian's stern gaze. "Nicanor thought wrong some advice Cestus Gallus had received as the 12th Legion marched from Antioch to Jerusalem. Nicanor believed that recommendations, and the commander's decisions based on them, had led to the legion losing much of its equipment and supplies to the rebel attacks on that march. When we reached Jerusalem, we did not have enough siege equipment and were forced to raid for supplies. At Beth Horon, we moved into the pass without clearing the higher ground...and we had not secured that as our line of retreat. The rebels held it, and their arrows and javelins rained down on us. Again, Lord Gallus had followed the counsel of his advisors."

"What advisors?" What the Syrian just said matched what he already knew from Nicanor.

"The senior military tribune, Galerius Senna, and the camp-prefect, Tyrannius Priseus... maybe others, sir, that I don't know about," Sayid replied.

"When their advice kept harming the legion, Cestius Gallus came to trust Nicanor, who had opposed some of what those men advised."

"How did you become a special messenger for Lord Gallus?"

"Nicanor, as a reward for his heroism at Beth Horon, was leaving to serve with the Praetorian Guard in Rome. Lord Gallus knew what would happen because of his failure and took responsibility for it. But he needed someone to take what he thought might be his last letters to his wife, Lady Octavia, in Antioch. My mother in Laodicea, near Antioch, was ill, and I had asked for leave to see her. Nicanor told Lord Gallus I could be counted on to deliver his letters to his wife."

"Lord Gallus did not trust the legion's couriers?"

"I don't know, general. Lord Gallus summoned me, and then I was on my way with orders. Once I delivered his letters to Lady Octavia in Antioch, I was allowed to see my mother and return when she was well."

Vespasian watched as beads of sweat appeared on the young Syrian's brow as he talked and wondered if the auxiliary was now hiding a lie. "That took you some time...."

"She was very ill, sir. I could not leave her until she was well enough to care for herself," Sayid paused a breath. "When I returned," he continued, "some men in the legion accused me of being a deserter... or a loyalist to Cestius Gallus. Most of the men in the legion thought him a weak and cowardly commander."

"But Nicanor... and you... did not?"

"No, sir. We thought him an honorable man but not an experienced soldier. His mistake was listening to—"

"The wrong men?"

"Yes, sir."

"Why does it appear to me Gessius Florus hates your and Nicanor's friend, Yosef? It seems it may be more than his being a rebel."

"I don't know, sir. After the shipwreck, Lady Cleo became fond of Yosef, though nothing came of that, though she was not yet married to Florus. They were just friends; all of us were. Sir, Nicanor... and I... dislike him—Gessius Florus. But Lady Cleo fears him."

* * *

"What did the general want?" Celsus asked the next morning.

That twinge of guilt he had felt when answering Vespasian's questions shot through Sayid again. "To ask me more about my friendship with Yosef."

"It's strange you and Nicanor can still like a Judean... after Beth Horon... and after Yotapta. I couldn't. The man's soldiers almost killed me there." Celsus shook his head.

"Yosef was serving his people."

"Yes, but he's an enemy."

Sayid kept quiet. He liked Celsus, who treated him well... much as had Nicanor when they first got to know each other. And he was a good officer to work for. Sayid still hoped he would help him find the legion his father served in.

"I heard that the general had his woman—his wife—removed from the camp."

"Yosef's?" It had stunned him that Yosef was married, but he had not been able to ask any questions about it. "What... why?"

"I don't know. It happened last night; she was gone this morning."

"Where?"

"I don't know, and it doesn't matter. Let's go." Celsus turned toward Sayid with a sheaf of parchment in his hand. "We have a supply ship at the port to check as it unloads."

An hour later, they were almost to the quay when Sayid glimpsed a man in front of a warehouse slip inside, one large hand pulling the door closed behind him. For a fleeting moment, he thought he had seen him somewhere before.

LXI

Caesaraugusta, the Road to Otho

It had rained for two days, and Nicanor and Graius approached the town feeling it had been much longer since they had been dry. "Easy, girl," Nicanor cautioned Carmenta. "Careful." He gathered the slack from the reins as she stumbled.

The cluster of buildings ahead, now coming alight with nightfall, were as alluring as the Sirens from the stories Nicanor had heard sailors tell during his days at sea. There they could dry off and eat something hot and not bread gone to mush from the steady rainfall. But the flats of the riverbank had turned to mud, and pools of water hid holes and washed-out areas with treacherous footing. He slowed Carmenta and scanned the area. Through sheets of rain in the graying twilight, he saw the surrounding heights. Rugged hills, some nearly mountains whose escarpments loomed over the valley formed by the Iber river and the confluence of two tributaries. Caesaraugusta sat on the Iber's north bank.

The first building was a stable, and there they unsaddled their mounts, hearing the rain splatter on the roof and glad to be out of it.

"Boy!" Nicanor called to the young man who had taken his coin. He rubbed Carmenta down with a rough blanket he had found hanging on a post. "Where's the closest inn where we can get a meal and a dry bed?" Though the rain had been warm, he had watched Graius shake as if with a chill for the past two days. The old man was still trembling, though he had donned a heavy mantle that had done nothing to hold out the rain. It now dripped rivulets onto the floor of the stable, and pools formed around his feet.

The boy, his paltry first beard a straw-colored fringe, pointed toward the rear of the stable and a wide door. "Through there." He hesitated and gauged the large man scowling at him from a scarred face. Then he added, "Sir. Just beyond the corral fence."

* * *

"The *Bona Dea*," Graius repeated the name they had seen carved in the wooden sign over the taberna's door. He pulled out a chair from the table closest to the low fire burning on an enormous hearth. On a spit above the flames turned a haunch of meat. Drops of grease and meat juice popped and sizzled in the fire. The girl turning the crank was as scantily clad as the one who now approached them with an amphora.

"Wine, sirs?" She gestured at the two *kylix*, decorative cups with handles, on the table.

Graius picked one up. "These are shallow, more like a *patera*, the libation bowl used in a ceremony than fit to hold a drink for a tired old man," he muttered. "Mulled wine, warmed..." he ordered and draped his sodden cloak over a chair.

"And some of that"—Nicanor pointed at the roasting meat and stooped to settle the two, wet and bulging *sarcina* next to the fireside but close enough where he could keep an eye on them. He had bought them in Tolosa once they were far enough from Narbo. The large legionary-style marching packs were stuffed with supplies and some clothing he hoped the cured hide of the bags had helped to keep dry. He shrugged off his cloak and hung it across another chair next to Graius's.

The serving girl returned with a different amphora showing marks on its base from sitting over embers to keep it warm. As she went around the table, the light of the fire behind her low-cut diaphanous gown revealed the figure of a grown woman, though her voice was high and sweet, and she seemed very young.

"What is it, Nicanor?"

Nicanor flushed, pulled his eyes from the girl, and looked at the old gladiator, who grinned at him and shook his head.

"Have you ever witnessed a festival for this taberna's namesake *Bona Dea*... the Good Goddess?"

"I've never heard of her." Nicanor shrugged, keeping his eyes on Graius and not behind him, where the girl turning the spit bent to carve slices of meat, she placed on two platters.

"I have... long ago on the Aventine in Rome. Some still follow her at a small temple there. The goddess is associated with chastity and fertility." Graius eyes swept the room. Each table had a young girl or woman serving food and drink to the seated men. "But I think this place is more bent toward the latter and less on chastity." He smiled again at Nicanor. "Is this one of the places your sea captain friend Marinus told you about?"

"No." Nicanor was glad to see the girl tending the meat spit was bringing them two plates. She set them on the table, smiled sweetly at both of them, and swayed back to the fire. His stomach growled, and he was heartened to see Graius turn his attention to the food. He had started to chew a large morsel—*lamb*, he decided and then stopped.

"How are the wine and meat?"

Nicanor looked up—but not far—at the short fat man with a very clean tunic. He could only be the proprietor and not a servant. Nicanor finished chewing and washed the bite of lamb down with a gulp of wine that emptied the cup. "Fine..." He recognized the two bronze disks and one silver pinned on the man's chest over the rise of his paunch and pointed at them. "Are those *phalarae* yours?" He doubted it.

"Oh no." The man's jowls shook with his head. "My grandfather served in the Legio XX, *Valeria Victrix,* and was awarded them and the land my taberna sits upon. May the gods still bless the long-gone Emperor Augustus. My grandfather fought for him in the *bellum cantabricum*, the conquest of Hispania. The emperor was grateful for his service." He studied Nicanor. "You have the look of a soldier... are you a legionary?"

"I once was...." The lie made it past his lips more easily than Nicanor thought it would.

The man's stomach now touched the edge of the table. "Have you heard the latest news... Lucius Rufus, the governor of Germania Superior, has defeated Julius Vindex, the rebellious governor of Gallia Lugdunensis. Vindex committed suicide after declaring again that Galba should become emperor." The man's jowls trembled again. "I think troubled times are upon the empire. But life here goes on," he said with a smile. "When you are through eating... we have rooms with comfortable beds."

The man stretched a short arm to pat the round bottom of the girl refilling their cups, and a sly expression spread over his moon face. "And some company for the night... if you wish."

"Just food." Nicanor gestured at his plate, wanting to get back to it. "And the beds."

The fat man's face sagged, then lifted with a smile as he bowed and left. "I'll see to your rooms."

"Look..." Graius pointed at the girl as she bent to clear the table next to theirs.

Nicanor glanced and closed his eyes to ignore the view of the cleft of her breasts. "We're not here for women."

"And it has been decades since I had a need for them," Graius replied. "Look again."

Nicanor did and saw it this time. On a leather cord hanging above the mounds of her breasts dangled the wooden shape of a fish. He thought of the man he had met briefly at the port taberna in Taernum on his way to Rome for Vespasian... and of Paul the Christian martyr.

"That religion spreads," said Graius.

"Is that a bad thing?" Nicanor asked, not believing it was.

Graius reached and checked their cloaks. "Still wet," he shook his head and sat back in his chair. "No. But I believe in our gods. Roman gods... and in Elysium."

"The Christians believe in an afterlife too, that their Christ has led the way for them. Perhaps to the same place?"

"I can't trust something so new... and unknown." A shiver shook the old gladiator. "When my *pneuma*, my soul, goes to Elysium... all I ask is for my ashes to return to the Temple of Hercules in Rome."

* * *

DIANIUM

The battered galley docked amid vessels loading with iron ore from the nearby mines, a strategic resource for the western legions whose exports reached all the way to Rome. The first man off glared up at another waiting at the rail. The man's face was red with anger that made the white of his dead eye and the scar bisecting it stand out. Quintus wished they had not run from that cursed pirate, Anicetus, and hoped they would another day and test who was the better. "Get the men. I'm going to check at the garrison for any messages from Lord Tigellinus and buy horses. We leave for Emerita Augusta immediately." Quintus hoped they had gotten ahead of a man—even a seasoned centurion—who was slowed by traveling with a woman.

LXII

Maius 68 CE

Jerusalem

The Lower City

The shop shutters were closed, and when Miriam cracked the door open, it was dark inside. She stepped in and blinked as her eyes adjusted. The closed shutters and darkness did not mean Hananiah was not there, and a faint glow from the shop's back showed the outline of a door. That must be where Hananiah slept. A tall shadow filled that doorway. When Hananiah called to her, she realized his eyes were as good as hers—maybe better—in the darkness.

"It's been a while. I'm surprised to see you, Miriam."

She walked further into the shop and could now see he held a drawstring bag in his hands. It was the same one she had seen him wear at his belt. Something about the way he handled it made her curious. He ran the palm of his hand across the bag, then pulled the cord to cinch it closed. He turned and set it just inside that door, on a shelf or table she could not see.

"It was the fighting... my parents were worried. They still worry about me being on the streets. My brother Matthew was wounded, and I had to help care for him. But the streets are quieter, and Matthew is better now." She had still seen groups of armed men at every corner and gate as she had made the trip to this shop. And the only reason she could be here—without directly confronting and defying her parents—was because of what had just happened.

The shadow moved, and a stream of sparks caught the wick of a hand lamp. A flame flared and grew. The light showed Hananiah's pale face as he straightened and turned. "And what of your other brother? People now call him a traitor." He walked toward her. "Earlier today," Hananiah waved a hand toward the door she had just entered through, "men marched in the streets burning a straw figure of him, a sign with his name around its neck."

"They came to my house... to insult my brother Yosef... and my family. Maybe even to harm us or our home. The leader who hates Yosef surely would have, if not for—"

"Who is this man that threatened you?"

Miriam had never heard such menace from anyone. It sent a chill through her. "Yonatan bar Hillel," she replied, without thinking why Hananiah wanted to know.

Hananiah's eyes glittered as a frown creased his face. "I suppose your *friend*, Ehud, stood up to him... for you and for your family."

"No.... he's gone—left the city." Miriam watched his scowl ease until she added, "He'll be back soon." As his brow puckered again, Miriam realized she hoped that Ehud would return quickly. *I must find out what was going on with him... why the Sicarii believed him a spy... and maybe it's time to let...* She shook that thought away.

"Then who stopped this Yonatan and his men?" Hananiah asked. "Or did they only threaten—as cowards do who are only brave against women?"

"A man came looking for my father. He commanded Yonatan to stop what he was doing. When my father came out, the man told him Yohanan ben Levi had betrayed the Moderates and joined the Zealots. The man was there to bring my father to a meeting with Yoshua ben Gamla and Ananaus ben Hanan. Matthew insisted on going along, too, so Mother went with them to help him."

"Your father and mother left... so you were then free to come here. Why did you?" Hananiah's voice softened.

"I wanted to thank you again for the dagger. And for that day when men were fighting in the streets outside. I saw you move to clear them away, to offer me the shelter of your shop."

"But you had your protector, *Ehud*." The edge came back to his tone, and the furrow in his forehead deepened, pulling the flesh of his face even tighter. In the flickering of light cast on his features, the crease looked almost like a cut, a wound the lamp's flame could not reveal but was made clear only by its shadowy cleft.

Miriam could hear his bitterness and regretted that he felt hurt. "Still, I'm your friend, Hananiah... and I thank you. I have little time and must get home before my parents return. But I'll visit again when I can."

* * *

Hananiah extinguished the hand lamp when Miriam left. He went to his room and, without looking, reached for the bag on the shelf above his cot. He took it to the small table and set it next to a sputtering oil lamp. Hananiah opened the bag and spilled its contents—the shriveled ears formed a pile next to a gleaming dagger. Picking that up, he turned it over so his eyes could enjoy the play of light on the metal. He ran a finger along its surface, and its touch soothed him.

253

The blade was a perfect twin to the one he had given Miriam. The two were the finest he had ever crafted. He slashed its keen edge across his scarred palm. As blood pooled in the cup of his hand, Hananiah dipped one ear until it was coated in red and set it aside, glistening crimson under the lamp's light. Perhaps it was time to add to his collection; this Yonatan had threatened Miriam... and Ehud, too. But that morning, he had picked up a message from Gessius Florus.

First, Florus wrote, Ehud must produce useful information or suffer the consequences. Hananiah would make Ehud deliver for Florus and earn his reward. Then he looked forward to the killing before he left Jerusalem: Yonatan would not hurt Miriam, and Ehud would never have her. The shadows on the tabletop stuttered and danced as the wick's flame wavered, shrank, and went out. But he kept anointing each of the ears with his blood. He had done it countless times, in light and in darkness.

LXIII

MAIUS 68 CE

JERUSALEM

THE LOWER CITY

Miriam had not gone far from Hananiah's shop when she had to slow and then stop. The mob of men grew thicker as she neared the steps she always took to go back to the Upper City. Rising directly to the Temple Enclosure from the Lower City, the steps were the safest way. Yosef and Matthew had taught her that when she tagged along on their childhood explorations of the city. The light there, especially in the morning and late afternoon as the day neared sundown, discouraged the street thieves who looked for the unarmed and unwary who walked alone. With the recent violence, Matthew—his expression full of questions he had not asked yet—had again warned her to not take the direct north path whose slope along the Tyropoeon Valley ran under the bridge and the viaduct that connected to the Temple Enclosure. It paralleled the foundation and walls and was in morning shadow until the sun rose high enough. In the evening, the setting sun became blocked by the buildings of the Upper City. Matthew had told her that lately, it seemed the men most involved in the fighting moved freely along that path, shrouded in darkness. She preferred not to encounter any of them. But the mass of men ahead, most armed and many carrying tools, some with beams of wood, blocked her from reaching the steps. Gathering her robe from around her feet, she bypassed them and started up the slope at a near run. She was surprised to find only a few men along the way Matthew had warned her against, and they hurried past and paid no attention to her.

As the slope reached the Upper City market area, Miriam noticed that the bright clear sky from earlier in the day had filled with clouds that seemed to grow thicker as she viewed them. *A shroud falls over Jerusalem*, she thought, *and the air has become so heavy.* Something in the stillness—a lull—alarmed her. The thinness of what would typically be a dense crowd in the market suggested that maybe others had the same foreboding. The people in the market also seemed not to notice her as she ran faster and still darted looks over her shoulder. Like the presentiments Yosef had told her he experienced, she felt the menace of something inexorably coming closer. Something yet to be, but inevitable. She shot another look. No. Nothing was behind her.

* * *

THE UPPER CITY

"Are they back yet?" Miriam panted as she came through the courtyard gate.

Ya'el turned from hanging a lighted oil lamp from a cord and hook tied to the limb of one of the larger trees near the table. "No," she said with a look of relief. "I did not look forward to explaining. I'm glad you're back." Ya'el called to Elian, "Come, light the torches."

Miriam shed her robe and straightened her clothing, one hand smoothing her hair. "Is Rachel still here?"

"She left right after you," Ya'el said with a shake of her head. "Rachel was lamenting her love for Yosef... it seems your brother has touched many hearts."

Miriam heard the sorrow in Ya'el's voice but had no answer for her. She was glad the boy interrupted the silence as he lighted the last torch.

"Now, can I go to the roof and watch the clouds?" he asked as he ran to Ya'el and tugged at her sleeve.

"Why... what's so interesting?" Ya'el looked down at him.

"They're funny looking." the boy pulled again. "Come with me and see them."

From the roof terrace, the storm clouds seemed even lower and bunched like misshapen and bruised grapes. They hovered just south of the city, clotted with a darkening purple at their centers and the western edges outlined in red from the setting sun. Movement along the streets caught her eyes, and Miriam shifted her gaze lower. She saw what must be hundreds of men racing through the streets toward the three towers along the city's western wall. The southernmost, Phaesel, was the tallest at nearly 150 feet high. The next was Hippicus, and then the northernmost and most decorative, Mariamne, was half the height of Phaesel. All three protected that side of the city and the traders' entry to Jerusalem. Beyond the walls, she could see broad whorls of dust whose tendrils twined around the parapets and were just fading in the twilight.

* * *

AT THE WALLS

"You should both go home. Right now." Mathias spoke sternly to Rebecca and watched Matthew, pale-faced, who had shrugged out of his mother's supporting embrace around his shoulders and stood without help. His strained expression slowed his pain. *Though,* Mathias thought, *that could also be because of what we've been listening to.* When he had spoken with Ananaus ben Hanan about Yohanan ben Levi's treachery, word had come of many Idumeans at the gates. They had gone with him to see the two thousand men, led by one of their generals, Shimon ben Calphas that demanded the Zealots be freed.

Rebecca, as white-faced as Matthew, shook her head. "He will not leave, so I stay."

"Yoshua will speak with them." Ananaus pointed to Yoshua ben Gamla, who, with a personal guard, climbed the stairs to the bulwark that ran atop the wall between the guard towers. "The Idumeans will turn away, or we have 6,000 men who can make them do so. I've ordered the Zealots in the Temple to be sealed in and all the gates barred. They cannot get out to help the Idumeans."

"I warned you, Ananaus, that Yohanan ben Levi would betray us. Simon bar Giora has already angered the Idumeans by raiding their towns. They were ready for a reason to do something against Jerusalem. All it took was for Yohanan ben Levi's lies to incite them to act."

Ananaus ben Hanan ignored him. "Listen."

"In this... your message to us," Yoshua's voice rang in the stillness, "you say Yohanan ben Levi, who now allies himself with reckless and murderous scum, has told you Ananaus ben Hanan and I have contacted the Roman general, Vespasian. You think we have offered to surrender the city... if he will remove the Zealots and leave us in power. That is false. I prefer peace to death for my own part. But this war has started, and I would rather die nobly than live as a Roman captive."

The men around Mathias, Rebecca, and Matthew turned to glare at them. *The lies about Yosef have poisoned them,* Matthew thought. Earlier that day, he had seen that look on the men carrying the burning effigy of his brother. Now he worried he was in no shape to defend his parents. Shouts came from beyond the wall, and the men looked away from them.

"See," Ananaus said as he leaned toward Mathias, "the Idumeans cast words, not spears." He spoke loud enough for Matthew to hear.

"You should not mock the Idumeans, Ananaus."

"Matthew is right, Ananaus. Treat them with respect, hear them out, and convince them Yohanan ben Levi of Gischala spreads such deceit only to serve his own purposes. If they do not peacefully withdraw, offer that they can enter the city without arms and serve as neutral judges to determine who tells them the truth. The Gischalan will hang himself with his own lies."

"What if they won't lay down their weapons?"

"Then have Yoshua tell them they can remain outside the walls, watch the city, and prevent any attempt to surrender to the Romans. Go now to Yoshua and have him tell them now before it's too late."

Ananaus shifted the torch in his hand, and Matthew saw the look of scorn on his face as he turned it up toward Yoshua on the wall.

"You have been lied to, Shimon ben Calphas!" Yoshua shouted down at the Idumean general. "You've brought your men—all in their shining armor—to the aid of scoundrels."

There was a rustle among the group of men as one man pushed through them, out of breath, to stand before Ananaus. "Our patrols report thousands of more Idumean soldiers nearing the city," he said. "They will be here, at our gates, soon."

Ananaus nodded and went to the steps leading to the parapet. He joined Yoshua, and the two bent their heads together. Yoshua straightened and stepped back as Ananaus moved forward and shouted: "Send away the men you've brought and those that are coming. The gates of Jerusalem are closed to you as long as you are armed."

The tumult outside the gates grew, the shouts becoming more strident. Ananaus's voice was rougher, ruder in reply: "You cannot enter the city. Jerusalem's gates are closed to you. The Zealots you seek to help represent a tyranny almost as bad as that of the Romans."

There was more shouting from the Idumeans.

"We do not care that you are fellow Jews!" he continued to shout. "You cannot enter carrying weapons... this city is ours, not yours."

The wails of anger beyond the wall grew louder and then were lost in the rising wind. A fork of lightning split the sky, accompanied immediately by a crack of thunder.

"We must go now," Rebecca said, taking Matthew's arm, and Mathias pressed through the crowd of men ahead of them as another stab of lightning cleaved the dark clouds.

LXIV

Maius 68 CE

Jerusalem

The Temple

Zerubabel laid the foundation of *Beit HaMikdash HaShemi*, the Temple, over 500 years before. King Herod rebuilt the structure itself and expanded the grounds over eight decades ago, and it took more than four decades to complete it all. And never had its stones trembled in a storm as they did now. Not since the quake of more than three decades back had the Temple been shaken so, and that had lasted only minutes. This tempest had gripped Jerusalem for what seemed like hours, like a beast hunched over, tearing at its prey. Talons of wind ripped at the city as lightning streaked the night sky, and roars of thunder shook the ground and walls. The Temple courtyards were flooded. A torrent of water spilled from the mount, pouring down the hills and into the Upper and Lower City. The guards at the Temple gates—trusting that the bars securing the gates would hold—fled the wind and the beating rain. To be out in that was to engage in combat against an opponent they could not defeat.

Inside the Temple, the floor was awash, and the movement of dozens of feet set off myriad waves across the surface. Unevenly spaced lamps and torches revealed eddies that shimmered on the wet tiles. Eleasar ben Ananias remembered a day in this room when Matthew's brother Yosef had told them of King Herod introducing that flooring technique, the *opus sectile*. In a pattern likely learned from the Romans, the floor was of geometric shapes and scenes on precisely cut and polished stone tiles of many hues and shades. The tiles were crafted and laid meticulously. A knife blade could barely be inserted between them. The water rippled over the stones beneath his feet as he closed his eyes and prayed. Eleasar heard his name called and looked up at a soaked man hurrying toward him, each step a splash.

"The guards have left the gates."

"You're sure they're gone?" Eleasar ben Ananias asked the drenched Levite named Caleb, one of his chief Temple guards.

"Yes, captain. I watched them go... and as soon as they did, Jabez appeared and told me the Idumeans are here, outside the walls. But

Ananaus ben Hanan and Yoshua ben Gamla have barred them from the city," said Caleb.

Eleasar turned at the sound of more splashing approaching behind him and frowned when he saw the source.

"I heard that, too," Yohanan ben Levi said as he joined them. "No matter, the Idumeans won't let that stop them. They come with 20,000 men, and with their help, we will throw out the Moderates."

Eleasar scowled at the man he had been forced to accept as a means to help break the Temple siege. "Do you always let others fight for what you say you believe in? You think swaying others with mere words will always get you what you want? I reached out to the Idumeans before you did. Now they have come... we must do our part."

"You may have contacted them first, but they've come because of what I've told them," Yohanan ben Levi scoffed. "And that's why they won't let closed gates stop them."

"What did you tell them, Yohanan?" Eleasar asked, his eyes flashing at the man's show of ego.

"Only what was needed to convince them to come to the aid of the Zealots. To help us gain control of this city before the Romans arrive." The Gischalan smiled. "You should thank me."

The misgivings Eleasar had always had and the distaste he now felt for the man wrenched his stomach. The Gischalan had fooled Shimon ben Gamliel with his lies. The Sanhedrin had accepted him only because they needed his Galileans. But Yohanan ben Levi had betrayed the Moderates, and now how could he and the Zealots trust him to be loyal? But with the Idumeans here, perhaps they no longer had to worry about the Gischalan's loyalty. Maybe Eleasar no longer had to swallow his disgust. He turned away from him. "Caleb, gather men with swords and shields to cover us while we work. We'll cut through the beams holding us in and try to help the Idumeans enter the city without letting them break through the city walls."

* * *

The next morning...

The storm and the Idumeans had raged through Jerusalem until just past dawn. Eleasar ben Ananias did not know if the coming of daylight had revealed enough to shock man and nature so much that they had stopped their destruction. Or maybe they were merely exhausted.

The men on the walls had assumed the Idumeans could do nothing during the ferocity of the storm and had not watched the gates closely. The tempest smothered sight and sound as Eleasar and his men, beaten by rain and whipped by the wind, found workmen's tools and sawed through the heavy crossbar beams securing the gates. Even though they had surprised the Idumean guards outside the gate by appearing suddenly through sheets of stinging rain, the guards had taken them to their commander and not killed them.

Shimon ben Calphas had been still seething at Ananaus ben Hanan's words and his rudeness. His people had been forced to assimilate the Jewish religion, and now generations had adopted it as their true faith. To be treated as a non-Jew by former high priests who professed to be Jerusalem's religious leaders had infuriated the Idumean general. He waited not a minute once he learned the city gate was unsecured. Mobilizing his men, Calphas had not listened to anything Eleasar said about wresting the city from the Moderates without harming the citizens. The general ignored his pleas that his men focus only on removing the leaders and then stand aside and let the Zealot leadership speak to the citizens of Jerusalem and assert calm.

Now it was too late for that. Thousands of bodies lay inside the walls and in the streets. People had been dragged from their homes; pallid corpses were washed bloodless by the storm. Only those who had died at the rain's end lay in red pools that had yet to dry in the morning sun. Countless more dead were inside houses and shops that had been looted. Eleasar had watched as the Idumeans, ordered by their general and with Yohanan ben Levi at his side, butchered Yoshua ben Gamla and Ananaus ben Hanan. They mocked their bodies as they cast them from the parapet the two Moderate leaders had spoken from the previous evening. The Gischalan had nodded his agreement as the general ordered the shocked citizens who stood blinking in the sun: "Leave them where they fell—anyone who attempts to retrieve their bodies for burial will suffer the same punishment."

Eleasar had turned away, not thinking where his feet led him.

* * *

The Upper City

The tears on Eleasar's face had dried by the time he reached Matthew's home. His own family had long ago gone to join the Sicarii at Masada. Matthew and his family, despite their differences coming to a head recently, were friends. He prayed they had all survived the night.

The first three bodies Eleasar came upon as he entered the rear courtyard had been killed by arrows. He stooped to study the odd shafts stuck in the Idumean soldiers. The arrows had been roughly shaped from thin, straight tree branches, the bark still on them. He pulled one out to find the point was of sharpened wood, no metal. Featherless, they would not have flown straight for very far. Their angle—slanted down and into the necks of the men, the exposed flesh not covered by their armor—meant they had been fired from above. He studied the home's second floor—knowing the bedrooms faced the courtyard—and the rooftop terrace, but he saw no movement. He rose and went to the shuttered entrance to the house. In front of it was the body of another armored Idumean. Kneeling, careful to avoid the puddle of blood, he moved the man's helmet that had come loose and lay beside his head, beneath his chin. The man's throat had been cut.

Standing, Eleasar pressed against the shutter, but it did not give. Something heavy must have been braced against it. He rattled and knocked, but there was no response from inside. He stepped back into the courtyard and called out: "Matthew... Mathias... it's Eleasar. I'm alone." A loud, angry squawk made him look up at a bird perched on the sill of a bedroom window above him.

LXV

The Road to Otho

The small village did not appear to have much to offer, but the horses and Graius needed rest. There had been little of that since the *Bona Dea* in Caesaraugusta. The next day should see them in Emerita Augusta by late afternoon. They planned to go straight to Marcus Otho's residence.

"I can ride longer... go farther, Nicanor." But Graius reeled in his saddle.

"I know you can, my friend." Nicanor did not hide his own grimace as he dismounted. His old wounds ached. "But we'll be in better shape to meet Marcus Otho if we stop earlier and rest a bit more than we have for days. I don't care to limp up to him... back sore and bent to one side as I ask him for his help." Still, if he had been on his own, *I would push on*, Nicanor thought. He knew Graius felt terrible for it, but whatever illness had ahold of him had laid him low and left him weak. Their one night in Caesaraugusta had turned into two and a late start on the third day. He had found a woman who sold medicines, and the ground bark bought from her had finally broken Graius's fever. But it had not lessened his stomach pain, and the medicine had run out days ago. The fever had returned.

The decurion-led men that had been behind them were now ahead of them, to judge from the words of travelers they met when they finally left the Bona Dea. Five of the legionaries were stopping and questioning people on the road. That meant the other men had pushed on ahead to seek them.

Nicanor had talked to a local trader who told him of a horse path south that would take them to another Roman road that ran west to Emerita Augusta. They had reached it, made the westerly turn, and come upon this village that sat astride the road in the twilight. Coarse laughter and shouts from the small taberna grew louder as they moved down the quiet street and closer to it. He had already decided to bypass the taberna. He saw what must be a stable further on, some distance from the other rough buildings. Beyond it, the forests thickened again on both sides of the road.

An old man with a two-tined pitchfork tossed hay into the corral to feed five horses inside and lined up at the railing at the stable.

Though their coats showed recent combing, the animal's backs and sides all showed the saddle marks of a long ride. "Do you have room for two more? But inside?" Nicanor asked the man.

The man nodded and pointed. "Two stalls at the back."

Nicanor dismounted and led Carmenta inside. Graius, still mounted, shaking uncontrollably, followed him silently, grimly. Nicanor was glad to see the width of the stall. He took a coin from his pouch and beckoned to the man, who came in behind them and leaned his tool against a wall. "We'll bed down with our mounts. Lay in some fresh straw and blankets for us... and," he untied an empty wineskin from his saddle, "take this to the taberna and have it filled. The best wine you can buy from what's left from this coin... and bring us two bowls of hot gruel."

A slyness came into the man's eyes as he nodded and took the coin. Nicanor squinted at the man and knew the wine would be poor quality, and the man would keep the difference. Still, he had no energy... nor desire to enter the taberna. He pulled his sword and thumbed its edge, locking his eyes on the man. "Return with what I pay for... and it had better be worth what I pay for. Do not make me come for you." The man nodded and took the coin. Nicanor turned to help Graius from his horse.

* * *

"You are far from Rome... and sleep so soundly, centurion."

Carmenta's shifting and warning nicker had stirred Nicanor, but it was the loud, contemptuous voice and barks of laughter that brought him fully awake. Two mounted men blocked the broad front entrance to the stable, the first light of dawn showing behind them. Nicanor rose and over the stall's low sidewall could see two more men, afoot, at the narrower back doors near their stalls. He recognized the sea captain and his men—the *speculatores augusti,* assassins Tigellinus had recruited from the Roman cavalry. Nicanor gripped his sword and wiped his mouth with the back of a hand. "You're far from Rome, too, Quintus." He peered up at the scar-faced sea captain and cast a corner-eyed glance at Graius in the next stall, who, wrapped in a sweat-soaked blanket, shakily stood, his eyes searching the ground at his feet.

"Looking for this, old man?" One legionary widened his stance and lifted Graius's sword. He pulled his shorter gladius with his other hand, took two quick steps closer through the opening, and lunged at the old gladiator.

Unsteady and tangled in the blanket, Graius was slow to dodge, and the thrust ripped across his chest and stomach. Blood pouring from the wound, he went down, rolling under his horse, who trampled him in fear. The old gladiator lay still.

As the first man attacked Graius, the second moved on Nicanor. Limited by the stall's side and back walls and Carmenta's bulk, Nicanor stood his ground. The legionary squared up in the stall's entry.

"You don't need to die here," Quintus lied as he walked his horse toward them. "Fortunately, I heard the stableman grumble about you at the taberna, cursing the big scarred man who rudely threatened him. It made me curious, and I had to see before we moved on. Now, answer my questions, and if they are what I need... you and your friend, if he is still alive, can go."

Nicanor knew the only way for him and Graius to live was to kill them all. He rested his hand on Carmenta's neck and seemed to consider Quintus's offer. He sheathed his sword, and the legionary, with a broken-toothed smile, took a step forward. "Now, girl," Nicanor's hand tapped a signal, and Carmenta reared, and her foreleg shot out. Hooves flashing, she struck the man square on his thick leather breastplate.

As the man fell backward into the man behind him who had attacked Graius, Nicanor was on him. The legionary straightened, and he kicked him in the stomach as the man's short sword came out and missed Nicanor's own stomach by a handsbreadth. A counter slash with the longsword's greater reach cut through the man's neck, nearly severing the head. He spun, and his blade speared through the second man's chest just as a mounted man crashed into Nicanor, spinning him into the wall. Stunned, he saw Carmenta charge from the stall, crashing into the rider, whose horse staggered. The man cut at Carmenta's neck as she careened off with a scream and splatter of blood. Nicanor brought his sword up to thrust at the rider, but he was off-balance, and he missed, and his blade stabbed up and under the man's horse's upthrust head. As the animal wrenched away, the sword ripped open its throat. The horse sagged; its rider leaped free as the animal fell on Nicanor, slamming the centurion's head into the ground.

The rider stooped and picked up his sword, careful to stay beyond his horse's flailing. Quintus dismounted and joined him to watch as Nicanor struggled to free himself.

Dazedly, Nicanor tried to pull his legs free and to get the dying horse's head in an armlock to keep it down and from rolling over on him. A shift in more weight onto his legs would likely break one, if not both.

"You can't escape, Nicanor. Lord Tigellinus has questions... and you'll give me answers to take to him."

"I think not," a voice grunted. Graius, bloody chest heaving, stood behind the men. He held the stableman's two-toned pitchfork. "I never fought as a *retiarius*, nor with a *fuscina*..." he shook the pitchfork, "and this is only a workmen's trident... not a true weapon." He adjusted his grip on the long handle. "But I think it will do." He thrust it into the upper chest of the closest man when he turned to face him. The man fell with a froth of blood on his lips.

"Kill this man and get the centurion from under that horse," Quintus ordered his remaining man and backed away.

The legionary went at Graius, who spun the pitchfork, and the tines—snake-strike quick—stabbed through the side of the man's face, tearing away an eye. Pulling out and reversing it, the bloody and torn tunic slipping from his shoulder, Graius thrust with the handle's rounded end into the second man's throat. With a crunch of bone, the man fell, clutching his neck.

"Carmenta," Nicanor called and pointed. The horse, a ragged wound in her neck, had moved clear of the men's blades and the kicking, dying animal that pinned Nicanor. She moved to the man Graius had taken down, stomped, and the choking man no longer had to worry about trying to breathe.

"Behind you!" Nicanor shouted and watched as the old gladiator whirled to block Quintus's sword. Graius stopped the arcing blow, but the sea captain held a dagger in the other hand. Right then, yanking its head free, the dying horse lurched and bucked a final time, striking Nicanor head-to-head, a bone-jarring impact. The horse's death throes stilled as Nicanor's sight dimmed. Before that darkness fell, he saw Quintus's dagger pierce Graius's gaunt ribs and thrust up. The old gladiator went to his knees.

LXVI

Maius 68 CE

The Road to Otho

Nicanor opened his eyes to bright sunshine shafting down through a canopy of trees. He lay within the circle of a dozen young trees, their boughs not grown enough to close out the span of the sky above. The sunlight touched the borders of their new leaves. He groaned, rubbed his head with both hands, and kneaded the muscles of his neck. He rocked his head side to side, trying to loosen his neck, but stopped. His head ached, and he felt a pounding as if he had drunk too much bad wine the night before. He sat up and discovered the throbbing extended to his legs. Carefully examining them, he found it was just the ache and not the stabbing pain of broken bone—then he rubbed his thighs as he looked around. At the next tree, Graius sat slumped against the trunk, his chin on his chest. A damp muzzle nudged the back of Nicanor's neck, and he painfully turned to see Carmenta, a bloody bandage roughly wrapped around her throat. Just beyond her was a small stream. There, he saw Graius's horse dip its head to drink.

He reached up to stroke Carmenta's nose. She nickered softly as he rose from the ground with a grunt of pain. He could see the edge of the road through the trees, but there were no sounds or signs of the village or villagers.

"Graius!" he called and went to the man and stiffly kneeled beside him. Beneath the old gladiator's cloak, he could see nothing but remnants of his tunic and a bloody wrapping. The cloth he had used to bind his own wounds had slipped, and Nicanor saw the terrible gash in Graius's chest and the jagged rip from Quintus's stab, the wound below his ribs curving down to his lower back. No bandage would have staunched those wounds. The ground beneath Graius was a slurry of blood, leaves, and dirt.

"Graius," Nicanor said mournfully, touching his shoulder, surprised when the old man's eyes fluttered open.

"Graius, wh-where are we?" he asked, bumbling over the words in his surprise.

"I killed him... the man with the scarred eye you called Quintus—who has killed me." Graius shakily raised his head. "The stableman came and boasted that he had told the others, the villagers, that we were wanted by the emperor. A few men then joined him. But I had donned my cloak and made little of my wounds. I lifted my sword—taken from one of those bastards we killed—and recited 'The Shield of Hercules' from the Greeks." Graius's eyes closed. "Do you know it, Nicanor?"

He gripped Nicanor's forearm and quoted from the epic poem: "'Though they were brothers, these were not of one spirit; for one was weaker but the other a far better man, one terrible and strong, the mighty Hercules.'" He paused and took a shallow breath; even that made him wince in agony. "They thought me crazed; none was brave enough to stop me as I readied our horses and got you up and loaded on Carmenta. I think we made four or five miles before I had to stop. I'm sorry I could not go further, Nicanor," he gasped. "I call you my little brother, now. But I'm the weaker man... and you the far better...." He lifted his hand to point above them. "It's not quite the temple's oculus, but still... it's beautiful. When you find Cleo, please tell her I love her as the child I could never have. But I must rest now...."

His hand fell as his *pneuma* left him.

* * *

EMERITA AUGUSTA, HISPANIA LUSITANIA

The city was at the junction of several vital trade routes and sat near a crossing of the *Flumen Anas*, the River of Ducks. The river was out of his sight, and Nicanor could not hear any of its namesake waterfowl. Roman roads connected the city west to Felicitas Julia Olisippo, south to Hispalis, northwest to the gold-mining region, and northeast to Toletum. The streets and markets were bustling with activity. Nicanor noted the clusters of people he came upon talking excitedly among themselves. He could not understand a word they said. Less often, he saw smaller groups, sometimes just three or four men, who seemed worried, fearful, watching the streets. The few times he caught snatches of their slower conversation, it was always about Galba or Nero and rumors of large bodies of armed men moving throughout the province.

Nicanor felt more than saw the stares at him as he led a horse, clearly with a body draped over its back, through the main street. Finally, that feeling grew too strong to ignore, and his stern glare, hand on his sword hilt, gave them pause and a reason to turn away. One man, curious and brave enough, asked his business in the town and then gave him directions to the governor's residence. He was nearing it.

Nicanor approached the walled-and-gated residence and the four sentries at its courtyard entry. "I must speak with Lord Marcus Otho on a matter of great importance."

One sentry, likely the guard or watch captain, came forward. "What do you wish to see the governor about?" His eyes swept over Nicanor, who no longer wore the trappings nor insignia of a centurion. He would see only a road-soiled, weary man but one with a soldier's bearing. "And what—or who—is this?" He pointed at Graius's body.

"He's a man worthy of your respect," Nicanor growled. "He served Lord Otho's family for years, and the governor will want to know of the man's death. And I must also speak with him about his sister, Lady Cleo."

The man locked eyes with Nicanor, who returned his gaze silently. He left and returned several minutes later with a dozen armored soldiers and a man in a patrician's robes. Despite the roundness of soft, noble flesh, his features had some of the same lines as Cleo's.

Marcus Otho stepped between two of the men leading his escort. "Where do you come from?"

"Rome, but—" Nicanor stopped as the soldiers bristled at the name, put hands on hilts, and two men readied to cast their *pila* at him.

"Hold! Lower your spears," Marcus Otho directed the men and spoke to Nicanor. "We're wary of men from Rome right now." He glanced at the body and back to Nicanor. "You claim Graius is dead, and you bring him to me." He ordered the captain of the guard without turning from Nicanor. "Reveal the body."

His eyes not moving from Nicanor, the man walked over to the horse and cut the cord used to lash the body to the saddle. Tugging at the cloak, he flipped the cowl back to reveal Graius's pallid face.

A shadow passed over Otho's features as he looked upon his former servant, and he turned to Nicanor. "He was a good man... and loyal. You must tell me how he died and who killed him. But first, what's this you speak of about my sister?"

"We should talk of it privately, lord."

"How do I know that you know anything of my sister?" Otho glanced at Graius's face again. "How do I know you did not kill Graius yourself... and this is some ploy to get within weapon's reach of me or to get me alone and unguarded? In these times, we—I—trust no one from Rome."

"I was with your sister on the *Salacia* that was wrecked as it carried us to Rome from Judea a few years ago. I'm one of the men who helped save her. I need your help to save her again."

"From whom?"

"Again, lord... that's better discussed in private."

"How can I trust you?" Otho shook his head, and the pouch under his chin quivered.

"Graius did." Nicanor searched for some way to prove it as four men with bows joined Marcus Otho's guards. Their captain signaled, and they nocked arrows. "Arrows..." Nicanor straightened.

"What?" Otho asked and took a step backward behind his men, who closed around him.

"Graius trusted me to save your sister, and I will not fail him. He told me you once caught Cleo—Lady Cleo—long ago, hunting the moon with her bow. Do you remember?"

Otho studied Nicanor for a moment. "Yes," he said and gestured for the archers to stand down.

"Then help me, Lord Otho, to save your sister."

ACT III

LXVII

Jerusalem

The Upper City

"After you eat, you should lie down, Matthew," Rebecca said again as she set fruit and water on the table. Before returning to the kitchen, she stopped at the head of the table to squeeze her husband's shoulder. "You too," she said.

"I will," Mathias said with a weary smile, but that faded as soon as she turned away.

Eleasar ben Ananias's eyes followed Rebecca, he waiting to report what he had learned during the day. He looked at Mathias, then Matthew. Father and son were both pallid, their faces strained. He knew they had slept poorly since the Idumean attack. "The killing has stopped, but the Idumeans have imprisoned hundreds... maybe thousands in the city. Yohanan ben Levi or his men pointed them out to be taken."

"We must help free them, and let's hope no more die." Mathias's voice quavered, and he wiped his brow with the back of one hand. Since the storm, the air had remained heavy over Jerusalem. The morning too still to break the heat that had come early, ahead of the summer.

"I pray so," Eleasar said, taking a handful of dates from the bowl. "Before... I was ready to fight Ananaus and his men. I thought them as much the enemies of Jerusalem as are the Romans. But now that I've seen thousands of bodies in the streets and not one of them a Roman, I know we must stop fighting among ourselves."

"How do we get the Idumeans to leave?" Mathias tugged his beard and looked from his son to Eleasar.

"Shimon ben Gamliel knows that Yohanan ben Levi deceived the Idumeans. I have spoken with him, and I plan to take him to meet with Calphas, the Idumean general. I've seen how Calphas has looked at the Gischalan as he harangues him to continue to purge the city. I think the Idumean leader's anger at us will be quenched by that disrespect. He has seen no signs that anyone has contacted Vespasian or any Roman, for that matter, about surrendering the city. Will you come with me, Mathias?" asked Eleasar. "Will you come and talk to him, too?"

"Yes." Mathias nodded. "But Shimon ben Gamliel must speak for the Sanhedrin and admit Yohanan ben Levi is a liar who has duped the Idumeans just as was done to him by the Gischalan."

"But now you must rest, father," said Matthew and called out: "Mother...."

Rebecca came from the kitchen. Mathias nodded and took his wife's arm. "I will go with you tomorrow morning, Eleasar, and do what I can to help."

Matthew watched as his father left the room and turned to Eleasar. "Do you think the Idumeans will listen?"

"I hope so. I have heard Calphas say he wants no more of his men killed in Jerusalem when he needs them to fight the Romans." The Temple Guard captain straightened his shoulders. "That reminds me—with all that has been happening, I haven't mentioned this to you. But the morning after the attack, I dragged away the bodies in the courtyard before the barricade was cleared so I could come inside. You did well and protected your family."

Matthew looked puzzled. "What?"

"The four dead Idumeans. That must be what reopened your wound." Eleasar gestured at Matthew's chest, the bandage showing beneath his robe. "But I see how tired you are. You must rest, too." He looked up at Rebecca, who had returned. "I can stay tonight and keep watch, if I may, so your family can better rest. And in the morning, Mathias and I will find Shimon ben Gamliel and meet with Calphas and try to convince him it's time for him and his Idumeans to leave."

"Thank you, Eleasar. Please do stay. I'll bring you some bedding for the divan, so you're comfortable." Rebecca replied. "Come, Matthew—first, I'll help you upstairs and change your bandage."

* * *

As his mother changed the dressing that wrapped his chest, Matthew considered what Eleasar had said. His wound had broken open during the Idumeans' attack on the city. But it had happened while securing the front entry. Miriam had been helping him, and when she saw the fresh blood, she had called their mother. Then she had insisted that he, their mother and father, and Elian go to the cellar. At the same time, she and Ya'el finished barricading the front and back entries. When they finally joined the family, they said nothing about any men.

His mother left, and Matthew looked from his window down into the courtyard as twilight grew. He heard the warble of some night birds and then a murmur of voices from Miriam's room. He could not make out what was said from behind her shutters and turned away. *Who killed those men?*

* * *

Miriam looked at the boy stretched on a blanket on her floor and the parrot perched in his cage on a stand. Both were already asleep. She turned to study Ya'el. The Roman lady had loosened her hair and was combing tangles from it. They had spoken of other things as Elian fell asleep and not of the men they had killed. They had yet to talk about what had happened that day.

She had been nearly done blocking the doorway and about to close and bar the shutters when the first Idumean entered the rear of the courtyard. Spotting her, the man had pulled a dagger from a sheath on his hip to accompany the sword in his other hand. He had walked toward her with a leer and told her things he would do—she shuddered to think of that now. She had told Ya'el, "Go... I'll face him," and slipped her blades from their forearm sheaths.

Ya'el had refused, telling her, "I'll stay by your side and fight." Then three more Idumeans had come into the courtyard. With barely a glance at her, Ya'el had wheeled and run toward the stairs. At that moment, Miriam's heart had fallen. She had stood there watching the man and three others come closer. Again the man said terrible things. When she did not move, standing her ground without fear, he laughed and called to the other men over his shoulder. That was when she had rushed him, and her first slash cut the man's throat as her second thrust stabbed through his neck just below one ear.

She had not heard or seen the first arrow streak from the bedroom window above her. But one of the Idumeans shouted as the man ahead of him fell with a shaft through his throat. His own cry had been cut off by another arrow that transfixed his neck as she stared at him. She heard the third pass above her on its way to skewer the last man. The Idumeans had died choking on their own blood. She thought of what the first man had said to her and was glad that the last thing they tasted was their death.

"I have not said this, but thank you." Miriam still had a twinge of regret; she had doubted Ya'el at that moment and had thought her a coward. She leaned toward Ya'el and grasped her shoulder to feel its tremble. There were tears on the Roman lady's face. Ya'el knew what Miriam meant.

"I've told you I will never be weak again—not before any man—but I'm not as brave as you are, Miriam. Still, I would not, could not... if there were another choice. So, for the second time, I've had to use my bow to—"

"To do what you must do. Kill a man... to save my life. I could not stand against four armored men. At best, they'd have killed me... and at worst... done other things and then killed me. And done that to you, too. They would've butchered Elian, my parents, and Matthew." Miriam released her shoulder. "But your aim was perfect."

Ya'el set aside the comb clenched in her hand and kneeled next to Elian. Her fingers brushed the hair from the boy's eyes and smoothed it with a palm. "It had to be." She looked up at Miriam and said, "Elian could find only three branches from your trees that were straight enough to shape for arrows." She straightened and sat next to her on the bed. "What will happen now? Will it be like this until the Romans come?"

Miriam shrugged; she had wondered the same thing since the day in the tunnel when the two Romans attacked her. The uncertainty and worry of what was next and what was to come. She did not know if it would ever leave her. "I don't know." Still, Ehud's return had kindled a spark of hope that one day she could live without fear.

LXVIII

JUNIUS 68 CE

JERUSALEM

THE UPPER CITY

"Yohanan ben Zaccai and I heard the talk about the Idumeans marching on Jerusalem, but never thought they would..." Ehud paused, and his shoulders sagged with more than fatigue. "What I saw myself and heard from others... we could never have imagined it. Nahum, the Essene leader, had warned us, so I should not have been shocked at what the Idumeans did."

"What did Nahum tell you?" Matthew asked.

"That the Sicarii now continually raid from Masada," Ehud replied. "When I arrived in Qumran, Yohanan and Nahum told me of the attack on Ein Gedi just two months ago. The defenders thought they wanted only to take food and supplies for Masada, for the Sicarii are readying their fortress for a lengthy Roman siege. But it was not just raiding for provisions—once the Sicarii overcame the defenders, they slaughtered 700, including women and children."

"The massacre here and at Ein Gedi are tragedies that should have never happened," Matthew said quietly.

"It is a stain... we can never remove," said Mathias. "History will condemn our stupidity," he rasped in a voice hoarse from Sanhedrin meetings that had become more shouting than rational argument.

"We were not... *are* not stupid, Father. Others were... and others are."

"No, son." Mathias shook his head, and his beard quivered. "We, too, share some blame. I, most of all, for not speaking out earlier... more forcefully. Years ago, I sensed how some were thinking and worried they stoked fear in others to get what they wanted. I should have done more then to stop them. Now we will all be judged."

"You are only one man, Father!" Matthew had raised his voice. His eyes darted to the darkened windows of the bedrooms above them, shutters open to let in any vestige of a breeze. His mother was asleep by now, Ya'el and Elian too, surely. He shifted his gaze to Miriam's window. No sign of light there or of movement... but he knew that meant little. His sister, he was now sure, was hiding something and likely was listening to them. He lowered his voice. "What can one man do?"

"One good man at a time can become many, Matthew. One good thing, one right thing... done every time it's needed and counted upon... adds up. And that can change fate." Mathias turned to Ehud. "When will Yohanan ben Zaccai return?"

"He is not far away. Tomorrow I'll go to Herodium and return with him." Ehud straightened in his chair.

"Why Herodium?" Matthew asked.

"When we heard the fighting in Jerusalem had stopped, we came here together from Qumran. We thought it best for him to stay someplace fortified and not out in the open while I made sure Jerusalem was safe."

"Nowhere is safe... not anymore," Mathias replied, sad and angry.

"Will the Idumeans really leave?" Ehud asked, looking at Mathias with what seemed somber respect. Matthew knew Ehud had always admired Mathias, lamenting that his own father was weak.

"The Idumeans have agreed to leave in a day or so," Matthew said. He took an angry breath and continued bitterly: "They released 2,000 prisoners once they were convinced that no one had contacted the Romans to offer them the city. Yohanan ben Levi now claims it all was a misunderstanding."

"He got what he wanted," Mathias said with a sigh. "His lies served to get the help he needed to break the Moderates. Those of us who still live have little power. The Zealots and Yohanan ben Levi and his Galileans now control the city. But they promise there will be no fighting between them."

"Then I'll leave in the morning to get Yohanan." Ehud rose from the table.

Mathias returned to the courtyard after walking Ehud out. "Will Eleasar ben Ananias help us once we have the locations and directions?" he asked Matthew.

"I'll see him tomorrow, but I'm sure he will." Matthew carefully stood, wincing, and followed his father into the house. A minute later, he paused outside of Miriam's door, and his ears caught what seemed a metal-on-stone rasping from inside. A board creaked as he shifted his feet, and the sound stopped. He waited a moment, but it did not return.

* * *

THE LOWER CITY

The streets showed the marks of the storm. The paving stones beneath Miriam's feet were more uneven, and some rocked, loosened when the fill dirt between them washed away. The murkiness of nightfall made it hard to see the worst areas, and she was thankful there were very few people out at that hour, so she could go slowly. Down several of the alleys lighted by torches, she could see more remnants of the storm. The fabric of awnings had torn from their frames over shops, and scraps of clothing, shafts of broken spears, and other objects had been caught in the flood's churn and wash and lay in piles. A tangle of them had yet to be cleared, just as the street she trod upon had yet to be re-leveled and smoothed. That work was well underway in the Upper City.

As she neared Ehud's glassworks, Miriam looked up from watching her footing. The lighter gray of a tall, cloaked figure stood in the shadows before the door, unlocking it. She stumbled on a loose stone, and the sound echoed on the nearly empty street. The person at the door stepped into the glow cast by the corner lantern that illuminated part of the face.

"Miriam?" he whispered.

"I heard you're leaving again," she said, not flipping her cowl back.

"What are you doing here? You should not be... your father and mother will be—"

"Mad. Yes, Ehud. They'll be angry with me. Matthew, too."

Ehud hurriedly opened the door and beckoned her inside. "Why are you here?"

"To see you... to talk where others are not around."

"I have to go right away," he said. "I'll come to see you when I return."

"I'm not leaving until we talk." Miriam went to the door he had unlocked, opened, and went inside. Ehud followed close behind.

Inside, Miriam watched him as he lighted an oil lamp. In the flare of light, she could see on the table a wrapped square of parchment tied with a cord. She picked it up. A puzzled expression on his face, Ehud took it from her, untied and smoothed it flat. He slid the lamp closer to read what was written upon it. As she bent toward him to study it as well, something in the slanting strokes—the writing—seemed familiar. With it in his hand, he turned from her before she could read it. With a sharp hiss of breath, Ehud crumpled the sheet into a ball in his fist. He pounded that fist on the table hard enough that she expected it to hurt him.

"What is it?" He ignored the question and her—face downcast—until she touched his arm. "Ehud, what's wrong?"

"What?" Ehud looked up, and his eyes were wide in the dimness. "Nothing, Miriam." He took her hand and pulled her toward the door. "I have to leave the city, and you must go home."

"But... let's talk for just a—"

"Go home, Miriam. Now."

She could not believe it as he gently but firmly pushed her out of the door and shut it. On the street, livid, she walked away.

* * *

Ehud watched her go, then took the crumpled parchment and smoothed it out to read again:

> You have two weeks to find out exact information on the plans to hide the Temple treasure. Or your family will die, one at a time.

The message was dated three days before. If someone had found it... he would likely have been killed on sight when he returned to the city from Herodium. And then there would be no one to save his family. He hurried and changed into the clothes he had come for. Yohanan ben Zaccai carried what he needed. He must copy or steal it to give to Gessius Florus and protect his family.

LXIX

Junius 68 CE

Caesarea

The Roman Encampment

"I never thought about how much work was done to move supplies and equipment to the legions," Sayid said near sundown when he entered the Legion Quartermaster's office and laid a sheaf of vessel manifests and warehouse inventories on Celsus's desk.

"It is largely thanks to General Gaius Marius, a century ago, that it can be done so well," Celsus said in greeting. "An old quartermaster in Ptolemais told me of how he and those before him were taught the methods and means Marius laid down when he reformed the deployment and supply of the legions. Without these improvements, Rome could not respond quickly to threats nor keep the empire's provinces secure. Our problem is the *impedimenta;* the standard provisioning that each legion carries is not enough for legions in the field this long. And the *commeatus res frumentaria* are not enough general commodities from Rome's *publicani,* the private contractors who help supply the legions in Italia. The northern and western provinces must help provide what we can't produce locally when we have a province and people in rebellion."

Celsus walked to the map on the wall behind his desk. "The legion's *abulatio* and *frumentario* have been routinely attacked by rebels and bandits. Here and here," he tapped with a finger in several spots, "and they can't get all we need. But with what we bring from Alexandria, we've stockpiled fodder for livestock and extra food supplies for the legion. Still, the *lignatio* and *aquatio,* who find wood and water and if needed, who also transport it, are hard-pressed to support each legion."

Celsus sat at the table, moved the stack of documents from Sayid to one side, and picked up a message the legion courier had delivered that morning. "I checked on what you asked and have something for you." He read from the message: "Marcus Sabinus serves in Legion XV Apollinaris. He was badly wounded at Gamala and was just released from the *valetudinarium* in Ptolemais." Celsus shook his head. "So, he was probably in the legion hospital there when I was."

"Thank you for helping me," Sayid felt a knot in his stomach tighten. "Where's his legion camped?" He knew Vespasian's son, General Titus, had spread the three legions under his command through different areas to suppress the raiding Celsus had just mentioned.

The newly-promoted centurion stood and checked the map or the wall behind his desk. "The Apollinaris cohorts and their auxiliaries are at Apollonia, Joppa, and Lydda." He turned to Sayid and said, "No new vessels are due for a while. We'll plan the supply caravan to them, and if you wish, you can go along and ask further about your father."

* * *

A day later...

The long day neared its end, and the taberna's lanterns were being lighted as Sayid entered to find it nearly full. He had finished checking on the loading of the wagons and knew the caravan's route there and back and time to unload at each camp would take 18 days. If he found his father at the first or second camp, he might return to Caesarea sooner if it proved safe enough to travel alone or with one of the camp couriers. He had eaten his meal and ordered beer often enough for the gruff barman to not give his table to better-paying customers. The beer seemed poor even to him. Nicanor would have had words with the barman about bringing something of better quality. Still, he cared little about that and was merely passing the time. He would leave early the next morning, and that could not come soon enough.

Waterfront tabernae, Sayid mused, *all smell the same.* The odor of brackish water was strongest when the doors or windows were opened. But open or closed, the stench lingered of sour wine, stale beer, and mostly of men who bathed infrequently. That mixed smell of seaports and legionaries. And there was tension in the air, too. The legion General Vespasian had kept close to Caesarea to protect the port, and his headquarters was idle and every man bored. It was more entertaining to be garrisoned in a secure province. Here, in a rebellious one—though Caesarea had not been part of the revolt—there were fewer opportunities for enjoyable activities after a day's work was done.

Sayid would not have noticed the man had he not spotted Celsus walking toward him. Just beyond Celsus, at a table near the portside door, sat a man holding a red-stained cloth to his cheek. His unobscured eye was locked on Sayid. He lowered his large hand to reveal furrows—deep gouges—in the flesh. The wounds were oozing blood, and smears of it had dried along his chin and jaw. Sayid jerked his gaze away from him. It was the man from the taberna in Ptolemais. The man who had attacked him.

"Sayid," Celsus rapped the table with the knuckles of his fist. "Sayid...."

Sayid looked up. "Sorry, sir. What?"

"I said I'm headed back to camp. If you're ready, we can go together."

Sayid nodded and stood. He looked for the man with the bloodied face, but he was gone.

* * *

Celsus and Sayid looked down on the body. It was facedown, but they could tell it was a woman wrapped in a threadbare cloak covered with dirt and bits of brush and grass. They had come upon her less than a hundred feet from the well-lighted main gate and could clearly see the sentries on duty.

Sayid kneeled as Celsus lowered the torch they had lighted once they left the town. The woman's head was bent at an angle, and when he swept aside the long hair freed from its loose scarf, he saw why. At the bend of the neck was a discolored bulge where bones had snapped beneath the skin.

"Her hand is bloody," Celsus said. He stooped and lifted her right hand, its fingers red-streaked and nails broken. "And her heels... one of them." He gestured at the one bare foot, the other still wearing a sandal, though it had twisted and nearly come off too. Her feet had left drag marks from where the road was more dirt than gravel to where she lay. She had to have been dragged some distance.

Sayid turned her over to reveal a face frozen in a grimace of rage or pain.

"A local woman, by her clothing." Celsus straightened and seemed impatient to leave. "I'll tell the guards to come to get her body."

Sayid did not move and kept staring at the dead woman in the torch's flickering light.

"What is it? Do you know her, Sayid?"

"It's Yosef's wife, Ariella." Sayid looked up at him and then back toward the town.

LXX

Junius 68 CE

Lydda

Sayid turned to one side in the saddle and unwound the cloth covering his nose and mouth. He shook out the dust and dirt and decided not to re-wrap the fabric since they were close to Lydda. After finding Yosef's wife dead, spending a sleepless night, and leaving early the following day, he found his thoughts swirling the way the gray powder of baked dirt eddied through the air as the wagons in front of him trundled along. From Caesarea to Apollonia, he thought about Ariella, so recently killed that her body had not yet cooled or stiffened when he and Celsus found her. The marks on her neck... the man in the taberna. Why did he kill her?

He knew why the man wanted him. The brute searched for Cleo. Sayid had ridden along half-dazed in the heat and worried whether Cleo... Ya'el... was still safe in Jerusalem. The approach to the first stop had made him more alert and anxious. But his father had not been in Apollonia. He went back to the cycle of thoughts and worries on the road to Joppa. But his father had not been there, either. And now they came to Lydda. As his anxiety had grown, part of him wished he would find that his father was not there, either.

The wagons in front of him slowed and came to a stop at the encampment gate. A pang of doubt shot through him. He should not have come. Maybe he should have stayed with his mother and aunt in Laodicea. Perhaps that would have been best. But when the wagon ahead of him rolled through the gate, he followed it.

* * *

The unloading done, Sayid stepped into the tent that served as the cohort's field office. He handed the supply manifest—checked off and signed—to the *tesserarius* assigned as the cohort quartermaster. "All done. Your centurion said that since it's late, we can stay overnight and leave at daybreak."

The first sergeant nodded, spread the manifest on the table, and began running a finger down the lines of items and quantities.

"Do you have an officer here," Sayid asked, "an optio by the name Marcus Sabinus?"

The man looked up. "Why do you ask?"

"He's my father, and I'd like to see him."

The sergeant studied Sayid from head to toe and looked doubtful. "Your father?"

"Yes. If he's here, I'd like to speak with him."

The legionary blinked and scratched his chin with a thumb. "He's with his men over at the city walls. Cross through the camp, and you'll see them."

"Thanks." Sayid turned to leave.

"Since he returned to the legion," the first sergeant warned, "Marcus has been testy at the end of a training day. You might want to wait until morning."

* * *

Sayid had not been with the 12th Legion when it razed Lydda on the march to Jerusalem, only one day's journey away. The 15th Legion had re-fortified the town and erected even higher walls. He did not understand why until he reached his father's unit. On the windward side of a stretch of the highest wall, teams of men clambered through dirt and sand, carrying ladders that they set against the walls and anchored at the base. A mix of other men, most from *Provincia Africa,* as was his father, worked alongside mules to push and pull into position the broad, flat sleds loaded with rocks to simulate a siege tower's weight. They made slow progress as a tall, lean-waisted, broad-shouldered dark-skinned man atop the wall cursed down at them to work harder... move faster.

Sayid stopped next to a handcart with a water barrel, manned by an auxiliary with a bandaged arm. "I'm looking for Marcus Sabinus."

The man pointed with his empty ladle at the cursing man on the wall.

* * *

Sayid watched as his father grunted and settled onto a folding camp stool and stretched his leg out. As Marcus Sabinus had stiffly descended a ladder held by his men, Sayid had seen the scars on his body. The long, now-healed tear started high on his thigh with a deep pucker that became a jagged seam running down to his knee and curled behind to end at mid-calf. At the bottom of the ladder, as he headed toward the water barrel, Marcus peeled his sweaty tunic from his torso and revealed another ropey scar that ran diagonally across his midriff. At the barrel, he took the ladle and drank. Twice. All the while, he kept his eyes on Sayid, whose head reached only to his father's shoulder.

Marcus finally said, "I had word from your mother that you were in the legions and would find me. You look like her." Then he had picked up a waterbag beckoned, and Sayid had followed as all the men, released from their detail, returned to camp, some squinting at their commander as they filed past.

* * *

Though it was now past sundown, the day's heat held, so the cook fire Sayid and his father sat beside was small. Their faces were shiny with sweat that dried as the night cooled and the silence between them grew. Marcus had not spoken since their walk to the camp, Sayid matching his deliberate pace, when he asked what Sayid was doing in Lydda. When Sayid answered, Marcus had compressed his lips into a tight line and not parted them except to take sips from the waterbag slung over his shoulder.

"The training I saw was good and needed," Sayid now commented to break the stillness, "but the walls of Jerusalem are near 40 feet high and eight feet thick. There are three walls around the city: 90 towers in the first, 14 in the second, and 60 in the third. It will be tough to breach them."

"You're a clerk," Marcus scoffed. "How would you know what wall is hard to breach?"

"I was in Jerusalem with the 12th Legion and once before that." *And I lived within them for a time,* he did not add. "I took careful note of those walls."

"I doubt you could even handle your share of a siege ladder," Marcus said, shaking his head.

A man standing across the fire leaned toward them. "I hear you, Marcus. Your boy lacks your stature... are you sure he's yours?" He and the two men next to him laughed.

Marcus lurched up, and the men stopped laughing and walked away.

"Thank you," Sayid said, glad his father had stood up for him.

"I sired you, but I'm not a father, boy," Marcus countered. "Legionaries can't marry... you know that, and your mother knew it."

"She still loves you... and I thought—"

"You thought you would find me, and I would suddenly *become* a father to you. Maybe even have you serve with me..." Marcus grimaced.

"Yes...."

"You're a clerk," he spat. "You know nothing of war or battle." Marcus slapped his scarred leg. "I can no longer fight... and I doubt you have the ability. We're both useless in battle. War is for men, and I doubt you can do even once what my men do every day."

"If it was my duty, I would do it. I can do anything your men can do. Scale any wall...."

Marcus turned from him and stared into the twilight that became evening as the sounds of men preparing dinner, laughing, and arguing filled the deepening silence between them.

Sayid stood. "Perhaps we'll meet again when I *become* a soldier." He walked away to where the mules and wagons waited for the morning. There he stood, lost in thought, wondering how his three years of searching could have ended in such a disappointment.

LXXI

EMERITA AUGUSTA

THE GOVERNOR'S RESIDENCE

The burning coals varied in shades from a roasting red to blistering orange and yellow shooting tongues of flame that flickered with the breeze that fanned them. The olive wood bier and plank the body lay upon had collapsed into the bed of the fire that had consumed them. At the last minute, Nicanor was glad he had thought to see if they had the wood that Hercules's famed club was made from. He thought the old gladiator would appreciate the ashes of that wood mingling with his.

Nicanor had studied Marcus Otho as they honored the first part of Graius's wish to be burned and his ashes taken back to the temple where Nicanor had met with him. He puzzled over how Cleo's brother had ended up in Hispania Lusitania, even as its governor. Life in the provinces was not near as luxurious as in Rome, and the man seemed not suited to be far removed from the delights found at the center of the empire. Cleo had told them—Sayid, Yosef, and himself—how Marcus had once been a friend of Emperor Nero and had married Poppaea Sabina, who became Cleo's best friend. Then Nero had become enamored of Poppaea and ordered her divorce so he could wed her. From Cleo's telling, it seemed Poppaea had willingly gone to Nero. Nicanor was not naïve; he knew the ways and wiles of men and women. Still, love should not be abandoned so readily—even for an emperor—at least that's how he felt.

In profile, the man's features showed how fine and plentiful eating and drinking had layered ample flesh over the lines and firmness of jaw he admired in Cleo's features. Nicanor closed his eyes and could still see her as she sat across from him in that port taberna in Ptolemais. Even with her face clouded with fear, worry, and marked by the wrongs done to her, she was beautiful. He shook his head and opened his eyes still on her older brother. Marcus seemed to lack the resoluteness Nicanor saw in his sister. But in their youth, Marcus Otho had done things to protect and help her be just herself. Their father thought differently. He saw women—even his daughter— as an asset to be bartered or traded for his own benefit. Marcus had

"

been long gone by the time Cleo's wedding to Gessius Florus had been arranged. But maybe now—Nicanor hoped—the brother could help save her from her husband.

"Let us talk more, now," Marcus Otho said as he turned from the flames. "Once all is done here, my servants will collect the remnants and bring them to us. Come with me." They crossed the courtyard to a terraced area leading toward the river. A graveled walkway led to what Otho had told him was the underground Temple of Mithra. Nicanor knew many legionaries who had served in the western provinces who were initiates into that religion's mysteries, greeting each other as *syndexioi* with a special handshake. He had no interest in that or any religion, though such thoughts often took him back to Paul the Christian.

It seemed to Nicanor that Marcus Otho was deep in his own thoughts as they approached the domus. Its masonry foundation, surrounded by a rammed earth buttress, was raised above ground level to the first floor. They climbed the steps to enter a four-columned atrium with an *impluvium*, a deep pond to collect water. Beyond it were rooms whose walls were plastered and decorated with paintings. Another set of steps and a stairway led to a second level, but they passed the stairs and stopped at the first large room beyond the atrium. Its floor was like nothing Nicanor had seen since his visit to the *domus transitoria*, Rome's imperial palace where he had met Emperor Nero to receive his reward for saving Cleo, Poppaea's best friend, from the shipwreck. That night had also been when he had first met Gessius Florus... and disliked him immediately.

"It's a mosaic of the cosmos." Marcus Otho pointed at the tiling that had caught Nicanor's attention, with its imaginative and realistic representation of men, terrestrial and celestial firmaments, and the elements. "See how all things revolve around *aternitas*... eternity? Sit..." He waved a hand at a chair.

Nicanor did not want to walk on the mosaic and skirted its cloud-framed border to reach the chair Otho indicated.

The governor had no qualms and walked across the colorful scene to sit next to him. "I've thought about what you told me. I have scant authority outside of my province and none in Judea." Otho held up his hand. "Now, hear me before you speak. I have little power to help my sister, but that might change soon. When Graius brought me what you gave him... the reports and letters from Cestius Gallus and my sister, with their suspicions, I shared them with Lord Galba. He is the governor of Hispania Tarraconensis, the largest of the three Hispanian provinces. After I showed him, he spoke with powerful people in Rome, and—with their support—he then announced himself as a *vir militaris* of the Senate and the people of Rome. He did not claim to be a military representative, but his imperial intentions were clear when he used phrases like *libertas restituta* and *Rom renasc*. The promise of restored liberty and rebirth of Rome drew men to him, and they continue to come. Then last month, Lucius Clodius Macer, legate of Legio II Augusta in Africa, revolted. He has cut off grain supplies to Rome and raised a new legion, I Macriana Liberatrix. Content within his own domain, Macer, will not support Lord Galba. And Lucius Verginius Rufus, who had defeated Julius Vindex—who called for Galba to become emperor—at Vesontio in Gallia Lugdmensis, has refused to accept his legions' request that he become emperor."

"I appreciate you telling me this, Lord Otho, but how does it help Lady Cleo?"

"Lord Galba has gathered men to form a new legion, the VII Gemina. He believes no one will oppose him becoming emperor and is coming here soon. We will speak with him about all that you have told me." Otho paused and seemed hesitant, then continued. "You say you served in the Praetorian Guard and now serve General Vespasian. I must warn you that Lord Galba fears—rightly—the Praetorians and strong legion commanders. Their men are completely loyal to them. Do you think Vespasian will support or oppose him?"

Nicanor had had little to do with the intrigues of politics and noblemen in his life, and that only since the wreck of the *Salacia*. But he knew men and their motivations, no matter their station. He sensed there was something unsaid in Cleo's brother's talk of Galba becoming emperor. Nicanor had heard Lord Galba was 70 years old and his wife and children dead. Marcus Otho was maybe in his mid-to-late 30s, just a few years younger than himself. *Perhaps...* He let the thought go and shook his head; it did not matter. Nicanor did not need to understand and sought to stay above the unseen undercurrents. All he wanted to do was get Cleo free from Gessius Florus and out of Judea to someplace safe. "I cannot speak for General Vespasian. I know that he is a soldier, and I think he only wishes to do his duty for the good of Rome."

"*Nero* cares nothing for the good of Rome or its people," Otho scoffed. "Your own experiences... and the suspicions told of in Lord Gallus's reports that you know about... reveal this, too. Rome needs a new ruler to save the empire.

"I don't wish to insult or anger you, Lord Otho. But is Lord Galba the man to do that? And will he help us save your sister?"

"Lord Otho," interrupted a servant, calling from the arched entry to the room. "A rider just delivered this." He waited for permission, then entered to hand a scroll to the governor, who broke the seal and read.

"We'll ask him, Nicanor," Marcus Otho said with a nod. "Lord Galba arrives tomorrow."

LXXII

EMERITA AUGUSTA

"What's this?" asked Nicanor as they approached a line of men and women entering a rectangular granite building fronted by six massive columns that rose from its foundation to a gabled roof high overhead.

"This," Marcus Otho gestured at their destination, "is dedicated to the imperial cult. It is fitting that Lord Galba would have us meet him here. He intends to return the empire to what it once was and what it should be again."

"No, Lord Otho... these people." Many of them carried torches. The sun had just dipped behind other buildings that lined the broad avenue west from the city's forum. "What are they doing here?"

"Lord Galba holds to the old traditions." Otho saw Nicanor's puzzled expression and continued. "Twice each day, one by one, the freedmen and slaves who serve him, and the legion he's formed... come to greet him. Now they bid him a good evening. They'll return after daybreak tomorrow to wish him a good morning."

Nicanor looked at the line of men and women again and shook his head. As a soldier, he understood how some men sought favor by fawning over their superior officers. He understood the freedmen and slaves had no choice. They must do as told or suffer the consequences. And he knew the importance to superior officers that their men respected them. Yet this—the freedmen's and slaves' daily greeting—was not done out of esteem. That measure of honor and respect had to be earned and not ordered. He did not comprehend any leader's need for obeisance such as this. But then, he was not a noble.

There was something else Nicanor did not understand that Otho had just said. "Lord, you say this building is for a cult. Is it a temple for their worship?"

"Not like what you're thinking, centurion. There are no costumed or cowled ceremonies held at *media nox*, no conjuring over entrails or midnight sacrifices." Otho seemed almost amused, then grew serious. "The imperial cult is a tradition and set of principles abandoned by emperors like Nero. Followers believe in Rome's original values and the principle that leaders should balance the interest of the people, the legions, and the Senate. And that we must have respect for our gods."

Nicanor and Otho passed through the two center columns and entered the building. At the end of the main hall sat a man on a dais. The line grew shorter as each man and woman greeted the robed figure, who nodded his acknowledgment and dismissal. As the line shortened to its end, Marcus Otho moved forward. Nicanor, who followed him, did not care for how it seemed they were in the queue for their own deference to the man in an esoteric tradition.

"Greetings, Lord Galba..." Otho bowed.

Nicanor did the same. He straightened and studied the man before him. While Cleo's brother was clearly overweight, Servius Galba was gaunt. Otho had hair carefully coifed and shaped—almost helmet-like on his head—but Galba was bald. Where Otho's full-cheeked face was split by a long blade of a nose, Galba's face had a large, distinctly hooked nose.

"Who is this, Lord Otho?" Galba asked and pointed at Nicanor with a gnarled fist of twisted fingers.

"This is the centurion I spoke of who sent me Cestius Gallus's reports, Lord Galba, and the letters we discussed. Otho glanced at the men flanking the dais. Nicanor saw that on the left was a centurion. A primus pilus, the VII Gemina's senior centurion, as designated by the insignia worked into the new metal of an ornate breastplate. On the right, an older man was dressed in the robes and markings of a tribune, with close-cropped gray hair. He had the bearing of a soldier.

"We should talk privately, Lord Galba," Otho said.

"Yes, let's hear what your centurion, this former Praetorian, has to say, and I have news from Gaius Sabinus in Rome." Galba dismissed the two men beside him and rose from the ornate chair with a grimace as he shifted his weight, favoring one leg.

Nicanor saw now that one of Galba's feet and both ankles were swollen. The skin was stretched tight beneath the leather straps of a sandal that cut into the flesh. It looked painful.

Galba reached for a staff leaning against the arm of the chair. "Come with me." He stopped and glared at Nicanor, then turned that scowl on Otho. "Marcus, do you trust this man?"

"Lord Galba, a man I knew for many years, vouchsafed his own trust for Nicanor." He nodded at the centurion next to him. "And so I trust him, too."

Nicanor was glad to hear no hesitation in Cleo's brother's reply. Then he felt Galba's fierce gaze turned on him, and he met it without flinching.

"I warn you," said the old man. "If I decide I do not trust you... I will have you killed. And it will not be an easy death."

LXXIII

Junius 68 CE

Jerusalem

The Upper City

Ya'el sat on the bed in Miriam's still darkened room, holding in her lap the sharpening stone and dagger Miriam had given her. Together they had listened to the talk in the courtyard until Ehud announced he would leave the next day for Herodium. Miriam had quickly changed into a modest ankle-length women's tunic, wrapped a veil to hide her hair, and took a plain gray cloak from a peg on the wall by the door. Then she told her, "Stay here, be quiet, and don't strike a light. I'll be back as soon as I can." Then she bolted.

After the conversation in the courtyard had ended, Ya'el heard the scuff of footsteps that stopped outside Miriam's bedroom door. She knew it must be Matthew and prayed he would not knock nor come inside. When he did not, she breathed a sigh of relief. She would do all she could to protect Miriam's secrets, but she knew nothing was hidden that would not one day be known. She thought about that for a long time as the quiet of the night deepened.

Sooner than expected, Miriam returned, startling her as she appeared in the room before Ya'el realized the door had opened. Only eyes that had been in darkness so long could have discerned Miriam's grim shape in the dimness. "Did you see Ehud?" she asked.

There was a pause and then a curt, "Yes." Miriam was signaling she did not want to talk.

Ya'el sensed her anger, but there was the sound of tears in her voice too. "What happened?" She waited for the tension she could feel more than see radiating from Miriam. How long had Ya'el held her own fear and anger inside and had no one to talk to or help her cope with it? "Talk to me... it will help." Miriam was silent for so long, she felt she would speak only to tell her to leave her alone. "Please..."

Miriam let out a deeply held breath. "He would not talk with me. I'm sure he hides some secret, and I now fear Elazar ben Yair and the Sicarii are right. When Ehud returns, I must follow him. I'm afraid that I won't find him innocent of what the Sicarii claim. I'm afraid I'll find him guilty of being a traitor."

Ya'el rose from the bed and hugged her. As Miriam silently wept, Ya'el thought, *Nothing is hidden that will not one day be known.*

* * *

BETWEEN JERUSALEM AND HERODIUM

Ehud's mind was as cloudy and full of dark thoughts as the day was clear and bright. A breeze swept across the countryside, swaying the sparse clumps of slender trees sway and turning broad swaths of the tall scrub brush into dancers in the wind. He did not feel the freshness that cooled his face as he looked around him, unseeing, as his mule plodded along. He was consumed by thoughts of the unexpected encounter with Miriam—he knew how badly he had upset her—and consumed by the contents of the message he had found waiting at his glassworks. Before leaving Jerusalem, he had written his reply to Gessius Florus, saying that he would soon know the locations where the Temple treasure would be hidden. He had taken the message to the spot in the grove of olive trees where three centuries-old trees had twined into a single colossal bole. Inside a concealed opening, he placed the message in a container knowing it would later be picked up and taken to Florus. Now, once he rejoined Yohanan ben Zaccai, he would have that information. He prayed that it would save his family.

He felt his mule pick up its pace without his prodding, and he shook off his inattention; that could get him killed out here on his own. The trail he had been on had joined a broader, more level road, and not far ahead, a cloud of dust showed the approach of many men. A few minutes later, he saw both horsemen and wagons. As they neared him, he saw Yohanan ben Zaccai riding on the bench of the first wagon. Four men on horseback, lightly armored, carrying *hasta*, moved from the sides to in front of the lead wagon. They came toward him and stopped just within reach of the long spears, whose bronze tips glinted in the sunlight as they pointed at his chest.

"He is no danger to us!" Zaccai called to them. "Boaz, I know this man... he is a friend." The old priest put a reassuring hand on the man's arm next to him, and the man brought the wagon to a stop and lowered the reins.

"Let him come forward and join us," said Boaz as his eyes left Ehud, looked beyond him, then scanned either side of the procession. "But we cannot stop long. We must keep moving."

The four men peeled back and split, two to each side. Ehud could now see four other outriders and a separate dust cloud behind the caravan that showed more riders trailed the merchant and his wagons. Boaz shook his reins to roll again, and Ehud turned his mule to walk beside the wagon at Yohanan ben Zaccai's side. The old priest leaned toward him.

"I heard more talk from traders stopping at Herodium that the fighting had stopped in Jerusalem, and the Idumeans were gone. And then my friend Boaz offered me a ride with men to protect us... So I decided not to wait for you."

Ehud gripped the mule with his knees and shifted closer to the old priest. "What of..." he hesitated and glanced at Boaz, whose attention remained on the road. Still, Ehud lowered his voice: "What of... what you brought from Qumran?"

"Don't worry," Yohanan replied. "It is safely hidden." He shook his head. "But let's not speak of it."

Ehud straightened, and his heart sank. Only the circumstance of Matthew's wounding had given him the chance to go to Qumran and be with Yohanan as he returned with the prize. So much depended on what must be a list of places where the Temple treasure was to be hidden. There would be a copy for Mathias and Matthew to use in directing the hiding. And another to be secreted away for safekeeping, but accessible and near Jerusalem. That was the information he had hoped to give Gessius Florus. Now he would have to either come back and search in and around Herodium or steal the copy the old priest carried with him now.

LXXIV

Cosa, Italia

Nicanor led Carmenta down the broad, heavy gangplank that had been put in place quickly once the *Favonius* had docked. They were both glad to be off the ship. Carmenta had not wanted to board the vessel in Dianium. He had coaxed her, step-by-step, with handfuls of salted grain. And he, too, remembered the wreck of the *Faustitas* and all that happened at Marianum... and the *Salacia* before that. He had no fondness for sailing and never looked forward to it. Over the ten days at sea from Dianium to Cosa, both had relaxed, but not completely. Nicanor realized that as he and Carmenta both let out deep breaths when feet and hooves stepped onto the stone of the quay.

Through Marcus Otho, Lord Galba had questioned Nicanor's insistence on taking a slower ship because it could carry his horse. Lord Galba wanted Nicanor in Rome as soon as possible to deliver his sealed letter to Gaius Sabinus, co-prefect of the Praetorian Guards. Nicanor had had no dealings with Sabinus, but the prefect had sent a dispatch to Galba via horse relay. Only the most urgent communications were sent that way on the *cursus publicus* throughout the empire. The message was that Emperor Nero had been deposed by the Senate and had disappeared, perhaps fleeing to Egypt and the protection of its prefect.

Nicanor shifted the *loculus* containing Galba's letter to Sabinus, so the satchel lay across his broad back, which freed his arms to saddle Carmenta. After securing his traveling pack and a waterskin he would fill before leaving the city, he gently rubbed around the puckered seam of the jagged scar on her neck. He had stitched the wound from their fight with Quintus and Tigellinus's men, and his workmanship was not as good as that of a trained medicus. But it had sealed the wound. And if Nero was no longer in power to protect Tigellinus, he swore a vow that Carmenta's wounding and Graius's death would be avenged. As would the wrongs done to Cleo if he ever got his hands on Gessius Florus.

Carmenta blew through her lips. She was ready to go, and so was he. They left behind the low fog that clung to the port as the road climbed to the town above them. Cosa sat over 300 feet above the *mare nostrum*, the sea whose waters—east to west, end to end—spanned the empire's breadth.

The road leveled as they passed through the southeast gate in the wall that encircled the town. At intervals along it were several watchtowers; Nicanor assumed they continued beyond what he could see as the wall curved in the distance to arc around the town. Minutes later, on the main street that would turn into his way east, he and Carmenta passed the city forum. It had been built adjacent to a *capitolium*—a sacred area of religious monuments and temple at the *arx*, the crest of the saddle between the town's two heights.

The joy of being off the ship and astride Carmenta faded. An aching emptiness grew; the return of the desolation never felt as a young man he had set aside during the sea crossing. He missed Graius and the companionship he had not known since being with Yosef, Sayid... and Cleo... before the war. He knew he would dwell on that ache over the three-day ride to Falacrine.

Once again, Galba and Otho had turned him into a courier—as Cestius Gallus and even Vespasian had. He had agreed to the task with the men's promise to do all they could to help Cleo. They had expected him to sail to Ostia, the closest port to Rome. But after what had happened to him and Graius on the road to Emerita Augusta, he had no interest in arriving at Rome's main military port, where Tigellinus likely had many men there watching for him. Galba and Otho, their legion, and those they planned to draw to them were a two-and-a-half-month march from Rome. He had time.

Cosa was a much smaller port but also quite busy for its size. Most importantly, it had a route to Falacrine, and one not likely to be watched. He must talk to Antonia Caenis before entering the hornet's nest Rome had become with Nero gone and so many jockeying for power.

* * *

FALACRINE

Antonia Caenis had greeted Nicanor the evening before, and the morning light revealed what lantern light had not. She was grayer and her face more lined as she joined him at the table on the terrace that ran along the back of Vespasian's rambling estate. "My sources confirm Nero has fled or is in hiding, but they don't know where. Yet. He might already be dead, perhaps by his own hand." She paused, and her face tightened. "I will not miss him and what he has done to the empire. But there is someone I've heard is dead who will be sorely missed. Lady Octavia. My men learned of a man with a scarred eye accompanied by four Praetorians in Praeneste—he sought directions to her villa. Neither she nor anyone from her household was seen in the days following. A local merchant delivering a wagonload of ordered goods found that Lady Octavia, her major domus, and the servants had been slaughtered. Those men must have done the killing."

Nicanor closed his eyes, recalling his visit to Octavia. "And they are now dead. Graius and I killed them all in Hispania. Lady Octavia and Cestius Gallus did not deserve to die." He shook his head and gritted his teeth. "Honest men and women die while the jackals who order their deaths live." A surge of anger coursed through him, and an urge to feel his sword in his hand, to find the men responsible and test his metal on their necks. He had to force down that impulse; those he wished to punish were far from Falacrine.

"This Gaius Sabinus you say you are to meet and deliver that message to... From what I've heard of him... he is not to be trusted." She pointed at the loculus still hanging across his body. "Are you sure you should not break the seal and see what it holds?"

"I gave my word, Lady, but I will be watchful for any betrayal." Nicanor hesitated. "Lord Galba has promised to help Lady Cleo. Do you think I can trust him?"

Antonia took a moment to answer. "I know Marcus Otho, despite his shortcomings, loves his sister." She studied Nicanor with a knowing eye. "And he is useful to Galba. Otho will make sure he keeps his promise."

Nicanor flushed at her scrutiny. How was it she could see what he could barely admit to himself? That he was more than just doing what was right to protect someone vulnerable, that he also deeply cared for Cleo as a woman. He cleared his throat before he could speak. "Then I will keep my word to them and deliver the message to Gaius Sabinus untouched. But I must also report to Vespasian all that's going on; he must know, or will soon know, about Nero. And I need to know his orders for me."

Behind Antonia, he saw Vespasian's youngest son, Domitian, halfway behind a column near the entry into the house. That morning the boy had joined him as he tended to Carmenta; he had even combed her and seemed to enjoy the moment. Now he watched them with a flat expression, his eyes locked on Antonia. When he saw Nicanor notice him, he turned away and went into the domus.

"I can get your report to him faster than any means you likely have use of," said Antonia, twisting in her chair to wave over a nearby servant. "Bring me my writing materials." She turned back to Nicanor as the servant set a wooden tray on the table beside her. "I must tell him others are maneuvering for power who will claim to be emperor. And none of them deserve it... none of them are the type of leader Rome needs right now."

"Thank you, Lady. After that, I must get to Rome."

"I'll give you an introduction to someone there you can trust. You will need someone to turn to who can help you." Antonia picked up her pen, dipped it in the inkpot, and bent over the parchment.

LXXV

Julius 68 CE

Jerusalem

Outside the Northern Gate, the base of the Mount of Olives

Passing through the Upper City twice each day, hours apart, going to and from the message drops outside of Jerusalem's walls, served another purpose for Hananiah. Miriam had promised him a month ago that she would return to visit him, but she had not. He worried that she had been harmed, maybe by this Yonatan bar Hilel she had told him had threatened her family. So he secretly checked on her and had also found where Yonatan lived.

Some mornings, Hananiah had seen Miriam in the agora, most often with the woman, her relation from Tarsus, who was Greek. The two seemed closer than when he had been introduced to Ya'el, and something about her still bothered him. Though he had only seen her a few times, the woman did not seem like the Greek women he had known in Alexandria. Perhaps it was her bearing... her manner, but Ya'el did not matter. What was important to him was Miriam. Hananiah believed she wanted to see him, but her parents must have convinced her to stay close to home. He had also seen her strolling with her brother, nearly healed from the wound Miriam had mentioned.

Hananiah had found the home of Yonatan bar Hilel but still had not seen him. When he had asked other shopkeepers about him, he learned the man had trade he still maintained outside of Jerusalem. But Hananiah had seen the woman who must be the man's wife. Her veil had slipped as she came out the morning he had found their house. The sun had been on her face. He had caught the twitch of a weak smile and noticed the mark of a fading bruise on her cheek. Just that morning, he had seen her again as she affixed her veil, but the smile was gone and the bruise—reborn—darkened her swollen cheek. The sight affected him only to the degree that he would not let her husband harm Miriam in such a way.

He climbed the mount as he slowed where the path wound through ancient trees leading up to the olive groves covering the ridge east of the city. Hananiah listened for others around him or further into the woods, but he heard only the wind. Minutes later, next to the gnarled, twined trunk of one of the oldest trees, he held a folded square of parchment. He moved from the shade of the trees and unfolded it to read:

The Essenes of Qumran have a detailed list of what you seek, and I am working to find a copy of that brought to a hiding spot nearby. Please do not harm them.

The message would have no meaning to others if found, and it was unsigned as it should be, containing the expected pleading. Ehud had returned, and he seemed close to delivering what Gessius Florus sought. Once that was done, Lord Florus would reward Hananiah, who would also do what he and Lord Florus wanted: kill Ehud. Then he would dispose of the body—*Most of it*, he thought as he patted the pouch at his waist—so it would never be found. Then Miriam would be his, and he would have the means to take her from Jerusalem. He refolded the message and sealed it to take it to where Florus's courier would pick it up. Then he would return to the city and keep watch.

* * *

THE UPPER CITY

Ehud arrived at the gate just as Yohanan ben Zaccai came out. "Yohanan... I'd hoped to see you this morning."

"I don't have time now, Ehud. We are going now to see Shimon ben Gamliel. There is news we must hear." The old priest turned as Mathias came from the house to join him. "But I can speak with you later if you wish."

"Matthew is inside, Ehud," Mathias said in greeting, "and Rebecca still has the morning meal out if you are hungry."

Ehud watched the two old priests walk toward the market and the street leading to the Temple Enclosure's viaduct.

* * *

THE TEMPLE

"Nahum often talked to me of what the Essenes thought of the Temple and its treasure," Yohanan ben Zaccai commented as they passed another storeroom full of incense. "... the material riches they deem unimportant. Much of it is not this easily seen... or accessed."

Mathias followed his old friend and nodded in agreement. "Most people see only the 13 trumpet mouths of the contribution chests along the wall of the Women's Court. Eleven for the Temple's voluntary offerings, and the two at the Gate of Susan, for the half-shekel tax from all who come to worship."

"Of course, all must pay to support the Temple, and the Essenes know that is needed. It is the accumulation of other treasures they object to, how some people—even the Temple's priests—worship material wealth above all... But they also understand the Temple treasure belongs to our people, and its theft by the Romans cannot be risked. So, Nahum still believes the Essenes must help us hide it."

Mathias glanced behind them and then ahead at the empty passageway that led to more storerooms. "I thought this was to be a meeting of the Sanhedrin in the Hall of Hewn Stone?"

"Shimon wanted to speak with us first, somewhere away from others. The meeting will be called afterward."

"If he has Yohanan ben Levi with him, I'll turn and leave. I've no desire to see that Gischalan traitor."

"He won't be with Shimon, who now prefers not to be around him."

"Naturally, now that he has seen the outcome of ben Levi's betrayal. Thousands are dead across Jerusalem at the Idumeans' hands. Still, responsibility for their deaths lies at the feet of Yohanan ben Levi. Shimon is also responsible for empowering the Gischalan."

"I think Shimon knows and regrets that." Yohanan entered a small chamber full of storage chests and walked between them to a curtained entry to another room. Holding the curtain aside, he waved Mathias in. "But someone is with him."

"How is Matthew?" Eleasar ben Ananias asked when Mathias stepped inside.

Surprised to see him, Mathias looked from the Temple Guard captain to Shimon ben Gamliel. "He's better. Why are you two together? I thought you now bitter enemies."

"Not bitter, though Eleasar would be right to feel so," Shimon replied. "Like many, I was fooled by Yohanan ben Levi. But no more... even with the followers he has drawn to him, I am not one of them. I cannot change what has passed, but I want to help do what must be done. There's little we can change in the course we are on"—he nodded to Eleasar. "The Zealots are in power. But there's news about Rome... maybe good news for us. If true, it no longer matters who is in power."

"What news?"

"An Alexandrian trader in Garza claims stories from Rome have reached the city that Emperor Nero has disappeared."

"What? Then who is ruling their empire now?"

"No one knows, though the rumors also said some Roman nobles are making a claim to the throne. There's news of other rebellions in Rome's northern and western provinces."

"Such tales are not something we can rely on," said Mathias. "How do we know they are true? Who brings them to us?"

Shimon shifted uncomfortably, looked away, then back, and started to answer.

Eleasar replied first. "Mathias, when Shimon came to me about this, I spoke with the messenger, Yonatan bar Hilel. I do not care for the man, and I know your family dislikes him, too, but I believe him. What he reports matches what I heard from another trader who brought his family from Joppa for their safety. He had heard the same thing from men in Caesarea who plan to come to Jerusalem." Eleasar paused and continued. "And the number of refugees coming here is another matter the Sanhedrin must talk about.

"Boaz, my merchant friend who brought me from Herodium, said the Romans are not attacking nor even preventing travelers from coming to Jerusalem," Mathias said. "They let them through without threat. Could the Alexandria rumor be the reason? Does Rome have other, more important problems to attend to, and will they leave us alone now?"

"I don't know, Yohanan." Mathias tugged his beard. "But we cannot assume so. Still, the Romans have yet to move their legions closer to Jerusalem."

"Should I convene the Sanhedrin and announce this news? Yonatan is probably telling Yohanan ben Levi right now. Once he figures how to use the news for his own purpose, it will spread."

"We can't let that Gischalan be the only voice speaking about this. Go to the hall now, and we'll join you."

Shimon looked at Mathias, then his eyes swept over Eleasar and Yohanan, who nodded at him. "I'll send out the call for the meeting, then," he said and left with a last glance at them.

"I believe Shimon wants to help," Eleasar said, waving his hand at the departing Sanhedrin president, "and to atone for believing Yohanan ben Levi... but still...."

"I do not fully trust him, either, Eleasar," said Mathias, "but we'll see." He turned to his old friend. "Does Matthew have what we need?"

"He has the list to break into separate locations and the directions to those," Yohanan ben Zaccai said with a nod. "He said he would begin on that today."

"We must continue with that work, then. Even if this news from Rome is true, I don't believe General Vespasian will take his legions and go back to Antioch. But perhaps it gives us more time," said Mathias, "and we cannot waste it."

LXXVI

Jerusalem

The Upper City

When Ehud knocked on the door, Rebecca opened it and greeted him, saying, "Matthew is in here. We've just eaten, but I have more if you're hungry." He noticed how her inflection changed when she added with the curl of a smile, "Miriam's in the courtyard." As he followed her inside, he wondered at the change in propriety from what would have been observed before the war. A mother of those days would not have offered that a young man could come into their home and see her daughter. But then, he had known Miriam and her family for many years, since he was a child. He was here for Matthew yet longed to apologize to Miriam, but that must wait.

"Thank you," Ehud said with a smile for Rebecca as she took away the plate of cheese and fruit he had pretended to have an interest in. He'd managed to eat half of it, though his stomach was in knots. Ehud squinted at his friend at the end of the table and wondered if he was still that... a friend. He had seen the flash of anger cross Matthew's face, and that expression told him he should have little hope his purpose would be accomplished. He barely got a glimpse at the scroll spread on the table, then Matthew quickly rolled the parchment, tied it with a cord, and set it aside atop a stack of flat sheets. Matthew had put his bronze-tipped pen on the stack and then greeted him.

Their talk had been only on generalities. Barely any of it about his trip to Qumran or the Essenes and none about what Yohanan ben Zaccai had brought back with him. Or what had been hidden somewhere near or within Herodium. Ehud had no plausible way to bring up that subject. Laughter from the courtyard broke an awkward silence, and he glanced at the open window.

Matthew looked relieved at the distraction. "You should go say hello to Miriam."

There was a moment as Ehud looked at Matthew when he wondered again, *What is Matthew thinking that has changed him?* He stood. "I will... I'm glad you're better, Matthew."

* * *

Matthew watched Ehud go outside and greet the women. Then he heard his mother's voice, a questioning tone he recognized, but not Miriam's reply. He gathered the parchment scroll Yohanan ben Zaccai had given him and his worksheets. Once Ehud had gone to the Essenes in his stead to return with Yohanan ben Zaccai, he had recalled Miriam's mention of Ehud asking questions. *I still must talk with her.* But first, he must focus on priorities. He needed no curiosity about what he worked on, especially now when there was more to keep secret about the safeguarding of the Temple treasure. They needed to make the locations secure enough and safe to hold the treasure. Then they must plan how much to move and where.

Matthew winced as he rose from the table, and one hand reflexively pressed to his chest. He would continue breaking down the locations into single sheets with directions for how to find them. Then, with the help of his father and Eleasar ben Ananias, he would use the Temple treasurer's information to allocate portions of the treasure suitable for each location. When that was done, they could assign trusted men for the work. Once the treasure was hidden, the details would then go back to the Essenes to inscribe on a copper scroll to be secreted away for safekeeping in a location known to only a handful of men. They must protect that information and its existence. And other copies should be burned in case the Romans took Jerusalem.

* * *

THE LOWER CITY

It was Elian who did it, Miriam thought, making that moment less painful for her. Her mother had been looking on expectantly but silently after announcing Ehud had stopped by to see Matthew and wanted to say hello. Ya'el had greeted Ehud pleasantly, but Cicero, from his perch of leather draped over Ya'el's shoulder, had glared at the tall young man. The golden orb of his cocked eye locked on Ehud had never strayed from him. Miriam had frowned, too—still angry at how he had treated her the night before he left for Qumran.

Then Elian, who had been picking figs from one tree, ran to Ehud and looked up at the tall man: "You can help…" He had grabbed his hand and pulled Ehud toward the tree and pointed above the lower branches he had already stripped. "Please lift me…"

With a grin, Ehud had swept the boy up to the higher branches and let him fill his hands… and mouth. He set the boy down, whose smile was now stretched around chewing the fruit. Ya'el had laughed, and the pure peal of joy made Miriam feel the weight—if for only that moment—roll off her heart. It had made her laugh, and Ehud, too, and her anger faded. With a smile, her mother had gone inside. That meant Miriam now must attempt a conversation. Then Elian had done it again—saved her from having to be the first to speak.

Elian had swallowed his mouthful and ran to Ya'el. "Mother, is this the man who makes glass you told me about?"

"Yes," Ya'el said, thumbing away fig juice from his chin.

Wide-eyed, Elian had walked back to Ehud and gazed up at him. "Are you a *magus*? Surely you must be. It is magic to create such a thing."

Ehud had kneeled in front of the boy. "Not magic... it's manufacturing.... a process known for many, many years."

"Is it a secret... can you show me?"

Ya'el had leaned closer to Miriam and whispered: "Ask Ehud to take us."

Miriam had done so, though she had been annoyed that Ya'el had spoken of Ehud to anyone, even Elian. Ehud had cheerfully agreed to show them the shop. After telling Rebecca where they were going, they had left for the Lower City. It had been pleasant to watch Ehud entertain the boy with his demonstration of glassmaking. As she watched them, she had wondered, *What would life be like with Ehud, with our own child?* The thought had filled her with a longing she had tried hard not to acknowledge. How could such a future ever be?

As they headed back to the Upper City, that thought came back, and it saddened her as they neared Hananiah's shop. When they passed his door, she could see a movement—a shadow within—and the wink of metal. She knew Hananiah was watching her and that she must come to see him. Somehow, she must tell him they could be only friends. Ehud was walking ahead of her with Ya'el, Elian talking animatedly at his other side. *How could such a future ever be?* What should she do about Elazar ben Yair and the Sicarii?

LXXVII

JULIUS 68 CE

CAESAREA

THE ROMAN ENCAMPMENT, QUARTERMASTER OFFICE

"It's been many days, and you have not spoken of your meeting with your father in Lydda," said Celsus. "What happened?"

"It's of no concern, sir, nothing to talk of," Sayid replied, though that meeting had weighed heavily on him ever since. He had not expected his father to greet him with affection or even a warm welcome. Still, he had not expected his disrespect. Finding his son an *immunes,* a mere clerk had disappointed Marcus Sabinus, and he had not shied away from saying so. "My father is bitter that his wound, though healed, will likely keep him from serving in combat again."

"I can understand his anger, and at first, I was like your father in that. I felt the eyes of other men, who expected me to be unsatisfied, angry. I did consider retiring. But I'm thankful I discovered I can do more for the legions with what I do now."

"Sir, you have education and found a new interest. My father has only been a soldier, which means to fight enemies and be a warrior. My mother has always told me that was his desire—and nothing more." A pang shot through Sayid, something he often thought but had never told his mother: *I wish he had wanted to be my father.*

"Your father thinks there is no value in what he does now?"

"I don't know what my father thinks, sir. But he does not seem happy that he has become an aide to a *tribuni angusticlavi.* Assisting the commander of an auxiliary cohort is not what he imagined for himself after so many years in the front ranks."

"Was he not glad to see you?"

Sayid had listened to Celsus speak of his family and his closeness with his father. Sayid realized even more what he had missed out on and how different life was for men like Celsus. "The glimmer of that feeling was gone once he learned I was even less than he. He called me a clerk, not a soldier."

"Did you tell him of what you've done... and that you fought at Beth Horon?"

"Sir, if he learned I fought in one of a legion's most embarrassing defeats, it would not help. Not in his eyes." Sayid did not say more, but he had felt more than once what he had seen in his father's expression... regret that he was no longer a soldier. And no matter how his officer professed the value of their work, Sayid could not disagree. Like Marcus, all he had ever wanted to be was a Roman soldier, to earn respect in combat and gain his father's esteem. He could not remain where he was—in Caesarea working for Celsus—and achieve either.

* * *

VESPASIAN'S PRAETORIUM

Titus reached his father's private office entrance the same time as Gaheris Clineas, smiling at the man he recognized with the aide as he stepped to one side.

"General, the governor of Syria is here... General Titus, too," Gaheris Clineas announced as Gaius Mucianus entered Vespasian's private office, Titus following him.

"You look thinner than when I saw you last in Antioch," the general said with a grin to greet his friend.

Gaius Mucianus sat without waiting for an offer of a chair and turned to Titus. "Your father, young Titus, seems no thinner and no older." Mucianus's smile twisted into a frown as he settled back in the chair and slumped. "The troubling events of late greatly wear on me and roil my stomach."

Vespasian sighed. "So, you believe the reports coming from Rome? Nero is no longer emperor."

"Much else confirms it." Mucianus smoothed his robe and tugged it free where it had bunched under one leg. "Vindex's rebellion ended with his death, but the man he proclaimed should become emperor, Galba, is forming a legion in Hispania and plans to draw others to him. Galba will no doubt march on Rome with them once they are all assembled."

"But will Lord Galba be good for Rome... for the empire, Lord Mucianus?" Titus asked, darting a look at his father, whose face was expressionless. When the first rumors had reached them, he had questioned his father's silence on the subject. Then Vespasian had explained it was better to learn more before forming an opinion or deciding anything.

"I don't know," answered the Syrian governor with a shake of his head. "Galba is old... and I'm told he is cruel, and that is not a good combination. If he feels the approach of *Morta*, the goddess drawing him closer to death, he might do things he thinks right at the moment. Afterward, the empire has to bear the results of any ill-considered decisions that become his legacy."

"Gaius," Vespasian asked his friend, "are you sure Galba will become the next emperor? Nero is clever; he has always flushed out treason and punished traitors."

"I've heard the Senate already supports Galba to assume the throne and have declared him emperor. So, Nero must be dead, or he is gone for good."

"I've heard that Galba's wife and children are deceased," said Titus, "and he's old. If he soon dies... who would be his heir?"

"One of his closest supporters is Marcus Otho, governor of Hispania Lusitania. My sources report he is with Galba and helping him raise more men. Otho is young and seems favored." Mucianus shifted and moved forward in his chair. "And Otho is one of the reasons I came to see you in person." He glanced at Titus and hesitated.

"My son can hear what you have to say," Vespasian replied to the unasked question.

Mucianus relaxed. "The centurion I met first in Rome with you—the one who carried the reports and letters from Cestius Gallus... he also knows Lady Cleo, Marcus Otho's sister. He could confirm what's going on. Have you heard from him... has he reached Otho?"

"I've not heard from Nicanor since he sailed from Ostia to Tarraco on his way to see Otho."

"Was that not some time ago?"

"In his message, Nicanor promised to report again as soon as he could. You and I have heard rumors of attempts to coerce the Praetorians to support others claiming the throne. And Ophonius Tigellinus has attempted to use Nicanor to spy on me. If it's discovered that he works on my behalf and not on behalf of Tigellinus, that makes Nicanor an enemy of the Praetorian Prefect. And likely the enemy of the new emperor, whoever that may be. With what's going on in Rome and the provinces, Nicanor must be careful."

"Then we must wait." Mucianus looked thoughtful. "And that brings up another thing. Though, with Nero gone, it may change circumstances for the man."

"What man... what do you mean?" Vespasian asked.

"Gessius Florus seems to wield more influence than one in his position as tax collector normally would. But with Nero gone—whether dead or having fled Rome—Florus's questions now have little weight."

Remembering earlier discussions with his father about Florus, Titus asked quickly, "What questions does he ask?"

"He routinely sends me couriered messages asking when you will assault Jerusalem and bring this Judean rebellion to an end. He says it is a matter of re-establishing Judean tax revenue for the empire."

"He is—I guess—doing his job, but you and I don't answer to him," said Vespasian.

"True, but others, men in the Senate, in Rome, have also commented on the delay." Mucianus pointed out, his eyes cutting warily toward Titus.

Titus had caught the governor's glance and knew its meaning. But kept silent. He was learning from his father to not rush to speak, even in defense of him. Words were best treated as game piece moves on a board; poorly considered rashness could lead to unwelcome consequences.

"And I have answered them in my official reports to Rome, to the emperor," Vespasian replied calmly.

"Some wonder why you are letting more Judeans enter Jerusalem. I admit I'd like to know, too."

"My son has asked me that, and I'll tell you what I told him and what I've put in my reports." The general unrolled the large map of Jerusalem that Pomponius Mela and Nicanor had prepared before he left Rome. The map covered the desktop. His legion cartographers had added to it, working with information captured by patrols or gathered by interrogating prisoners. "The more people who come to Jerusalem seeking safety within its walls, the more the city will feel the pain of the siege I plan to inflict on it. Most fleeing to that city are women and children, and few of the men with them are experienced fighters. All of them require food and water, and the city cannot stockpile enough to support that many people in a lengthy siege."

Mucianus sat back, scratching his chin. "So, that will help you take the city."

"Yes." Vespasian rolled the map and set it aside. "The weight of Judea's own people will hasten the city's fall."

"In his career, my father has captured over 20 enemy cities, governor," Titus commented. "When it is time... he will take Jerusalem, too."

* * *

IN THE CITY

The inn was away from the port and not as crowded as the other tabernae, which is why Sayid had picked it. The quiet made his own thoughts louder still, and he would not drink to silence them. *As if that would work.* Celsus's questions had stirred what he would rather not stir. He had spent the hours on horseback to Apollonia, Joppa, and Lydda, anticipating finally seeing and speaking with his father. It had not gone as he had hoped. Since returning, he had considered what to do next and wished he had a friend to talk to. There was little chance General Vespasian would let him speak with Yosef again. And that made him think of Ariella. Did Yosef know someone had killed his wife?

A clatter at the entryway made him raise his head. Two men came in wearing leather cuirasses and carrying at their hips Thracian *sica*, the short swords he had seen some wear in Antioch. The two mercenaries—that was all they could be—surveyed the room. One of them turned to the innkeeper, and after a brief conversation, he stepped outside after the clinking of coins changing hands. Almost immediately, he returned with four more Thracians and two other men. The taller of them wore a Roman patrician's robes, and he had his back to Sayid as he talked with the innkeeper. In the tunic and breeches of a workman, the second man was much shorter, broad-shouldered.

The Roman noble straightened, half-turned, and bent to say something to the shorter man. Sayid recognized the profile. The last he had seen this man—the man who had beaten Cleo—Sayid had kicked him backward into a burning room at his residence in Ptolemais. *Gessius Florus!*

The shorter man reached to grasp the shoulder of one of the Thracians, motioning toward him to follow. Seeing the massive hand—evident even on the shoulder of the much larger man—Sayid thought of the bruising on Ariella's broken neck and the grip of those hands on his own throat. The short man and his Thracian companion left, and Gessius Florus's eyes turned toward Sayid.

LXXVIII

ROME

Nicanor reined Carmenta to one side once they were through the *porta collina* gate and inside the *murus servii tullii*, the wall constructed by King Servius Tullius centuries before. The *via Flaminia* was the closest and best road to Rome near Falacrine. It surprised him how infrequently he had encountered travelers on it, other than traders and merchants. And no soldiers. But that changed once the Flaminia joined v*ia Salaria* near the wall. The road ahead, beyond the gate, boiled with soldiers, afoot and horseback, most of them Praetorian. But then, just to his left, on a broad, connecting gravel road, was the *Castra Praetoria*, the primary barracks—virtually a fortress—for the Praetorian Guard. He knew it well, having been there when he had served as a guard and watch captain at the Tullianum, a prison near the city center. Sitting on the high ground outside the wall, the camp's twelve-foot-high masonry walls were almost square, more than 1000 feet on each side enclosing a vast plot of land. Its facing of red brick had shaded pink in the slanting rays of the coming sunset. The two-story barracks could hold 4,000 men, and other buildings stored the Praetorian's arsenal of equipment and weapons. Several stables housed their horses and mules.

Nicanor shook the dust from the light linen traveler's cloak Antonia Caenis had given him and adjusted the hood. It matched what many on the road wore to shield their heads from the scorching summer sun. He loosened the cloth where sweat had stuck it to his sides and back, and his fingers brushed the hilt of the sword sheathed between his shoulders. It was hidden snugly beneath the slip of additional fabric that formed the mantle draped across his shoulders.

It was better—safer—for him to appear to be an itinerant trader or craftsmen traveling on his own than as an armed soldier with a sword at his hip or sheathed from the saddle. But his pugio was where it needed to be. When he was awake, the dagger was always in easy reach on his belt. He sometimes missed the weight of a sword at his waist or the feel as it tapped his thigh when he rode. But Graius had taught him the benefit—besides disguise—of the back harness sheath, and he had become used to it. He patted the pouch of supple hide affixed next to the dagger and gauged the sun in the sky. By the time the light of day faded, he would render honors for his friend.

"Let's go, girl," he said, stroking Carmenta's neck and kneeing her forward. They joined the stream entering Rome with a watchful eye on any soldiers drawing too near them.

* * *

The underbellies of the low, darkening clouds were shading to a sullen crimson with a setting, orange-red sun as Nicanor and Carmenta approached the Temple of Hercules. Unlike the city center they had just passed through, the surrounding area was tranquil, with few people on the grounds surrounding it and none near the temple. He could not help but recall the times he had met Graius at this spot. He'd never thought Cleo's old retired major domus could prove to be a freed gladiator and still a formidable fighter. *He saved my life,* Nicanor thought as he dismounted. "Come, girl," he said as he led Carmenta up into the temple.

Nicanor knew someone might complain if they were seen. Graius had once told him they allowed only sacrificial animals within the temple. But Carmenta was not a mere animal; she was their companion of the road. She was a fighter as steadfast as Graius had been, and she would remain at his side for this. He stopped beneath the oculus and looked up at the opening. The sunward edges of the white-stoned rim had the last vestige of a reddish tint. The sky directly above was the gray-purple of twilight.

A westerly wind picked up, and Nicanor could smell the rank water that lapped the nearby Tiber's riverbanks. He took the leather pouch from his belt and loosened its drawstring. Reaching in to cup a handful, he waited for the wind to lessen. He did not want Graius's ashes carried too far from where the old gladiator wished them placed. Carmenta nickered and nuzzled his shoulder. She shifted, and he heard the echoed clink of hooves on a stone-covered opening. He looked down at the massive drain and the face of the grill covering it. Carmenta could not know, but she had shown him what he should do. He kneeled and poured Graius ashes into the mouth. "Rest, my friend."

Nicanor closed his eyes and remembered Graius's other wish. He would honor that one, too. "I'll find Cleo... make sure she's safe from Gessius Florus... and tell her you loved her as if she were your child," he vowed.

Nicanor stood and led Carmenta out and onto the grass. The treetops swayed as he studied the sky over the city. The wind was still blowing just as hard but had changed direction. It carried smells of cooking fires and other things that only come from many humans living close together in a large city. He had sensed earlier that the city's night did not promise peace or a good sleep for some. The streets full of people had been abuzz with either dread or anticipation; he could not tell which. But he had the sensation he often felt in a legion camp before a coming battle. He shook off the edginess.

"Time to go, girl," Nicanor said. He planned to stay at an inn where Carmenta could be stabled close by. In the morning, they would see this Gnaeus Batiatus, Antonia Caenis's friend. The letter from her he carried asked the man to provide him a safe place while in Rome as he waited to secure a written proclamation from Marcus Otho and Galba to protect Cleo. And he prayed for orders from Vespasian to return to Judea once that was done.

LXXIX

ROME

The *argentarii* was located near Graius's former *insula*, the old gladiator's apartment, and the same side street. Thanks to Marcus Otho's connections and personal confirmation it was Graius's signature on the rudimentary, hastily-written document, Graius's *codicillus*, testifying that Nicanor should receive his money, was accepted as valid. The banker had shown Nicanor the transfer was complete. Otho had seemed relieved Nicanor had not asked him for reward or compensation for trying to help his sister. *I'm sure Lord Otho thought I wanted Graius's money for myself*, Nicanor thought, and it was best to let him think so. *He doesn't need to know I'll give it to his sister, so she has some money of her own, as little as it was.*

Nicanor crossed through the city, skirting the forum and civic buildings where Praetorian officers might recognize him and ask questions he would rather not answer. It would likely be dangerous if he did. He would soon need to find Gaius Sabinus and deliver Lord Galba's message. But first, he must see how Antonia Caenis's contact could help him. That would bring him nearer to fulfilling the vow he had made to himself. After doing as Galba wished, he would figure out what to do about Tigellinus. The Praetorian Prefect must pay for his role in the deaths of Graius, Lady Octavia, and likely that of her husband and Nicanor's former legion commander, Cestius Gallus. Once done with that, Nicanor looked forward to the day he returned to Judea and dealt with Gessius Florus. That man, most of all—now that Nero was gone—needed killing for hurting Cleo.

Reaching the Via Appia, he turned Carmenta south. According to Antonia Caenis's directions, Gnaeus Batiatus lived at the southern edge of the city near a centuries-old temple and shrine dedicated to *Fors Fortuna*, the Goddess of Luck, and some believed... Destiny.

* * *

Nicanor slowed Carmenta to a walk when he saw the sign telling him he was near the *horti caesaris*, the Tiber River gardens that originally belonged to Julius Caesar. According to Antonia, the garden's southernmost point was where he should find Gnaeus Batiatus's estate. He recalled Yosef once telling Cleo that her namesake,

Cleopatra Thea Philoraptor—the last ruler of Egypt before it became a Roman province—had stayed at a domus within the gardens during her visit to Rome over a century before. Yosef, a Judean, had heard even in his land the stories of Cleopatra's beauty and of her tragic end with her lover, General Marcus Antonius. Nicanor had put that story out of his mind, but not before thinking, *No woman is more beautiful than the Cleo I know.*

Carmenta's snort broke his reverie, and then he heard the familiar sounds, too. At the end of the gardens, they came to a wide cobblestone lane, and several buildings were in the distance. Most were squared off, but the largest was columned and domed and looked like a temple. Opposite that lane was a small path of gravel and packed earth. An engraved sign mounted on a thick wooden post at eye level for anyone on horseback at the crossroad.

Nicanor mouthed the words: "*Uri, vinciri, uerbarari, feroqque necari*—to endure burning with fire, shackling in chains, being whipped with rods.... and to be killed with steel." Graius had told him that was the oath sworn by all men entering a *ludus*, a training school for gladiators. Beneath the motto was the name: Batiatus.

The clash of weapons and shouts of men... noises Nicanor readily recognized even from a distance... came from the gravel lane. Nicanor nudged Carmenta into the road and forward toward the sounds.

LXXX

Rome

Gnaeus Batiatus's Villa

The servant escorted Nicanor to an atrium; just beyond it was a central courtyard with a fountain. Near every entrance to the atrium stood a large slave wielding a stiff fan of plaited leaves to move the air in the room.

Nicanor studied the two men lounging in the breeze on a *biclinium*, two couches joined at a right angle and appreciated the coolness it brought to his face, too. He wiped sweat with the palm of one hand as the older man looked up from their game of *tali*. The four four-sided dice made from a goat's knucklebones showed a score of 14, a Venus throw.... the highest possible roll. Years ago, Nicanor had thrown a dog, the lowest roll, and lost a month's pay. That day he had sworn off gambling. The graying man set down the *fritillus*, the tiny box from which he had cast the die, and picked up a sheet of vellum. Its wax seal was broken and falling away.

"So, you come from Antonia Caenis?" he said.

"Yes. She told me you could be of help." Nicanor stepped into the atrium. "You are Gnaeus Batiatus?"

The man nodded and turned to the younger man. "Marcus, your bad luck has only put you deeper in debt. But you have other skills I can use. Think about my offer." Gnaeus gestured his dismissal and waved Nicanor to a seat across from the table.

"So," he said as he studied Nicanor, "you're a centurion under Lord Vespasian's command but not attired as your rank befits." He raised an eyebrow, then continued when Nicanor remained silent. "Antonia says you are wanted by Lord Tigellinus, and I have heard indirectly that he offers a reward for some man. You, it seems."

Nicanor tensed but did not reply.

"Relax, centurion... Nicanor. Antonia and her friend Claudia Acte were my father's friends, and they have helped my family and me. We—I—owe them a great deal. Antonia and Lord Vespasian," he waved the letter, "think highly of you... and of your purpose in Rome. Whatever that may be. I would never betray their trust... so I will not betray you. How can I help?"

Nicanor knew he must have help to accomplish what he must. "I have to deliver something to Gaius Sabinus—the co-prefect of the Praetorians—as soon as possible, on behalf of Lord Galba. And it must be done secretly."

Gnaeus studied Nicanor, and the moment stretched into a full minute. "Galba," he said with a nod as if something had become clear to him. "Gaius Sabinus uses my services, as other nobles do. I can arrange such a meeting."

Nicanor eased back in the *sella*, the chair legs scraping on the marble floor, and his thigh muscles relaxed, and his stomach unclenched. "Thank you. Would it be possible to meet with him tomorrow or the next day?"

"Not tomorrow and the next day after is unlikely. I have to speak to my man, and he then has to approach Gaius when he can be spoken to privately."

"Of course." Nicanor asked further, "What services do you offer?" He looked around the room and thought of what lay beyond the walls. "This seems a gladiator school."

"It is... and my gladiators have had success in the arena. Some have fought even for the emperor... for Nero. Now, in these troubling times, many nobles hire my fighters for protection."

Nicanor shifted in his chair and felt his stomach tighten. "I must tell you that, besides delivering what I must to Sabinus... I seek Ophonius Tigellinus."

"The man who searches for you?" Gnaeus's eyebrow raised even higher than before. "He has been seen hardly at all since Nero's..."

"Death?"

"They officially still say he has merely disappeared. But I believe he is dead. And I expect to confirm that this evening." Gnaeus rose from the couch. "Come with me, and we'll get your horse settled in my stable and then get you to the baths before dinner. You can join me to hear what has happened to Nero."

* * *

That evening...

A servant cleared dinner plates and bowls as Gnaeus poured more wine from an amphora. "One of my men is Batavian and became one of Nero's *corporis custodes*—you know he gets all his personal guards from Germania. And all of them—all but my man—have disappeared at the same time as Nero. My man came to tell me yesterday that he had found someone who had been with Nero when the Senate proclamation was delivered." He beckoned to his major domus, who waited at the entrance to the *triclinium*. "We're done eating; bring him in."

A slender, pale-skinned, round-shouldered young man entered. His head, under a cap of oiled curls that reached his ears, was bent as if he studied his own clasped hands at his waist.

"This is Sporus... who says he was with our emperor. Tell us what you know."

"And you will reward me?" The young man raised his head.

Gnaeus tossed a small bag of coins on the table.

Sporus nodded and twisted his hands without releasing them. "I cannot be gone long. Gaius Sabinus... he has taken me into his household and will expect me to be waiting for him when he comes to...." His voice trailed off.

Nicanor shook his head, knowing what that meant.

"Then speak quickly but completely," Gnaeus poked the bag with a forefinger, "and this is yours."

"A messenger from Phaon—the emperor's personal advisor— arrived saying the Senate had declared that Nero was *hostis publicus*, an enemy of Rome and its people." Sporus began, words spilling out in a rush. "Nero tore it from the man's hands and read it himself. He asked what it meant that the Senate called for him to be punished in the ancient style. Neophytus told him that the executioners stripped their victims naked, thrust their heads into a wooden fork, and then flogged them to death with sticks. Nero took out two daggers he carried, and it seemed he would try their points. But the emperor threw them down again, protesting that his last hour had not yet come. Neophytus, Epaphroditos, and I insisted he try to escape." Sporus's eyes filled with tears. "But all the emperor would do was lament: 'Dead! And so great an artist!'"

"But he wasn't dead yet, was he?" Gnaeus commented to prod the young man to continue.

"No. Then the emperor begged me to weep and mourn for him but also pleaded that one of us set an example by committing suicide first. He kept moaning and muttering: 'How ugly and vulgar my life has become!' Neophytus, who had been at a window looking out, cried out that a troop of cavalry was coming up the road. Soon we heard the pounding of their hooves. Nero gasped and was afraid to be taken alive. Then, with the help of Epaphroditos, he stabbed himself in the throat and was already half dead when a cavalry officer entered. The man pretended to rush to the emperor to staunch the wound with his cloak. Nero's last words were: 'Too late.' Then his eyes glazed and bulged from their sockets, a horrible sight."

Sporus covered his face with his hands. "He had made us promise that whatever happened, to not to let his head be cut off. To have him buried in one piece. So—the next day—they laid Nero on a pyre, dressed in gold-embroidered white robes. That's all I know, sirs."

Gnaeus leaned forward, picked up the bag of coins, and threw it to him. "You may go." As Sporus hurried out, he turned to Nicanor. "So, Nero is dead."

"Why does the Senate not announce it?"

"There are powerful men who would rather not have that news out yet. Nero has become popular with the common people. Those powerful men do not want any unrest while they position themselves for whoever becomes the new emperor. Your mission here is part of the proof for that. But all will come out soon; too many know of Galba's march to Rome."

Nicanor cared about who became emperor only because Galba could then help Cleo. That's all that mattered to him... and one more thing. "Where is Tigellinus now?"

Gnaeus rubbed his chin and squinted at the centurion. "Tigellinus sought you for some reason—I care not what it was or is—but why would you seek him?"

"A personal matter." Nicanor shook his head.

"Keeping your own counsel is wise..." Gnaeus nudged the amphora toward Nicanor. "Did Antonia tell you about me, about my family?"

"No. Only that she trusted you."

"My great-grandfather, Lentulus Batiatus, once owned a gladiator school in Capua... and also owned a slave-turned-gladiator you may have heard stories of. Spartacus. Some powerful men blamed my great-grandfather for Spartacus's revolt as if he could have stopped such a man. And that cost my family its reputation. Claudia convinced Nero to sponsor some of our fighters. She and Antonia referred us to those who could re-establish our status. That was beyond price; I owe a great deal to them and to anyone they name. So, wherever your issue with Tigellinus leads you, whatever happens, I offer not just room and board... but protection."

LXXXI

JERUSALEM

THE UPPER CITY

It was barely past dawn, and the scant cool of night gave way to the cruel sultriness of late summer. The air filled with fine dust dried people's throats and labored the breathing for the old and the ill. The stupor affected even the young and healthy.

The courtyard trees screened the family from the rising sun, and the rich aroma of their ripened figs and pears was thick in the air. Elian would be out soon for his daily chore of harvesting the best fruit of the day. Matthew wished for any hint of a breeze to relieve the heat and carry away the cloying scent now long past its pleasant fragrance of earlier weeks.

Even the southeastern *siroccos* to come in another month would be welcome, though they could be fiercer than the spring winds and more destructive. He used one end of the damp cloth around his neck to wipe his face. That respite was only temporary. Matthew fluttered his hand fan, moving the tepid air about, as did his father, Eleasar ben Ananias and Yohanan ben Zaccai. The squares of thin wood affixed to a bone handle offered some relief, but his father's hand fan was clasped to his chest. "Father?"

Mathias stirred and reached for his cup of water, took a drink, and waved the fan to cool his perspiring face. He looked around at the questioning expressions of the others around the table. "Just thinking, son, about the Sanhedrin's endless arguing, day in and day out. And about the Romans—what does this news about the emperor mean for us?"

"I've heard again that Yosef still lives. I believe we should contact General Vespasian and ask *him* that and Yosef," said Yohanan.

"I'm glad you did not say that in any of those meetings," Mathias said with a shake of his head. "Besides, you would never get any message to him, old friend."

"I know men—traders—who still enter Caesarea. They stage goods at Herodium for towns west and south of Jerusalem. They've told me that Vespasian—through his staff—listens to news or information from locals. So, there's a chance...."

"Vespasian might not even be in Caesarea now," commented Eleasar, who had spoken little since arriving at daybreak to see Matthew. "I've received a report that he and his personal escort went to Lydda and from there rode with two cohorts of legion cavalry to Lake Asphaltitis."

Matthew straightened in his chair, pulling the damp tunic from his chest and tugging it free from his back as he leaned forward. "Why would he go there?"

Eleasar shrugged. "They've taken Jericho and Perea... The area is safe for Romans, and the report said he seemed to want to see the waters... and to test them."

"Test?" Mathias asked.

"The watchers say he threw bound prisoners into the waters—men who could not swim."

"To drown them?" Mathias asked and shot a hard look at Yohanan ben Zaccai. "And you think we should try to speak with him!"

"No, Mathias," Eleasar said as he half-turned and pulled at his own tunic. "Apparently, he wanted to see if the waters would make them float more than usual. It did, and he had them pulled from the water. Though the Romans have killed thousands and thousands, Vespasian stays his hand from advancing on Jerusalem."

"Humph..." Mathias smoothed his beard and turned to his friend. "Yohanan, perhaps we should send a message to this General Vespasian."

"Father, Yohanan... you cannot even think this!" They alarmed Matthew. "The Zealots will kill you!" He glanced at Eleasar, who shook his head as a reminder that he had told them repeatedly he was done with fanatics. But Matthew continued: "They will kill you... all of us, if they learn we have even spoken of sending messages to the Romans."

"But what if a new emperor in Rome changes what Vespasian is ordered to do?" Yohanan scanned the faces of the others at the table.

"Why would anything be different?" Matthew scoffed. "We have killed too many Romans to expect leniency. Simon bar Giora—who continues to raid outside of Jerusalem—still parades around with the 12th Legion's *aquila*... as if that eagle standard were his own. Yosef himself told us once we had gone too far to hope for peace—Rome would let no province get away with what we've done. Else why would he choose to lead the men of Galilee to fight the Romans and lose his freedom? He must have had no hope of reconciliation."

"Yet Vespasian keeps him alive. Why?" Mathias mused. "I am thankful for it. But why?"

The silence made the air even more stifling. The clucks of Ya'el's parrot could be heard from a bedroom above them.

"Please think no more of contacting the Romans," Matthew said, standing in worry and grim resolve. "Eleasar and I must go. We have men from the Temple Guard to meet with, for they will become the teams to move the treasure." He wiped his face again with the cloth. "We can't load wagons and mules within the Temple Enclosure. I'm not sure what we'll do, but we must come up with something."

He looked above Eleasar, who was now standing, at Miriam's bedroom window, where she and Ya'el sat just within. Pausing their own conversation, Miriam caught his eye and raised her hand in a slight wave. Matthew waved back, his thoughts shifting to his ever-growing suspicions. Who killed those Idumeans in this very courtyard?"

* * *

Once Matthew and Eleasar were gone, Mathias leaned toward Yohanan. "Are you sure you have someone you trust to give this message to—and take it to Caesarea? And they would somehow get it into Vespasian's hands?"

Yohanan ben Zaccai nodded. "I'm certain. So, you've decided to send such a message?"

"I could not let Matthew nor Eleasar—nor anyone else—think I was considering it. But I think we must try. Notify those you know who are watching Caesarea. As soon as you can confirm Vespasian has returned there, we'll write the message. But Matthew is right—if anyone here finds out... we'll all suffer."

"I'll leave now."

"And Yohanan"—he stopped his friend. "When you go to Herodium... bring back what you hid there.

"Of course."

325

LXXXII

Augustus 68 CE

Caesarea

The Roman Encampment

This *castrum* has grown to become more like a fortress, Sayid thought, than a temporary camp... and it hums like the plucked strings of a Greek lyre. The men chattering about why they had yet to attack the Jews' strongest city had started talking about the rumors of Nero's death instead. The buzz of it was everywhere in the camp. Some men said the new emperor would not pursue a war started under Nero. While others were sure they would soon receive orders and the assault of Jerusalem would begin. Many stated even more loudly this rebellion could only end with the destruction of Jerusalem and the death of all who would stand against the empire. As much as he regretted that future reality, Sayid knew it was likely the truth. There would be no retreat from Judea. The conquering commander would depart, leaving behind a subjugated people... that is, if any survived.

Knuckling sweat from his eyes, Sayid knocked at the quartermaster commander's office doorway. He stuck his head inside and reported: "Sir, we loaded the supply wagons for Legio Apollinaris. They will leave tomorrow just before dawn."

Celsus nodded and looked questioningly at Sayid. "You will not accompany the caravan... to Lydda?"

"No, sir," Sayid answered, knowing his commander had been concerned—before the last trip—that he might ask for an assignment with his father once he found him.

"Good," Celsus said as he waved Sayid in. "You are useful to me. General Vespasian is back from Jericho, and you can help me with these inventory reports for the staff meeting he's called."

"Yes, sir," Sayid said with a grin. *This work is vital after all*, he thought and pulled a camp stool closer to the commander's worktable. He reached for the stack of scrolls tabulating all the supplies that had come in. What had been distributed to the legions and what remained in the warehouses and supply yards. "Why does General Vespasian attend those meetings? I would think he would have General Titus or others hold the logistics and supply review, and then they would report to him."

"The general believes it's worthy of his personal attention that all senior officers who serve under him are accountable to perform their duties as he expects. When I received this promotion, I was told he likes to look his officers in the eye when they report. He disapproves of waste. Everything must be accounted for, and he always asks questions and expects answers."

"Do you speak with him in these meetings, or perhaps afterward?"

"Sometimes. If I'm spoken to or asked to explain the reports."

For several minutes the only sound in the room was the scratching of pens on parchment transcribing amounts from each legion's current supply inventory to the single report encompassing all legions and headquarters units under Vespasian's command. Familiar with the accounts and the routine but careful not to make a mistake, Sayid switched from thinking about his father and mused again why Florus had not seemed to recognize him that day at the inn. The Roman nobleman had looked squarely at him, after all. They had met the first time at the emperor's domus in Rome—when Sayid was introduced as one of Lady Cleo's saviors on the *Salacia*. Later they had encounters in Caesarea when Gessius Florus had been the Judean Procurator, and then in Ptolemais. The man surely knew his face.

Sayid had expected Cleo's husband would send one, two, or all of those Thracian mercenaries to do something. Maybe not kill him then and there but certainly secure him and plan to kill him secretly. But perhaps Florus planned to send them later once Sayid was in a less public place. Or maybe he would send just the short Hercules with the strangler's hands. That man connected Gessius Florus to Ariella's death and the previous attempt on his own.

Sayid could understand why Cleo's husband would want to kill him, but what was his intent in killing Ariella? When the former procurator's gaze had swept over him without immediate recognition, Sayid had hurried out and back to the camp thinking someone would follow. But they had not, and he had remained within the encampment since. *Surely Florus is not still in Caesarea*, he thought, but chances were the other man—Florus's killer—was.

"Sir, has there been any news about the dead woman we found?" he asked Celsus.

The officer looked up from writing. "Why would there be?"

"Well, sir, she was killed outside the camp gate."

"She's a local," Celsus shrugged, "not our concern."

"So, no one reported it, sir?" Sayid said, understanding his thinking. Most Romans felt the same way about those who were not citizens of Rome. They weren't one of 'their' people... so not important, especially if they revolted against the empire. But Ariella was not unknown, at least to Sayid... he thought Yosef's wife deserved better.

"The gate sentries noted it in their log," Celsus said, "and the watch captain had the body picked up."

Sayid pressed, though he sensed he should not. "To identify and bury her, sir?"

A frown creased Celsus's face. "I don't know, Sayid... and why does any of that matter? Turn back to your work."

Sayid let it go; he did not want Celsus angry at him. The officer had saved his life and had enabled him to find his father, though that might not have been the good fortune he once believed it would be. He blotted away the drops of perspiration that had fallen on the sheet of vellum and focused on preventing any ink smears. Sayid's reading and writing quality were unusually good for an auxiliary since most could not read or write. That was thanks only to the time he'd spent with Lady Cleo, and he took pride in it. *Cleo, I pray to the gods you are still safe in Jerusalem.* That made him think of Yosef. He had seen him recently a few times outside his cell, always with four guards, and other than a brief exchange of glances, they had not been able to communicate. Did Yosef know his wife had been killed? "Sir..." He waited for Celsus to raise his head. "Would you ask General Vespasian if I could speak with my friend Yosef again?"

LXXXIII

ROME

GNAEUS BATIATUS'S VILLA

A wall twice Nicanor's height encircled three-quarters of the arena. The only unwalled portion was opposite where he and Gnaeus sat—upon a platform raised slightly higher than the tiered three rows that radiated in an arc to either side. An iron latticework gate as high as the wall spanned that opening. Beyond it was a cluster of buildings surrounded by a broad expanse of packed earth dotted with clumps of dying grass that at its boundary climbed the browned shoulders of the foothills.

"I've not seen many villas around Rome, but those I have seen... do not have this." Nicanor gestured at the arena and the men sparring within it.

"Do you like the Games?" Gnaeus waved a horsehair whisk against the flies.

Nicanor cursed the pests and used his hand to wave them away from his face. "I've seen them."

Gnaeus noted the curt reply. "But are you not entertained by them?" He beckoned a slave boy to adjust the awning over their heads.

"No," Nicanor shook his head and turned to his host with impatience. "Gnaeus, it's been days. Has your man spoken with Gaius Sabinus yet?

"Sabinus just returned yesterday—I know not from where—and yes... he now knows you need to speak to him privately."

"So, when can I meet with him?"

"Sabinus told my man to tell me... to tell you... he will let you know when."

"What?" The waiting and the biting flies made Nicanor snap. He stood up impatiently. "If he's back, I'll go to him now and be done with it."

"Sit, Nicanor, and be welcome. I've told you what Sabinus said. You have done what you can do. Besides, you told me you would remain here and wait for Galba. Is it long before he reaches Rome?"

Every night Nicanor thought of that very thing: two legions with auxiliaries—over 10,000 men—1400 mules, hundreds of wagons... at a steady pace from Hispania. "They should reach here in... October."

"So, sit back and watch my men spar... there's time." Gnaeus beckoned to the girl behind them holding an amphora, and he handed her his empty cup to fill, then pointed at Nicanor's sitting on the low table between them. "I thought you would enjoy seeing my fighters. I know it's much different from the battles you've fought. Is it not much better to be an observer?"

"Still men bleed... some become crippled for life... and some die." Nicanor held silent a moment thinking of Graius, then changed his tone. "So, what of this?" Nicanor inclined his head toward Sextus, Gnaeus's *lanista* on the floor of the arena. The gladiator trainer had the men paired off against each other with wooden swords similar to the *rudis* Graius had shown him. There was no glint of metal in the sun, but the sharp cracks echoed of hardened wood on wood. In the stillness of the morning, amid the scuffling of feet and muttered curses came grunts from the men when an opponent got past their guard and landed a blow on the padded leather protecting their torsos.

"Your observation is right... this is no place for a *ludus*. I've plans to move the school into Rome... near the Circus Maximus. I need backers. So, I'm holding an exhibition and inviting some prospects."

"Do you worry about there being a new emperor who might make changes?"

Gnaeus nodded. "You mean Lord Galba?"

"It seems to be him... the Senate has said so."

"Nicanor, I've thought long about that... but I don't believe it matters who rules Rome. Men, whether common, noble, or emperor... all enjoy the Games." A leer spread on Gnaeus's face. "Noblewomen love gladiators, the comelier ones anyway, and do not mind paying for their... attentions. And that pays almost as well as does my men guarding their husbands, fathers, and brothers from harm."

"Since you are doing so well, and with the temple of Fortuna nearby, wouldn't it be wise to stay close and not make any changes?"

"The goddess has been kind to me here," Gnaeus acknowledged. "But I must expand, and there is providence in being near where the most rewarding Games are held and where the rich live and conduct business. I will always honor Fortuna... but I seek what Fama can bring me, renown."

* * *

The sun had sunk below the foothills when Nicanor slowed Carmenta from a canter to a walk to cool her. Near the rear courtyard terrace, he recognized the man he'd seen with Gnaeus Batiatus during their first meeting. He was loading a cart from a storage room built into the rear of the domus. He had passed several times by the door built into the exterior wall and had wondered, but never asked, about the heavy iron bars and locks securing it. He dismounted next to the cart and, in the slanting sunshine, could see the broad-shouldered freedman inside. "You're Marcus, right?"

The man turned from inspecting something hung on the wall. "Marcus Attilius...."

"This seems an odd place to store armor. Should it not be closer to the gladiators?"

Marcus came out with a massive breastplate adorned with translucent reddish-gold fittings that glowed under the sun. "These need more secure storage. Now I take them to a man who will clean and polish them." He set the breastplate in the cart and went back inside and returned with another, exactly like it, that he put in the cart. Then he covered both with a blanket.

Something in that sight teased Nicanor's memory. "They're massive..."

"They're worn by Gnaeus's two best gladiators, two brothers. He hopes they'll be back in time." Marcus wiped his brow with a palm, then wiped that on his tunic.

"For the exhibition?"

"Yes." Marcus leaned into the cart to make sure all was covered.

A cord had slipped from Marcus's tunic, and Nicanor saw an *Ichthus* dangled from it. "Are you a Christian?" Nicanor asked.

Marcus followed Nicanor's eyes, gripped the fish symbol in his fist, and hastily tucked it beneath the cloth. His expression turned wary as he studied Nicanor. "Who are you?"

"I'm Nicanor." He raised his hands, palms out, toward Marcus. "Don't worry. I have nothing against it. I knew a man once who talked to me many times about his belief."

"A Christian?" Marcus asked, and when Nicanor nodded, he asked another question. "How did you meet him?"

"He was a prisoner when I served as a watch captain at the Tullianum."

"You mean Paul... you spoke with Paul?" A surprised look replaced the wariness on Marcus's face.

"Many times."

Marcus took a deep breath and let it out, his features settled, and he shook his head. "He has been dead for some time now. Executed."

Nicanor's expression matched the freedman's. "I know...."

"That saddens you... why?" The surprise had come back to Marcus's face.

"He seemed a good man, and I was curious about his religion."

"He was a fine man. I never heard him speak, but my mother did before she died. I think—I pray—that gave her peace at the end. Before she died, she moved me to accept the faith, too. Are you interested in becoming a Christian?"

Once, Nicanor would have burst out laughing at such a question or replied with profanity. But time and events had changed him. "I don't think so," he answered thoughtfully.

"I understand," Marcus nodded. "It is dangerous. The Christian message is still considered sedition and is forbidden, officially at least. But it has changed me. I'm a much better man for it." He reached in to straighten the blanket over the armor, though it did not need straightening. "Or I try to be..."

In the silence that followed, Carmenta nuzzled Nicanor's shoulder twice. Curious about the young man, Nicanor rubbed her neck to appease her—she was hungry, so he knew he must tend to her soon. He said, "So, this is work you do to earn money to pay your debtors."

"Just one debt. Gnaeus bought all my debt from those I owed money to... so I pay only him."

It puzzled Nicanor. "Why would he do that?"

The few lines in the younger man's face tightened, and that aged Marcus beyond his years. "Because Gnaeus hopes I will grow tired at the slowness of repaying him with this kind of work," he replied.

"What kind of work does he want you to do that pays more?"

"Fighting... Once while I was drunk, and to win a bet with him... I bested two of his better gladiators. Since then, he hounds me to fight for him."

"But Christians don't fight... there are no Christian gladiators I know of." Nicanor's eyes gauged the thickness of Marcus's forearms, corded muscle slick with sweat, and the tunic stretched taut across biceps and chest. *But perhaps this one can*, he thought. "Does Gnaeus speak against your beliefs?"

"No."

"Then tell him your belief means you cannot fight."

"Oh, I can fight." The sternness hardened. "But I choose not to. Gnaeus knows I'm Christian, which frustrates him because a

Christian gladiator would make for a profitable spectacle. But I will not become a show for him." Marcus grew quiet as he turned and secured the door, then climbed onto the cart and picked up the reins. "Have you heard of the night of Nero's torches... when he bound Christians to poles, doused them in oil, and set them afire to light his new gardens at the domus aurea?"

At the time, the news of that had made even Nicanor's gut wrench. "Yes...."

"My mother was one of them." Marcus slapped the slack of the reins against the mule's rump and rode away.

LXXXIV

AUGUSTUS 68 CE

JERUSALEM

THE UPPER CITY

"Where are we going, Miriam?" Ya'el asked and hurried to keep up. "You promised your parents you would not go to the Lower City unless we were with Matthew... or Ehud." Miriam's brother had healed and returned to his duties, and Ehud had been visiting them more. But lately, Matthew had been focused on something with Eleasar ben Ananias from morning until night. And Ehud had not invited them again to his glassworks, though Elian often hinted he would like to go back to watch glass being made. Time had grown heavy for both women in the ordinary routines of life, and any change was welcome.

Miriam looked over her shoulder and replied, "Don't worry. We're remaining in the Upper City, but I can't just stay at home or wander the market every day."

"Well, where are we going?" Ya'el asked again.

"I decided we should explore..."

Any change is welcome, Ya'el thought. Still, she detected a hint of trepidation, of uncertainty in Miriam. *But what is there to explore?* They had often walked the Temple Enclosure—the Women's Court, the Upper City, and even Bezetha—and the Fortress Antonia up to the city's northern gate. *What is left to see?*

They reached the last of the merchant stalls in the agora, near the street at the base of the Temple Enclosure's outer wall. Miriam turned down an alley between two buildings and followed as it bent toward the Temple and came to a dead end. Behind a shoulder-height shrub thick with thorns was a cleverly fitted trap door in the ground.

"Watch out... the thorns are sharp," Miriam cautioned as she stooped to sweep dirt away and find the finger holes to lift the trap door. Sunlight showed the top part of a ladder below, and Ya'el followed, full of curiosity.

Several minutes later, a lighted lamp in Miriam's hand, they were down the ladder and far into the tunnel.

"Careful, here."

But Miriam's warning came too late. Ya'el stumbled over the chunks of stone strewn on the hard-packed earthen floor.

"There's more rubble here than I remember," said Miriam. "I haven't been in here since Zechariah...."

Ya'el got her balance, took a step, and more stones rolled beneath her foot. Flailing, she fell into Miriam, knocking the handlamp to the ground. Darkness shrouded them.

"Don't move, Ya'el..." Miriam steadied her friend, then let her go as she set Zechariah's staff down and kneeled to feel for the lamp.

"Miriam..." Ya'el's questioning voice echoed.

"Shh... be quiet..." Miriam snapped. "Sound carries here..."

"Do you think someone is down here?" Ya'el whispered.

"That's not likely, but we must be careful. I first saw your husband here, up ahead in this tunnel."

"What?" Ya'el almost yelped, her eyes wide in the intense blackness underground.

"Shh..." Miriam said, and Ya'el heard her grope around on the ground until she murmured, "Got the lamp, but it's spilled." Ya'el heard the plop of a plug being pulled free from the goatskin bladder of oil that Miriam had slung over her shoulder. Then the sloshing sound of the oil going into the lamp. With a click of the sparking stones, soon the wick caught.

Ya'el let out the breath she'd been holding as Miriam raised the lamp, and within its blessed arc of light, she could see more debris around them. Standing and lifting the lamp higher, Miriam pointed out sections of the ceiling that had fractured in places. *Probably in the storms*, Ya'el thought. Fallen pieces littered the way ahead, but none so big it obstructed the tunnel. They could step over or around what she saw before them.

"Let's go," said Miriam. "But watch your footing."

"Miriam, wait." Ya'el gripped her arm. "What do you mean you saw Gessius Florus down here?"

Miriam pulled her arm free and took Ya'el's hand. "Come on."

"Answer me, Miriam."

"I will..." Miriam squeezed Ya'el's hand and held tighter onto it. For several minutes only the scuffling of their feet, the occasional rattle of a kicked rock, and their breathing broke the silence. They could breathe without strain in the cool below the streets. The current of air was sensed more than felt, and it had the taste of dirt and dust, but it wasn't stale or thin. "That bit of breeze tells me that somewhere along here is an opening to the outside," Miriam said. "Zechariah taught me to pay close attention to things like that."

Soon they came to an area where she paused and raised the lamp, revealing soot on the walls almost obscured by the shifting shadows. "It happened here," Miriam said with a gasp, one hand pressed to her chest as if she could stop the pang of an old wound.

"What... this is where you saw my husband?" Ya'el asked.

Miriam raised the lamp and half-turned toward her. The gold-tinged warmth of the lamp's glow could not bring color to Miriam's face. She could not speak.

Awareness flared on Ya'el's face. "This is where you were raped!" Shocked, Ya'el found her hands had flown to cover her mouth.

The memory must have flooded over Miriam, who staggered a step, then raised her head and spoke. "I walked for some time, remembering only some of how this tunnel was situated because the only time I'd been here before, I was young. In those days, I mostly just followed Yosef. Ahead of me, I saw the glow of more than just the one or two handheld lamps I expected from the Romans I'd followed. The tracks of their sandals with studded nail soles led me to the tunnel's hidden entrance. I heard a voice and slowed, shielding my lamp with one hand as I moved closer. I stumbled, just as you did a while ago, Ya'el. I stopped, worried that they'd heard me. Then I slipped behind a pile of rubble near their circle of light and put out my lamp. I listened, and a Roman voice became distinct: 'These are men I trust, and they're couriers,' the man said: 'They'll post and retrieve messages between us.'

"I peeked over the pile of stones to see the Roman, a nobleman, to judge by his robes and bearing. He pointed at the two soldiers—the ones I had followed—and then at a spike driven into the stone wall just above shoulder height. He hung a cylinder of leather sealed at one end and open at the other to hold the messages he mentioned. The Roman nobleman turned his head, and his face came into the lamp's light. He spoke to someone in the shadows in the entrance to one of the adjoining tunnels: 'I expect you to live up to your side of our agreement. Or...' The Roman stopped, and the man in the shadows replied, 'I will not fail you.' The man sounded Jewish but spoke Latin—and I thought his voice familiar. But the echo on stone made it difficult to tell. I moved and brushed against some loose rocks that rolled and clattered. The shadowy man, I thought a Jew, stepped back into the darkness. I saw the flash of the Roman nobleman's ring and arm cuff as he waved a hand at the two soldiers: 'Find out what made that sound and take care of it,' he ordered and then hurried into one of the side tunnels.

"I ran blindly back the way I had come. Over my shoulder, I saw the two soldiers' torches that lighted their coarse faces. They grinned as if chasing me was some sport that pleased them. They were much faster than I was. I had no light and stumbled into the pitch-black ahead of me. The two men caught me... dragged me back to that spot... and... and..." Miriam stopped, then, after a pause, said one thing more. "The Roman nobleman... I did not know who he was until I saw the new procurator when he came with you to Passover three years ago. It was Gessius Florus, your husband."

"My gods, Miriam... why come here?" Ya'el was too shocked at what Miriam had recounted to register that Gessius Florus had been in this same tunnel. And he had essentially ordered Miriam's rape— the violation of dear Yosef's sister.

"I had to," Miriam explained. "Zechariah told me—taught me—to accept my fear. To acknowledge it exists. But I must never let it stop me from doing what I must. He taught me that I cannot—should not—ignore the fear... even when I know it's always there. I can move beyond it. Here..."

Miriam slowly pivoted with the lamp outstretched like a shield. "Here is where my life changed. Here is where I learned about fear, where fear found me. I got no further in this tunnel, and now I must see what's beyond... at its end." She reached for Ya'el's hand.

LXXXV

Augustus 68 CE

Jerusalem

The Tunnel Beneath the Temple Enclosure

"We should have brought another lamp," Ya'el said as they entered the first of the side tunnels.

"Here," Miriam said, handing the lamp to her, knowing she could see better in the murkiness than Ya'el could. "This passage is wide enough for us to walk side by side."

"Is this the one Gessius Florus went into? After he ordered the two soldiers—"

"No." Miriam appreciated how Ya'el avoided saying anything hurtful to further remind her. And she noted how the former Roman noblewoman tried not to call Florus her husband. She did not blame her for denying that relationship. She prayed that one day soon, Ya'el—Lady Cleo no more—would become his widow. "He entered the next one. I think that way leads to Antonia Fortress. Yehudah ish Krioth entered this one."

"You knew the man!"

"Not then... but later I recognized him when he came to meet with my father. Then I knew he was a Jewish traitor secretly meeting with your... with the Roman procurator."

"Did you tell your father or Matthew?"

"No..." Miriam slowed. Her sense of direction told her they must be well inside the Temple Enclosure... maybe beneath the Temple itself. The passageway seemed wider. She studied the walls and the floor, trying to judge width and height.

"What happened then... what did you do?"

"I killed him." Miriam took the lamp from Ya'el, seeing her questioning expression in the arc of its light. She recalled Yehudah ish Krioth's much different countenance as her blade shot up under his chin. The blood spilling from his lips and torn throat had drenched the silky groomed beard he had been so vain about. "I had to." She raised the lamp to inspect what had caught her eye. There was a large shadow on the tunnel's ceiling a few steps from them.

"What is this?" she said aloud. The shadow became an opening, a vertical shaft. Its inner surface was lighter where the lamp's glow reached and darker gray as the lamplight faded and then black from that point upward. She could not see how far it went.

"I wonder where it goes?" Ya'el asked as she joined her, looking up to see what little the lamp revealed.

"I'm not sure, but it could be to the Temple or its cisterns or storage rooms. Zechariah showed me many of the old tunnels beneath the city and told me of others."

"But not this one?" Ya'el asked. When Miriam did not reply, she touched her shoulder. "Miriam?"

"There are many I don't know any details about." Miriam shook her head. "We'll have to come back with a ladder and torches to see where it goes." She lowered the lamp, unsure how they could do such a thing without being noticed. "Let's go. I want to see how far the main tunnel goes." She hefted the goatskin of lamp oil and shook it, assessing the sloshing sound and its feel. "We have enough to go quite a distance before we have to turn back."

* * *

NORTHWEST OF JERUSALEM

Miriam moistened thumb and forefinger to snuff out the lamp's wick when the passage darkness ahead lightened. Twenty paces later—after a slight bend in the tunnel—in front of them was an opening filled with sunlight achingly bright to their eyes that had grown used to nothing but a hand lamp's glow.

"What place is this?" Ya'el blinked as her eyes adjusted. Before them was an open field, a small valley surrounded by four hills, two on either side that half-overlapped each other and stretched into a ribbon of varying height and slope. Winding among them was a path that looked wide enough to be considered a road but overgrown. It had been many years since it had been used.

"I think we're just northwest of the city. But I don't know what this could be." Miriam gestured at a few buildings that hugged the hill on either side of the opening. Weather-worn, their steps, and entries were half-buried beneath drifts of sand and dirt, and the structures appeared to be as long-disused as the road. "I want to see what's beyond these hills."

"What if it's only more hills?" Ya'el was uncertain. "Shouldn't we go back now?"

Miriam watched Ya'el study the sky and followed her eyes to gauge the sun. "We have time enough... and I think the hills end just there." She pointed in the distance at the last craggy peak with no others beyond it. "Do you remember overhearing Matthew's concern about loading wagons and pack animals inside the Temple Enclosure?"

"Yes, but for loading what?" That had puzzled Ya'el, though she hadn't listened in to as many conversations as had Miriam.

Miriam held up a hand as if to delay answering that question. "If the shaft we found reaches the Temple, it's big enough to raise and lower things to and from it. And the tunnel was wide enough for a narrow cart. Maybe that's what the tunnel was for—to bring things to and from the Temple without being seen." She left the tunnel's exit and entered the clearing. "Larger wagons could be loaded here. I hope the road is good enough and leads to others or to a flat, open plain. Come on...." Miriam walked across the clearing and pushed through the scrub, clogging the old road.

Ya'el followed.

* * *

Less than hour later, Miriam's hope was realized. Standing on the lower part of the north-facing slope of the outermost hill, both women were soaked in sweat. Dust and dirt had turned their light cloaks the grayish-brown of the summer-dry foliage and ground around them. Thick with bushes and brush, the road had proved to have a roughened yet still firmly packed earth bed beneath the overgrowth. If someone cleared away the thickest scrub, any donkey or mule-cart, or wagon should be able to traverse it. And the hills ended at a level plain where four well-used rutted paths—from four equal directions—converged.

"The southerly road we passed, the road that skirts the hills, must lead to Jerusalem." Miriam wiped her brow with the back of a hand. "I think Matthew and Eleasar can use this"—she gestured toward the rough road, hidden by the shoulder of the hill and the valley behind them. "And the tunnel will take care of their other needs."

Ya'el was surprised. "You'd tell Matthew about us going into the tunnel?"

"My brother already suspects I keep secrets from them all. So, I'll reveal one to him." Miriam turned back toward the secluded valley and half-slid down the lower slope they had climbed to get a better view. At the bottom, she set off at a quick pace. Ya'el caught up with her, and she continued: "Maybe that will satisfy my family's curiosity, and they'll leave me alone."

* * *

340

Hananiah, eyes lowered, felt more than saw where the road's low section rose to join three others branching in different directions. Looking around, he crossed to the southerly route and searched again for a sign of any other travelers. Not that other Judeans worried him. Romans could be a problem. He knew there were likely no other Romans around, other than Florus's courier from the 12th Legion picking up and delivering messages at the drop point just north of where he stood. Tyrannius Priseus, the 12th Legion's new First Centurion, controlled the men performing messenger duty. So far, he had kept patrols—even those from Caesarea—clear of that spot. To his right, two plumes of dust lingered over the slope of the nearest hill. He gave it little thought—some animal loosening rocks that then tumbled down the heights of the steep hill.

The message from Gessius Florus occupied his mind. The Roman nobleman said he would soon know whether Ehud's information about the Essenes had proved true. If they had what Lord Florus sought, Hananiah would be rewarded handsomely. Then he would not need to remain in Jerusalem and would have enough money to escape what was to happen when the Roman legions finally arrived outside the city walls. He knew Miriam had feelings for Ehud, but once he had killed him, Hananiah would show Miriam she was better off with him. Together they would leave Jerusalem behind them.

LXXXVI

Augustus 68 CE

Caesarea

Trader's Inn

"Lord Florus..." Drusus had knocked and waited at the entry, and Gessius Florus glanced up, squinting, and saw the man's eyes sweeping the room. Likely checking if any of the Thracians were within other than the one in the hall outside the door. Drusus had served with Thracian auxiliaries, respected their prowess, and knew them as unruly and impatient, all characteristics he had reported to Florus. Tales were told of their disobedience even to their own kings. Taking the counsel of Drusus, Florus, too, held back from trusting them mercenaries. But these Thracians of the Odomanti tribe were said to be the best if the most expensive. Loyal as long as they were paid.

Still, Florus had instructed Drusus not to speak of certain things with them around, so the man's glance suggested he had news that needed privacy.

"What is it, Drusus? Come in." He set aside the crystal lens recommended by a Pompeian engraver. The disc helped him read the writing on the scroll spread before him, but still, after a while, his eyes burned. "Have you found that Syrian auxiliary?"

"I'm sorry, lord, but no. He remains in the camp. Two others are watching for him with me. If I could only enter the camp and—"

"No, that would bring too much attention." Florus re-rolled the letter he had received from Rome, from Tigellinus's senior *evocati augusti*. Evidently, the Praetorian Prefect had delegated the message be sent by one of his hand-picked senior Praetorians. A sign that his support in Rome was weakening with Nero's death. The note said that a servant—hearing of the search and reward—had said he had witnessed a centurion named Nicanor arriving in Emerita Augusta but without a woman. He had met with Marcus Otho to discuss how Lord Otho's sister could be protected.

Florus's mind had raced as he read it. Was Cleo elsewhere in Rome, or had she even left Judea? Where could she be?

How I still burn to find and punish her, he thought as he gritted his teeth and squinted again at Drusus. "Don't go near the camp, but get more men to watch for the Syrian. And make sure you take him alive."

"Yes, lord." Drusus nodded. "I also have a report from Sycaminum that the construction changes you ordered to the warehouse you purchased there have been completed. And the new private dock is under construction."

"Good... good. Leave me now. Focus on finding that Syrian and bring him to me." Once the man had left, Florus sat back and rubbed his eyes. Now, he needed only for Vespasian to respond to Galerius Senna's request. He wanted cohorts from the 12th Legion to investigate reports that Judean rebels were gathering at Qumran with a plan to retake Jericho. It was a chance for the 12th Legion's redemption while they awaited the attack on Jerusalem. *Then we'll see if these Essenes have the locations where the Jews are hiding their treasure*, he thought, recalling the report from Ehud ben Meshulam, his spy in Jerusalem. If he got his hands on that information, it would not matter when Vespasian attacked the city. Hananiah would take care of what needed to be done there. Ehud, the young Jew, would live only until his father—upon Florus's order—moved one of his cargo vessels into Sycaminum.

* * *

Vespasian's Praetorium

Vespasian did not move as Gaheris Clineas returned from escorting out the 12th Legion's commander. The aide held a lighted beeswax taper to the wick of a large lantern. Its glow brightened the room but did not lighten his mood. Resting his square chin on his enormous fist, he asked, "Anything else for today?"

"Only one more, sir," said the aide. "Celsus Evander of the quartermasters has asked twice to speak with you."

"About what?" Vespasian's eyebrows twitched with irritation. There were too many important things on his mind for him to deal with questions of logistics. Though his forces were ready, he would not march on Jerusalem until he confirmed the identity of the new emperor, and if it was Galba, await his orders. He knew his men would not be happy at the further delay.

"About his clerk, Sayid," Gaheris replied. "You may recall this request in the past. He wishes to speak to your prisoner, Yosef ben Mathias."

"I recall him. He and Yosef are—were—friends. I don't see any need to foster their friendship."

343

"Centurion Evander says this Sayid wants to be sure Yosef knows of his wife's death."

"The Syrian's wife?"

"No, general. Your prisoner Yosef's."

Vespasian's head rose from his fist. "What? I did not order her death... when did this happen?"

"I don't know, general. All the centurion said—other than to make the request on Sayid's behalf—was that her name was Ariella, and he and Sayid found her dead outside the camp gate."

"Send Celsus Evander and his clerk to me first thing tomorrow, *prima diei hora*. And send Titus to me now."

* * *

YOSEF'S PRISON CELL

Yosef rinsed his hand in the bowl of water and slid the *novacila* from it, knuckles catching in the round holes for his fingers to grasp the razor. He gingerly touched his face and traced the scrapes along his jaw and throat, then held a damp cloth against the raw flesh to lessen the sting. Raising the polished bronze mirror that had accompanied the iron blade Romans used for shaving, he studied his face beardless for the first time in over ten years. He had been surprised at Titus's offer of both implements, even more at himself for accepting and using them. But then he had felt a distancing from the past—from himself—as he filled page after page in his journal. He had experienced much the last few years. And he recorded all of it with his thoughts about his people and what had led to this war. General Vespasian approved of the writing. He had given Yosef the materials and even some insight into the Roman details of events to include.

He yawned, and the gaping of his jaw made the abraded skin sting anew. Yosef was tired but had no interest in sleeping. He pondered again where Ariella was. She had announced her anger was spent though she believed him still responsible for Levi's death. But having been close to him—hearing his thoughts, his explanations—unless the Romans forced her, she would no longer see him. She would live with her hurt, she told him and no longer sought retribution. Oddly, he missed her company. Since then, his nights had been disturbed with dreams. The vision of Vespasian becoming emperor was one of them at first, but it had been replaced by a scene of the destruction of a Jewish community. It seemed familiar but was not Jerusalem or anywhere in Galilee, the two places he had witnessed fighting against the Romans. Maybe it was just the result of hours of writing and reliving some of that experience. Still, he must try to sleep. As he extinguished the lamp beside his cot, he prayed for a night with no dreams.

LXXXVII

AUGUSTUS 68 CE

ROME

GNAEUS BATIATUS'S VILLA

"Marcus, have you seen Gnaeus?" Nicanor asked as he entered the stable. Gnaeus had told him late the evening before to come to see him in the morning; he had news of Lord Tigellinus and Gaius Sabinus. Carmenta greeted him from her stall, spotting the bag of millet with bits of dried fig he had brought with him, nickered, and tossed her head. Opening the drawstring on the sack, he poured some into a wooden bowl and carried it to her. "You've become spoiled," he whispered in her ear and held the bowl under her nose.

The freedman turned from saddling a horse. "He left with Sextus to meet with the man he's considering hiring as a *summa rudis*, senior referee, for this exhibition and future Games."

"So, death won't decide the match winners?" Nicanor cupped the last of the millet for Carmenta, who lipped it from his hand and nosed him for more.

"Patrons of the Games sometimes pay more for a death match and also compensate for the cost of the dead gladiator. But most matches are not to death. Gnaeus has spent good money acquiring and training his group of slave-gladiators; he won't waste them. There are always wounds—some severe—but the fights will be stopped before they go too far."

"That's what the referee is for..." Nicanor said.

"Yes, and to score the match and grade each fighter. How well each does could be the difference in whether he remains here—a better place than most—or gets sold. And it determines their reward."

"Reward?"

"Better quarters, privacy... women." Marcus shrugged and turned back to the horse.

Nicanor thought of Graius. "What of their chance for freedom?"

The freedman nodded without looking at the centurion, "There is that, but not until Gnaeus has made his money back and a sizable profit."

Nicanor had debated asking, though of late, he had talked often and long with Marcus, and he seemed worthy. But despite Antonia

Caenis's confidence, the thought of having to rely on men he did not know made him restless at night. *Is Gnaeus trustworthy?* He was unsure whether he could even trust Marcus to answer that question, but he had to know. So, he asked it aloud: "Can I trust Gnaeus?"

Marcus finished tightening a girth strap and turned to the centurion. "Gnaeus always has his eye on an opportunity for profit or to add more to the rebuilding of his family's reputation. Other than his looseness used in bargaining, Gnaeus does not lie or cheat. You can trust he will do as he promises, but Gnaeus has grown used to talking, selling... pitching, and promoting. Sometimes he too easily says things that seem right to him. He assumes that an arrangement and agreement are understood... but that may prove not to be understood the same way by the other person. Always make him state things clearly and that your understanding is the same as his."

"You talk as if you know him well."

"All my life. I grew up around him. My family is connected to his."

"Yet he holds your debt?"

"Yes."

"To get you to fight for him."

"That and to save me. Some men I owed money to had declared my death their last recourse. Were it not for Gnaeus, I'd be another dead body in the Tiber." Marcus led the horse outside.

Nicanor followed him. "If you're such a good fighter, and the bouts are not to the death... why not fight just long enough to get out of debt?"

"Because not all fights will be that way... and because of my family and its legacy. Some will want to see me cut down and would not mind it unjustly done." Marcus grew quiet as he mounted. "Did you really speak with Paul about the Jewish Messiah Yesous Christos and his teachings?"

"He talked about them... I listened." Nicanor was curious about what he meant about his family but needed to find Gnaeus. He started to leave.

Marcus stopped him. "Wait. I have errands to do for Gnaeus... come with me part of the way, and if you want... I can show you where many of us believe Paul is buried."

* * *

VIA OSTIENSIS AT VIA VALENTINIANA, JUST OUTSIDE THE CITY WALL

Marcus reined his horse to a stop soon after turning down what seemed a private lane. "Paul was beheaded at *Aquae Salviae*, close to here. Lucina, a Christian matriarch, had his body brought here to her family burial plot, which is located beyond the city wall, as the *pomerium* requires."

Nicanor looked at the many small *mausolea;* the tombs were square masonry structures with low roofs. "Do you know which holds Paul?"

"No, and Lucina and her family will not reveal it. They worry the grave will be desecrated, especially if Nero returns and continues his oppression of Christians. He has made others in Rome hate Christians. We all fear that...."

"Nero's dead, Marcus... but I hope others won't persecute you. Your belief seems a harmless one." Nicanor leaned forward to stroke Carmenta's neck. A breeze kicked up, and he smelled the river. They were only a short distance south of the Temple of Hercules. He bowed his head and thought of his friend.

"Nicanor?"

He had missed what Marcus had asked him. "What?"

"Do you want to continue with me, or do you have things to do?"

"No, I'll go back now and see if Gnaeus has returned. I must speak with him."

"Were you saying a prayer for Paul?" Marcus sounded encouraged.

Nicanor smiled inside. Paul, too, had seemed hopeful he would convert to his belief and reverence for their divine prophet. "A prayer, yes, but for another friend. One day I might tell you of him."

LXXXVIII

JERUSALEM

THE UPPER CITY

On the rooftop, Ya'el smiled. She saw a small grin form on Miriam's face as they watched Elian in the courtyard below. The boy loaded square wooden trays with figs and grapes to bring to the terrace and set upon tables near them where they would dry in the sun. Near sundown, he would get them inside to rinse away the dust and the next morning repeat the process. Though late summer heat still shrouded the city, it was also time to prepare for winter.

"Sun-drying fruits used to be my responsibility, and Yosef and Matthew's before me." Miriam seemed to dwell on those memories.

Perched on Elian's shoulder, supervising, was Cicero, who occasionally quivered, fluffing his feathers before preening as he bobbed in rhythm with the boy's pace. Ya'el had already saved quite a few of the bird's feathers to use for fletching when she had a private place to work on arrows. She studied Miriam, who still watched Elian. Now that she'd confessed her tunnel exploration, would Miriam give up going to Zechariah's or the tomb?

Ya'el was afraid of what would happen if Miriam continued in the tunnels. Still, she also wanted Miriam to continue and include her. Elian was happy with the daily chores Rebecca had given him and kept interested and busy with both of Miriam's parents teaching him. He had picked up Aramaic quickly. Though thankful for her safety and the home provided in a time of war, Ya'el was bored and wanted to better understand Yosef's sister. She thought she'd glean more from Miriam's thoughts and leaned toward her. "Your mother and father seemed relieved when you told them you've been secretly exploring the tunnels for some time."

"But not Matthew..." Miriam shook her head, her veil loosening and the end of her headscarf trailing in the wind. The sirocco brought with it a haze of desert dust and grit.

"Not entirely," Ya'el replied, "but I think telling him it was his and Yosef's fault made him relax a little. Even your mother had to admit she had tried to make you stop doing that but had failed."

"It's the truth. Leah and I used to follow my brothers and Ehud everywhere when they explored."

From Miriam's remarks before, Ya'el knew childhood had been the happiest time for her and her brothers. But there was no hint of fond remembrance in what she'd just shared. She seemed troubled, and Ya'el thought she knew why. "Miriam, what will you do about Matthew?" Ya'el did not tell her that Matthew had asked her if his sister had other secrets. Ya'el had told him she knew of none. So now she had joined Miriam in the lie.

"Nothing," Miriam said. "I hope he has little time to do anything with his worries about me. After I gave him information about the tunnel and shaft we found under the Temple, he and Eleasar ben Ananias met with Ehud to ask for his help in looking into it."

"Why do they need Ehud?"

"Though it's been years, he knows that tunnel, too. Until they see if they can use it for what's needed, they cannot talk about it with others. That's what they've been working on. And..." Miriam shook her head and stopped.

"And what?" Ya'el asked, curious at Miriam's expression... not one of worry but of unease. It was the unease she had felt when Miriam proposed exploring another tunnel. Ya'el had confessed she feared falling into a crevice or becoming lost underground. She doubted she could ever enter a tunnel as boldly as Miriam did. "What is it?" Ya'el pressed. Something shifted in Miriam's eyes, and she lowered them.

"Each day, there are fewer people my father and brother can rely on. And now—because they need help—they've decided to trust Ehud."

"Why?" Ya'el asked.

Miriam's eyes lifted to Ya'el's, flared, and then dimmed. "Because he loves me..."

"Ehud told you that?"

"Not in words to me... but to my father, when Father asked Ehud his intentions toward me."

"If you give Ehud a chance, I know he will tell you what he feels." Ya'el paused. "Do you love him?"

"Yes. But I don't know if I can save him."

Ya'el sat with her in silence, knowing what weighed on her mind. The Sicarii believed Ehud a spy. Now he was included in one of the most important Jewish secrets of all. His loyalties would surely be tested. "Nothing is hidden that one day will not be known," Ya'el whispered.

"Yes," Miriam replied. "All becomes revealed in time, and that's what frightens me."

Ya'el understood Miriam feared being loved would expose what had happened to her, disclose her true secret. The truth, Ya'el had learned, was full of pain. Her own truth as Cleo was that her father had arranged her marriage to Gessius Florus to benefit himself, not for his daughter's good. And now Cleo believed Florus had accepted her because it aided him in being assigned as the Judean Procurator. Her friend, Poppaea—knowing Cleo's fondness for Judea and the Jewish people—had gone to her husband Nero to ask for that position for Florus as a wedding gift.

Now, what Miriam had told her in the tunnel shocked her. Just a couple of years ago, Gessius Florus had met with a Jewish traitor in a tunnel beneath the city he planned to destroy, just to steal its treasures. She wondered what her husband did now, without Nero's support. One thing was sure—he would not stop hunting for her. That was another painful truth, not that it mattered. Another certainty was that the legions would eventually march on Jerusalem and accomplish what her husband wanted. The destruction of Jerusalem would mean her death. It had always been that her life seemed in others' hands: her father, Gessius Florus... now, the charity of Yosef's family. But when the legions breached Jerusalem's walls—as she knew they would—and entered the city, she would fight to protect the Jewish family that had become all she had. And if it must be, she would die by her own hand. She would not be taken as a slave nor executed as a traitor to the empire.

Ya'el raised her head and looked around, startled. The sound of dozens, maybe hundreds of voices carried on the wind. "Who are they?" Ya'el asked.

"Those are people entering the city."

"What do they sing?"

"It's the Song of Ascents."

"I can't hear the words, but it sounds beautiful." *Yet the voices sound sad*, Ya'el did not add.

"It is beautiful," Miriam said, turning her back to the wind and singing: "I was glad when they said to me, let us go to the house of the Lord! Our feet have been standing within your gates, O Jerusalem! Jerusalem, built as a city bound firmly together. To which the tribes go up, the tribes of the Lord, as was decreed to give thanks to the name of the Lord. There thrones for judgment were set, the thrones of the house of David. Pray for the peace of Jerusalem. May they be secure who love you. Peace be within your walls and security within your towers!" Miriam took Ya'el's hand—the Roman still knew little Aramaic—and finished in Greek: "For my brothers and companions' sake, I will say, O peace be within you. For the sake of the house of the Lord our God, I will seek your good."

* * *

In the courtyard below them, Mathias looked up, eyes closed, listening. "I have not heard her sing in… I'm not sure how long." He put his arm around Rebecca's shoulders. "We have many things to worry about. But I think Ehud's love for Miriam—and her finally telling what she had hidden for so long—is returning our daughter to us."

"So I pray, Mathias…." Rebecca could not keep herself from pulling at a thread of doubt in the fabric her husband thought had been sewn back together. "So, I pray."

LXXXIX

SEPTEMBER 68 CE

CAESAREA

VESPASIAN'S PRAETORIUM

"Return to your duties, centurion," Vespasian ordered. "Your clerk will stay." Celsus hurried as if glad to be leaving. He had seemed surprised at Vespasian's questions and darted looks toward the young Syrian. But his forthrightness suggested there was no secret to cover up. Celsus had not known the woman's identity, though Sayid clearly did. "Titus," Vespasian motioned to his son, "bring Yosef here." While he waited, Vespasian studied the young Syrian across from him. At first, the auxiliary did not meet his gaze, then Sayid's eyes lifted and fixed on his. "When Nicanor told me of you," Vespasian remarked, "he spoke of your intelligence and loyalty and of things you had done for Cestius Gallus. What he said struck me as honest and that you had acted with good intent. But I do not understand how any of it would lead to you being attacked in Ptolemais and to the death of a Jewish woman here. Yet my sense is that they are connected."

* * *

Yosef entered the room with Titus, who said to Vespasian, "I ordered his guards to remain outside, general." The young general looked frankly at Yosef and said, "They're not needed, right?"

"No, Lord Titus," Yosef replied. Lately, he had talked more with the general's son than with Vespasian himself. But news of Nero's death had likely created quite a stir in the upper ranks of the Roman military and the empire's political structure. There was much for men such as Vespasian to be concerned with. He was surprised to see Sayid and nodded his greeting with a smile but spoke to the general. "You sent for me, lord?"

"Your friend here," he pointed a thumb toward Sayid, "has brought news that concerns me and will likely distress you. I know we have not spoken of something you've asked me about. That's because no explanation was needed—I felt she was no longer necessary."

"She, lord?" Yosef asked. "Is this about Ariella? I've asked my guards why I have not heard any news of her, I know you must still hold her to serve your purpose, but they will not answer me. I was about to ask to see you about her."

"I ordered her freed, and she stayed in Caesarea, apparently." Vespasian's eyes narrowed at Sayid, then at Yosef. "Your friend has reported that he and his commanding officer found her dead outside the camp's main gate."

Yosef visibly paled; he had no beard to hide that pallor. "What?"

"I did not order her killed," Vespasian said.

Yosef rubbed his face with both hands as he looked from Sayid's sad expression to Vespasian's stern curiosity.

"Would her own people kill her?" the general asked.

"For marrying me, general?" Yosef shook his head. "No, sir. But I think I know who would... and why."

"Tell me." Vespasian uncrossed his thick arms and placed both hands flat on his desk.

"When Ariella was a prisoner in Ptolemais, she told others she held me accountable for her husband's death in Yotapta. She was full of anger and hatred."

"For you?"

"Yes, lord." Yosef hesitated then continued. "She told me a man took her before the 12th Legion's Camp-Prefect—men from that legion were assigned to guard prisoners from Galilee—who asked her if she hated me enough to kill me. And she did. Ariella then met with a Roman nobleman in Ptolemais. He asked the same thing: if an opportunity came up and she was close enough to do it, would she kill me to avenge her husband's death? She told him yes. He asked, 'Even if it meant marrying the man you hate?' She told him yes because she would soon be the man's widow, my widow."

"So, she married you to kill you?" Titus asked.

"Yes, lord."

Vespasian leaned toward Yosef, "Why didn't she, then?"

"Sir, at first, I think Ariella waited to be sure she could do it without interference. I kept talking to her, trying to explain her thinking was wrong. We argued many times—I'm sure the guards reported that—and then Ariella realized deep in her heart I was not a traitor." Yosef lowered his head, "But as commander, ultimately, I am responsible for her husband's death." Yosef raised his head. "He... Levi was my friend and saved my life." Yosef looked away, thinking of how his own grief had been swallowed up in her rage so that he'd hardly had time to consider these things. "Then Ariella no longer came to my cell. I expect that for the man who sent her to kill me, she no longer served a purpose." *Florus would have been enraged, but there's no use in mentioning that,* Yosef thought, *Vespasian would not hold a fellow Roman accountable for a rebel's death.*

"The man who arranged the marriage—suggested it strongly—was Gessius Florus. He persuaded me that your responsibility for a wife would keep you from escaping, would provide leverage for our questioning. You know the man, do you not?"

"Yes, general."

"Why would he want you killed?"

Yosef was silent. So much was at stake. Could this man be trusted to protect Cleo?

"Answer me, Yosef." Vespasian's voice betrayed irritation, though he was usually slow to anger.

"Yosef," Titus shifted in his chair and then stood, "answer the question."

"I can tell you," Sayid said, ignoring the warning look Yosef darted at him. "I was assigned as an auxiliary in Lady Cleo's escort when she toured the eastern and southern provinces before marrying Gessius Florus. On the return to Rome, a storm wrecked our ship...."

* * *

Vespasian sat back. He had listened to the Syrian auxiliary though he had heard the story before from Nicanor. "Is that all?" Vespasian interrupted Sayid.

"Almost, general... that's how we all met: me, Lady Cleo, Nicanor, and Yosef."

"Go on."

"After the shipwreck, we survived after many days at sea, and then afterward in Rome, I could see Lady Cleo and Yosef had grown fond of each other. We all grew to care for Lady Cleo, but there was a closeness between her and Yosef." Sayid's eyes returned to Yosef, who glared at him, and then quickly returned to Vespasian. "My reward for helping save Lady Cleo was to return to Judea in her service. Once we were here in Caesarea, Lord Florus mistreated her in small ways. After I returned to the 12th Legion, I learned his abuse of her had grown. It seemed Lord Florus believed that Lady Cleo was in love with Yosef. He took it out on her, and that's why she ran from him. In my own time around him, I found Lord Florus to be vengeful. When Yosef was captured and not executed, Florus attempted to carry out the killing his own way. As Yosef has reported from the woman, in Ariella's own words."

The room was quiet as Vespasian studied Sayid for some time. He had spoken with auxiliaries countless times in his military career but never so long to one of such low rank. But what Sayid said made sense. Florus struck him as a man who would not let any slight or insult go without retaliation. It would enrage him that a foreign subject—in his eyes a lesser man—could be loved more than he.

"Would he really kill a prisoner in my custody?" He said aloud what he marveled at in his mind.

"I think he was aflame," Sayid blinked, and Vespasian immediately thought of Florus's burns, "with hatred, general. I was glad to hear Lady Cleo had left him."

The two things he thought connected now proved linked. "Did you and Nicanor help Lady Cleo escape him?" asked Vespasian.

"No, sir."

The Syrian lies, but let's see what more there is from him, Vespasian thought.

"But as Celsus told you, general... I was attacked. Celsus did not know—I did not tell him—but it was because Lord Florus believes I might know where she is."

"Do you?" Vespasian glared at the Syrian and glanced at Yosef, who had remained silent.

"No, sir."

He lies again. Vespasian drummed thick fingers on the tabletop. He had too many things to worry about without being drawn into some tawdry drama. But he also could not ignore the clear signs of Gessius Florus's involvement. What Sayid told him rang true, which meant Florus had no problem interfering in matters under others' command, even his own. "That will be all," he said, dismissing Sayid, who turned pleading eyes toward Yosef before leaving. As Vespasian scrutinized the departing auxiliary, he resolved to monitor Gessius Florus closely if he remained in Judea. *Perhaps the new emperor will replace him with a man of his own choosing.*

He turned to Yosef, who still sat stiffly as he had while listening to Sayid. "You've kept silent while your friend spoke a great deal. Do you have anything to add about Gessius Florus?" When Yosef shook his head, he continued, "Then I'll hear no more of Lady Cleo and Gessius Florus's marital issues." He tapped a forefinger twice on his desk and glanced at his son, glad to change the subject. "General Titus tells me you've mentioned you spent time with a group of your people called the Essenes. We've had reports of Judean rebels massing at one of its communities, Qumran. General Titus will accompany a cohort to investigate and deal with them if that's needed. What can you tell me of them?"

* * *

Yosef surfaced from beneath his guilt at Ariella's death, his concern for Lady Cleo... and his anger at Sayid for revealing such a personal observation about her... and him. But with time to consider, he now understood why Sayid had done it. If Vespasian became more watchful of Florus's intrigues, that could prove helpful to Cleo at some point. And Vespasian's question solved the puzzle of his latest dream. He had told the general: "The Essenes are peaceful, general. They prefer to lead simple, spiritual lives. Their communities are not a refuge for Judean troops or rebel forces to gather to strike against you." Vespasian's grim expression told him his words did not dissuade the Roman general from what he had already decided. *I've seen Qumran's destruction*, Yosef thought and closed his eyes. Memory took him back to his time with Nahum and the other Essenes.

XC

SEPTEMBER 68 CE

ROME

GNAEUS BATIATUS'S VILLA

Nicanor squinted at the morning sky and thought of his Greek mother's stories of Aeolus, the keeper, and controller of the winds. Bunched clouds broke apart, revealing the sky's deep-sea blue that brightened as he studied it. The gleam of gold on the clouds, the gift of Sol, made him think of Paul the Christian and his belief in the light of his god. In Syria, while with a legion cohort in Palmyra, he heard of the local worship of Sol Invictus, the unconquered sun... their chief god. Some soldiers had been swayed to worship that god, and he wondered if it was related to Paul's. Perhaps that was why, as he watched the sun, he had a curious wish to hear Paul's reassuring voice speaking to him again. He wished Marcus had known which tomb held the Christian. As with Graius's ashes at the Temple of Hercules, it would be good to know the resting place of Paul's remains. *But maybe*, he thought and squinted again at the sky, *Paul's pneuma is above me right now as the Christian believed.*

"How goes it, centurion?"

Nicanor turned to see the *lanista* with four gladiators with training gear and wooden *spathas*, long swords. "*Semper idem*, Sextus... each day always seems the same."

"Then come with me and shake that 'sameness' from you. You're a fighting man, or I'm no judge. I vow my men won't bore you."

Nicanor looked at the metal sword sheathed at Sextus's hip and the wooden versions the fighters held. There was a hint of challenge in the trainer's tone that he did not care for. "I'm afraid I don't fight using mock weapons. And never for points, Sextus, or for someone's entertainment."

The trainer bristled, and his knuckles whitened on the hilt of his sword.

"Nicanor!" Marcus called from the stable path, his hurried step crunching on the gravel and coming to a stop as Nicanor shifted his gaze from its lock on Sextus. "I have something to show you... for Carmenta."

Nicanor glanced at the lanista, eyes flicking to Sextus's grip, his blade showing inches out of its sheath, and his lips curled as he met the man's icy stare. "Be with you shortly, Marcus," he replied to the young freedman.

"Maybe another time, then, centurion." Sextus took his hand from his sword, spun on his heel, and marched toward the arena, the fighters following him. Two of them shot hard looks at Nicanor over their shoulders.

"Perhaps, Sextus," Nicanor replied, then went to Marcus, who had not returned to the stables.

"That man does not like me." Marcus nodded to Nicanor as the centurion stopped in front of him.

"I don't think he likes me, either... and I don't care." Nicanor pointed a thumb over his shoulder toward the arena. "But why does he dislike you?"

"He's one of Gnaeus's fighters I bested, and he won't let go of it." Marcus shook his head.

"Ahhh..." Nicanor grinned. "So, he wants a rematch."

"No." Marcus shook his head again. "He was one of the better fighters but lacked heart. That deficiency came out in our bout. I embarrassed him and probably should not have." He shrugged. "The man never fought again."

Nicanor understood. "And those that cannot do, or can no longer do..."

"Teach." Marcus finished for him.

"Right." Nicanor rubbed the scar that bisected his brow and creased his cheek. "Still, he acted as if he'd pull his sword and have at me if he had the chance."

"Only with fighters there to get him out of trouble. He would have reconsidered, though, since you are Gnaeus's guest."

Nicanor studied the smiling freedman, the only one he could talk to who seemed genuine among the posturing men he had met in Rome. "I haven't seen you lately."

"I just returned from Puteoli... Gnaeus is moving equipment from his school at Leptis Magna. With Nero dead and no imperial sponsorship, he plans to focus everything here. I met the ship to arrange the transfer to a storage warehouse near the Circus Maximus."

"What did you have to show me for Carmenta?"

"Nothing. I just wanted to stop what might have happened with Sextus and his men." Marcus stooped to pick up a thick stick at his feet and picked bark from it. "Where do things stand on your meeting with Gaius Sabinus? How much longer will you be here?"

"I don't know." *And that begins to anger me*, Nicanor thought. The last Gnaeus had told him was Tigellinus had contacted Galba, as the new emperor, to secure his place under him. Gaius Sabinus was already maneuvering, too. When Nero went missing, Sabinus told the Praetorian Guard he had fled to Egypt. But when Nero's death was confirmed, Sabinus claimed others vying for the throne were treacherous liars, but he could be trusted. Nicanor's gut told him none of them were honest. Gnaeus believed Sabinus lobbied for the Praetorians to back him as sole prefect before he accepted the letter from Galba. "Why do you ask how long I'll be here?"

"When I returned last night and reported to Gnaeus, he made me an offer. His two best fighters return on the next vessel sailing from Leptis Magna, and the exhibition will be held when they arrive." Marcus paced, his head down. Gripping the stick, he snapped it into two pieces.

"What is it, Marcus... what does that have to do with me?"

"It will take me a year or more to repay Gnaeus working for him as I have been. I grow frustrated, just as he planned. Last night, he offered to consider a third of my debt repaid."

"That sounds good—"

"No," Marcus interrupted, "he wants me to fight in his exhibition and...." Marcus stopped pacing and stood in front of Nicanor, raising his head, but did not continue.

"And?" Nicanor asked.

"I told him I would, but only as in a training match. Still, I do not trust any man Sextus puts against me to limit it to just sparring. He will promise some reward to the man for my killing and then explain it away as 'accidents will happen.' So, I proposed an alternative.

"To fighting?"

"To whom I fight..."

"A fighter from a different *ludis*? I understand there are several gladiator schools."

"I thought that at first, but it occurred to me Sextus has connections and could make some similar arrangement with another. I did not have a resolution for that, but Gnaeus was like a dog with a bone and would not let go. He said he knew a trustworthy man who might think a favor was owed him and who might be willing to take part under the conditions I wanted.

"Sounds like there's your solution."

"I won't know until I ask and get his answer."

"Well, I wish you luck with him." Nicanor clapped Marcus on the shoulder. The man flinched, though the touch was light.

Marcus drew in a breath, "Will you match against me in the exhibition?"

Nicanor blinked, not sure he had heard the question.

The freedman continued. "I told Gnaeus I would be in his exhibition but only against you."

"You told him what?"

XCI

September 68 CE

Jerusalem

The Upper City

Ya'el had been watching Miriam at breakfast when Ehud had shown up at Rebecca's open invitation to eat meals with them. He had teased Elian about how round he was becoming from all that Rebecca fed him. Then he had conferred with Mathias and Matthew about the tunnel's adequate size and stability. Now they discussed the work ahead to use it with caution. The glances between Miriam and Ehud were neither questioning nor wary. Instead, the two seemed to share some acknowledgment of unspoken words.

Before dawn, Ya'el had heard Miriam go downstairs and through the courtyard to the rear entrance. Then as the first hint of daylight crept over the wall, she had seen two figures under the trees near the gate, the two shadows coming together as one. Minutes later, more visible in the growing light, Miriam had crossed the courtyard, her eyes searching the upper windows.

Now both of the young women were back upstairs, and Miriam sat upon the corner of Ya'el's bed.

"You saw me this morning?" she asked.

"Yes. Was that Ehud with you?"

Miriam nodded. "He apologized for every time he'd hurt my feelings, even for the times when he hadn't but thought he might have."

"Did you tell him why you were wary, that you thought he hid something from you?"

"Yes, and my tongue burned with having to keep my secrets while demanding he tell me his own. His family in Alexandria is in trouble, and it's something to do with his father's cargo ships. People want to use one of them for something illegal; he couldn't say what because they are waiting for something to happen first."

"Who is it? Romans?" Ya'el, for the first time, felt she spoke of Romans as being separate from her—and different from her.

"It must be since he worries the arrangement makes his father a traitor. And he worries that someone here watches him too, to keep his father in line until Ehud has done as they demand. That's why he has been elusive and reluctant to speak. But he says he can't let things between us stay unresolved. Who knows what tomorrow brings? He wanted to tell me today, at dawn, that he loves me."

The news pleased Ya'el, but she could still hear the concern in Miriam's voice. "What will you do now?"

"He's concerned I'll draw the attention of whoever is watching him, and that could put me in danger. But he also believes it will be over soon. Then he'll be free if only to face the Roman legions with everyone here in Jerusalem. But we'd be together, at least. He plans to talk to Father about a betrothal as soon as he can."

Ya'el leaned forward to take Miriam's hand. "I'm so happy for you!"

"For the longest time, I've thought I never would be happy again," Miriam said as she squeezed Ya'el's hand in return. "But now I must keep him safe from the Sicarii, and whoever else is watching him." Miriam shook her head. "I want to keep my promise to my parents... but I can't stay away from the Lower City if I must watch Ehud."

"There's someone else there you must consider..." Ya'el said.

"Who?"

"Hananiah. I saw the knife maker watching this house twice recently... I think he watches for you."

* * *

THE LOWER CITY

Miriam entered the shop carrying two old carving knives wrapped in a cloth. She could explain she was getting them sharpened if an explanation was needed.

"It's good to see you," Hananiah said, looking up from writing on a square of parchment. His voice was as devoid of emotion as she had become accustomed to, but his dark eyes glittered.

"I've heard that you watch my home... I want to know why." Miriam stepped to the work counter, determined to be forthright.

He kept writing with slashing strokes like he was cutting letters into the sheet, strong slanting characters.

A moment's recognition passed over her. *Where have I seen...?*

"You told me of someone who threatened you... so when I can, I watch." Hananiah folded the note and tucked it into the sash at his waist.

"There hasn't been any more concern... not really. But I thank you."

"Was it your cousin," he studied her, "who saw me?"

"Yes." Miriam saw his expression harden, then relax, as if by will.

"Will you come with me?" he asked.

"I just wanted to thank you and tell you—you don't need to watch over me."

"Will you come with me?" he repeated.

"Where?" Miriam asked.

* * *

Hananiah led Miriam through the Lower City almost to the Upper City's steps near the Temple Enclosure and stopped at a series of large limestone support columns. He kneeled before the center pillar and touched the words carved into it.

Miriam recalled his mournful sigh that morning a year and a half ago when she had followed him to this column. She had watched as he traced the engraving on it with a long thin finger and then bowed as if in thought or prayer. After he had gone, her own fingers had traced the chiseled inscription: *Hananiah bar Dodalos mi-Yerushalayim...* Hananiah, the son of Dodalos from Jerusalem.

Hananiah rose and dusted his knees. "I told you of my father—this is some of his work"—he gestured to the inscription. "I come here sometimes to tell him things... my thoughts. Just now, I told him I found a woman I care for that I think favors me. If all works out, I'll no longer be alone." Hananiah reached for her hand. "I can soon take you from here, Miriam. We can leave and go far away from the Romans and the fighting. You will not have to obey anyone again. You'll be free."

His eyes softened, and the appeal in them startled her. "I... I..." she did not want to hurt him but—

"Miriam!" A voice called out.

She turned her head and recognized the old priest coming toward her with a stiff, waddling gait. "Yohanan, you look tired," she said.

"I am. I've spent too much time in a donkey cart. Who was that with you?"

Miriam turned to find Hananiah had disappeared. "A friend—he had to finish his errand."

"And I must finish mine. Walk me to your home so I may see your father and Matthew." Yohanan ben Zaccai rested his hand on her arm as they walked.

"I see road dust on you this morning. Where do you come from?" Miriam asked.

"Herodium."

* * *

Once they were far enough away, Hananiah stepped from behind the column. *I'll do more than tell you of my love, Miriam. I'll show you,* Hananiah vowed.

XCII

Sᴇᴘᴛᴇᴍʙᴇʀ 68 CE

Cᴀᴇsᴀʀᴇᴀ

Vᴇsᴘᴀsɪᴀɴ's Pʀᴀᴇᴛᴏʀɪᴜᴍ

Vespasian did not let his aggravation show as he read. After what he had heard about the man recently, he was cautious but curious. Had Florus become aware of Vespasian setting one of the *areani* who had served him in Britannia to pay attention to the man's activities? Not even Titus knew of those secretive agents on his staff, and until now, he'd had no purpose for them other than their mundane duties. But, as always, his intuition that he should bring them to Judea proved helpful. He set the sheet down, and it curled into its former shape.

"You should go to Antioch," he said, "and meet with Governor Mucianus or the Judean Procurator Marcus Antonius Julianus."

"But General Vespasian, you've seen success as a legate, as a consul, and as governor of a province. I merely want your opinion."

"Lord Florus, it's too soon to discuss taxes on the Judeans." Vespasian slid across the desktop the scroll the imperial tax collector had given him. *Would he still be in that position with the new emperor?* "My opinion of your *fiscus judaicus*, clearly a vengeful tax to further punish Judea, matters little. The emperor decides."

Gessius Florus used the palm of his hand to roll the scroll back and forth on the desk. "And who will the emperor be?"

"The Senate has declared Galba—"

"But that's not official until he reaches Rome." Florus stopped rolling the cylinder of vellum. His fingers tented over it, and he began tapping the two of them in rhythm on the wood.

Vespasian silently resisted the urge to bring one of his mallet-sized fists down on Florus's hand as if squashing a spider.

"I've heard some prefer Aulus Vitellius. Do you know him?" Florus asked.

"I know *of* him," Vespasian replied. "A governor—before me—of *Provincia Africa*. By accounts I've heard, he did well at that."

* * *

"Yes, I've heard that about Vitellius," Florus agreed with Vespasian, *and much more*, Florus thought. In his insulae, guarded by one of his

Thracians, he had a note from his men in Rome. The document was secured by his own variation of Caesar's cipher. The man had secretly approached Vitellius with Florus's offer to form an allegiance of mutual benefit, replacing the one he had lost with Nero's death.

Florus could not accept Galba as emperor. The man was too close to Marcus Otho, Cleo's brother, and if Otho gained a place of power besides the throne, there was little hope for Florus's plans. Who knew what would be dredged up to charge him under *lex maiestatas*, the Law of Treason? That law had long been used against any who committed crimes against the empire. Florus had colluded with Jews before the war started—in fact, perhaps partially *caused* the war. *My dealings with the Idumean Esau ben Beor could come out, too,* he thought.

And he had advised Nero to set the great fire. Rome was rife with *delatores*, professional informers. Who knew what they or Ophonius Tigellinus might tell any new emperor? What might result if Florus did not establish an alliance to protect himself? But Vitellius had a quality familiar to Florus: greed. As emperor, Vitellius would be willing to offer his protection for an imperial share of the sizable Temple treasure.

"Well," Florus said, breaking the brooding silence, knowing Vespasian was too wise to speak his true thoughts. "I'll do as you say, general. I'll discuss this with Governor Mucianus. Thank you for your time."

* * *

Vespasian watched him leave, noting the scars on the back of Flores's knees and calves. The burns undoubtedly must have caused great pain. He could not help but think it was likely deserved. The more he knew of Gessius Florus, the more he disliked him. Now he had a task for his other areani. To watch Vitellius.

XCIII

Sᴇᴘᴛᴇᴍʙᴇʀ 68 CE

Rᴏᴍᴇ

Gɴᴀᴇᴜs Bᴀᴛɪᴀᴛᴜs's Vɪʟʟᴀ

Nicanor could not get used to the feel of it; it had been decades since he'd last used a wooden sword on the exercise fields. His body, long trained to wield a metal sword to hew a death blow at an enemy, missed the weight and balance. Each thrust and counterthrust was unsettling, and Marcus used every opportunity to make him pay for over-swinging. He was well padded, but he would have new bruises added to those from the previous days. Still, the workouts had certainly loosened the stiffness of his joints and reduced the slackness he had felt growing in his arms, legs, and stomach since leaving Hispania. Still, the *thwack* of wood on wood did not give him the martial thrill he always expected with the ring of metal on metal. Sparring like this was play, and he liked the freedman, who had yet to give him any gut twitch of distrust. That was what made him feel better at telling Marcus he'd go along with his plan.

Gnaeus Batiatus sat in the shade of the atrium watching the two men practice in the inner courtyard. He was pleased with Nicanor's decision and called to him from the long divan he stretched upon. "Antonia Caenis has arrived in Rome and will come to the exhibition; she says she looks forward to speaking with you." He saw the centurion's curt nod of acknowledgment, his eyes not straying from Marcus's movements. "It's cool and pleasant where I sit... you two make me sweat. Come, leave that and sit with me. Some wine will refresh you." He waved a hand at a table loaded with plates of fruit and an amphora with three cups, two unused.

"That sounds good to me," Nicanor said, lowering the wooden gladius and nodding at Marcus. "I'll ask again since you've not answered me yet. Where did you learn to handle a sword? You move better than most legionaries I've served with, and they have the experience of dozens of battles."

Marcus shrugged and followed Nicanor into the atrium, and an attendant brought them towels and bowls of water. They laved their faces, arms, and hands and dried them with the cloths.

"Ahh..." Nicanor sat and breathed a sigh, rubbing at an ache in his thigh. Marcus had pressed him harder with each bout, but he suspected the younger freedman was still holding back. He reclined and studied him as he took the opposite seat. "Well?"

Marcus shrugged again, filled a mug, and drank deeply.

"Our young friend has not told you, centurion?" Gnaeus sat up to refill his cup, glancing at Marcus.

"Told me what?" Nicanor asked.

"If you don't want to, Marcus, is this man someone I'm allowed to tell?" Gnaeus lifted his cup at Nicanor, then sat back and waited for Marcus's reply.

Marcus leaned toward the centurion. "Nicanor, was what you told me of your friend Graius true? That he was a gladiator who earned his freedom?"

"Yes. I owe my life to Graius... at least twice; I believed him. And Lord Otho confirmed he had earned the *rudis*. He died a freedman."

"My great-grandfather did not...."

"I don't understand; he was a gladiator?"

"You tell him, Gnaeus... you're better with stories."

Gnaeus set his cup on the table and sat up, his forearm on his knees. "Marcus's great-grandfather was a Thracian soldier, captured and enslaved. But he was unbreakable. That spirit was channeled into the Games. Few had his skill, and he was indomitable in the arena. As a reward, he took a woman—one of my great-grandmother's servants—to be his. He chose, and there's was not just a mating, not merely a man's lust sated by a young maiden, beautiful as she was. He treated her with respect. With love. The man could not bear for that love to be bound by slavery. The woman was of the same spirit. So, with 70 other slave-gladiators, he fought himself free from the man who owned them, my great-grandfather. The man raised an army of 30,000 men, and soon his followers numbered over 120,000 men, women, and children. His revolt lasted two years. It took eight legions—48,000 infantrymen, 12,000 cavalrymen, and 3,000 auxiliaries—to defeat him."

"Spartacus...." Nicanor said, now understanding.

"My great-grandfather," Marcus nodded. "His wife—my great-grandmother—was a Thracian captive, too, from the Maedi tribe. She came from the line of a prophetess and foretold the defeat to her husband, but he would not abandon his men to flee with her. To save her from what was to come, he made her go alone to save their child she carried. She sought a place to hide and protect her baby from reprisals, bringing the newborn to the Roman woman who had treated her kindly."

"My great-grandmother took her in and freed her," Gnaeus said, gesturing at Marcus. "Our families have been close ever since. Marcus here, family tales have it, looks like his great-grandfather and inherited his dexterity and power. I was raised in the business of fighters and gladiators, and I've never seen his equal." He refilled his cup and reclined.

As if an afterthought, Gnaeus added, "I also received a message from Gaius Sabinus, Nicanor. He will come to the exhibition too, and you'll get to speak with him then."

XCIV

September 68 CE

Rome

Gnaeus Batiatus's Villa

Nicanor gauged the late-afternoon sky as he and Marcus awaited their bout. Each man wore a leather helmet and padded chestplate and backplate to protect his torso. "It still seems an odd time for this." The sun on the horizon had begun to shade into a lurid blood-orange light, and even that was fading into twilight.

"Gnaeus wants to finish the exhibition at sunset. He and his guests will then turn to their serious drinking and eating... that's when he plies his skill in convincing them to back his venture."

Music began playing, and Nicanor looked up. The sound came from behind the curtained-off platform next to Gnaeus and his guests. He watched as Gnaeus gestured at a servant, who then pulled back the curtain. A man stood at a waist-high pedestal, and upon it was a curious assemblage of vertical pipes of varying heights, the tallest rising just above the man's head. Behind the pipes, he pressed something that caused them to give forth music. At his feet kneeled a female servant who worked a lever attached to the pedestal's base as the reedy sounds echoed. "What's that?"

"Gnaeus's new organ... he's quite pleased with it."

The music grew to a flourishing crescendo and stopped. Gnaeus stood and faced his guests. "We've come to an end, and the best is last," he said. He turned and pointed to Nicanor and Marcus on the arena floor. "I give you a man with decades of experience in the legions fighting against Rome's enemies. And a man whom I believe is the finest fighter I've ever seen. Sadly, these two are not gladiators like the others you've watched today. Even so, they've been gracious enough to agree to display their skill."

"Gracious, he says," Nicanor muttered only so Marcus could hear. The freedman grinned.

Gnaeus continued. "But I also have my two best gladiators just returned from triumphs at Leptis Magna." Gnaeus raised a fist over his head and faced the arena. "I give you... Castor and Pollux!" Across the field, two figures walked through the gate. As they neared, their size was apparent; they were massive men made even more so by their protective gear. They stomped to a stop next to Nicanor and Marcus.

Marcus nodded, for he knew them. One took off his helmet and leaned toward Nicanor, a fierce frown forming.

"You!" The man's roar shook the ground.

"Futuo," Nicanor swore and looked up at the giant, noting the eye patch he knew hid the wound he had made at a makeshift arena in Marianum. He looked at the wooden *spatha* in his hand and shook his head. "Futuo...."

"What is this?" Marcus was confused as Castor and Pollux closed on Nicanor, who was backing away. He stayed with the centurion. "Gnaeus!" he called up to his friend. Sextus, the gladiator trainer, was at the side of Gnaeus, whispering in his ear.

"Stand your ground!" Gnaeus shouted at the men in the arena. "Castor, you lost an eye in an ill-advised match in Marianum. I did not have you punished for that, as you've proven you can still fight. Nicanor, are you the man who took his eye?"

"Yes. I fought to earn money to save my friend Graius, who had been hurt in the wreck of our ship." He glanced at Marcus, who stared at him.

"Let me fight him, now!" thundered Castor. "I want my revenge." He shook the wooden sword that seemed small in his massive fist.

Nicanor's eyes swept the stands on either side of the platform Gnaeus stood upon. He now saw Antonia Caenis, who sat just behind the host with a puzzled, concerned expression. Sextus was at the gladiator owner's ear again. Gnaeus listened, nodded, and spoke something in return. The trainer left his side and came down to the arena floor.

"This must be resolved," Sextus announced loudly, "and an idea how has come forth. Castor will 'spar' with Nicanor and you, Marcus... with Pollux."

Marcus shook his head. "That's not what was agreed on, Sextus. I must speak with Gnaeus."

Sextus lowered his voice. "He already knows you object and offers this. Instead of one-third of your debt paid, he'll consider it two-thirds paid."

"I can't ask Nicanor to do this..." Marcus rocked his head and glared up at Gnaeus.

"Are you not a man of pride, Marcus? Or do you like being in debt to a friend whose charity saved your life?" Sextus jeered.

Marcus bristled, "Let's you and I fight, Sextus. Here and now..."

"That's not what Gnaeus wants, and it's him you owe," Sextus said with a smile.

Nicanor stepped between them and waved over the referee who had remained to one side. The man joined them as Nicanor turned to Castor. "I had to beat you to save my friend. But also, so I could continue my journey to save someone I care for—a woman. Blinding you was the only way. My journey to save the woman has not ended. I'll spar with you, and you'll likely beat me. But my mission cannot end here. After my mission is finished, I will find you and give you the fight you want, to whatever end it leads."

"Nicanor..." called Marcus.

"Marcus, I'll do this," Nicanor said and turned to the referee. "You understand it's to be how it was arranged before: we will be stopped at sundown and the winner decided by points?" The man looked at Castor with wary eyes, then back at the centurion, and nodded. "Castor... do you believe in honor and agree?" Nicanor asked, turning to the twins. The giants looked at each other, and both nodded. Nicanor thrust a finger into Sextus's chest. "Tell your master."

* * *

In the eastern and southern provinces, Nicanor had experienced sandstorms that formed suddenly and lashed at him from all directions. He did what he could to get through them. The fight had become like that. The two separate engagements had coalesced into one, and he had blocked and parried as many blows from Pollux as he had from Castor. And were it not for Marcus's speed, the two giants would have already bashed his head until it split like an overripe melon. A flare of light caught his eye, and he stole a quick glance around. Men lighted great bronze bowls of oil-soaked wood, while others took flaming tapers to lanterns raised on tall posts. The gray twilight had lessened, and he looked for the referee's signal that it was over.

The melee had beaten and buffeted the man. There was no way that points could be assessed, but sundown was certain. The referee signaled. "It ends!"

Breathing heavily, bearing long scratches on arms and thighs where points of the wooden sword had scored their flesh, Marcus and Pollux lowered their weapons. Nicanor was about to, but Castor did not. He charged, and Nicanor frantically blocked the man's thrusts, backing out of the arc of light from the lanterns and past the place where shadows deepened. He stumbled as he barely caught another blow that numbed his hand and arm. His sword fell to the ground as

Castor loomed over him. He tried to scramble away. Pain shot through his thigh, for the old wound, though long healed, still hampered him. He heard the thunk of a sword over his own gasps—the blade had been turned broadside to strike flat against the back of Castor's head. The immense man crumbled and fell to reveal Marcus behind him. The freedman, one eye on Pollux, tossed his sword at the feet of the referee and called up to Gnaeus: "They win."

* * *

Marcus and Nicanor stood with Gnaeus, the warriors still in the stained and torn knee-length tunics they'd worn in the fight. But both had washed their faces and arms, removing sweat, dirt, and blood.

"Are you sure?" Gnaeus asked again. "I can have the baths readied now." He had apologized for the circumstances that had developed and thanked them for their service in the fight. Several guests had been impressed at the exhibition and his gladiatorial training school. They had agreed to become patrons of the ludus in its planned new location.

Nicanor did not care. "I'll bathe after I give this to Gaius Sabinus," he said, holding up Galba's sealed letter. "Call him over, Gnaeus."

Gnaeus left and returned with the Praetorian co-prefect. "Quite an inspiring bout," Sabinus said as he greeted them. "I'm ready to accept the letter you have for me." He held out his hand to Nicanor.

"Lord Galba said to tell you when I gave you his letter that he looks forward to your support." Nicanor gave it to him.

"I'll consider what's in this message," said Sabinus, who tucked it inside his toga, turned, and left without another word.

Nicanor stood there, bewildered. "What does that mean?" He looked from Gnaeus to Marcus, who shrugged. "I thought he'd already agreed to support Galba...."

"It means...." Antonia Caenis's voice came from behind them. They turned to her as she continued. "Sabinus has gotten the Praetorian Guard senior officers to speak to the Senate and demand he be made sole prefect of the Praetorian Guard for life, irrevocably. The Senate has agreed, and their support gives him leverage with Galba." She wrinkled her nose at Nicanor. "After you clean up, I must speak with you privately, Nicanor."

XCV

October 68 CE

Jerusalem

The Upper City

"Rachel!" Rebecca exclaimed, surprised to see no one with her. "Come in... you should not be out in the evening alone." When the young woman came in, Rebecca asked, concerned: "Leah—?"

"She's with Yonatan... she's fine—you'll soon understand."

Rebecca nodded. "We just finished eating, but you're welcome to come in." She turned toward the family room. Ya'el and Miriam were entering from the courtyard, bringing in bowls and plates from the table. Mathias, Matthew, and Ehud followed them. Elian's laughter and the clucking of Cicero filtered in through the window. "Why do you call on us?"

Miriam set the dishes she carried down and greeted her friend with a smile. Rebecca was pleased to see a flash of joy on her daughter's face. Ehud now stood near Miriam, and her hand was on his arm. "I thought you should know; Yonatan was attacked while returning from the Temple."

"Where?" Matthew asked. Rebecca knew he'd be worried the attack signaled new fighting among the factions. Her husband had told her how the few Moderates remained had become fearfully silent. But the Zealots led by Eleasar ben Ananias and the Galileans led by Yohanan ben Levi were still at odds with each other over who would lead Jerusalem.

"At his own door. Were it not for Leah hearing the noise and coming upon them and startling the attacker, she thinks Yonatan would have been killed."

"Was he hurt?" Again, Matthew was the only one to speak though he cared little for Yonatan, Rebecca knew. Leah—and the city—would be better off without him. But attacks here, in the Upper City, were cause for all to be worried.

Rachel nodded. "The attacker cut off one of his ears."

Rebecca caught Miriam's sudden grin and scowled, making the smirk fade. "Thank you for telling us, Rachel," Rebecca said. "But you should not be on the streets. Especially with such violence happening again, it's not safe."

"I'll walk her home, Mother," Matthew said, "I have to meet with Yohanan ben Zaccai at the House of Caiaphas."

"Tonight?" Rebecca asked. If the attacks had started again, it was as dangerous for men as for women to be out unaccompanied.

"Yohanan leaves early tomorrow to meet Boaz in Herodium," Mathias replied for his son. "We must see him before he goes."

"Mathias," Rebecca gave her husband a stern look, "you must rest." Then she softened and put a hand on his shoulder. "Please."

"Father, there's no need for you to go." Matthew took his cloak from a peg on the wall. "Come, Rachel...."

Rachel hesitated. "Has there been any news of Yosef?"

Rebecca saw Rachel's eyes dart toward Ya'el and almost started in alarm, for that was a dangerous connection for any to recognize beyond their household. Without thinking, Rebecca took two steps toward Rachel to move between her and Ya'el. "No, there's not been any news."

"Come, Rachel, I must go." Matthew walked to the door, and Rachel followed.

"I'll come with you part of the way," Ehud said. "I've some work to tend to at the glassworks." He donned his cloak and reached for Miriam's hand, and she walked with him to the door.

Rebecca's heart warmed when Ehud was reluctant to pull his hand from Miriam's as Matthew and Rachel left. Perhaps this love between them she watched rekindling would fix what troubled Miriam. As her daughter turned back into the room, she caught the quirking of an eyebrow, but not at her... it seemed at Ya'el behind her, who called out.

"Miriam, will you come upstairs to study with me? I need your help."

Amused and a bit bemused by the young women in her house, Rebecca turned to find Mathias had trudged upstairs, and not all the dishes and clearing of the table had been done. She would be on her own to clean up that evening, it seemed. But.... "Elian, come here...."

* * *

THE LOWER CITY

Upstairs, Ya'el went into her room with some study materials and talked to herself as if Miriam were with her. Miriam had gone to her own room and pulled out the clothing and beard she had brought from Zechariah's. She decided against the belly padding since she needed to move fast to catch up with Ehud and follow him to the Lower City. She was sure she'd made good time, but she could not

376

find him. She waited in the shadows near his glassworks and wondered where he was.

* * *

Ehud followed the slope down to the Lower City. Lost in thought, he stumbled a few times. He had seen Yohanan ben Zaccai something, and his heart had thumped in his chest. *It must be! The list from the Essenes in Qumran!* At the House of Caiaphas, he could not get close enough to hear them. But the thick scroll was easily seen exchanging hands in the torchlight of the small upper terrace. Now he must decide what to do. Should he steal the copy from Matthew or the original from Zaccai? Could he do it without them knowing? Then he must somehow make a copy without getting caught. If the original was missing, they might alter the plans, making the information worthless to Florus, who would then kill his family. *Betray my people? Betray Miriam?* He prayed and hoped he could get Gessius Florus what he wanted with no one being harmed.

Behind him, shadows followed without a sound.

* * *

Miriam heard steps echo on the uneven stones of the road. A tall figure holding a small lighted lantern approached the glassworks. From her location in the alley at that corner of the street, she heard the movement of someone in the darkness opposite, along the row of closed shops. Without hesitation, the figure closed on Ehud, who was plodding along with his head down. She saw a gray shape silhouetted briefly by a distant lighted torch in the alley it passed. The person pulled out a curved blade that glinted in the dim torchlight. The form slowed as Ehud approached the glassworks door.

Miriam shot from the alley as Ehud opened the door. The shadow loomed, arm raised, the dagger ready to reach around Ehud's neck and cut his throat. Silently, in movements that mirrored the assassin's, Miriam's left hand smothered the mouth and slit the throat with the blade in her right hand. She lowered the spasming body to the ground. Ehud was inside now, unaware that death had been at his door. She took the assassin's dagger from the clenched fist. It was the same kind as hers. A Sicarii.

Clouds parted, and Miriam stared down at the body in the moon's glow. She kneeled and pressed her hand in the pool of blood from the man's torn throat. Angrily, to show Ehud was protected, she raised her dripping hand to the wall over the body. *No*—she cleared her head—*that would be taken as choosing to stand against Elazar ben*

Yair and retaliating for his ordering Ehud's death. Miriam wiped her hand clean on the dead man's black robe. Taking his dagger, she disappeared into the night, hoping it would be thought a random killing.

Hananiah emerged from his vantage point. He had followed Ehud from the Upper City and backed away when he realized someone else was following the man, too. He was even quieter than the shadow he followed and only closed on the man when he saw what was clearly a Sicarii dagger. Ehud could not die. Not yet. When he did, it would be by Hananiah's hand and not someone else's. He had been about to intervene when yet another shadow shot from the opposite alley and, in deadly silence, beautifully killed the Sicarii. Shockingly, the bearded figure had also proved to be Sicarii. As Hananiah watched, the killer started to lay a bloody handprint on the wall—*The Hand!* He had thought The Hand either dead or long gone. But then the killer had instead wiped the blood on the robe of the dead.

Hananiah's next message to Gessius Florus would be about the return of The Hand and to confirm he would still receive the bounty for killing that notorious assassin.

XCVI

Oᴄᴛᴏʙᴇʀ 68 CE

Cᴀᴇsᴀʀᴇᴀ

Tʜᴇ Rᴏᴍᴀɴ Eɴᴄᴀᴍᴘᴍᴇɴᴛ

Celsus Evander found Sayid in the newly constructed grain warehouse within the camp. Vespasian, preferring that vital food supply be better guarded and distributed, had ordered one of the larger three-masted cargo vessels intended for Puteoli re-routed to Caesarea to supply the Judean legions. Muddled rumors continued from Rome. Perhaps the general wanted to ensure some unexpected demand did not disrupt or divert legion supplies. Still, it made for considerably more work. As Celsus had seen the previous day, Sayid was not merely supervising—he labored with the men to unload the wagons and transfer the grain containers into the warehouse. It was backbreaking work. He called to his clerk and motioned him over.

"Yes, sir," Sayid answered, walked over to where Celsus stood by a wagon, and wiped his hands with a cloth draped there.

"You have men to do the unloading. All you must do is keep an accurate count."

"I can do both, sir." Sayid reached around to his lower back, into the small pouch strapped there, and brought out a *diptych*. Its stylus was dangling by a leather cord attached to the wooden-framed wax tablet. He tilted it to show Celsus. On it was the vessel name with its load count, the day's date with rows of marks for the loaded wagon count, and under the warehouse number, the unload count. "I keep the count from the ship to the wagons to stock inside the warehouse, sir. The tally will balance when we're done."

"But why take on such hard labor when you don't have to?"

Sayid lifted the waterskin hung on the corner post of the wagon bed. He offered it to Celsus, who shook his head. Sayid then drank and wiped his mouth with the back of his hand. He looked up at the sun almost directly overhead. He held up a finger to ask leave of Celsus, who nodded, then called to the men returning empty-handed to carry more from the wagons. "*Cibus meridianus*, take your lunch now."

With sighs of relief, the men settled against the wagon wheels with their bags of salted bread and fruit. Groups of two or three shared skins of water.

"Do you have time, sir?" asked Sayid, lifting a small bag from beneath the driver's bench.

Celsus nodded. "I'll sit with you." Sayid dropped right there to sit cross-legged within the little shade provided by the wagon, with the waterskin on his lap.

"You've asked me about my father," Sayid said as he opened the bag and took out a cloth-covered loaf of bread.

"Yes." Celsus shook his head at Sayid's offer to split the loaf.

"Sir, my father is the reason I decided to work with the men and will continue to do so with every labor detail. My mother told me my father's father was a Roman in Utica who married a Numidian woman who was also a citizen. Together they farmed a tract of land, one of many farms providing grain for the empire. Soon they had children, the first a son... my father, Marcus Sabinus. He grew up working the farm but wanted more than that life. When he was old enough, against his parents' wishes, he applied to the legion stationed there to protect grain supplies to the empire. My father was tall, taller than most his age... even full-grown men. And he was strong from all the work on the farm. That made him a prime recruit for the legion."

Celsus thought, *And you've had to prove yourself beyond what men first see.* The Syrian was lean; perhaps he took after his mother.

"He joined, and after training, he served in Antioch. That's where he met my mother. She told me he loved her, though, of course, he could not marry. When he had an opportunity to rise in the ranks, he followed it to serve where it led, leaving her behind. I was born to her in Laodicea ad Mare and raised there. So, I'm city born. My father—proud of his own strength, thought me weakly and told my mother I'd never be strong enough to do soldiers' work."

Sayid reached up and slapped the side of the half-unloaded wagon. "So, I will get stronger and prove him wrong."

XCVII

OCTOBER 68 CE

ROME

GNAEUS BATIATUS'S VILLA

"So, you have his decision?" Marcus asked as he rose from the table, brushing crumbs from his tunic.

Nicanor nodded and stood, too. "And a threat."

"A threat? From whom… Gaius Sabinus?"

"He told me he would not ally with Galba until formally confirmed as sole Praetorian Prefect for life. Then added: 'Do not think to warn Lord Galba I choose not to support him, yet.' Sabinus did not refer to him as emperor and warned me: 'I do not know your loyalties, centurion… but if you cross me, I will have you killed.'"

"He wants the throne for himself."

"It seems many do… so Antonia Caenis told me."

"Did she have orders for you from General Vespasian?"

"Yes, but they were to do more of what I've been doing. Wait for Galba. And once Vespasian feels secure about Rome, he will send his son Titus to meet with Emperor Galba to get orders for the Judean campaign. Lady Antonia passed me General Vespasian's written orders to remain here until then. So at least I won't have to worry about being thought an *emansor*, absent without leave."

"I know you're bored with waiting," Marcus said, "and if that's what angers you… I could rouse Castor and Pollux. They're not happy Gnaeus has ordered them to not confront you. And he's also instructed Sextus to not stir things up with you… or me. Besides, he's keeping them busy with the new site he's building near the Circus Maximus. That should occupy them for a while." Marcus studied the centurion, who did not respond to the teasing. "What is it?"

Nicanor tossed his head back and paced. "I grow tired of the people—Romans, my own countrymen—who threaten or try to kill me." Nicanor gripped the hilt of the gladius at his hip.

"Will you meet with Antonia Caenis again?" Marcus watched as the centurion took his cloak from the stone bench he had set it upon and swirled it around his shoulders.

"She has asked me to ride with her to her villa in Tibur, a short distance east and north of Rome."

"Why?"

Nicanor shrugged.

"Will you stay there with her?"

"No. Galba and Otho, with their legion, are getting close. Lady Antonia told me an *eques legionis* arrived yesterday morning with a message for the Senate from Lord Galba. He remains with his legion, and they are only a handful of days from Rome. So, I'll escort her to Tibur, stay the night, return tomorrow, and be ready for the arrival of Galba and Otho. I'll see you then." Nicanor turned toward the stables. He and Carmenta would both enjoy leaving Rome, even if only for a day or two.

* * *

THE ROAD TO TIBUR

"The *via Tiburtina* is a good road all the way, and we'll make good time." Antonia Caenis turned and waved Nicanor alongside her. Ahead of them were three heavily armed and armored men, and behind, four more. All had the taciturnity and alert demeanor of retired legionaries. Serious about the business of protecting the one who had hired them.

"Now that we're away from Rome, the road is less congested," Nicanor said. *The air, too*, he thought and admired how Lady Antonia—once outside the city—had unbound her hair, not complying with expected behaviors. Now it flowed behind her in tangled coils of black and gray shot with skeins of near-white silver. She rode easily, with authority, and seemed to grow younger as they got farther from Rome.

"You know where all those soldiers were going, don't you, centurion?" Antonia gave Nicanor a sideways glance.

Nicanor knew. He had heard of the scratched-together legion of dissipated men Nero had formed to protect himself but had lacked the courage to use. Or perhaps he had tried, and they obeyed a different master. Many men in Rome were nervous that they had not disbanded. Instead, they had stayed together in several ill-formed and disorganized encampments around the city. Still, as motley, as they were—with a wide-ranging mix of clothing and equipment— none of their weapons appeared dull or rarely used. "They're moving west and north."

"There are men who want to prevent Galba from entering Rome. They send them to block the road... to kill or capture the man.

"Who commands them?"

"At the very top? Aulus Vitellius, or maybe Gaius Sabinus." She shot another look at Nicanor from under her heavy brows. "I'm not sure who... but will soon know. I must tell my general."

* * *

THE ANIENE VALLEY, TIBUR

As they entered the valley formed by the confluence of the Aniene and Tiber rivers, Nicanor reined in Carmenta alongside Lady Antonia. His eyes followed hers to the crag of the acropolis. Prominently perched on the very edge of the cliff was the Temple of Vesta. Eighteen Corinthian columns surrounded its circular *cella*. That inner chamber built upon a high brick podium of travertine blocks overlooked the drop to the Aniene River that flowed before them. Next to the temple poured a cascade of water whose spray formed rainbows in the sun.

Antonia pointed at the play of colors hung in the droplets of water in the air. "The goddess Iris dances here... she forms a path joining Terra and Elysium. There are also man-made things of great importance here. The three principal aqueducts of Rome—the Aqua Anio Vetus, Aqua Anio Novus, and Aqua Claudia—have this valley as their source." Antonia Caenis added, "Lord Vespasian would appreciate, and I'm sure you do as well, that strategic importance."

"It's beautiful here." Nicanor had not looked away from the tumbling cataract of water.

"There's a yearning in your voice I did not expect," Antonia said and nodded approvingly. "This place reminds me of my homeland as a young girl."

"Why have you come here and not returned to Falacrine?"

"I fear a hard year is upon us. Perhaps not as harsh as in Judea when that war continues as it will at some point. But in Rome, throughout Italia and the provinces... we face growing anarchy. Who knows when I'll see my love again... and under whose rule Rome will be when that happens? Here I'm close to Rome when Lord Vespasian makes his return without having to endure the city." Antonia sighed. "Falacrine is Vespasian's, but this small villa I've arranged here is mine."

"A place where you feel at home... and at ease?"

Antonia blinked and studied the centurion. "You surprise me, Nicanor..."

"I seek such a place too, my lady."

"And a lady of your own to share it?" She studied his expression. "Is there a lady you think of?"

"Yes, but I don't know if she lives or not. I pray..." Nicanor almost said to the gods, *but which, or should I pray to a single one?* "I pray she lives, but I doubt she can ever be mine."

XCVIII

JERUSALEM

THE HALL OF HEWN STONE

The meeting of the Sanhedrin was nothing but the arguments and bickering Mathias had expected as it turned to the allegations and lies cast by Yohanan ben Levi. *Still, we had to try*, he thought. He had remained seated upon the front row in the Hall of Hewn Stone, now empty but for himself, his son, Eleasar, and the Sanhedrin president.

"Shimon," he said, "some will not listen to me now. They are certain my son has betrayed Jerusalem, though there's no evidence of that. Yosef is a victim of this war and the fighting within our own factions as much as is anyone in Jerusalem. You must convince the Sanhedrin to allow fewer people into the city or, better still, to stop letting in any more at all. When the merchants Yosef ben Gurion and his brother Nikadimon died during the Temple siege, the Idumean attack, their flow of supplies ended. The city is becoming too overcrowded, and we will not be able to feed everyone when the Romans lay siege upon us."

"Many believe that under the new emperor, Rome will not attack," Shimon ben Gamliel answered. "They believe we must bring more people in to make the city stronger."

"Then they are fools. Yohanan ben Levi is spreading and feeding that rumor to serve his own interests. He wants more people to come under the sway of his lies—he wants to claim he has become the sole leader of Jerusalem. He will never go hungry while others starve. We must do what we can to make sound decisions without his interference."

"Are you sure he is not in the city now?" Shimon asked. But if the Gischalan were in Jerusalem, he would have been at the meeting that had just adjourned.

"Yes, I'm sure," Eleasar ben Ananias said with a nod, frowning at the Sanhedrin president. "And while he is gone, we must discuss the sacrilege he has committed with his men. You and the high priest must speak out against it. You must condemn him."

"But Yohanan ben Levi stood before the Sanhedrin and said he believes in the sanctity of—"

Matthew and Eleasar's harsh laughs cut him off.

Mathias's tone was somber, tired. "The Gischalan says only what he thinks others want to hear him say. The man believes only in what power he can draw into his own hands." Mathias did not know for how long he would hold his seat, his position among his people. "A Jew rejects idolatry... Jews are modest, compassionate, and benevolent. So, our sacred books teach us. But we know there are those—not just the Gischalan—who have not learned and choose not to learn those lessons. Yohanan ben Levi and his other Galileans have stopped the daily sacrifices, and they dress up as high priests and as women and parade around the Temple." Mathias's beard bristled with his anger. "He and his men are less Jewish than the *gerei toshav,* the foreigners who live among us and have adopted our beliefs and practices. And he and they are far less than the *gerei tzedek* who have fully converted and that proselytize to spread our beliefs. Yohanan ben Levi never learned from the story of Hillel: 'What is hateful to you, do not do to your fellow man.'"

"He is not the only one who presumes to lead our people and has not learned that lesson," said Eleasar. "Simon bar Giora has left Masada to Elazar ben Yair. He now controls most of southern Judea with his 40,000 followers. Hebron has become his base, and rumors are that he plans to take our city and install himself as our leader."

A clatter turned them toward the entrance to the hall.

"Captain!" a Levite Temple guardsman called out and hurried to them. "A rider just brought this"—he handed a scroll of parchment to Eleasar.

He read, "Yohanan ben Levi's Galileans have attacked men escorting Simon bar Giora's wife to Hebron. They have captured her, and he brings her to Jerusalem."

"That explains where the Gischalan is, then. He thinks to use Giora's wife to bargain with Simon. That will only enrage him, and now he will surely march on Jerusalem to get her back." Matthew shook his head and took his father's arm to help him stand.

"If only we would learn we must become one people," Mathias said as unshed tears pooled in his eyes. "If only...."

XCIX

OCTOBER 68 CE

CAESAREA

VESPASIAN'S PRAETORIUM

It was early when his son entered Vespasian's office, and Titus seemed surprised to see Yosef sitting there. Titus had returned from Qumran late the previous night and would want to report what he had seen. "Sir, I'll come back later."

"I heard of your return and expected you," Vespasian said, with a glance toward the Jewish prisoner, "and we'll talk now." The general inclined his head toward the Jew. "Yosef asked to see me two days ago and told me of another dream he had. Go ahead, Yosef, tell him what you dreamed."

"I... I dreamed of legionaries killing men and women." The words again came slowly from Yosef's mouth as if they were too heavy to speak. "Then they searched through Qumran's records... the writings of my people. A shackled man with them, a translator, looked at what was found and told the centurion leading the men which to keep and which to..." He closed his red-rimmed eyes, and his chin dipped. "Which to burn."

Titus slowly nodded. "That is how it happened, sir. A cohort from the 12th Legion was led by their First Centurion, a man named Tyrannius Priseus."

Vespasian saw Yosef's head come up when he heard the name. "You know the man, Yosef?"

"No, sir, but I know of him. Nicanor briefly mentioned him as Cestius Gallus's 12th Legion camp-prefect."

"And?" Vespasian sensed there was more to it.

"He did not care for the man."

"Hmm..." Vespasian turned to his son. "Were there any rebel forces there, as was reported?"

"No, sir. Just the locals... fighting to protect their town."

"Did the 12th Legion's men destroy everything?"

"Not all, sir. Once I was sure no rebel troops were hiding or poised to counterattack, I ordered the First Centurion to stop his men. They were about to spread into the hills and search for more in the caves, but I saw no reason for it. The rebels would have come out and fought us if any more had been there.”

Vespasian nodded. “Where were the documents taken?”

“The First Centurion had orders from his legion commander to bring them to Ptolemais to be better translated and then delivered to you, sir.”

“There are—were—writings in Qumran with portents for my city, Jerusalem,” Yosef said softly, as if to himself. “I saw that, too, in my dream.”

“Portents... what kind?” Vespasian asked.

“I don’t know, general... But something—not a voice but a presentiment. Something in that vision told me the writings are important and would not be among what was burned. The Essenes at Qumran are known for of making predictions about Jerusalem and a coming war between the forces of good and evil.”

Vespasian turned to Titus. “Send a message under my name to Galerius Senna and tell him I want all that was taken from Qumran sent to me as soon as it’s translated.” He watched Titus leave and shifted to study his prisoner, who sat silently lost in his thoughts. There, on his desk, he had still to read the letters from Antonia Caenis and Gaius Licinius Mucianus, reports on Galba, Vitellius... perhaps others. Each message—he was sure—also had omens for them all.

C

ROME

GNAEUS BATIATUS'S VILLA

Marcus Attilius sat on the top rail of the corral, watching Nicanor adjust the set of new leather-and-metal *hipposandals* on Carmenta. "Do you know how to put those on?"

Nicanor, trying to attach the cup of grooved metal with clips and leather laces to one of the horse's hooves secured between his knees. Carmenta stood patiently, her head turned to watch him. "Yes," he said, but *maybe,* he thought. It had looked simpler when Antonia Caenis's man in Tibur had shown him, saying all Lady Antonia mounts now wore them for protection and a better grip on the damp earth and slick grass of the new estate.

Gnaeus Batiatus came down the path toward the stable, reins still in hand and his mount trailing behind him. "Gaius Sabinus is dead," he announced.

Nicanor lowered Carmenta's hoof and straightened up as Marcus dropped from the rail to the ground. Gnaeus Batiatus reached the fence and rested his forearms on the rail.

"What? How?" Nicanor asked.

Gnaeus drew a finger across his throat. "The Praetorians killed him. I was at the new training school site when the news spread among my new financial backers."

"I thought the Praetorians were on his side," Marcus commented and stepped back for Nicanor to climb through the rails.

"They were, but I guess Galba promised them something even greater. With what happened to Sabinus, Galba should know he must keep any promise he makes, or...." Gnaeus wagged his head from side to side. "And there are other things the new emperor has stirred up that should concern him. I understand being confronted by Nero's ragtag legion badly shook Galba. Still, his order to slaughter its men seems a bad omen for the start of his reign."

Nicanor wondered if Tigellinus was the one making promises for Galba. Antonia Caenis had said Tigellinus was at work to secure a place of favor with the new emperor. Nicanor had heard of the battle shortly after returning from Tibur but had little of the detail. "What happened?"

"Lucius Licinianus, my most significant *patronus*, led one group ready to greet Lord Galba, and hundreds lined the road and witnessed what happened next. Nero had raised his 'legion' by levying 5,000 sailors and marines from the navy—ordering them from their port at Misenum. Those men met Lord Galba and his legion just north of Rome. I'm told it was not to fight but demand that Galba honor what Nero had promised them: pay, colors for their legion, a standard, and new barracks for their quarters. Galba tried to put them off, saying he would consider the matter later, and he rode on. The men did not accept that and demanded Galba confirm their status as legionaries—that would give them the citizenship they sought, primarily. Some pressed forward toward Galba's column with their swords drawn while the bulk—most of them unarmed—blocked the crossing at Milvian Bridge over the Tiber. Galba ordered his cavalry to ride over them. Nero's 'legion' was routed, and thousands were killed trying to flee Galba's horsemen. The story already spreads that Galba has made his first entry to Rome through much blood and over dead bodies." Gnaeus straightened, his usual half-smile and good humor missing. "It is an ill omen."

"I hope not," Marcus said. "Rome needs no more turmoil."

"Lord Galba and Otho will be in the forum tomorrow, and Galba will address the Senate. Hopefully, that will put some fears to rest." Gnaeus turned back to the stables.

"Then I'll be there to hear him," Nicanor commented, "and I must meet with him and Lord Otho." Carmenta reached her nose over the fence to nuzzle his shoulder, and he patted it. "Well, girl... now there's finally some hope to get done what I can for Lady Cleo."

CI

NOVEMBER 68 CE

JERUSALEM

THE UPPER CITY

Miriam, Ehud, and Ya'el were sitting in the family room while Elian in the courtyard played with a spinning wooden top next to a small brazier of charcoal, its wisps of smoke twining upward. Miriam noted Ehud's preoccupation with thoughts. He seemed to want to leave as he sat with her. But Ehud had recently spent much time with her and Ya'el in the Upper City... and with Matthew, to her brother's consternation. Still, she was thankful for not having had to follow Ehud around the Lower City, where she worried about running into Hananiah. Only Yohanan ben Zaccai's arrival had saved her from having to tell the knife maker she did not feel for him as he seemed to for her. He was a friend, yes, no matter what he had told his father's ghost.

She had wondered at Hananiah's speaking with his father's soul. She remembered Yosef having long talks with their father about the Sadducees' disbelief in an afterlife and the resurrection of the dead, but the Pharisees believed in both. Whatever Hananiah's dreams might be... she had no part in his future. Also, she wanted to avoid Kefa, who likely had messages to give her from Elazar ben Yair. Or worse, notice that the Sicarii leader demanded a meeting with her. But with what Matthew had told her and Ya'el about Simon bar Giora and the Zealot's capture of his wife—her father had been at Temple all day discussing that predicament—perhaps Elazar was now focused on Masada and had no time for Jerusalem.

"Where are Mother and Father?" Matthew asked as he came upon them from upstairs.

"At Temple," Miriam answered. "Are you going back out?"

"For a while. I must meet Yohanan ben Zaccai." Matthew pulled his cloak on, for the nights were becoming cooler.

"I should go, too," Ehud said as he stood.

"Mother and Father won't mind if you stay," Matthew said as he glanced at Ya'el, who was always cast as the watchful matron if Matthew could not be around in their parents' absence.

"No. I really must go." Ehud looked down. "I'm sorry, Miriam. I've some work I should get to..."

Miriam rose, too, regretting his leaving, and touched Ehud's arm. "I'll walk you out."

Back inside, as the door closed behind her, she whirled to Ya'el. "If Mother and Father return before I'm back, tell them I'm asleep. Get Elian inside so he doesn't see me leave." She ran upstairs, and only minutes later, in disguise, with beard and belly padding in place this time, she slipped out of the courtyard's rear gate.

* * *

Ehud stood at a corner watching Matthew at a merchant's stall buying a hand lamp and cured-skin bag of oil. They had parted at the agora where the slope to the Lower City began. Ehud had gone far enough down the street to be out of sight and then crept back to follow Matthew. He prayed the man's meeting with Yohanan ben Zaccai would be an opportunity for Ehud to get more information on where the Temple treasure would be hidden. He *must* get something more substantial for Gessius Florus. His family depended upon it.

Just that morning, in the overcrowded market, someone had bumped into him and dropped a small cloth-wrapped bundle at his feet. He had heard the whispered, "For you." The surrounding people were so many that it took a moment for him to stoop and pick it up and then move to one side of the square so he would not be jostled as he opened it. Inside had been another wrapping of cloth, this one crusted with what could only be dried blood. He had peeled back the layers to reveal a severed, rotting finger. Upon it was a *hotam* he recognized, the ring's *bullae* inscribed with his father's favorite sigil, the *shekhinah*—representing the dwelling of the divine presence and its protection. But the guard against evil had failed.

The message he had held in shaking hands that morning was clear. Now his mind was clouded, but his hands were steady as he rotated the ring on his finger and closed his eyes. *Father!* When he opened his eyes, he saw the old priest join Matthew and hand him several scrolls bound with a cord.

* * *

I was so warm sitting with Ehud, Miriam thought. *Now I shiver.* Twilight had come with a chill, but she did not believe that was what made her tremble. What was Ehud doing? She had come out of an alley between houses that led to the market, expecting to turn toward the Lower City and catch up to him. But then she saw Ehud trailing someone in the other direction and trying to not be caught doing it. Now he had stopped where a small street separated two shops. Her eyes followed his stare to... Matthew and Yohanan ben Zaccai! As her brother and the old priest went different ways, Ehud began following Matthew. She trailed Ehud.

* * *

Ehud's eyes were wide, adjusting to the sun's fading light, and he was jittery as he considered what he must do. Would he have to sneak up on his friend and then—where he would not be seen—knock him unconscious and steal what Yohanan ben Zaccai had just given to him? His stomach wrenched as he blindly followed Matthew into an alley and stepped around a merchant rolling barrels from his shop and standing them up along the wall. Turning sideways to slip by the man and his containers, he hurried down the alley until he slowed where it came to a familiar turn. He now knew where Matthew was going, the tunnel. In the stillness behind him, he heard a curse and complaint and the sound of hurrying steps. Worried it was one of Gessius Florus's people coming for him, from inside his cloak, he pulled his only weapon, a pair of bronze shears he used for snipping hot glass. And waited.

* * *

Miriam's false belly caught again as she squeezed past the last barrel, shifting it out of place as the merchant glared at her and cursed again. Moving quickly, she reached the corner and crashed into the man waiting there. Behind her, the merchant lighted a torch that blazed as he lifted it to set it into a bracket. In the flare of light, Miriam's eyes caught the flash of metal in a raised fist. Thinking of the assassin who had attacked Ehud in the Lower City, her left-hand dagger came out of its forearm sheath. With a cry, but without thinking, she thrust and struck the shadow in the chest. In the torchlight, in a near-endless moment, Ehud's eyes met hers.

"Miriam?" he gasped and sank to the ground, the knife buried in his chest.

She realized her beard was askew as she kneeled by him. The blade came free, and she pressed her hand to Ehud's heart. "I'm sorry," she sobbed, feeling it beat and pump his blood over her hand. Trying to lift him, she reached out and used the wall to steady herself as she untangled the belly padding and freed her cloak from beneath her knees. She heard the merchant behind her, back with more barrels. From up the alley, she heard Matthew call out, "Who's there?" The noise drew him back to investigate the cause. She bent over Ehud, touched his face with bloody fingers, and cried. "Ehud... I... I...." She had to go before Matthew reached them.

"Miriam... I... I'm sorr—" He reached for her face and gasped in pain, unable to speak.

"I'm sorry... too...." She pressed the beard in place and darted a glance at the glow of hand lamp coming nearer, revealing Matthew with his sword drawn. And she ran.

CII

November 68 CE

Sycaminum

Port, Florus's Warehouse

Gessius Florus re-sealed the message from the 12th Legion commander with his duplicate of Galerius Senna's personal seal.

"You're sure no one followed you from Ptolemais?" he asked. He did not care that the Tyrannius Priseus had seen him open and review his commander's correspondence. After all, Priseus was the one who had provided him Senna's seal to be copied.

"Yes, lord. I have two riders ahead and two behind me to sweep and check for followers or spies," replied Tyrannius Priseus. "As you directed."

Florus nodded and handed the message to the 12th Legion's First Centurion. "Then continue your delivery to Titus in Caesarea." Lord Titus had requested from Senna the documents that had been taken from Qumran.

"This man will remain here," Florus said, beckoning with a hand the shackled man behind the centurion. The man shuffled forward with several scrolls in his arms. "Are those all that you found that mention anything about Jerusalem and a request to find locations to be used for some purpose?"

"Yes, lord. There were hundreds to go through." The man's voice quavered. "I discovered these"—he waved the scrolls, which trembled in his hands. "They are mostly just rough survey notes of the sites."

"Hand them to me...." Florus stepped forward for the scrolls, then turned to the centurion. "You may go, Tyrannius. Deliver the message and the other documents and their translation. Be alert for any unusual attention or questions."

As I am so alert, he thought. Vespasian is now too interested in me.

Drusus and the Thracians had observed and reported the men they saw too often near Florus in Caesarea. Watchers. And he suspected even the taberna girl he favored kept attentive eyes upon him. Perhaps that was the best reason of all to indulge his impulses and treat her as women should be treated. *Hmmm...* he mused on what he would plan for her during her next visit to him.

"Lord Florus..."

The vision of the girl cowering at his feet vanished.

"Yes, Drusus," he said. Florus looked at the squat man who had just entered.

"The men report that the street outside, and the road beyond, are clear of anyone who seems to loiter. Do you want them to go now and scout further ahead to Caesarea?"

"Yes, we're leaving now. But have two men remain here to hold this man." Florus gestured at the Jew Tyrannius Priseus had left behind. "General Vespasian will no doubt have the documents reviewed, maybe even by his pet prisoner who continues to enjoy his favor."

Wishing it were Yosef in chains before him instead, Florus turned to the prisoner: "You will stay alive as long as you are useful to me. And if I should learn you have missed something in those other documents that could have proved valuable to me... your death will be long and painful."

Florus tucked the scrolls into the satchel draped over his shoulder. He watched as Drusus shoved the Jew into a storeroom. When he had arrived at the warehouse, he had been pleased to see the large Alexandrian cargo vessel—one of the sand carriers vital to his plans—at the dock. Unlike some of the other ships whose men crawled over them like ants rigging new lines, cutting away damaged wood and decking, and replacing it all with new materials, this one was being repaired by only a handful of workers who seemed in no hurry. He approved of their pace. The sand carrier actually needed little work, but it must remain in place until he required it.

Once they got back to Caesarea, Drusus and the new mercenaries Florus expected from Alexandria would investigate the locations on the scrolls he now had in his possession. Still, he needed further details from Jerusalem. The latest message he had sent to Ehud through Hananiah should be a great incentive to produce results. Or the next would include a more vital body part from the Jew's mother. He had also confirmed for Hananiah his reward for killing the Sicarii assassin—The Hand. That man had reappeared and was responsible for eliminating his other agents within Jerusalem.

But Hananiah, his killer in Jerusalem, need not know his further payment would come only once the Jews' treasure was safely in his hands. And if that happened without Hananiah's help, then the man would suffer the same fate as would all in that cursed city—when Vespasian destroyed it.

Florus regretted that Yosef would likely never be within his reach. But that left him with two others to settle accounts with: his traitorous wife and the man he was sure had helped her run from him. If what Vitellius had told him was true, Galba, the new emperor, had but a tenuous hold on the throne and work had already begun to loosen it completely. Vitellius waited for his moment to take the throne. Then he would order Vespasian to start his assault of Jerusalem. Florus had to be prepared to move quickly, so he must cut loose ends.

"Read to go, lord?" Drusus asked, returning from chaining the prisoner within what had become his cell.

"Yes. When we get to Caesarea, I have something important to discuss with you. And I want you to select the best fighter among the Thracians. His only task will be to watch for that Syrian, Sayid—you've been slack in getting this done—and next time he leaves the legion encampment, take him so I can question him. I'm certain he must know something about where my wife is hiding. Before I finish with him, he will tell me, and only then will I let him die."

CIII

Rome

The Forum of Augustus / The Temple of Mars Ultor

Nicanor stood before the pediment, a broad, low-pitched gable surmounting the facade of the temple. Inscribed upon it was the name of Augustus and the carved reliefs of the divinities that influenced the outcome of battles and wars. The figure of Mars in the center was flanked by the goddesses Fortuna and Venus. Next to these were the seated figures of Romulus—in the guise of an augur—and the goddess Roma, who personified not just the city but the Roman state. In the gable corners were figures of the personification of the Palatine Hill. *Palatua is the guardian, if I remember correctly,* he thought. Though he was sure, the other was Tiberinus, God of the River.

In Tibur, Antonia Caenis had told him of others she wanted him to meet who were also loyal to Vespasian. A city courier had arrived the day before from one of them, Marcus Antonius Primus. Once a member of the Senate, he was banished by Nero. Who had believed—but could not prove to the Senate—that Primus had conspired against him.

"You must be Nicanor... have you been inside, centurion?"

Nicanor turned and saw the man who spoke to him and understood why Lady Antonia had said, using what must be the man's nickname: "Beccus will be a useful ally." The nobleman's nose was truly an eagle's beak. Broad and hooked, it pushed down the corners of the man's mouth.

"Twice, sir. The last time with General Vespasian before we left for Judea."

"Ahh... of course. This is one of his favorite places in Rome. I've been here with him many times." Marcus Antonius Primus turned to gaze at the expanse of the *Forum Augustum*. "I admire it, too... though the man who erected it, Octavian who became Emperor Augustus, was responsible for my ancestor's death."

"Your ancestor, lord?"

"Marcus Antonius... Julius Caesar's general."

"And the lover of Cleopatra of Egypt."

"You know history, centurion?"

"I have a friend who does, sir, and once we had a lot of time together here in Rome. I knew a little about the story of Marc Antony, but my friend knew more of the details and told me of Antony and Cleopatra's love."

"I'd probably enjoy talking with him."

Nicanor smiled at the thought of Yosef discussing Roman history with the man, but he kept silent.

"Let's talk inside," the nobleman said, gesturing with a toga-draped arm.

Within the temple stood three statues. In the middle, a colossal *Mars Ultor* depicted in full military dress, holding a giant spear in his right hand and a shield in his left. To his right was a statue of the goddess Venus with Cupid. She was the goddess of the *gens Julia*— one of the oldest patrician families, with many members leaders in the Republic. From her, they claimed descent. To the left of Mars was a statue of *divus Julius*. After a star appeared in the daytime during the funerary Games of Julius Caesar and slowly crossed the sky, Augustus had claimed it was Caesar riding in a chariot of the gods, and he was thus deified.

The nobleman studied the massive statue of Mars and spoke without turning from it: "Antonia Caenis tells me she and Vespasian think highly of you. I have great respect for their opinion."

"I am thankful for that, and I have great respect for them, too, sir."

"How long will this Judean war take? How long to defeat the rebels?"

Nicanor was—at first—surprised at the shift, but he reflected on how that often happened when he talked with Romans outside the legions and above his station. Their questions had another layer to them, more than was revealed in their surface simplicity. Lord Primus's two questions contained a tone of some subtle urgency. "You mean General Vespasian's ultimate objective... the sacking of Jerusalem?"

Marcus Primus nodded.

"That city will not fall easily... it could take months from when a siege begins."

"What do you think of Galba as emperor?"

This was another unexpected subject change, *and it seems intentional as if he is testing me*, Nicanor thought. He had enough self-control not to frown at the question, though it was not as straightforward as it first seemed. "I'm a soldier, sir, and obey the emperor, and now that is Lord Galba."

"Yes, of course," said Primus, and the corners of the nobleman's mouth fought the downward push of his nose and lost. Still, there was a hint of humor in his words. "We all serve the emperor. Lord Galba has honored me with command of Legio VII and reinstated me to the Senate."

"Congratulations, sir."

"Yes. Still, I look forward to the day I see my friend Vespasian in Rome again. I'm sure we'll talk more in days to come, centurion."

Nicanor watched as the nobleman gathered his toga about him and walked away, and he wondered at the conversation. The truth was that Nicanor was dismayed at how frail Galba had seemed when he addressed the Senate. And afterward, in Nicanor's private conversation with Lord Otho, he had even more doubts. He had asked Otho if Galba would now issue a proclamation to protect Lady Cleo, and the answer had alarmed him. Otho had said, "Galba says he will… but not when. The new emperor has many important things to see to… many people ask favors of him." Holding onto his temper, he had told Otho, "That does not help your sister!" Otho had replied, "Galba is old… and has no family. I'm close to him… and soon, I'm certain I'll be able to protect Cleo." Nicanor would never mix in the intrigues of Rome, but he could not help but wish it would happen soon. For the thousandth time since leaving her behind in Ptolemais, he worried about Cleo and prayed to the gods she was alive and safe. And now, though he would never express it, he wished Otho were emperor, so he *could* save her. *Hopefully, they will not be too late.*

CIV

NOVEMBER 68 CE

JERUSALEM

THE UPPER CITY

Matthew reached the man on the ground, as did the merchant he had passed by only moments before. The merchant's torch cast his shadow over the man as he bent down. Matthew set his hand lamp on the ground next to him. In its light, he could see the man's tunic front was soaked in blood, his head turned toward the alley wall and in the shadows. Matthew touched the man's face as he weakly stirred and muttered something. His chest spasmed in a stuttering breath. Kneeling, Matthew lifted the man's head and turned toward the light.

Ehud!

His friend tried to talk again.

"What?" Matthew asked. He leaned closer to hear, knowing the rattle within his friend's chest was a death sign.

"Miriam...." His eyes distended, staring, as Ehud tried to raise himself. One blood-slick hand tugged at Matthew's tunic... and he brought the other up in a loose fist as if offering something to him. "Miriam," he said for the last time and sagged as the lurching breaths stopped.

Matthew settled Ehud's hands on his chest, and something rolled out. He picked it up and stared. Was that what Ehud had tried to give him?

"Look..." The merchant pointed at the bloody handprint on the wall just over the body.

Matthew looked at Ehud's hands and compared them to the smudge on the wall. It—the handprint—was smaller. Had the Sicarii assassin returned? And why would the Sicarii want to kill Ehud?

* * *

Not realizing she had lost her false beard, Miriam stripped off her bloody cloak as she rushed through the courtyard, draping it over her shoulder, its cloth bunched around her neck. Numbed by what had happened, she barely caught herself in time but paused outside to listen first. There were no sounds from inside the house, so she slipped in and rushed upstairs. In her room, fumbling, hands shaking, she lighted a lamp. She took off the man's tunic and loosened the sash of the linen man's undergarment she wore, and pulled it off over her head. She balled it up in the bowl on her small table and poured water from the clay pitcher. Getting it wet and then wringing it out, she used the cloth to wipe away bits of sticky gum she had used for the beard and cleaned the blood from her hands and forearms. Ehud's blood.

Her hands knotted into fists that spasmed and began to cramp. Something inside—a clawed hand—tore at her chest and gripped so tight she had to force each breath. Willing her hands to unclench, she stuffed the undergarment, tunic, and stained cloak far under her bed. Her still-trembling hands lifted and held before her the clean sleeping tunic her mother always laid upon the foot of her bed. Now the pain ripped through her, and she could not breathe no matter how hard she tried. Only once before had she ever felt such agony—not just heartbreak, but a heart's death—and Zechariah had been there to help her get through it. Now she had no one. She shuddered, but not from the chill in the room.

"Miriam?" Ya'el's voice came from outside the door, followed by the rap of a knock.

Miriam did not answer; she did not even look toward the door.

* * *

Ya'el had heard the hurried steps and now the sound of Miriam's gasps. It was the heavy, can't-catch-a-breath labor of someone trying to compose herself and failing. She didn't wait or ask permission—she entered the room. "Miriam... what is wrong?" She went to her friend and said, "You're shaking... put this on." She took the garment from Miriam's unsteady hands and raised it to pull over her head as if helping a child dress. Reflexively, Miriam—white-faced, quivering—found the sleeves and pushed her arms through. She still did not speak.

Ya'el heard the front door bang open in the stillness and then the sound of heavy steps on the stairs that stopped at the first bedroom. Then there was knocking and Matthew's voice—low, tense, and sharp: "Father... Father, I must talk with you."

Ya'el saw the blank stare on Miriam's face change. Into fright? They listened and heard a muffled response. *From Rebecca*, Ya'el thought. She felt Miriam take her hand and squeeze so hard, it hurt. Though she could feel the pain of that grip, when she looked into Miriam's eyes, her friend was there... but not there. Something haunting jittered and flickered within her.

She sees something but not me. Ya'el wondered what had happened. She watched eyes full of tears that did not fall; instead, they pooled until the wells of Miriam's eyes could no longer hold them. They spilled down her cheeks. More murmurs and shuffling from the hall were followed by steps descending. Moments later, Rebecca's sharp cry came from below.

Miriam stirred, drying her wet cheeks with a sleeve. She reached for her night robe, putting it on as she walked to the door.

Ya'el followed her. Downstairs, the sitting room was alight with two lanterns. Mathias stood with Matthew, both men's faces in tight, worried expressions. Rebecca sat, wiping her eyes with a kerchief.

"Mother, I heard your cry. What's wrong?" Miriam rubbed her eyes with the back of her hands as if just having risen from sleep.

Ya'el almost looked at Miriam, surprised at how steady her voice was, though there remained a faint tremble to her shoulders. She saw Rebecca glance up at her husband.

"Come sit, Miriam." Mathias gestured at the divan; the space next to his wife. "There is bad news."

Ya'el's heart jumped. News about Yosef? Had he been executed? *No,* she thought, *I know how much Rebecca loves her children.* That news would have prostrated her.

Miriam joined her mother, who took her hand and clasped it to her chest. "What is it, Father... what's happened?" Miriam looked up at him.

Mathias's beard bristled and then sank onto his chest. "Ehud has been murdered..."

In the light of the large lamp on the table next to the divan, Ya'el saw the cords in Miriam's neck strain as if bearing a weight. In that illumination, on her pale skin was a hand's span smear of something dried to a reddish-brown.

Gods... I know what that is, Miriam thought, and she saw it had caught Matthew's eye, too! As he stepped toward his sister, brow furrowed with a frown, Ya'el walked between them to sit next to Miriam and put an arm across her shoulders, covering her neck. What Miriam had kept inside broke free, and she rocked back and forth, crying the lament of a soul... of love... lost.

Ya'el stared up at Matthew, hoping to get his attention. "Matthew, do you know who killed him?"

"The Sicarii..." Matthew blinked, the lines in his brow deepening. But his words sounded as much a question as a statement.

CV

November 68 CE

Caesarea

Near Vespasian's Praetorium

"I'll join you shortly for dinner," Vespasian said to his son and continued his walk on the sparsely lighted promenade. He enjoyed the view here and had had the walkway constructed to run along the shore above the high tide mark. He considered calling Titus back to bring Yosef to join him for dinner and a talk. But that morning, the Jew had requested more writing materials and was probably busily filling sheets of parchment. He approved of the man using his days in such a manner, recording events for posterity. He had even provided some Roman records for the Jew to work into his accounts.

Strewn at the water's edge were tumbled piles of cast-aside blocks, now washed by the phosphorescent surf. As the sun dipped to touch the water, men moved along the breakwater to light the massive bronze bowls of oil and wood that marked at night the open arms of the port. But the last ship of the day—an Alexandrian merchant vessel to judge by its markings—had docked not an hour before. He and Titus had watched it enter the harbor, its oars plying the water and working to angle in and tie up at the quay.

Vespasian was tired of Caesarea... of Judea and longed for the green hills and mountains surrounding his home in Falacrine. Still, he enjoyed that sunset flood of colors on the waters of the seaward horizon. He had just witnessed a sunset of vermillion that rippled into an almost Tyrian-purple shade that tinted the wind-formed white-caps before fading in the darkening troughs.

The thuds of an approaching galloping horse turned him. His inclination was to look toward his praetorium and the castra beyond. The camp was the likely source of any rider. But the sound came from the port road. The last vestige of slanting sunlight framed the horseman, his mantle flowing behind him, as he angled his mount onto the gravel path and directly toward the general.

Odd, he thought. A courier coming from the port would head straight for my headquarters. Or has someone told them I walk the promenade this time of day and can be met here? He faced the rider and waited, tapping his vine-staff in his hand.

The horseman bore down on him without slowing. Alarmed, Vespasian stepped off the path onto the grass as the rider veered and raised an arm wielding a sword. The rider's harsh voice declared, "The emperor sends his regards!" as the weapon swung in a downward arc.

The general twisted his torso and thrust at his attacker with the three-foot staff, cursing his camp complacency and that it was the only weapon at hand.

The rider's first strike missed its target, and the man spun the horse. The hooves of its hind legs kicked up a spray of gravel that scored bloody streaks on the general's face. Vespasian recognized the curved sword in the arc of light from a lantern on the walkway. The horseman charged him again, leaning from his mount as the Thracian sica flashed. When the rider reached him and swung his blade, an arrow struck the man in the shoulder. His aim was thrown off, and the sword cut in two the staff Vespasian had defensively raised.

The general heard the shouts of several men behind him and staggered backward from the horseman. Two more arrows hissed through the gloom, one snagging the horseman's cloak and the other narrowly missing. The rider yanked the horse's head around and thundered back onto the path and away into the deepening twilight.

* * *

The next morning...

THE QUARTERMASTERS' OFFICE

Celsus entered the office. "Cancel the supply wagons for the legion *vexillations* in Apollonia, Joppa, and Lydda. General Vespasian is pulling those units back to Caesarea."

"Why?" asked Sayid. He had spent the previous day loading them all and had just prepared each camp's manifest for the caravan.

"Someone tried to kill General Vespasian last evening."

"What? Where?"

"Here. Just outside the camp, on his walk."

"Did they catch the man?"

"No, but units of cavalry are still out searching. I've never seen the general so angry. He's increasing the routine patrols and adding more men to port security. All ships will be searched, and crew and any passengers questioned before they leave the ships. We will have to wait for that before we can unload them. More work for us." Celsus sat down and studied his clerk. "But with your father's unit moving here, perhaps you can see more of him."

Sayid wasn't sure whether or not that would be a good thing. Marcus Sabinus had seemed clear about what he thought of his son.

CVI

December 68 CE

Jerusalem

The Lower City

Hananiah knew the ways of human beings. He had often worked for those who exploited people's weaknesses to answer their own hatred, envy, greed, or lust. And he counted on those he hunted to have flaws, too, for that made their killing easier for him. Jerusalem was a large city where killings were common, especially with the recent upheavals and the pressure of all the people seeking shelter within its walls. The differing factions had not stopped attacking each other verbally and even physically. And some used their ideological differences as a reason to settle personal conflicts.

So, few things surprised him. But Ehud's death surprised him, and the news was spreading throughout the city. The dead man had been Hananiah's means of earning money and potentially an even greater reward. Ehud's chief value to him—that possibility of that tremendous financial reward—was conditional, to be realized only if Ehud produced what Gessius Florus needed. *Now that opportunity has died with Ehud.* Or had it?

He had been surprised at the mark left by the killer. He had witnessed The Hand save Ehud... from another Sicarii. Had there been a falling out within that extreme faction? Was The Hand no longer a Sicarii? Were the Sicarii trying to get details on hiding the Temple treasure for their own benefit and using Ehud as Hananiah was? Had Ehud finally gotten that information, so he was no longer of use and thus had been killed?

So many questions whirled in his head as Hananiah donned his cloak and left his shop.

* * *

The Upper City

"Here, you can still see it." The merchant showed Hananiah the crusted brown-red handprint on the alley wall.

The knife maker bent to look more closely. "Who was it you said was with the body?"

"Matthew ben Mathias... the Temple Guard officer. I'm friends with a Levite guard, and I have seen this officer before at the Temple."

"Was there anyone else around?" Hananiah straightened, his eyes locked on the merchant.

The man blinked at the intense look. "Another man... he was running from Matthew. I think."

"What did the man look like?"

"About my height, but..." the merchant passed a hand over his girth.

"Fatter?" Hananiah glared at the man.

The merchant nodded. "He had quite a belly on him, and his beard seemed grown strangely...."

"What do you mean strangely?"

"I don't know... it just seemed... odd." The merchant shrugged.

Hananiah nodded and left him. Had the last message to Ehud driven him to act foolishly and alarm Matthew? Had Matthew then killed him and then, to misdirect others, left the bloody handprint? Or had the other man been the killer... the real Hand?

Regardless, it made no difference in what he had decided as he walked from the Lower City. Starting now, he would spy on Matthew. He did not know why Gessius Florus had chosen Ehud, other than that his past friendship with Matthew offered a means of contact. But his relationship with Miriam could serve his two purposes. He knew she was a kindred soul who wished to be free. And his other purpose would be to provide financially for their freedom. Florus need not know of Ehud's death, not until he had details on the treasure locations in his hands. Now he would find Matthew and the places where the Temple treasure was to be hidden. Then Lord Florus would pay.

CVII

* * *

DECEMBER 68 CE

CAESAREA

Gessius Florus studied the Thracian and almost regretted the man's failure to kill Vespasian, but that had not been the primary aim. The odds had been against him. It was enough that he had come close enough to plant the seed of threat, and from here, it could grow into a spreading suspicion. "Krateros, you're sure General Vespasian heard you?"

The mercenary nodded. "He heard me, lord... that's certain. But by now, the town and camp are sewn up tighter than a miser's purse. So, I doubt there'll be another chance."

"One attempt is enough." Gessius Florus lifted a small bag that clinked with coins. "That is if he heard you."

"Unless the general is *inauritus*, lord... unless he's deaf." Krateros shrugged with only an involuntary wince of pain from the arrow wound. "As your orders delivered to my ship instructed, I called out the 'greeting' and struck at him quickly but did not linger to press my attack." The man eyed the pouch. "Drusus said you have other work for me."

Florus tossed the bag to him, and the man caught it. The back of his hand bore a crocodile tattoo, a symbol of the ferocious beast of the river Nilus in Aegyptus. Florus had seen some at the lesser Games in Circus Flaminius in Rome. The beasts had torn apart two men foolish enough to come close and taunt it, prodding the creature with their spears.

"You were wounded in the shoulder," said Florus. "Are you able to serve as I require?"

"Drusus and I went to the port, and he pointed out the Syrian to me. I can easily take him... unless he is among many others willing to help him. But I can kill him even if he is helped; I've found that a bloody blade scatters a crowd not willing to spill their own blood. I'll deliver the Syrian's fate however you choose, lord." Krateros leaned forward, his tattooed fist shaking the bag of coins. "Before Drusus left with the other men from Alexandria, he told me you paid well, Lord Florus. So, what will you pay for this Syrian, this... Sayid Sabinus?"

* * *

THE ROMAN ENCAMPMENT

The smaller final ship had carried a load of spices and garum. Which required a separate, smaller *horrea piperataria* to be built next to another larger storage warehouse with its rows and ranks of *dolia.* The six-foot-high fifteen-foot wide fired-clay containers sunk into the ground for storing local merchant's wine and olive oil for the legions. The spices needed special care and included what had become a favorite condiment for many Romans: the much-craved pepper. Sayid was unloading the last wagon when the Lydda unit entered the camp. When he hefted one of the heavy sacks of pepper up and on his shoulder, its fumes crinkled his nose, and he sneezed.

Looking up as he recovered from the sneeze, Sayid saw his father pass, leading a column to the accommodations for the incoming cohorts, which had been set up behind the new warehouses. Marcus Sabinus sat straight, much more so than the men trailing behind him—mounted and marching—who showed the signs of a long day on the road. Sayid balanced the weight on his shoulder. Shifting his stance to steady himself, he stared at his unresponsive father until he was abreast of him. Sayid turned and walked into the warehouse.

* * *

Marcus had been watching his son from the corner of his eye and twisted in the saddle to watch him walk away. The African centurion did not turn back to face ahead until he was well past the warehouse.

CVIII

Dᴇᴄᴇᴍʙᴇʀ 68 CE

Rᴏᴍᴇ

Tʜᴇ Rᴇɢɪᴀ

The building along the Via Sacra sat at the edge of the Roman Forum had served initially as the residence or one of the principal offices of the first kings of Rome. It was actually two separate structures joined to become one and was far older than the surrounding construction and set far back from the street. At the Regia's main entrance, Nicanor crossed into an irregularly formed, enclosed court paved in volcanic rock and bordered by a wooden portico. Passing through the courtyard, he entered a vestibule with wings that branched east and west off the large central room. The room he had been directed to was on the right and had two large, closed wooden doors—framed and banded in bronze.

Nicanor had been surprised by Otho's message to meet him in this same room where he had worked on Vespasian's campaign planning before leaving for Judea. It had not changed. The walls were decorated with terracotta friezes, and the one he remembered most portrayed a minotaur. On the wall facing him was the *ancilia:* the 12 sacred shields believed to guarantee the continued imperium of Rome—and the *hastae*, lances arranged above and below the shields. Nicanor had recognized the hastae at first sight from the stories he knew about them. When he was last here, he had been told that they would shudder just before something terrible happened. On the night of 14 Martius, 124 years before, the story was that Julius Caesar had witnessed their tremor. The following morning, he attended the Senate meeting at which he had been assassinated by a man he thought his friend, aided by others who also wielded blades. Nicanor wondered if the lances had recently shaken or even twitched—with all that was happening in Rome. Or was it just a legend?

The two men at the table wore *toga picta*, elegantly embroidered noblemen's attire in different patterns. "My brother, Titianus," Marcus Otho motioned to the older man next to him at the table, "is a former senator and consul and also the *promagistrate* of the Arval Brethren. You've heard about them before. I did not know that until

I mentioned you and General Vespasian to Titianus, and he recalled notes in the brethren's private records of your meetings here."

"Yes, Lord Otho. I first met Pomponius Mela here. We worked together on Judean campaign maps for General Vespasian," Nicanor said, recalling what he had learned about the *fratres arvales*. The Arval Brethren believed in the old ways, the *pignora imperii*. Its members vowed to uphold and honor both the rulers and the sacred objects that had made Rome strong and kept her that way.

"Centurion, this meeting, too, is about a campaign... of sorts." Titianus rested his forearms on the tabletop. "It is one far more important than the one you recently served in."

Nicanor knew little of Cleo's family: only some about her father, who she abhorred, and Otho and the grandmother she adored. Titianus was much older than Otho and Cleo. Still, in him, he saw even more of Cleo's firm countenance than in Otho's soft, round visage. "What campaign, sirs? And why am I here?"

"Does it matter to you who becomes the emperor?" Titianus asked.

Nicanor hesitated, and his apprehension flared. *There's danger in answering him.* He weighed his words and fleetingly considered he had done that more in the last few years than in the entirety of his life before. "No matter who it is, I want our emperor to do what's right for Rome."

"Not what's right for you... or for us?" Titianus asked, his head tilted toward his brother.

"I can speak only for myself, lord. I serve the emperor... who should serve the needs of the empire. But he does not serve me. Nor should I expect him to."

"You are as reported, centurion. Steadfast and loyal. At least your words are...." Titianus sensed Nicanor's affront by the centurion's involuntary tightening of his jaw. Titianus raised a hand, palm out: "I mean no offense to you. So many people around my brother and me say things and then—either openly or secretly—do something else. Their words, said aloud, often include others in plans for the benefit of the citizens of Rome. They convince people to align with their aims and support them to achieve that 'greater good' for the benefit of all. But then they do what they planned all along: whatever best helps them, their cronies, and their sycophants. You know this. I'm sure you have seen it even in the legions."

"Why am I here, lords?" Nicanor would not engage with that comment.

"Lord Galba is not fulfilling his promises, Nicanor," Otho said. "He has not paid those who helped him, as he agreed to. They grow angry. I was shocked at the decimation of Nero's legion at the Milvian Bridge—on his orders. And that, too, has made people angry."

"Galba has executed many of his enemies—and those he perceives as such—no matter their rank or privileged status, without evidence or trial. That has alarmed our peers and us." Titianus glanced at Otho, who nodded. "He has canceled the Games, saying they're a waste of money, and placed hefty levies on the provinces that did not immediately support him."

"I know Lord Galba better than most," said Otho, whose face was creased with a frown. "I don't know if it is his age or ill health, but now that he has become emperor, he cares little for the daily demands of being a ruler. He has turned those duties over to others." There was bitterness in the words and in Otho's expression.

"To three pedagogues, you mean," Titianus spat out. He raised a hand to enumerate them on his fingers. "Co-consul Titus Vinius; the new Praetorian Guard commander, Cornelius Laco; and Galba's insidious personal advisor, Icelus Marianus, a freedman. And," his eyes danced sideways at his brother, "he has grown close to Lucius Piso, who has influence within the Senate to mollify several senators who worry about Galba's age and infirmities."

"Lords, why am I here?" Nicanor asked again, but he had an inkling. His own thoughts and concerns about Galba were becoming a reality. Though he could not have prevented what was happening, he regretted being drawn to where this conversation was headed.

"You've traveled long and far to tell my brother you wish to help our sister, Cleo. Do you really?"

"With all my honor," Nicanor answered, swallowing his misgivings about what he sensed was coming. But he kept his genuine feeling—*and with all my heart*—to himself.

"Good. Then we need you to use your lower-level contacts or connections within the Praetorian Guard. See if the men of the Guard are angry with Galba enough to support my brother, Otho... so we can save Cleo."

Nicanor looked past the men to the lances on the wall to see if they quivered.

CIX

DECEMBER 68 CE

JERUSALEM

THE UPPER CITY

Matthew watched as his mother lit a taper with the *shamash*. The center *servant* flame that rose between and over the eight others on the menorah's branches had been lighted seven evenings before. It served to ignite the others, and now was the evening for the ninth and final wick. It was the eighth night of Chanukkah and the last night of the Festival of Lights. This holiday had always been his sister's favorite. But now its celebration of the Maccabean revolt to free their people from the Seleucid Empire and Jerusalem's repossession reminded that the Second Temple—reclaimed and cleansed by Judah Maccabee and his fighters—now faced another despoiling. It was in danger not just from another empire but from within, from men such as Yohanan ben Levi.

The death of Ehud on the eve of the holiday had dampened everyone's spirits but Miriam's most of all. Since that night, Matthew had only briefly seen her at dinner and the lighting of the menorah. She stayed downstairs only long enough to give wan smiles of encouragement to Ya'el and Elian as they sang the songs they had only recently learned in an unfamiliar language. The boy sang too loudly as the parrot on his shoulder bobbed its head, eyes glittering in the lamplight.

As she had each night of Chanukkah, Ya'el sat next to Miriam, holding her hand. Matthew took from the pouch at his waist the ring that had fallen from Ehud's grip as he died. He had not told anyone about it or about Ehud's final moment. But it must have been Ehud's intent for Miriam to have the ring. He lifted Elian from the couch he was sharing with Miriam and Ya'el and took his place. The boy immediately settled on the floor between his feet.

"Miriam, I have something I think Ehud wanted you to have." He held out the ring on the palm of his hand. "I think his last wish was for you to have it."

At the mention of Ehud, Miriam's eyes skittered away. Not meeting Matthew's look. Not seeing what lay on his palm. "Wh... Wh..." she stuttered, "why would you think that?"

"It was gripped in his hand... and I think he was giving it to me to give to you."

Miriam closed her eyes but faced Matthew. Then, jaw clenched, she opened them to look at the ring. She picked it up to hold it closer to the lamp on the table before them. "I can't take this."

"It seemed too big for Ehud, so it will be much too large for you," Matthew misunderstood her, "but I could have it resized for you if you wish."

"That's Meshulam's, Ehud's father's ring. He was a large man, as was his father before him. That ring's been handed down for generations," Mathias said.

Rebecca added, "You meant a lot to him, Miriam."

"Here, Miriam," Elian stood, "Matthew carved this for me for the holiday," he held up the four-sided *sevivon* by its stem used to spin the top. "So, you can have this one." He unwound the twine from the Roman spinning top. Taking the ring from Miriam, he ran the coarse string through the ring's loop and tied the two ends in a knot. He slipped the ring on the cord over her head, and it rested just over her heart. Her hand rose to grasp it.

Miriam's lips trembled as she asked: "How do you know Ehud wanted me to have this?"

"His last words were your name, several times." Matthew regretted telling her as he watched his sister's composure crack, then crumble.

* * *

Next day...

Ya'el watched the morning sun through the slats of the shutter cast stripes of light and dark on Miriam's face as she sat staring through the shutter, her hand gripping the ring on its cord. Ya'el felt the coin that hung beneath her own robe; the *kinyan* was Leah's love keepsake given to Miriam's brother. Ya'el had it now because Yosef had given it to her to validate his message that she carried. He had asked his family to take her in and offer a sanctuary and protection. *For as long as that lasts*, she thought.

Ya'el believed Yosef had fallen in love with her, just as she had with him. It was a wishful dream both of them knew would never come true. Now she and Yosef were prisoners—he of a Roman general and she in her marriage to a twisted Roman nobleman. But, thanks to Yosef, thanks to his family, she did not expect ever to be at Florus's mercy again.

415

Mathias and his family were the only people she could run to that would take her in, and now they all had nowhere to go. They were all prisoners awaiting the Roman army. Ya'el squeezed the coin on its cord. She thought of Leah and the pain of the woman's marriage to Yonatan, of Yosef with his lost loves and imprisonment. And now of Miriam—who had become her sister—stricken and scarred by an unspeakable assault. Crushed even further by the pain of killing the man she loved.

"Miriam..." Ya'el started to tell her again Ehud's death had been a tragic accident, but she didn't. "What do they talk of?" she asked instead, motioning at the shuttered window and the courtyard below.

"Shh...." Miriam eased the shutter open a little and bowed her head, listening.

* * *

"We cannot move the wagons from the valley near Motza with Simon bar Giora's 20,000 men stationed outside Jerusalem's walls," Matthew declared, frustrated.

"We must be patient, then," said Yohanan ben Zaccai. "Eleasar ben Ananias has men guarding the wagons. The valley is well hidden, even more with the work that's been done to replant brush and scrub to screen its opening. Simon and most of his men are to the west and camped before the Gennath gate. So that's where their attention is."

"How could Simon bar Giora convince an Idumean general to join him and provide so many men?" Matthew wondered aloud.

"Because he is a proven warrior and leader, at least in fighting the Romans. He still uses the *aquila* taken from the 12th Legion at Beth Horon—he parades it as his own standard. The Idumeans might hate him, but they respect that he has led men against the Romans—and beaten them. No other in Jerusalem can claim that. If they help him take Jerusalem, they believe he will remain here and leave Idumea alone."

"Will he?" Matthew asked.

"Take Jerusalem? Or if he does, leave the Idumeans alone?"

"Both."

"No, neither. But until there are Romans, he can easily fight, Simon bar Giora will be a thorn that continues to prick the flesh of this city," Mathias said, scoffing. "Shimon ben Gamliel says Yohanan ben Levi has—unsurprisingly—decided not to confront Simon. Today at sundown, ben Levi will release his wife. When that happens, Simon has agreed to leave."

"For how long, Father?" Matthew asked.

Mathias shrugged. "I don't know, my son. These days seem to give us more questions than answers."

Matthew nodded. He and his father had talked long into many nights about all that needed answering. He turned to his father's oldest friend. "Did you learn anything of why the Sicarii killed Ehud?"

"I asked those I know but got nothing in return." Yohanan ben Zaccai shook his head. "Those who are real Sicarii... do not speak."

"Why were they after Ehud? And now I feel eyes upon *me* since his death." Matthew was sure of it. "I know someone follows me, and the feeling grows stronger each day. Then, just when I think I'm on to them, I turn to catch them or sidestep into an alley or shop to watch for them. But they're never there, nor anyone who seems could be the one watching me. So if it is the Sicarii, why do they follow me?"

The sound of rasping wood made him look above them.

* * *

That evening...

NEAR ANTONIA FORTRESS

Miriam had heard all that Matthew said, and that last question was one she now kept asking herself. With her accidental bloody handprint, she had done something that was the only good to come from Ehud's death. Elazar ben Yair, the Sicarii leader, now knew she had done as he wished. Whether Ehud was innocent or not—and with him secretly following Matthew, she now believed he was not innocent—the Sicarii should be satisfied and leave her and her family alone. But the cooking pot that Leah's husband Yonatan had stirred had come to a boil. His voice condemning her family had quieted only for a while, and now other voices joined his. She wished whoever had attacked Yonatan had done more than take his ear.

Yohanan ben Levi was also out to do more than just brand Yosef a traitor. The Gischalan, from what she'd heard Matthew say in conversation with her father, wanted to ruin her family's credibility. Her father had still not regained his strength and could not fight him. Matthew had to focus on protecting some of the Temple treasure because Ya'el was adamant that Rome would punish Judea no matter who was emperor. The legions' full wrath would fall on Jerusalem.

Miriam wondered if someone should deal with Yohanan ben Levi, but now she must defend her brother. So here she followed Matthew while Ya'el—again—screened her absence from her parents. She needed to do what she could to ensure Matthew was not at risk from the Sicarii. And she must somehow shake the haunting vision of

417

Ehud's face as he realized she had stabbed him and was abandoning him to die.

In her man's garb and guise and carrying Zechariah's staff, Miriam followed Matthew into the Temple Enclosure to where the western and northern porticoes met at the northwest corner, where stone steps rose to the fortress. Matthew had told her father about going to the armory to arrange a cartload of shields and more arrows for delivery the following day to Eleasar ben Ananias and his men. She slipped from shadow to shadow and drew closer to her brother. She had never been inside the fortress and worried she would lose him once he entered. Or worse, inside, it would be impossible for her to follow him furtively. But he would be safe there, and perhaps she should wait here for him to come out.

Miriam slowed as she saw Matthew reach the steps. *What was that?* Someone ahead of her had stepped from the porticoes to slink behind Matthew. No longer seeking the shadows, she hurried to cut them off. The sounds alerted the follower, who turned toward her. It was the man she had seen the night she had killed Esau ben Beor. Tall, lean, in a dark mantle covering a black tunic and breeches. A headdress wrapped to cover his lower face, leaving only his eyes visible.

"So, perhaps the Sicarii are not done with Ehud's death," the man jeered. "Now they are after his friends. Or are you acting on your own? It seems we meet again, Hand!" He stepped sideways into a column's broad swath of shadow, leaving Miriam in the remnants of sunlight. A dagger in his hand danced out from the dimness, gleaming in the sun's last rays, and it beckoned to her. When she did not move, he charged toward her.

The man's knives slashed in arcs that flickered and traced a pattern in front of him. His first pass missed as Miriam twisted aside. The next—a one-two double thrust—sliced across and cut through her tunic above her breasts. One blade cut the twine around her neck and scored a red furrow across the base of her neck. Miriam scrambled to the side, stumbling to her knees and bringing Zechariah's staff around to chop at the man's ankles, sending him staggering backward. Sprawling, she saw the man recover and lunge toward her as he brought both blades down to drive into her chest.

A figure shot between them. *Matthew!*

She heard a gasp as one of the man's blades, rather than reaching Miriam, sliced her brother's flesh. Matthew fell away, gripping his arm. With a scream, she surged up with Zechariah's staff. Its iron ferrule she sharpened every day, as Zechariah had taught her, speared through man's cloak. It just missed his contorting torso as it spun him backward from her brother. Yanking the staff free, she used her other hand to pull a knife from her forearm sheath.

Breathing heavily, her heart in her throat almost choking her, Miriam darted a glance at Matthew behind her. He kneeled on the stone, blood pouring from between his fingers, staring at her.

The man, breathing easily, stood in front of her and glared until from above came shouts and the echoing of footsteps on the stone. Two of Antonia Fortress's guards rushed down the steps toward them as other men approached from the nearest courtyard. The man waited, and seeing she would not leave first, he slipped into the growing darkness.

As the guards reached them, she cast a last look at Matthew, whose wide eyes had not left her. He now held the severed twine from Elian's spinning top and Ehud's ring in his bloody hand. She ran from him.

CX

DECEMBER 68 CE

CAESAREA

GESSIUS FLORUS'S NEW DOMUS

Gessius Florus preferred to be closer to the sea, but any such residences available would put him too close to Vespasian's praetorium and the legion castrum. His newly hired major domus Irad had once been an administrator for a builder and had promised to find something suitable for his tastes—and more private, for meetings and for his resurging appetite for entertainment inappropriate for a public taberna. This villa, abandoned by a wealthy Jewish merchant fleeing angry Greeks, sat at the end of the city's *decumanus maximus.* That major road started at the port and warehouses. It ran through the city forum and due east until it ended, where a north-south trade route crossed not far outside the Herodian walls of the city.

"How long will you be here, lord, before we move to Sycaminum?"

"It's too soon for that, Drusus. And from what you've told me, it will be longer than I wish." Florus glanced at the man who always reminded him of the Molossi that accompanied some legions into battle. He had seen those hulking war dogs in Italia and heard of their use in the northern provinces. They were violent animals with a sole brutal purpose... to rend and kill. He wished he could see them used against the Jews. Drusus had become his own war dog. Even the Thracians respected his strength and cruelty. He had already heard their talk of how easily Drusus had disjointed a Jew, an unfortunate soul who lived near one site listed in the translated scrolls. The Jew—when not screaming—had told them nothing, and the site was barren. There was no sign of any treasure.

"You're sure the Jew had no information before he died?" Florus asked.

"Yes, lord. He said only that some time ago, men he thought were Essenes had been in the area but did not know why and he had not seen them since."

"How many men did you leave there to watch?"

"Two, sir. They have orders for one to report if anyone should appear who seem to transport goods."

"Goods?"

"Yes, sir... as you told me, these Thracians do not need to know more than necessary. Shall I continue to check the other places on the list?"

"Yes. Those that are closest and quickest to reach. If that's also unfruitful, leave two men at each of those sites as well."

"For how long, lord?"

Florus glared at the man. "Until I say so...."

Drusus nodded. "I'll need more men, sir."

"I'll arrange it... now leave me." He watched as the man walked to his enormous horse and sprang into its saddle. Florus noted the repairs underway as he passed through the atrium inside the villa and crossed the inner courtyard. He heard the woman's sobbing coming from his bedroom and paused, smiling before he turned down a short hallway to his private office. Drusus's report followed what he had recently learned—that a Jewish leader and commander, Simon bar Giora, with 20,000 men, had sealed Jerusalem and threatened those within its walls. Was that why he had not heard from Hananiah? Were these things connected, this Simon bar Giora blockading the city and the empty site?

More and more, it seemed the Jews were like Romans in that many of their leaders sought even more power and wealth. And had few qualms about how to gain it. Had the honorable Jews in Jerusalem trying to save their Temple's treasure been prevented from moving it out of the city because they feared their own people? Or were they instead hiding it in a secure hiding place within Jerusalem's walls? Perhaps they had a place far more secure than the Temple, a place that an invading army was not likely to find. He sat at his desk and took out a bronze-tipped pen and a small inkpot, breaking its wax seal and removing the stopper. Then, sliding a sheet of vellum to him, he dipped the pen and wrote to Hananiah:
"Find out if any of the Temple treasure has been moved or if it is being hidden within Jerusalem. Make this your priority, and Ehud's."

He folded the sheet and sealed it with wax. Then he called for one of the new servants. "Find Irad and tell him to come here," he said. Florus drummed fingers on his desk and waited in thought.

"Yes, lord?" Irad stood at the entry, catching his breath.

"I hired you in part because I discovered your brother still trades with Jerusalem—and profits—despite the prohibitions."

Then, seeing the man's face whiten, Florus continued: "Do not fear. Bring him to me. He can be of use to me, and I will reward you both." He did not add *or kill you if you are not helpful.*

CXI

JANUARIUS 69 CE

ROME

THE CAPITOLINE HILL

Nicanor climbed the steep Gemonian Stairs from the Roman Forum to the Arx Capitolina, where he had served the nearby prison as a watch captain. On the southern summit, a flattened boulder on an overhang brooded over the sheer cliff, and there he could stand and view the city. But the one time he had done that, the man he was with had warned him to be loyal, or he would be cast from it, suffering the fate of traitors.

Nicanor reached the top and looked around as clouds parted and shafts of sunlight slanted down upon him. On the southwestern part of the hill, to his left, several buildings, temples, and worship areas were grouped. Over the uneven retaining walls that followed the hillside contours, Nicanor could see the Temple of Jupiter had been completely reconstructed after the great fire. The Corinthian colonnade that stretched down the sides of the hill had been replaced, and its roofline frieze was re-plastered and shone a brilliant white under the sun. Before him were the Tullianum he had served in and the Arx Capitolina garrisoning the Praetorian guards of the central city.

To the right was the *Auguraculum*, a roofless temple where priests practiced their augury and ornithomancy, divination from the movement of birds. Within the temple walls, the priests lived in tents or huts. They watched the sky to see from what direction the birds came and then marked it with stones placed along the temple's perimeter. From this observation, the priests believed they could predict the future. Nicanor believed in the gods—and prayed to them… mostly in times of battle, but he had long had his doubts any priest could foretell the future. He also had concerns about how a *haruspex* could glean wisdom from looking into an animal's guts.

Other than Yosef and his dreams, Nicanor had not been around any who claimed to predict the future. Not since Cestius Gallus had brought Spurinus, a diviner from Caesarea, to their camp at Gibeon during the 12th Legion's march on Jerusalem two years before. The soothsayer had read in a bowl of rooster guts that they should continue their assault on Jerusalem. Despite the rebel raids having taken the supplies and siege engines, they needed for that attack. The gods or chicken guts had given them poor advice that day.

Nicanor headed down the slope, bypassing the field of prophesying priests, and followed the gravel path that bent left to the Temple of Juno. That was where he was to meet Florin. The auxiliary had once served as his clerk-courier during his night watch at the prison. After meeting with Titianus and Marcus Otho, he called on the young man and enlisted his help. He knew men talked more easily around auxiliary subordinates than they did around legion superiors. Florin had big ears but spoke little.

The young auxiliary stopped pacing when he spotted Nicanor and looked up expectantly.

"What do you hear among the Guard?" Nicanor asked by way of greeting.

"Anger, Nicanor," Florin said with some anxiety. "Emperor Galba still has not honored his promises, and the new Praetorian Prefect, Cornelius Laco, attempts to placate the senior officers with nothing but more words."

"What about the officers at my level and the men beneath them?"

"They resent these who still believe Prefect Laco and the emperor."

"Will they do anything?"

Florin scanned the area.

"No one is close enough to hear us," Nicanor assured him.

"If they—the emperor and Praetorian Prefect—stood there"— Florin pointed back across the plateau toward the edge where Nicanor had just been overlooking the city center. "Many I overheard would shove them off in hopes of finding better men to replace them."

"And do they think Lord Marcus Otho one of the better men?"

"They would support him..."

* * *

THE REGIA

Nicanor sat as still as the hastae upon the wall and thought again about the Tarpeian Rock he had seen that morning. Upon that rock, Lord Tigellinus had told him years before, "This is the spot from which the most traitorous are thrown." Tigellinus was then the Praetorian Prefect. He and so many others Nicanor had met in positions of authority seemed to believe much of life was like a transaction in the market. One did not pay and receive goods, but one remained loyal and lived. Or abandoned honor and profited. But integrity and loyalty existed inside a person and were not garments to be donned or doffed. Nicanor had frowned upon the thinking of men like Tigellinus and Gessius Florus. That thinking and those men were offensive to his beliefs.

"Bad company ruins good character," Nicanor muttered. A grim smile came to him at the thought of those words from the Christian prisoner, Paul, as he sat in a dank, dark cell—facing an unknown future—in the Tullianum. *Sitting there talking to me, a man who served those who had imprisoned him, as I perched on a rickety stool in the late hours of the night and early morning.*

Now here he sat, waiting to tell men he doubted were moral what they could use and turn to their benefit to gain even more power. But he needed them to wield that power to save Cleo. Even thousands of miles away from him and so many months gone by—he cared for her deeply. So, he would transact with these men and not think of whether they had honor. Instead, he would focus on his loyalty to do as he promised Lady Cleo. And he would reflect on that love he had unexpectedly discovered, though he might never see it realized. Paul had spoken frequently of love, and his words had remained with him: *Love is patient, love is kind, and is not jealous; love does not brag and is not arrogant, does not act unbecomingly; it does not seek its own will, is not provoked, does not consider a wrong suffered, does not rejoice in unrighteousness, but rejoices with the truth; bears all things, believes all things, hopes all things, endures all things.* Despite the truth behind such words, no one seemed to live that way.

"What have you learned, centurion?" Marcus Otho interrupted his reverie as he and his brother, Titianus, entered the room.

Shaken, Nicanor took a deep breath and let it out. His next words would increase the current imperial instability... and could provoke a civil war. "The men of the Praetorian Guard would support you if any of the legions in provinces near Rome protested against Galba." He saw the smiles appear on the two men's faces. And he hoped and believed that what was coming would help Cleo.

CXII

Jerusalem

The Lower City

Miriam awoke at Zechariah's, not remembering how she got there but recalling vividly what had driven her there. After what had happened at Antonia Fortress, Matthew had not been far behind her as she ran from him. He had caught up as she paused at the gate at the rear of their home courtyard to strip off her disguise. In her blind panicked run, it was not until then that she realized she should have stayed with Matthew and tried to explain, tried to convince him to keep her secret. She should not have led him back home for such a confrontation. But he was upset and angry. Blood streamed down his arm when he had dragged her into the courtyard before their parents. They came out at the sound of her cries to Matthew to let her go. Feeling her forearm sheaths, he had yanked up her sleeves to reveal the Sicarii daggers strapped there and had tossed Ehud's bloody ring to the ground before them. He had slapped his bloody hand on the front of her tunic and demanded, "No more lies!"

Those three words from her brother had torn open the fragile shell that contained all Miriam's pain, all her hurt... and her guilt. Everything spilled out before her family, and she told them of her rape... the men she had killed.... and the stabbing of Ehud.

Her mother's and father's expressions had grown more shocked with every word; their faces became drawn tight and whitened. Her mother's knees buckled, and she had sunk to the ground sobbing. Ya'el had come out and stood with tears streaming down her face, and Elian also cried, frightened by what he did not understand.

Then, finally, Mathias, shaking and swaying, had pointed at her and hoarsely ordered, "Leave! I don't care where you go... but leave! Now!"

His words had cut her deeper than could the sharpest blade. Miriam had turned and staggered from them, snatching up her disguise from near the gate, and then run into the night. She ran to the place where, in her darkest moments, she had found some measure of solace. Zechariah had been her rescuer... her redeemer. When he had been killed—saving her one last time—she had felt more alone than ever before. Ehud's return into her life had lessened her pain, but with his death by her hand, the pain had roared back. All Zechariah's shop held for her now was the memory of how the old, blind Sicarii had saved her life and taught her how to fight. And those two things Zechariah had done for her had resulted in her killing Ehud and the cruelest loss of all—the loss of her family.

I can't stay here, she thought. Whether the Sicarii remain in Jerusalem to fight the Romans or not, I'm no longer one of them. I'll fight, but not for them. I have to live until the fighting begins. There was only one place for her to go. She went to the hidden compartment, took out the tunnel maps—Zechariah's and the ones she had worked on—and fled the shop.

* * *

Miriam shifted the bag over her shoulder, feeling the weight of the two *minae* she had taken from King David's tomb. Each bar weighed over a pound. At 1/60th the value of a *talent,* it was still too much to use to buy food and lamp oil in the market. It would attract too much attention. The only tradesman she knew who could exchange or convert the bars to coin—the only one she could convince to keep it a secret—was Hananiah.

Miriam had misgivings about using him and taking advantage of his feelings for her, but she had no choice. She entered his shop to find it dark except for the usual dim glow in the back. She followed the light to the small room and peeked inside. His small table with writing materials and the lighted lamp, a stool, and a thinly padded cot covered by a rough wool blanket were the only furnishings. She turned to leave, and the strap of her bag caught on a low shelf, jostling a draw-stringed purse onto the ground. Stooping to put it back, she saw what had dropped from the loosened purse and picked it up from the dimness near the floor. It had a crusty, leathery feel. She held it under the lamplight. It looked like...

The sound of the street door opening startled her, and she dropped the human ear. Then, thinking quickly, she blew out the lamp.

"Hello. Anyone here?"

Shocked at what she had found and at the voice she recognized, Miriam held her breath. After what seemed an eternity, she heard Matthew leave. He must be looking for her and—as he had done once before when she had gone missing—wanted to check whether Hananiah had seen her.

427

Miriam's thoughts went to what she had just found. *Hananiah was protecting me—he had been the one who attacked Yonatan!* She would come back later to see him about the gold and ask about Yonatan. Now, worried Matthew was still on the street searching for her, she must get away. She slipped out the rear entrance and followed the alley to where she could reach Zechariah's. Her next task required that she don her disguise at least one more time.

Among the myriad thoughts and regrets whirling through her mind, it had occurred that her parents might hold Ya'el to account for not telling them about Miriam's secret. Ya'el and Elian, too, needed a safe place to go. And money to live on or even a means to leave the city. The second small gold bar in her bag was for them. With it, Ya'el could pay someone to take her and the boy from Jerusalem.

* * *

THE UPPER CITY

Hananiah watched the Caesarean trader continue through the agora toward the northern gate of the city. The man, a dealer in fine goods, had called on him that morning with a surprising announcement: he carried a message from Gessius Florus. Hananiah had unsealed and read it as the man waited. Lord Florus's new instructions were that he and Ehud watch for any signs that the Jews were hiding the treasure within the city and report anything new or suspicious about Yosef ben Mathias's family.

The trader was to wait for his reply and return to Caesarea with it. The man would have heard of and would report Ehud's death. In his response, Hananiah included that Ehud had been killed by the Sicarii assassin. He explained that many in Jerusalem thought Yosef ben Mathias's family were traitors. The city was filling with people seeking shelter, which created increasing tension within its walls. Even Matthew's family had a woman and boy with a pet bird come to live with them. With Ehud's death, he now directly watched Matthew for leads to the treasure. He would report anything he found out about it being moved within the city. Hananiah sealed the message and handed it to the trader, who he followed to the Upper City market as he left Jerusalem.

The knife maker finished his own deliveries. Before turning toward the residential area to watch for Matthew, he saw the ruffle of color from beating wings rise from one of the lower terraces of the Xystus near the Temple Enclosure. Curious, he walked closer. He heard a boy calling to the bird. The parrot's predominantly green feathers, with a red, yellow, and blue-gray band, caught the sun as the bird made small circles in the air. As the boy and bird played, a dozen feet from them stood Miriam's cousin Ya'el talking with a broad-bellied, bearded man of her height he immediately recognized. This woman, Ya'el, knew The Hand!

Careful of being seen watching them, Hananiah saw a glint of gold exchange hands. The two separated, and he soon lost sight of the man he believed to be The Hand in the crowd. That did not matter. He could not confront him here... and the gold bar he had seen flash had remained with the woman, who had slipped it into a purse at her waist. That made him cautious and even more suspicious. Was Lord Florus right to suspect the treasure was not being moved from Jerusalem but taken by someone within? He followed the woman and boy. Through them, he would trap The Hand and find out where the gold bar came from. Then he would kill them.

CXIII

Januarius 69 CE

Caesarea

Florus's Villa

"Did you have a reply, sir?" Irad asked nervously, seeing Lord Florus's features change while reading the message. He had been with the Roman nobleman long enough now to know his smile meant ill for some around him.

"No reply for your brother, but have him see me before he goes again to Jerusalem. Is Krateros back from the legion camp?"

"Yes, lord. I saw him enter the stable as I came at your call."

"Send him to me."

"Yes, sir." Irad held up a rolled cylinder of soft leather tied with a cord and sealed along its seam by a blob of wax at the center. "A rider also just brought this for you."

Florus took it and broke the seal—the one he had given Drusus—and unrolled it. Inside was a folded square of parchment, also sealed. He opened that and unfolded it, and his smirk broadened. He looked up, and a flash of anger erased the grin with a frown.

"What do you wait for? Go. Send Krateros to me now." He watched the man scurry away, and his smile returned.

* * *

Sycaminum

"Wait outside," Gessius Florus ordered the six men as he dismounted. Drusus had said in his message to enter the warehouse alone. He glanced at the enormous cargo vessel at the nearby dock. With Hananiah's news of Ehud's killing, that leverage with the vessel owner was gone. If Meshulam learned of his son's death, he could disrupt Florus's use of the vessel by bringing attention that could lead to questions from General Vespasian about why an imperial tax collector was involved with an Alexandrian glassmaker. He would have to seize the ship and replace its crew soon, especially if he found out shortly that what Drusus had reported was true. He entered the *horrea* and passed several small rooms, hearing the clink of chains from the Jewish prisoner still held within one, and he came to a large, open space. In its center, lighted by four large post-mounted lanterns commonly used in courtyards, was a wagon, its bed covered by a heavy cloth.

"Well, what's this?" he asked, walking over to Drusus, who stood next to the rear of the wagon.

"The men near the town the Jews call Shechem reported it, sir. They watched the site at the base of the mountain, Har Eival—one of the sites from the Qumran list. The wagon came in from the east on the road to the river they call Nahar ha-Yarden. Our men followed when they saw that the accompanying Jews were armed. They stopped the Jews as they backed the wagon into a limestone cave."

"What's in it?" Florus tugged at one rope lashing the covering.

"I don't know, lord. But the Jews planned that once they had it inside the cave, they would let go a rockslide that had been engineered above the opening. The massive fall of stone and dirt would have completely buried the wagon. One of our men, an archer, killed the Jews before they could trigger it. Then they pulled the wagon out, and one rode to report to me. I sent a team with mules to bring it here. I thought you should see it opened, lord."

"The men don't know what's inside?"

"In the wagon, sir? No, I hired and sent draymen from Ptolemais. The two men who captured it I sent on to another of the list locations near Tiberias." Drusus pulled the dagger sheathed at his belt and gripped one line. "Ready, lord?"

Florus nodded.

Drusus cut the ropes at the back and sides. Then, since he was too short, he climbed onto the end of the wagon and whipped away the heavy cloth as if it were a thin blanket. He stared. The ruddy gleam of copper sheets covered whatever the wagon contained. Puzzled, he looked at the nobleman. "The metal is to protect it?"

"Open it." Florus motioned and stepped back.

Drusus jumped down, pulled a *dolabra* stuck in one post, and climbed back. He took the spike end of the pickaxe, jammed it under the edge of the end sheet, and pried it loose. Then he worked his way around the edge and loosened it so he could get his hands under it. Slipping the pickaxe into a loop at his belt, he gripped the sheet and lifted it. The metal groaned as it peeled back to reveal another cloth underneath. He flipped that off. Beneath, in neat stacks, were bars of silver and gold that shone dully in the lantern's glow.

Florus smiled. Two lovely things had finally happened. First, Hananiah had mentioned a woman, boy, and bird that lived with the family of Vespasian's Jew, Yosef. That told him Cleo had run to the

Jews in Jerusalem, the provincials she had always admired. Florus would make her into the most hunted person in that city. By now, Krateros would have spread the rumor throughout Caesarea. Second, a Roman noblewoman, sister of one of Emperor Galba's closest advisors, Marcus Otho—a traitor to the empire—was hiding in Jerusalem. A reward was offered for her. Every woman who had sought refuge there, little known and new to the city, would be a suspect. And the Jew-against-Jew conflict already burning within Jerusalem's walls would have more fuel. Hananiah would take Cleo and smuggle her out of Jerusalem to him. Then he would have his vengeance.

If Hananiah did not capture or kill her, men in Jerusalem would find her and use for leverage when the legions arrived at their gates. Either way, ultimately, Cleo would die. *And now,* Florus thought as he eyed the stacks of gold and silver bars whose gleam illuminated his dream, *I have this badly needed money. I need nothing from others to continue. I can accomplish what I've wanted since arriving in this gods-forsaken land—to take the Jews' treasure and become one of the richest men in the empire.*

CXIV

JANUARIUS 69 CE

ROME

IANUS GEMININUS

The temple stood within the forum near the Basilica Aemilia—a place of business, full of shops and tabernae—that fronted the court along the Argiletum, the main route into the city from the northeast. Nicanor entered to find Antonia Caenis standing next to a bronze statue with two faces.

"Janus, the god of boundaries and beginnings," she announced with a smile as if introducing Nicanor to the god. "He is not attended by *flamen* or *sarcedos* assigned to him. When you come here," she turned a full circle, her arms stretched out, "without priests, it's just you and the god."

"My lady, why did you send the message to meet you here this morning?" Nicanor asked.

Antonia pointed at the two faces. "He is the god of duality... of transition and endings. Rome is facing one or—I fear—the other. I know you have thought about the changes in the direction your life has taken. So, I thought this a good place to meet and tell you what I've heard." She paused to emphasize the importance of the information. "Four Germania legions refuse to swear loyalty to Galba. Instead, they've thrown the new statues of him into the Rhenus, and they demand their governor Vitellius be declared emperor."

"Does that mean—"

"Yes. Soon Galba himself—his body—might be found in another river, the Tiber. He has no friends, no supporters in the Senate. Everyone there fears the Praetorians. None will stand with Galba against their wishes nor for him. So, I needed to warn you about being ready."

* * *

GNAEUS BATIATUS'S VILLA

"When I got off watch, I heard the news, centurion, and ran here." The auxiliary gasped, catching his breath.

Nicanor handed the young man a cup of water and rubbed the sleep from his eyes. After meeting with Antonia Caenis, he had not slept well. A servant had wakened him to tell of Florin's arrival and his demand to speak with Nicanor. A crack of lightning streaked in the sky above the atrium, and thunder rolled. The air became still as the last of the stormy night abated, and the sky began to turn gray with the coming dawn. "What's shaken you, Florin?" He eyed the Tullianum clerk's unsteady hand sloshing water as he drank.

"A legionary from the Castra Praetoria reported that Lord Otho has been killed there... by Julius Atticus."

"What?" Nicanor felt his stomach wrench and push bile into his throat. "Who is this Atticus?" Marcus Otho's will was not as flabby as his physique, Nicanor had learned. Since their last meeting, Lord Otho had recruited and paid well two *praetorian speculatores*: a tesserarius, Barbius Proculus, and an optio called Veturius. These provocateurs had been spreading dissent and discord in Galba's reign.

"Atticus is a Praetorian, one of Emperor Galba's personal guards," Florin said.

Lord Otho's either overstepped or misstepped, Nicanor thought. Galba's public announcement just days before at the Castra Praetoria had pushed him over the edge. Galba had said that the young Senator Lucius Piso would be his heir.

And now, what will I do to save Cleo?

Gnaeus Batiatus entered the atrium, yawning. "You are popular this morning, Nicanor. Someone else asks for you."

Nicanor, Florin trailing behind, followed Gnaeus to the porticoed entry. On tree-trunk legs and half a head taller than Nicanor, there stood an armored member of the Praetorian Guard. "You are the *tribunus* Nicanor?"

Nicanor nearly corrected the grizzled warrant officer. But Vespasian's recent orders Antonia Caenis had given him announced his promotion to a senior officer within the legions and among the general's staff. "Yes," he said with a nod. Then, gesturing to Florin to step behind him, he rested a hand on the hilt of his pugio, the dagger always at his belt.

"I'm to take you to the emperor."

Nicanor felt Florin stir as if to move forward and stand beside him. He motioned the auxiliary to stay back. Though warmed by the young man's courage, Nicanor knew the clerk was armed only with a bronze stylus and wax tablet. He caught the anxious expression on his host's face. He must not draw either Gnaeus or Florin into what he thought was about to come.

"Gnaeus, I go with this soldier. I thank you for your hospitality."

He turned to Florin. "Return to your duties." He saw the clerk hesitate and added—regretfully—in his field commander's bark, "Now!"

After another scant pause to search Nicanor's face, the young man left. Nicanor hoped the young auxiliary would not linger outside. He stalled for time by sending for his cloak and gladius. A servant brought them, and he pinned the mantle in place at his right shoulder. He then belted the short sword onto his right hip. "Let's go..."

With a final nod of thanks at Gnaeus, he waved the Praetorian to walk ahead of him.

* * *

THE TEMPLE OF SATURN

Nicanor had been surprised to leave Gnaeus Batiatus's villa and not see at least a decanus of Praetorians accompanying the massive *evocatus augusti* who rode ahead of him. He had intentionally called to have one of the stable horses saddled, not Carmenta. He knew Marcus Attilius would care for her if he did not return. And that is what he expected. Nicanor did not regret helping Marcus Otho, but he did regret that Graius had died trying to reach him to save Cleo. The old gladiator had saved Nicanor's life so he could get that done... to get Lord Otho's protection for her. Now he had failed in his vow to them both. *Graius died for nothing, and now what will come of Cleo?* he thought.

The Praetorian warrant officer reined to a stop at the Temple of Saturn at the foot of the Capitoline Hill and the western end of the Forum. About two dozen Praetorians in full armor and bearing arms stood in ranks on its steps. Two stepped forward and took the reins of the mounts. The huge Praetorian beckoned to Nicanor to follow him.

It's an odd place to die, Nicanor thought as he passed the massive altar to enter the temple atop its pediment of travertine blocks. He had never been inside. But Yosef had told him years before, during his first time in Rome, it was the second oldest temple after the Temple of Jupiter Optimus Maximus. Long ago, it had housed the Aerarium, the Roman treasury that stored the legion standards and laws and all Senate decrees, engraved in brass.

Two fine-robed men stood before the statue of a veiled god holding a scythe.

"Hello, Nicanor," said Marcus Otho in greeting.

435

Letting out a breath he had not realized he held, Nicanor replied, "It's good to see you, Lord Otho... your brother, too." He nodded to Titianus Otho, who looked past him to the Praetorian.

"See to your men, Statius," said Titianus. "Then spot your man and take your position. Then, when you see the signal, be ready to act."

Nicanor glanced at the broad back of the Praetorian walking away, then faced the two nobles. He was relieved Otho was alive but wondered at Titianus's commands to the departing Praetorian. But he asked no questions and just waited.

"Come with us." Marcus Otho told him.

Leaving the Praetorians at the Temple of Saturn, they crossed to climb the Palatine, where it steeply sloped toward the Circus Maximus. The Temple of Apollo Palatinus had been built upon a man-made terrace. On its northern part, the temple was raised on a high podium of tufa blocks, travertine, and, where not load-bearing, cement. The temple was constructed of blocks of Carrara marble, with full columns across the front and half-columns along the outside of the cella. The structure was surrounded by a portico of Danaids. Its columns were fashioned in *giallo antico*, golden-toned marble with black flecks. The Danaids were of black marble between the column shafts of the portico.

Inside, at the altar, was Emperor Galba with his closest advisors: Titus Vinius, his legion commander from Hispania; the new Praetorian Prefect, Cornelius Laco; the freedman Icelus. He was surprised to see also the general Marcus Antonius Primus, whom he had not seen since that day at the Temple of Mars Ultor. Next to him was Lucius Piso, Galba's new heir. Behind them, Sempronius Densus, a Praetorian centurion Nicanor recognized, led the bodyguard detail for the deputy-emperor Piso. Within the unit was Sulpicius Florus, an auxiliary he knew had recently been granted citizenship by Galba.

The emperor stepped to the altar and waved a servant to bring forward his offering. The cloaked soothsayer stood before the two bowls and flipped his cowl back. Nicanor recognized Umbricius, a haruspex who had accompanied Galba from Hispania. With the flashing thrust of a curved-bladed *carnifex*, the butcher's knife disemboweled the fowl. Umbricius filled the water bowl with its entrails, rinsing them and placing them cleansed in the second, empty bowl. Then, in the flare of torchlight around the altar, the man lifted and rotated the entrails, seeking signs. He looked dismayed and leaned to whisper in the emperor's ear. At his words, Galba became upset. A rustle at Nicanor's elbow made him half-turn to Marcus

Otho, whose personal aide, a freedman named Onomastus had appeared next to him. He overheard the freedman's muttered words: "All is ready and in place, lord." Nicanor's eyes caught movement among the group with the emperor. He watched Marcus Antonius Primus separate from them and walk to stand beside the emperor without speaking.

"Nicanor," Marcus Otho said as he touched his elbow, "my brother and I must go. Stay here, and when the emperor is *done*, join us at the Regia."

"Must you leave now, Lord Otho?" Marcus Primus quietly asked.

"We are buying a large tract of property, the remnants of what was damaged in the great fire. It has finally been surveyed, and we must speak with our architect."

The words puzzled Nicanor as the two nobles left the temple.

Nicanor and Marcus Primus watched Umbricius repeat the sacrifice and review of the bird's entrails with the same results, to judge from his and the emperor's expressions. Then, finally, the emperor and his group exited the temple, and Nicanor and Marcus Primus followed at a distance. Silently they had reached the base of the hill and turned into the forum near the *lacus curtius*. This deep basin had once been a lake that many Romans venerated, while others believed it cursed. Nicanor, about to break the silence and tell the general he must part ways with him, was startled to see a man he knew. Atilius Vergilio reached up and ripped Galba's *imago*, the bronze likeness of the emperor from the staff he carried for the Praetorian escort.

Vergilio cast the metal piece upon the ground and the ranks of Praetorians that had closed around Galba's imperial litter dissolved into a roiling mass of men fighting. The six burly auxiliary litter-bearers dropped their burden, and Galba was thrown from his chair. The Praetorians closest to him pulled their swords and slashed him to pieces, slaughtering the prostrate emperor. Nicanor watched as Sempronius Densus, gladius in one hand, pugio in the other, fought to protect Lucius Piso as Galba's heir fled into the nearby Temple of Vesta. Statius—the huge Praetorian who had come for him that morning—cut Sempronius down and went after the deputy emperor. A minute later, Statius came out holding Piso's head by a tangle of hair, the severed head still dripping blood.

Nicanor was sickened by what surrounded him. Not at the sight of the butchered men strewn about, nor the stench of bowels voided when death takes hold. He was familiar with such scenes and smells. That it was in the Roman Forum stunned and repulsed him. This time the chicken guts had not lied... whatever ill-portent Umbricius had delivered to Galba, not an hour before, had quickly come true.

* * *

THE REGIA

Nicanor had once seen an enormous dirt mound broken and thousands of ants boil out. Some seemed to seek to attack the offender in the bright sunlight, others scurried about without purpose... and some ran from the devastation, seeking escape and safety. What he had witnessed after Galba's assassination had been like that. Leaving the bloodshed at the forum, he had unthinkingly followed the general, Marcus Antonius Primus, to the Regia. He had not realized until he stood before Marcus and Titianus Otho, surprised to find Antonia Caenis with them, that the he and the general had been expected.

"By now, Galba and his heir are dead. The Senate will convene shortly and proclaim me emperor," Marcus Otho had announced as he and the general entered the room. *Either the legend of the lances was a lie, or they had done their dance when I wasn't watching,* Nicanor thought. "Tribunus... centurion... here is my edict that Lady Cleo, has imperial protection." Marcus Otho had handed Nicanor sealed scrolls, official copies of the proclamation. "The Senate will also issue this order once I'm proclaimed emperor."

He had been relieved, "Thank you, Lord—I mean Emperor Otho... I will leave now for Ostia and the next ship to Judea."

But now the new emperor continued. "I cannot let you go, Nicanor." His voice was firmer than his jowls. "I need people around me I trust... to help protect me until I can secure the throne and put down the unrest within Rome. So you must serve me now."

"Nicanor," Antonia Caenis had said, "Lord Titus arrives tomorrow morning in Ostia. The emperor, Lord Otho, has orders for Vespasian to hold in place, for now. He is to suspend the Judean campaign while Emperor Otho consolidates his military and political position. I will go with you to meet Titus and give him these orders and the imperial decree protecting Lady Cleo. Then you can return to serve Emperor Otho."

* * *

The next morning...

OSTIA

THE PORT

Nicanor and Antonia had greeted Titus, informing him of the new emperor's orders. At this news, Titus then sought a ship headed to Judea, finding a *quinquereme* that sailed on the afternoon tide. As Nicanor watched Antonia Caenis exchange a few final private words with Titus before he boarded the vessel, he listened to the talk of the sailors exchanging news and gossip.

"Gods' truth... I swear it. I heard it myself, and it has spread from Antioch to Alexandria." The sailor slapped the back of his hand against the shoulder of the man standing with him. "A Roman noblewoman, close to this new emperor you tell me of, some say—but a traitor—now hides in the Jews' capital city, Jerusalem. She's been aiding the Jews against us. First, she helped defeat Cestius Gallus and the 12th Legion... and now she works against General Vespasian. There's a reward... a right large one, too... for her capture. Some greedy Jew hoping to save his own ass will turn in the *mecha putida*. Plenty of the rebels there will think her a spy anyway. Then the treasonous slut'll be executed."

"*Futuo!*" Nicanor spat. He prayed for fair winds and calm seas. Titus must get Marcus Otho's declamation protecting Cleo to Judea quickly!

CXV

Januarius 69 CE

Jerusalem

The Lower City, King David's Tomb

Shivering in the damp wool cloak gathered close around her, Miriam poured into the cistern the last of the rainwater she'd collected in the traps set near the hidden entrance to the tomb. It had rained for days, and after she found the cistern in an antechamber, she knew that at least she would not thirst. But her stomach growled. The food Ya'el had passed to her the last sunny day before—when she had met to give her the gold *mina*—had run out.

Setting the now-empty hide bucket aside, she went through another entry to a larger room that narrowed at its far end, where a passageway led deeper into the tomb. This chamber—a vestibule of sorts—smelled of smoke and charred wood. One wall showed the soot marks of the fire pit she had dug and bordered with mud brick and chunks of stone from a collapsed wall she had found inside the tomb. A crack, perhaps from the earth shake three decades ago that her father had told her about, started at the top of the wall and ate into the stone overhead. The flickering of a hand lamp had helped her discover the current of air swirling from the fissure. It drew the flame... and the smoke from the fire she built with rotted cloth kindling and dried wood from chests and shelves within the many rooms and main gallery. She had even left the tomb long enough to check whether the smoke could be seen outside. But with the past days' iron-gray sky, wind, and rain, there was no sight of it. The air moved well in much of the tomb, so perhaps it disbursed before reaching the outside.

But she was cautious about some sections that remained sealed. Breaking through a sealed passage at the other end of the tomb had nearly been her death by fire, the foul air ignited by her torch. When the weather cleared, she would look again to make sure there was no plume of smoke to reveal her hiding place.

Miriam settled beside the fire, feeling its welcome warmth reflected by the wall. She pushed aside thoughts of what was next for her. If she drew no attention, there was safety in the tomb. She even planned—once she could get more lamp oil—to explore the tomb's tunnels. She had returned to the treasure chamber to take some of the gold *minae* but had not retraced the route that had first brought her to the tomb. It led back to Zedekiah's Cave and Solomon's Quarry at Bezetha, the northern part of Jerusalem. And there were other tunnels and passages she might use to reach other parts of the city without traveling the streets. Zechariah had used them for that and told her of tunnels that led beyond the walls. Because they were hidden and used to enter and leave Jerusalem, they, too, could be of use.

She hugged her arms tight to her sides, partly because of the chill but also because of the ache within her. The past and present hurt badly enough, and she did not want to think about the future. She leaned against the wall and turned her face toward the flames. The wall's warmth felt pleasing on her cheek and her ear, chilled from fetching the water. She reached up to brush her hair back, and her fingers grazing the ear made her think of what she had found at Hananiah's shop. The knife maker's past, she knew, had left him with his own pain to bear. She had sensed he contained a dark rage at the abuse he had suffered. That—and his fondness for her—had surely driven his attack on Yonatan when he cut off his ear. She understood the need to punish those who hurt others and would tell him that when she took the gold bar to him. She would ask for his help to convert it to shekels.

"Miriam…"

The call echoed and brought her to her feet. She pulled her daggers and went to the entry.

"It's Ya'el!" the voice called again.

Miriam took the brief passage to a small gallery, the open area before the outside tunnel where she had found the two dead Romans, the place she had shown Ya'el once before. She stepped from the dark passage to see Ya'el and Matthew standing there with water dripping from their cloaks and cowls, holding two sputtering torches. Surprised that Ya'el had remembered the way into the tomb, she demanded, "Why did you bring him here?"

"Sister… I…" Matthew took a step toward Miriam and stopped. "I came to ask you to listen to me and forgive me and to come home. Mother has not stopped crying… Father has not slept. They forgive you, Miriam."

"Do you, Matthew?" Tears came into Miriam's eyes, and she angrily wiped them away.

"Of course. I should have acted differently... I..." His voice broke. "I did not know about what had happened to you... Or I would have—"

"What? You could not save me from what had already happened."

"I would've helped you. I could have shown how much we love you no matter what had happened."

"But how can I love myself, Matthew? After what the Romans took from me... after the killing I've done?" Her shoulders shook. "After killing Ehud!"

"Come home, Miriam. Yohanan ben Levi now calls for all Moderates to be imprisoned. Many listen to him. You shouldn't be alone."

"I'm safe here..."

"What of Mother and Father? What of Ya'el here, and Elian? Your family loves you, Miriam. We should be together."

"Jerusalem sits on the edge of a precipice...." Ya'el said quietly but firmly. "The city faces growing anarchy, Miriam. The only way to survive it... is to stick together. Your family needs you, and you need your family." She went to Miriam and gripped her shoulders to steady them. "You knew Ehud had some secret and was up to something he felt guilt over. Elazar ben Yair and the Sicarii suspected it, too. And they were right. He died because of that. All you did was protect your brother. Ehud's death is not your fault; it was his own."

Miriam knew what Ya'el said was right, and she tried to push down the darkness that had been reborn in her with Ehud's death.

"Come home, Miriam," Matthew pleaded. "I have to meet Eleasar ben Ananias in the rift valley now. But please come home and let me find you there tonight."

Miriam nodded, though she was not sure.

"I must go, too," said Ya'el. "I left Elian with your mother, and he's bored with staying inside. Your father will get no rest with no one there to keep the boy occupied. Please come home soon." Ya'el kissed her on the cheek.

Miriam nodded again, but just as uncertainly.

* * *

THE UPPER CITY

"Hello? Rebecca... Mathias?" The home was silent. Ya'el looked at the overturned chair next to the divan and the table that was skewed out of place. A cup and its spilled contents lay on the floor next to them. The courtyard was empty and quiet, save for the dripping sound of water from the roof and the tree limbs after the rain had finally stopped. She went back in and upstairs to check the bedrooms, then to the rooftop terrace—no one there under the brooding, overcast sky. Downstairs in the kitchen, she called out: "Elian... it's Ya'el." She heard a rustling sound and turned to the storage area near the pantry. "Elian?"

The lid of the large bin of charcoal lifted, and she saw his eyes peeking from within. He climbed out. Elian was covered in charcoal dust that had smeared on his face from his crying and collected thickest where his nose dripped. He wiped it with the back of his hand, spreading more across his cheeks. "Men came and took them! Before Rebecca told me to hide here, I saw one with just a scabby clump where he'd lost an ear...." The boy began crying again. "They said they were going to look for Matthew and Miriam."

"Shh... shh... Elian." Ya'el wiped his face with the damp sleeve of her cloak. "Grab your cloak. Hurry. I'll get Cicero, and we must go."

* * *

THE LOWER CITY

Though some had taken advantage of the weather break to go out, the street was not so busy that she could not tell someone was following them. Ya'el made a turn away from where she was headed, away from the secret entrance to King David's tomb. She could not lead whoever was trailing them to Miriam. Drawing Elian closer, she slipped into an alley to search the street. Beneath the boy's cloak, the unhappy parrot squawked.

"Why are we at Ehud's shop?" Elian asked.

Ya'el looked to where the boy pointed. The small sign next to the alley door still marked the glassworks.

"Yes, why?" The voice behind them had more of a chill than did the wind.

Ya'el turned from the door. The tall man, lithe and lean even while wearing a heavy cloak over his dark mantle, slid his cowl back to reveal glittering black eyes.

"Hananiah, why do you follow us. What do you want?" She thought the man was going to ask about Miriam, as he cared for her. But still, she did not feel settled.

"I want you to tell me how to find the Sicarii Hand and how to find more of the gold bars like the one I saw him give you at the Xystus." A blade appeared in his hand, and he gestured with it. "Let's go inside for your answers."

* * *

Ya'el watched the knife maker rotate the gold bar he had taken from her under the lamp's light. Its yellow glint reflected in the man's eyes. "So, you say you know who The Hand is, but not the name nor location?"

Ya'el had become good at lying to Gessius Florus but prayed Elian would be quiet. "I know nothing more about him," she said, spinning the falsehood. "The Hand paid me to spy on Matthew."

"Why?"

"I don't know... I was just to report what I knew of where Matthew went and who he planned to meet with."

"Are you not family? Why would you spy on them?" Hananiah lifted the blade and used its tip to score a groove in the gold.

"I'm Greek... I married into their family. I came here when my husband was killed by the Romans. But I worry that they will cast me out, and I needed money if they did." The words soured in her mouth as she said them. But they were words he might believe. He seemed driven by greed.

"How did you meet with The Hand? Did he arrange the meetings?" Hananiah set the gold down and ran a thumb along the dagger's edge. It left a thin thread of blood that he rubbed between thumb and forefinger. "Tell me... or...." He moved to Elian. "Don't twitch, boy." The knife maker's fingers traced the edge of Elian's ear and lingered to daub the ear with blood. Elian flinched, and Cicero squawked louder beneath his cloak. "Give me that bird... it won't make any noise when it's headless." Hananiah grabbed at the parrot as Elian twisted away from him.

"Do that, and I cannot contact The Hand," Ya'el said to stop him. Three times during their visits with Ehud, Cicero—in one of his sulks—had flown from the glassworks to the rooftop terrace at home and perched above her room window. If Miriam were there, a message could get to her. Then maybe, being forewarned, she could find Matthew and bring help to save them. She prayed Miriam had come home.

* * *

THE UPPER CITY

The soft rumbling in the sky slowly drew nearer, or so it seemed in the stillness as Miriam entered the rear of the courtyard. She saw that the door-sized wooden shutters to the courtyard were open, and one askew as if struck from the inside. The house was unlighted and silent. She went in and found the furniture had been knocked around. "Mother, Father!... Matthew!" A raucous screeching came from the courtyard. She went to its entrance and called out: "Ya'el..." just as Cicero streaked through and up to land on the terrace. She ran upstairs to find him above Ya'el's room, peering down at the closed shutters. Cicero was upset, his feathers ruffled and quivering. The parrot shook his leg, and Miriam saw the cylinder strapped to his leg. "Easy Cicero... easy..." she went to the bird and carefully—avoiding a snap of his beak— removed it and unrolled it to see the message: "Hand, I have the woman, Ya'el, and her boy. Bring gold to Ehud's glassworks tomorrow morning, or they die."

Who could do this? The bird shook his wings and emitted a screech. Gently lifting him from the terrace balustrade, she carried Cicero to Ya'el's room and settled the bird in his cage. She must think of what to do. Downstairs she stepped out onto the silent street, wondering at its quiet and why her mother and father were not home. *Should I search for Matthew and ask for his help?*

The sound of someone calling, no shouting... came nearer. Coming down the street from the agora, Miriam saw Yeshua ben Ananias, the old man Matthew had told her had been released from prison. He had been jailed for years for doing as he did right now. He cried out: "A voice from the east, a voice from the west, a voice from the four winds, a voice against Jerusalem and the holy house, a voice against the bridegrooms and the brides, and a voice against this whole people! Woe, woe to Jerusalem!"

As the echoes of his lamentation faded, a stab of lightning split the sky and struck so near that its rolling thunder shook her and the house behind her. In the moment's lull after, she heard the raucous cries from Cicero, scared or angry at being alone. Then the sky released a torrent of rain, and the wind howled, carrying away a last cry from the man: "Woe to Jerusalem...."

IF YOU ENJOYED THIS BOOK, PLEASE CONSIDER LEAVING A REVIEW. IT IS THE PRIMARY WAY INDEPENDENT AUTHORS GET THEIR WORK NOTICED.

THE STORY CONCLUDES IN BOOK FOUR.

For updates, please visit the author's website at:

WWW.CRYFORJERUSALEM.COM

ABOUT THE AUTHOR

Dr. Ward Sanford is an internationally renowned hydrogeologist who has spent over thirty years studying and writing journal articles on the availability and sustainability of groundwater around the United States and the world. He has given professional advice on a number of sites across North America, Europe, and the Middle East, as well as undertaken missions with the International Atomic Energy Agency to Thailand and the U. S. State Department to Libya.

More recently he has developed a keen interest in the first century history of Israel through the writings of the contemporary historian Flavius Josephus. His desire is now to bring those recorded events to life through dramatization in a series of novels entitled *Cry For Jerusalem*. Dr. Sanford is a member of the Historical Novel Society of North America. He and his wife, two grown sons, and daughter-in-law live in the Virginia suburbs of Washington DC.